Nikki's Secret

William Malmborg

Darker Dreams Media
Chicago, IL

Darker Dreams Media
Chicago, IL

Publisher's Note: This is a work of fiction. Names, characters,
places, and incidents are a product of the author's imagination.
Locales and public names are sometimes used for atmospheric
purposes. Any resemblance to actual people, living or dead, or
to businesses, companies, events, institutions, or locales is
completely coincidental.

Nikki's Secret/ William Malmborg. -- 1st ed.
ISBN 978-0615808130

Dedicated to
Sarah, Shannon, Katie, Maggie, Megan and Jen

Tuesday, August 9, 2011

1

"It's not bad," Kimberly said while attempting to maneuver the car around a sharp corner with one hand. "The carpets are a bit aged, and the fridge had the most god awful smell since it had been unplugged for several weeks, but aside from that it's big, it's cheap, and I really like it."

"And better than living at home?" Melissa asked.

"Oh, God yes!" Kimberly cried. "You have no idea how crazy it was getting living there again. Neither one of them could seem to wrap their minds around the fact that I was an adult and began treating me like a teenager."

"I bet that was fun."

"Yeah, so much fun that Dad decided I should have a curfew and then tried to ground me for breaking it. Can you believe that?"

"Sadly, yes."

Kimberly shook her head and then quickly tried to twist the steering wheel to the left as a large pothole appeared. Her wrist couldn't make the necessary pivot, however, and within seconds, groceries were bouncing off the seat and onto the floor.

"Shit!"

"What happened?" A worried film coated Melissa's voice.

"Ah, nothing, I just hit a huge pothole that probably killed a carton of eggs. You won't believe the roads up here. Winter was a real bitch. Did you know we got almost two feet of snow one night in February?"

"Yeah, it was all over the news. Hell, we even got some down here with that storm and I can pretty much see Mexico from my apartment. It was great. Everyone was freaking out like it was the end of the world or something and it was only two inches."

"Really?"

"They even shut down the schools. I couldn't believe it. I remember times when we got six or seven inches and still had to go to class."

"Unless you went to St. James or St. Francis, they always shut -- oh fuck!"

"What now? Your tire busted?"

"No, no, I think I made a wrong turn. I still haven't fully figured out the roads in this neighborhood yet."

"You know, maybe Mom and Dad were right to treat you like a little kid, I mean, if you can't even find your way home from the grocery store -- "

"Shut up."

"Do you at least know what street you live -- "

"Shut up!"

"Okay, okay," Melissa said, and then, after a few seconds of silence, "So, you all settled in yet or do you still have a lot of unpacking to do?"

"God, I've barely even made a dent and am royally pissed off because Kyle hasn't come to help me once. He didn't even show up to help me move like he said he would."

"Are you serious?"

"And get this, he told me it was my fault because I gave him the wrong day and time which is complete bullshit since we had been talking about it for weeks." Kimberly felt the anger of that moment returning and quickly tried to smother it.

"Is this the same guy that caused you two to miss a movie because he lost track of time while playing a video game with his roommates?"

"Yeah," she confirmed.

"And the one who sets limits on phone calls and will simply hang up on you if he feels you two have been talking for too long?"

"Yeah."

"Wow, sounds like a real winner. You should have Cosmo do a write up on him so other guys know how to behave."

"Hey, come on, he has good qualities too," Kimberly said.

"Really?"

"Yes!"

"Well, I hope they start to show."

Kimberly resented the tone and unspoken implication. It was one thing if she complained about Kyle; it was another for those she was talking with to start bashing him as well.

"So, who ended up helping you move?" Melissa asked.

"Just some friends from school." She pulled the car to a stop at another unfamiliar intersection. "Had to bribe them with the promise of free pizza, but it was worth it."

"That's good."

"Yep."

Silence settled.

Kimberly decided to continue forward, her mind hoping to see something that would pinpoint her location. Nothing upon the street stood out, however, and she soon found herself sitting at another intersection, panic rising, eyes desperately searching back and forth.

"You still there?" Melissa asked.

"Yeah, I'm just having one hell of a -- " the words halted as she looked up at the stop sign for the crossing traffic, her eyes settling on a very distinctive piece of artwork that had been added to it -- artwork that most guys would probably claim they had modeled for given the unrealistic size that was displayed. "Oh snap, I figured out where I am."

"Really?"

"Yep, believe it or not I've got a penis pointing the way."

"What?"

"Someone painted a giant white penis on the stop sign near my place. I noticed it the first time I ever drove this way to the apartment."

"Nice, and it points to your place?"

"Well, no. My street is the next one down. South Street to be exact." She made the turn while talking. "It's the second to last house on the right. Hey I completely forgot to tell you, guess what's within walking distance of my backyard?"

"Um, an endless desert with cacti, tumbleweeds and rattlesnakes?"

"That's your backyard you brat."

"Oh right -- sorry. What's in yours?"

"A really big graveyard."

"No way, honest?"

"Yep, and get this, the guy that lives in the apartment above me is a horror writer."

"Seriously?" Melissa asked. "Like a real writer that has published books and stuff, or a wannabe who calls himself a writer and brings his laptop to Starbucks?"

"A real one I think. If not then he must have some other work at home job because he like never leaves the place."

"Hmmm, well that's pretty cool."

Kimberly relished the excitement that carried across the phone connection. Her little sister had always had an obsession with the horror genre and seemed to crave everything within it.

"So, what's his name?" Melissa asked.

"Oh, hmmm . . . good question."

"You don't know his name?"

"I only met him once when he came down to say hi and asked if we needed a hand moving my stuff. I'm sure he introduced himself, but I was so busy that I can't remember." She took a right into her driveway and parked next to the side steps that led up to her kitchen. "I guess he's pretty shy too, at least that's what the landlord told me."

"Shy as in 'I'm socially awkward' or 'I have several bodies in my closet and don't want to draw any unwanted attention to myself?'"

"Wow, as if I didn't have enough on my mind already, now you try to add a crazy horror writer killer living above me to the mix." She looked over at the steps leading up to the writer's second floor apartment, her mind picturing him carrying a bloody garbage bag down to the cans in the middle of the night. It was a ridiculous image.

"Hey, at least you didn't live there during the blizzard," Melissa said. "He might have pulled a Jack Torrance on you."

"Do I even want to know what that means?" She shifted her attention toward the backseat and reached her free hand into one of the fallen bags to see what was inside. Relief soon followed. Nothing within those bags had been breakable.

"*The Shining* by Stephen King," Melissa said. "It was made into a classic horror movie by Stanley Kubrick. Any of those names ring a bell?"

Kimberly sighed. "Yes. So, not only are you suggesting I have a crazy killer horror author living above me, but now the place is haunted too. Super."

"Well, Jack was a play writer, not a horror writer, and one never really knows if the hotel was haunted or if it was just him, so you're in the clear on those two fronts. However, you might want to find out if he has published any super violent novels under a pen name because you never know when that half of him will start to take over -- oh, and check his marriage record."

"Is that a Stephen King one too?" Kimberly asked.

"All the great ones usually are."

"Good point. Well, if anything crazy happens I will know where to turn for guidance. In the meantime, I better start unpacking these groceries before the heat kills them. It's hotter than hell up here right now and I only bought like a hundred dollars worth of stuff that needs to go into the fridge."

"Okay, yeah, I actually need to run too and get some lunch before the DFAC shuts down. Tell Mom I said hi if she calls to pester you in the near future, and find out his name so I can buy some of his books, and then fawn over him when I come up to visit at Christmas."

"You fawn over someone? No one will ever buy it. Talk to

you later."

"Haha, yep, bye."

Kimberly closed the phone and started to step out of the car, but then leaned back in to grab the keys, her mind realizing she couldn't leave the car running because she needed to unlock the apartment door. Unfortunately, this act triggered memories of living in Champaign, Illinois and the hell that had encompassed the last few months of her life there before moving back in with her parents.

Don't, she warned herself. *It was two years ago.*

Holding back painful memories wasn't easy though, and within seconds, she found herself completely engulfed.

Footsteps echoed.

Kimberly turned and watched as the young mailman rounded the corner, his feet quickly taking him from the overgrown grass of the front yard to the scarred up concrete of the driveway.

"Well, hello again," he said with a smile, his feet gliding around all the potential trip points between the yard and the second two mailboxes without incident. "Still moving in?"

"Nah, all finished with that," Kimberly replied. "Just unloading groceries now."

"Ah, the big stock up," he said. "I remember doing that myself many times. It's always amazing how many things you have to buy when you have absolutely nothing in the kitchen."

"Oh, I know." In all honesty she hadn't really been all that amazed or surprised since this was her second time around. "So, was there anything for me today?"

"Actually, yeah, quite a bit."

"Oh, really?"

"Yep, almost had trouble fitting it all into the box too, mostly since you got a big padded envelope."

"Wow, okay." She hadn't been expecting anything, especially something that would be in a padded envelope, and had figured it would take at least two weeks before all the junk began to arrive.

The mailman smiled and then went about filling her neighbor's boxes, one of which was positioned next to the stairs leading down, the other on the stairway leading up.

Kimberly, meanwhile, went about unloading her groceries, which took about eight minutes, and then pulled her car around to the garage. While walking back she watched as the writer guy hurried back up his steps, a bundle of mail in his hands.

It's almost like he times everything so we don't ever come face to face, she noted as he stepped back into the apartment above, the wooden balcony groaning with relief as his weight disappeared. *Or is it just coincidence?*

Kimberly thought about this for a second as she went around to retrieve her own mail from the front of the house, her mailbox still being the original box that had been bolted beside the front door when it was a single family home, and then contemplated forcing a face to face meeting by simply heading up the steps and introducing herself again as she walked back around to the side door.

Not now, she told herself. *You have groceries to unpack.*

Before heading in she glanced at the junk mail to see if there were any coupons worth keeping, and dropped the rest into the green recycle bin next to the steps. She then began to rip into the large envelope, curiosity on what it could be getting the better of her as her fingers struggled to get beneath the tape that helped seal the flap. Once open she paused to step into the kitchen and then reached inside. Tissue paper met her fingers, something soft and clothing like beneath it. She pulled it out.

What in the world? she silently asked as her fingers unwrapped a very risqué piece of black lingerie, one that left more skin exposed than it covered. Then, *In your dreams, Kyle.*

Anger followed as memories of their Valentine's Day dinner several months earlier arrived. First Kyle had flat out told her he hadn't gotten her a card due the amount of money he had already spent on her gift -- another risqué undergarment -- and because of how pricey dinner was going to be -- anyone who thought Big Bowl was pricey needed to get out more. He then had suggested she not eat too much because he didn't want her to become so full that she couldn't proceed with their after dinner 'fun', where, he told her, she would be able to wear the sexy

lingerie he had gotten her and show him how much she appreciated him.

The worst part of all, however, had been her indulgence in his
wishes. Once back at his place she had taken a moment to put on
the lingerie and then given him a blowjob. Later, back at her
parent's house, she had thrown up, the constant thought of his
semen mixing in with the shrimp dish she had eaten causing her
stomach to purge itself. Tears had followed, along with a decision to break up with Kyle the next day.

But you didn't, she said to herself.

Fear of being single kept intervening every time she worked
up the courage to break it off with him. Fear of . . .

She pushed the thoughts from her mind and quickly carried
the lingerie into her bedroom; a toss from the doorway allowing
it to land on the bed.

After that she headed back into the kitchen to start unpacking
the groceries, her mind debating on whether or not she would
call Kyle afterward or wait and see if he called her.

2

Kimberly forgot about her decision to call Kyle for several
hours, a problem with her TV and Internet connection following
her distribution of the grocery items forcing her to call Comcast
and find out what the issue was. Naturally human error was to
blame; someone on their end having switched off her service for
a lack of payment. Unfortunately the person on the phone
couldn't fix the issue himself and informed her that she needed
to go down to the local Comcast office and show them her lease
to prove that she actually was the new resident of the house on
South Street.

"But I was just in here the other day getting everything all set
up," Kimberly told the lady behind the counter once she was at
the office. It was located on Route 23, about fifteen minutes from
her apartment.

"We still have the Roberts listed as the residents," the grumpy
lady said. She had a pillow behind her on the chair and kept

shifting it around to better cushion her lower back. "Are you sure this is the right address?"

"Yes," Kimberly said. Keeping her voice calm wasn't easy -- not after having explained all this the Friday before to another employee. "The Roberts moved out last month, and I moved in last week. And this isn't a house with one owner, it's a house divided into three apartments, one of which I am now renting."

"Well, the address is still listed as a single family home," the lady said. "And the Roberts are listed as the tenants."

Kimberly shook her head and pointed to her lease. "That is an official renter's document that lists me as the person living there. Now, I brought this in the other day and everything was set up without a problem. My TV and Internet has worked since then until this afternoon. Why has it now suddenly been switched off and why is it once again listed under the Roberts name?"

The lady didn't have a good explanation, yet she continued to be difficult for nearly twenty minutes. During this time a line grew behind Kimberly, the lady being the only employee at the desk. At one point she actually suggested Kimberly come in the following day when there would be more employees working so that she didn't cause such a hold up, but Kimberly refused, the idea that the lady was almost saying this was her fault nearly pushing her over the edge.

"I'm going to have to make a copy of this," the lady eventually said while taking hold of Kimberly's lease. "And you need to tell your landlord that he needs to list the house as an apartment building rather than a single family home now that he's decided to start renting it out."

"Fine," Kimberly said. Truth was she wouldn't do any such thing, not when verifying such information was between Comcast and her landlord. She did, however, call her landlord just to let him know that Comcast might be getting in touch with him, and, in the course of the conversation mentioned the trouble she had just endured.

"Ah, you know what," Mr. Ludlow said, "for several years we just ran one cable into that place and had all the TVs and computers hooked up to it through the ground floor apartment and everyone paid a third. Last spring, however, someone bought a whole bunch of adult movies that added a hundred dollars to the bill, and no one would claim responsibility. After that, everyone agreed it was time to separate the service. Unfortunately, Comcast has never been able to fully understand the situation. Brian, the guy that lives beneath you, got so frustrated that he switched to DISH network, which is why you have a satellite dish sticking out of the side of the house, and Bill, the guy above you, decided after a month of fighting with them to just go without TV and Internet because he realized he was getting much more work done without them."

"And I'm guessing the Roberts just kept the same plan that had always been with the place," Kimberly said.

"Yep, and that wasn't a problem for Comcast since the ground floor address was always where the service went anyway."

"Okay, wow." She didn't know what else to say.

"At some point some of their paperwork must have gotten all mixed up," the landlord continued. "And when no payment went through under their name they shut everything down."

"Yeah." Kimberly had already figured this out herself earlier, but didn't want to be a jerk. "You're probably right."

"So, aside from that is everything okay over there? Any issues with the apartment I should know about?"

"Nope, nothing I can think of. The place is great."

"Wonderful. Of course, if anything should come up please let me know right away. Always best to catch things early."

"I will." Given his tone Kimberly had a feeling things had happened in the past that no one had informed him about. It also sounded like he expected more things to happen in the future, probably given the age of the house.

A double beep echoed from her phone.

She pulled it away from her ear and looked at the screen. A call was waiting. Kyle.

"Um, I don't mean to be rude, but I have a call on the other end I need to take," Kimberly said.

"Oh sure, no problem. Talk to you later."

"Okay." She ended that call and opened the next one.

"Hello."

"Hey Kimmy it's me," Kyle said.

Jesus Christ, she said to herself. Over and over again she had told Kyle not to call her Kimmy, yet the message never seemed to register.

"Kim?" he asked. "You there?"

"Yes, I'm here," Kimberly said.

"Okay good. For a moment there I got worried that you changed numbers on me or something without telling me, which would suck because your Mom probably wouldn't give me the new one since she hates me."

Kimberly didn't reply to this.

"So . . . what's up?" Kyle asked.

"Nothing really. Just unpacking groceries and getting ready to watch TV *all by myself.*" She emphasized the 'all by myself' part in hopes that he would realize she would like it if he would come to visit her sometime soon.

"Well I should hope so. I'd hate if you had someone else there to watch TV with." He laughed.

Kimberly shook her head.

Silence settled.

"Hey, what's up with you?" Kyle asked.

"Nothing."

"Really? Because you don't seem all that happy to hear from me and your voice is telling me something is wrong."

"Do you realize you haven't been out to see me once yet -- "

"Gas is expensive and I'm busy with these summer finals -- "

"You also haven't sent me a card, or offered to help me un-pack anything," she snapped.

"I don't know your address!"

"Really, then how were you able to send me a sexy little piece of lingerie?" she demanded.

"What?"

"And you didn't even bother to have a note or anything in-side, yet I guess one wasn't really necessary since I know exactly what you wanted me to do with it. Wear it for you the first night you finally come to visit, right, because in your mind the only reason I got a new place is so we can fuck each other without having to worry about my parents or your roommates."

"My roommates don't care if we -- "

"Your roommates don't care!" Kimberly shook her head. "Nice." She hit END and tossed the phone onto the couch, anger and frustration mixing together within her bloodstream.

The phone rang.

She didn't answer it.

No voicemail.

It rang a second time.

Though tempted to pick it up, she resisted.

This time the silence lasted nearly a minute before the phone beeped.

It better be an apology text, she said to herself while walking up to the phone.

CALL ME BACK WHEN YOU'RE READY TO TALK LIKE A MATURE ADULT. PS: I DIDN'T SEND YOU ANYTHING!

Bullshit!

Then, without much thought, she hurried into the other room to take a picture of the tiny sexy outfit, and sent it to him.

IT'S NICE AND I'D LOVE TO SEE YOU WEAR IT BUT I DIDN'T SEND IT, was his reply.

Why would he continue to lie about it? she asked herself.

The question didn't sit well and she quickly went into the kitchen to examine the package the lingerie had come in, her mind starting the process of saying, *who else would send something like this,* but not really finishing the thought.

Instead the next inner statement was: *Oh shit!*

A startled laugh followed.

The package wasn't for her, the name Nikki Smith sitting above the house's address -- above *her* address. From there Kimberly looked up at the return address. No name was given, just a San Francisco location.

He really didn't send it.

Guilt followed, but then she dismissed it because she had plenty of other things to be angry about.

Curiosity came next. She wanted to know who Nikki was and

why she had had something sent to this address when she didn't live there anymore, and probably hadn't for a while given that the Roberts had been there for a couple years.

Unless . . .

She considered the huge mistake Comcast had just made and wondered if a similar mistake could have happened with whatever company had sent the package. From there she wondered if there was anything she could do to help, a thought about asking her landlord what Nikki's new address was so she could bring the outfit to her arriving within her head.

Would she even want it after it has been open?

Kimberly knew if the situation was reversed she wouldn't want the item, not if there was a chance it had been worn by someone else.

Still, you should probably find a way of letting her know it arrived here so she can contact the company and get another sent.

She looked at her phone. Placing another call to the landlord just seemed too exhausting after everything she had done today.

It can wait.

Another thought crept in, this one concerning Kyle and the idea that she should probably apologize for snapping at him.

Ah, fuck that, a voice said. It belonged to Melissa. *He probably deserved it for something else.*

Kimberly agreed.

Thursday, August 18, 2011

1

Kimberly never did take the necessary steps toward finding out whom Nikki Smith was, the need to unpack, find a job, and prepare for her upcoming semester occupying most of her time. Had more items arrived then maybe she would have added finding out whom and where Nikki Smith was to the *August Tasks* list, but the one garment was all that showed up so she figured the situation had resolved itself.

Not that she would have minded getting more outfits in the mail, the temptation to try it on one day proving it to be a perfect fit, but better that she didn't because then she would have felt obligated to correct the continuing mistake.

"Why?" Kyle had asked her one night when she voiced this thought to him -- at his place since he was still hooting and hollering over the cost of gas to drive out to her place after his first visit.

"Because they're expensive, and I would hate for her to be out that kind of money," Kimberly had replied.

"Hey, not your fault she can't put the right address down," he said. *"Plus they make me so hot for you."* He had pressed her hand

to his groin. *"See and this is just with me thinking about you wearing one."*

"Then part with some cash and buy me some," she said and pulled her hand away. *"They're cheaper than these Play Station games you buy every couple of weeks."*

"You know we all split the cost of the games," Kyle said, the 'we' meaning him and his two roommates. *"But hey, we could all go in on lingerie next time and take turns enjoying you in it."* Then, before she could voice her disgust with him at that comment, he added, *"Actually, you have three holes, so we could all -- "*

"Kim," a voice called. "Hey Kim, your foods up."

Kimberly looked over at the expo counter and saw the three plates for table five waiting, the memory of her breakup with Kyle fading as she grabbed the order and carried it out. "You need anything else?" she asked once the food was placed in front of the hungry customers -- two guys and a girl -- and waited a moment for a reply. None arrived. "Well, enjoy."

Kimberly returned to the expo area where Sandy was waiting, a drive-thru headset around her neck.

"Still thinking about him," Sandy asked; her ability to read Kimberly a tad unnerving.

"Little bit," Kimberly said.

"Well, don't let it get you down, from what you told me he was a real piece of shit."

"Yeah," Kimberly agreed. "It just feels weird, though, you know. I was with him for almost two years, so to be single again . . ." she shrugged ". . . but with classes starting and now working here it's probably for the best."

"You got that -- " a *beep* echoed from her earpiece, which she pushed back in place, the words, "Welcome to Steak and Shake," leaving her lips as she walked to the drive-thru register.

While Sandy was taking care of that customer, Kimberly made her way through the dining area to check on her three tables, all of whom needed drink refills, and then went up to the waiting area to seat the newly arrived couple, a practiced smile in place.

"Well, at least it's something, right," Bill said as his fingers carefully tore open the envelope that promised to have a check within, one that would be over a hundred dollars given the minimum payment the Adult Friend Finder affiliates required before mailing a check.

Toby looked up at him but didn't reply, and then hurried into the kitchen to sit by the treat drawer.

Bill looked at the cat and shook his head, the words *I've created a monster* echoing within. He then looked at the check total and saw it was well over two hundred dollars, which was more than he had expected from this company, but less than he was expecting from the Amazon check he was waiting for. Actually, just getting a check from the affiliate program was more than he had expected since he had pretty much quit updating the various sites he had been running, the need for the money they provided him having vanished once his Amazon sales finally began to take off.

A meow reached his ears.

"Oh come on!" he urged. "I just gave you some!"

Another meow, followed by the sound of Toby jumping up onto the counter, came from the kitchen.

Bill sighed. Two years earlier he would have scolded the cat for jumping onto the counter, but now he knew it was a useless battle and instead just made sure to keep all his food secure. He also was quick at putting the drying dishes back into their spots within the drawers and cabinets, therefore making it less likely that Toby would rub up against them while on the prowl for something edible.

Check in hand he went to his desk in the main room of his apartment and sat down. On screen, the curser waited at the end of the last sentence he had typed, his attempts at writing his daily movie review for his blog having stalled. It just wasn't working today. Thankfully he had nine movie reviews scheduled for posting, along with four book reviews and ten miscellaneous posts that he would space between them, thereby making it so he had a variety of posts hitting the web every day. Still, even with so many posts ready to go, he hated failing to complete a review, mostly because it would then push back the review he would want to write for whatever he watched that night -- he still hadn't checked the Netflix sleeve to see what he had received that afternoon -- which in turn could make the movie a waste if he watched another movie the next day and started a review for that one instead.

In the kitchen he heard a *THUMP* as Toby jumped down to the floor. Not long after that he was jumping up onto the desk to sprawl out next to the laptop while Bill worked; his tail positioned perfectly to land upon the keyboard whenever such a distraction felt warranted.

"I don't think it's happening today," Bill said.

Toby looked up at him and yawned.

"I know, I know. I did a lot this morning." *A lot* was an understatement. He had gotten twenty-two pages of fresh type into his latest novel, his mind having easily fallen into the story a few minutes after sitting down at his desk a little after five this morning; his daily goal of ten pages having been reached by seven. At that point his normal routine would have seen him getting up to go eat something, and then returning to the desk to write the movie review, but instead he had skipped eating, made more coffee, and continued with the novel until about ten forty. By then his fingers demanded he take a break, one that his stomach concurred with. A little over an hour later he had sat down to write his movie review, but rather than typing something up quickly as was his norm, he just stared at the screen, his finger occasionally distracting himself with the radio which he had set to 101.9 The Mix.

Now he flipped on the radio again, the music from the Chicago station filling the room without any static -- sometimes it just didn't reach him, which was always depressing -- his eyes having realized the *Kill a Half Hour* question of the day was about to air.

"Think we'll get it this time?" he asked Toby.

Toby didn't reply, but he did look up when Bill pushed away from the desk and started pacing the apartment, his mind trying to think up a way to write the review so that he could finally close the computer for the day and --

What, read a couple hundred pages, watch a DVD or two, go to the library before they close and check your book sales?

It all sounded dull.

Go cash the check?

He would have to drive to either St. Charles or Sandwich to do that since Chase didn't have a branch in DeKalb -- something he had been shocked about after moving in two years earlier and going in search of his bank given how many of the suburban kids from the Chicago area came out here to go to college. It was a forty minute drive to either location, so it didn't really matter which he decided upon. The only thing was he didn't relish making the drive when he would have to make it again once his Amazon check arrived. Plus it wasn't like he could go on a spending spree with the check, not when he was still knocking down the credit card debt he had accumulated on one of his two cards before the Amazon books had finally began to sell.

Thoughts on how close he had come to being made homeless, and what that would have meant for Toby caused him to shiver, all because he had quit his job and moved into this apartment when Dorchester showed considerable interest in his first novel during the fall of 2009, his thinking being he had finally broken through.

You were lucky.

He looked at the blinking cursor again and realized nothing was going to come of him sitting at the desk.

Just go cash the check.

Or just get out of the apartment for a while.

It was a good idea. The last time he had actually gone any-where had been . . .

Shit, Monday, because it was when you went grocery shopping. It was now Thursday.

Yeah, time to get out.

The trouble was he didn't know what to do or where to go. Nothing appealed to him.

Which is why you haven't gone anywhere in four days.

Start with the bank and then the library and go from there.

It was the best he could do.

3

Two dollars! Kimberly silently shouted once the group of college students left the table. *Fucking cheapskates!*

From two to four the place had been pretty much dead, the seating area seeing a total of five tables filled while the drive-thru got hammered. Things then picked up after that, the five to eight part of her shift always being busy no matter the day. It was a pattern Kimberly had started to recognize fairly quickly, her week on the job having been enough time to learn everything she needed to know about working in the semi fast food burger joint. Another thing was that college kids never tipped well.

"You should have seen it when I worked at Borders," Max Benning said while the two were waiting for some shake orders. "They'd come in with their books and notes and take up tables all day and only order water, or coffee back when it was self-serve. They also complained about the wireless being slow or not free back when one had to pay for it."

"Um, I hate to admit it, but I was guilty of that too when I was going to school at U of I," Kimberly said with a faint smile.

"Oh, I didn't mean to imply that -- " he started.

"No worries," Kimberly said with a laugh while putting the three shakes on a tray. Five seconds later the place was filled with false cheers and statements of 'put it anywhere sweetheart' as the shakes splashed across the floor, a kid having charged around the seating area and smashed into Kimberly's hip.

One of the few not laughing, aside from the staff, was the mother of the boy who scolded Kimberly for not looking where she was going while attempting to cradle her crying brat.

"He ran into me!" Kimberly replied. She would have said more but the manager got between the two, several different offers for free food and future discounts leaving his lips in an attempt to soothe the angry woman.

4

Visiting the library that afternoon turned out to be a good idea because Bill discovered an email from his book cover artist waiting for him, one that had a concept cover attached to it. Unfortunately, the library's computers didn't allow him to open attachments or upload anything from his external hard drive, which meant he needed to get online with his laptop. Such a connection was actually possible at the library. Whenever he needed to upload a weeks worth of posts to his blog or a novel to Amazon he would sit at one of their tower room tables and connect to the wireless system they provided. Going out and then coming back in felt odd though so he decided to simply head over to the Panera on Route 23. While making the stop at his apartment for the laptop he noticed someone standing by the front door of the house with flowers, but didn't really think much of it until the person, a young man, called up to him from the driveway as he was heading up his steps.

"I'm sorry to bother you, but I was just wondering, do you know the young lady that lives here?" He pointed to the ground floor while speaking.

"No, not really," Bill said. Inside he was asking himself where he had seen this guy before, the face having triggered something within his memory.

"Oh, um, well, you have any idea when she'll be back?"

"No, I don't. Sorry."

"Hmm, okay." For a moment it looked like he was going to say something else, but then he quickly turned and started to walk away.

"Hey, do you want me to leave a message with her?"

The young man stopped and considered it. "No, that's okay. I'll just come by later." With that he rounded the corner of the house and disappeared.

A few minutes later Bill was leaving the house as well, the thoughts about the flower-holding young man gone, his mind only able to focus on one thing: the book cover. *Would it have the look he was going for, or would he have to ask for changes? If the latter, how long would the changes take? Would it be ready in time for his promised October release, or would he have to wait week after week for the cover to arrive, his readers constantly sending him emails asking why the new book wasn't out yet?*

The questions couldn't be answered until he saw the book cover concept, a moment which arrived five minutes after he pulled into a parking spot outside of Panera, the process of connecting to their wireless needlessly slow.

Yes, I agree to all your silly little rules for connecting, he said to himself while hitting the log-in button and waiting for the screen to change over to his homepage. During this wait, he thought back to the first time he had ever connected to the Panera wireless from his car, his goal of downloading several hours worth of porn to his other laptop foiled by a page restriction. After that he had driven all over Sycamore and DeKalb looking for an unsecured wireless connection, his desperation for some new videos after having gone a week with all the old videos getting the better of him. Concern about not being able to log into his Adult Friend Finder profile had also been present because it would kill a necessary source of income -- *all because someone in the house didn't want to admit to buying the adult videos and ruined our wonderful internet agreement.*

The resentment he still felt about this was short lived because his homepage appeared. The fact that his two Kindle novels had started selling really well that month, and his realization that his porn addiction had been slowly killing his ability to write also played a part. Losing the web connection last spring had been a blessing.

Connecting to his Gmail account from his homepage didn't take long, and soon he was looking at the downloaded cover concept. As with the four previous covers this artist had created for him, this one was beautiful, yet right away his mind began thinking up some changes he would like to see.

Rather than sending those suggested changes from the car, however, he decided to sit on the cover overnight and see if he still thought they were necessary come morning. Last time they hadn't been, this time . . . well, he would know in the morning when he looked at it again.

Satisfied he started to move the mouse cursor to the X at the top of the screen, but then decided to check the sales on his Amazon Kindle Publishers Dashboard even though he had just looked at it while at the library. Four books had been sold since his last check, a total that used to represent a good day of sales back when he had uploaded his first two novels, but now represented a typical evening hour. Fifty to seventy five book sales a day was his average daily total, which, when earning seventy cents a book, made for a decent check each month. Well, decent when living in the DeKalb area. His goal of moving back into the suburbs was still a long way off, the average rent for a single bedroom out there being around a thousand dollars a month before expenses. Actually, given the money he was now making, moving back to the suburbs was doable, but the fear of suddenly having a bad month or two kept him from making that move a reality. He also wanted to knock down all the credit card debt and build up at least six months worth of rent and living expenses into his savings account beforehand.

And who knows, maybe by then you will have enough to start considering buying a place rather than renting a place, especially if you raise the prices to two ninety-nine so you can make two bucks a download rather than seventy cents.

This thought stuck with him as he shut down the laptop. He then contemplated going into Panera and having dinner here rather than making some instant pasta dish at home. It wasn't often that he treated himself to a meal that cost more than five dollars, and while the idea did cause a small bit of discomfort to settle within him due to the credit card debt that still needed to be paid, it wasn't enough to overpower the angry rumbles from his stomach.

5

Mark got back in his car, his mind once again questioning whether or not coming out here had been a good idea. Something about it just didn't seem right -- hadn't seemed right from the beginning -- but he couldn't put his finger on what. He also couldn't just toss aside the opportunity to have sex, not when he was on his way to being a real life forty-year-old virgin. Nope. Just going into his freshman year at college without ever having officially touched a boob was embarrassing (he had bumped plenty, his elbow always savoring the moment of contact, but that wasn't the same), and now he was heading into his junior year in the same condition. Even his friends couldn't help him out, and some were female. Why they didn't just lay back and let him fuck them was a mystery. It was, after all, the twenty-first century, and it wasn't like any of them were still intact down there. Well, maybe sex was going a bit too far, but he would settle for a simple handjob, or, if they were feeling generous, a blowjob. Hell, they could even just rub him with his pants still on while watching a movie and he would probably burst with pleasure and think of the experience as the greatest moment of all time -- until he finally did have sex.

He shook his head, and then looked over at the flowers sitting on the seat, the words *don't call it quits just yet* filling his head.

She probably just had to run out for something and will be back soon.

He looked at his phone and wondered if she had left a message on his profile or in his email about having to postpone their meeting time. Things like that happened and given the time it had taken him to drive out here from his parent's house -- he wouldn't be moving back into an apartment in DeKalb until September, his idiot friend and school year roommate having been evicted from their usual place in late July -- he could very well have missed such a message.

No internet connection.

Gah, best network my ass.

A debate on whether to leave his spot on the street and find an area where he could hop online with his phone or to simply stay and see if she showed up in the next few minutes began to unfold.

You don't want her thinking you stood her up.

At the same time he didn't want to sit here on the street like an idiot if she had canceled on him, especially if it resulted in him approaching her after she arrived home and finding out she wanted to fuck him another time.

You'd look like a fool; a flower carrying fool.

The fear of such a thing was too much so he quickly switched the car back on and started heading toward the NIU campus, past experiences guiding him toward an area where he knew his phone would work.

6

Kimberly didn't notice the pink stain from the strawberry milkshake until she was in her bedroom getting ready for a shower, her eyes spotting it just as her fingers tossed her work pants toward the bed. Thankfully no shake residue landed upon the sheets.

What a night, she silently said.

A reprimand from her manager for the way she had snapped at the mother had followed the shake incident. After that the customers who had ordered the dropped shakes had refused to tip her due to poor service. Things had then calmed down and for a while it had looked as if the night would end without any further incident, which was when some summer youth sports team had showed up, and, *surprise surprise*, had sat in her section due to need for movable tables that could be put together.

At least they tipped well, she noted. With that she grabbed her bathrobe from her bedroom door and started toward the shower.

A knock on the front door echoed.

Ah shit, her mind cried as she hurried back into the bedroom to grab a shirt and pants, her hand selecting items from her hamper rather than donning her work clothes.

Another knock, this one a little more forceful, appeared.

I'm coming, she mentally projected and headed to the door, a question of *who could it be* arriving as she wrapped her fingers around the doorknob.

Hesitation hit.

No peephole had ever been installed on the door. Instead she simply had three rectangular windows side by side, a brown curtain providing privacy. It was something she hadn't thought much about when being shown the place two months earlier.

No chain either, she noted.

Hmmm.

She pulled a corner of the curtain from the window and saw a young man standing on the front steps with a bunch of red roses in his right hand.

He smiled as their eyes met.

Who in the world is this? she asked herself and then opened the door a few inches and said, "Hello?"

"Hi," the young man said. A happy ring was present within his voice. "It's Mark."

"Mark?" she questioned.

"Yeah, Mark, um . . . *shy-college-guy22*." The happy ring had been replaced with concern. "I'm here to see Nikki."

"Oh -- " *Nikki again?* " -- I'm sorry, she doesn't live here any-more."

"What?"

"She doesn't live here," Kimberly repeated. "I'm sorry."

The look that appeared on his face was hard to describe -- almost a mix of fear, sadness, and confusion. "Are you sure?" he asked, voice fading on the last word as if he already knew the answer.

"I'm sorry," she said again, the flowers bringing on the state-ment. "I don't know what to tell you?"

"I guess . . ." he started, the flowers slowly lowering.

Kimberly waited, embarrassment for the guy beginning to fill her head. He looked as if he was going to cry.

"Are you really not her, or are you just telling me this because you now have second thoughts?" he asked.

"I'm really not her," Kimberly said. "I did get some mail for her a while back though, so . . ." she realized this wouldn't help him because if he didn't know what she looked like then that meant this was his first time trying to visit her, so a sudden change in address wouldn't mean anything. Plus she was pretty sure the Roberts had lived at this address for quite some time before leaving in July, so she wasn't sure how this mix up could have gotten started.

For a moment it looked like he was going to say something, but then he just shook his head.

"Sorry to bother you, then," he muttered.

Kimberly didn't really know how to reply to this and simply gave him an apologetic smile and shrug. A second later she closed the door, his body having turned and started back down the steps.

Poor guy, she thought. Then, *You need to figure out who this Nikki girl is and get her to change her address somewhere because obviously it still lists this place.*

Talk to the landlord.

It was the only thing she could think to do.

Or maybe Mark here will inform her of the mistake? After all it seemed like the two would have had to have communicated recently for him to pick her up for a date or from here (the flowers were making her think the two had planned on going out).

Or maybe it wasn't even Nikki's fault, she thought. *What if someone had set the two up on a blind date and gave the wrong address?*

At that very moment Nikki could be waiting for Mark to show up, her mind growing emotional as she started to consider the possibility that she was being stood up.

How awful.

7

I knew it! Mark mentally shouted while throwing the flowers into the backseat, his mind not caring if they were damaged, not when he would just be throwing them away once he got home. *I fucking knew it!*

8

Bill spent several hours that evening reading a used paperback horror novel that he had ordered through Amazon a few weeks earlier. It was a title he had first seen on the Too Much Horror Fiction website which was dedicated to horror fiction of the sixties, seventies and eighties (occasionally a book from the early nineties as well), one published by Zebra Horror in 1981. Once done with the book, he would review it for his own website. Like his novel writing, his website popularity had increased dramatically after he had been cut off from his constant porn stream. A part of this might have had something to do with the changes in html code that he had put in place last March because they had made it easier for Google to crawl his posts and recognize the titles. Most likely, however, it was the result of more posts being produced. The quality of those posts was probably better as well. After all, writing, like any art form, was something that improved with practice, and practice was all he did now thanks to the lack of stimulation his apartment provided. Of course this wasn't to say his writing had been lacking before, one didn't get a publishing deal with a major publishing house if they couldn't write, just that the ability to produce anything had been getting worse and worse as the porn addition had gotten more and more intense.

His eyes paused in mid-sentence and looked over at his desk. Only one laptop sat atop it -- his main writing one -- and it had been off for hours. Back in his Internet days a second laptop would have been up there, both of them vibrating with life, his eyes and fingers constantly moving from whatever writing project he was trying to work on to the second laptop to click the download button on a dozen little thumbnail video boxes, his mind not even really considering what those boxes displayed. All day long he would have done this until he couldn't take sitting at the desk any longer, his writing output having barely totaled three pages by the time he called it quits.

Disgust at himself had always been present, not because he liked looking at porn (every guy did), but because he could no longer segment it into his life. It was one thing to spend an hour or two every couple of nights watching various adult videos while slowing building up the pleasure within the penis, it was another to spend all day everyday downloading video after video onto a computer screen that couldn't even show the latest video icons due to the lack of space. Most of the time he didn't even get a chance to watch the majority of the videos because there were just so many. In fact, he could probably view one video a night for the rest of his life and still never see everything that had been downloaded. It was ridiculous.

The worst part of all, however, had been his lack of recognition of the problem when trying to understand why he couldn't finish any writing projects. One day he had even gone so far as to rearrange his apartment because he had read online that pointing his desk in a westward direction would help his creativity. When that had failed he had then researched what foods and vitamins would help stimulate creativity, his thinking being that one reason he had been able to write while living with his parents and not when living on his own was due to his mother cooking nutritious meals.

He shook his head at the memories and then went back to his book. Ten minutes later he was moving Toby from his lap so he could go replenish his tea, and then, rather than going back to his book right away, decided to check and see what DVD Netflix had sent him.

House on Sorority Row.

Excellent, his mind echoed. For quite some time he had wanted to watch this one, but every time a copy arrived he discovered the stupid remake sitting in the sleeve rather than the original. Last year the same thing had happened to him with *Black Christmas,* which had been even more infuriating because he had wanted to watch the DVD during the holiday season, and had been relieved to see it arrive on the twenty-second (it had been in high demand). Once he realized the mistake, and understood that Netflix would never get the original to him in time for Christmas, he had jumped onto I-90 and driven into the northwest suburbs to the Park Place Mall where he fought through the Christmas crowds to the small video store to buy it. From there he had decided to browse the mall a bit, but then got fed up with the mindless shoppers who were moving at a snail's pace from window to window and called it quits, his mind thinking that an hour or two of website browsing would be more enjoyable than mall browsing.

And naturally the hour or two of website browsing had turned into a

*'downloading porn until two in the morning' situation, which made it
so you didn't watch the new DVD until the following night.* If his
memory served him correctly the porn laptop had been hit by a
particularly nasty virus that night too, one that was worse than
the standard viruses he frequently experienced on that laptop,
and had forced him to wipe the hard drive, and thus delete thousands of videos he had never even watched.

"What do you think," he said to Toby. "Should we watch this
tonight or wait until I finish today's review tomorrow?"

Toby stared at him for a moment and then shifted his attention to the back window. On cue light illuminated it, the motion
sensor on the garage having been tripped.

Knowing this meant something was moving down there;
something that he probably would have hunted had he been an
outdoor cat still, Toby hurried to the perch that stood before the
window and looked down upon the rear part of the driveway
and backyard.

Bill followed and made it to the window in time to see a figure
running by the garage.

What the -- his mind started.

Downstairs a scream echoed.

9

Kimberly had just finished her shower, her body clad in fresh
t-shirt and pajama bottoms, when someone pounded on the front
door.

Startled, she headed to the front room, a warning about simply opening the door echoing through her mind given the time of
night.

"Who is it?" she called out.

Nothing.

The pounding did not recommence, which was odd.

Hesitation hit.

*Did someone realize at the last second that they had the wrong
house?*

A few days earlier this had happened, not with her, but with the writer upstairs, a pizza delivery guy having gone up there to knock on the door rather than down to the basement. Kimberly knew about it because her windows had been open, the air temp outside being just low enough that it made more sense to cool the place down that way than with the air conditioning.

She decided to peek out the window and see if a pizza delivery car was parked on the street. Rather than looking out at the street, however, her attention was snagged by the corner of something that had been stuck to one of the door windows.

Pulling the curtain further from the window revealed an envelope that had been taped to the glass.

An unexpected chill followed.

Why would someone put an envelope on the window at this time of night?

No answer arrived.

What's in the envelope?

Kimberly didn't really want to open the door, not when someone could easily be waiting behind one of the bushes, but the urge to see what was inside was too great and couldn't be denied. She also knew if she moved quickly enough she could open the door, reach up, grab the envelope and shut the door again without giving anyone time enough to even think about charging up the steps.

Do it.

She took a deep breath first. Less than ten seconds later the door was slamming shut; the envelope safely in her hands.

Nothing was written on it, but something was certainly inside.

She twisted the lock back in place and then opened the envelope.

Several pictures were within, pictures of her taken during the last few days: some of her working, some of her simply running errands. On the back of each the word WHORE or SLUT was written in big bold letters. Seeing this she couldn't help but let out a scream.

An odd sound followed. It was coming from the inner stairway that separated her apartment from the apartment upstairs. A knock on the door leading to the stairway echoed along with the words, "Are you okay?"

Kimberly realized it was the writer from above.

Without really thinking, just knowing she suddenly didn't want to be alone, she unlocked the stairway door and opened it. A second later the writer was standing in her front room, the question about her being okay leaving his lips again.

10

"At the very least they could make a report and use it as evidence if stuff like this continues," Bill said.

"Do you think it will?" Kimberly asked.

The two were sitting across from each other in the family room, him on a leather chair, her on the couch. On a box in front of the couch sat the pictures. According to Kimberly the box was just there until she could find a decently priced coffee table. The fact that she had felt the need to share this with him after he had looked at it while sitting down despite the circumstances was a good sign. It meant she wasn't completely scared out of her mind. Fear was present, however. That could not be denied.

"I don't know," Bill said. He thought carefully on what to say because he didn't want to add terror to the situation, but also didn't want to lead her to a false sense of security. "I've never really dealt with anything like this before, but it seems to me if someone went far enough to take pictures of you, and then write things like 'whore' and 'slut' on the back of each then this probably isn't going to be the end of it."

She didn't reply right away.

The silence made Bill uncomfortable.

"I guess you're probably -- " she started and then yelped as something behind him caught her attention.

Bill twisted around and saw Toby's head peeking around the stairway door. "Toby, what're you doing down here?" he asked.

Toby stepped into the room, eyes darting back and forth.

"You don't mind cats, do you?" Bill asked.

"No, I love cats," she said with a weak smile. An odd sense of sadness followed the statement, but faded quickly.

Bill turned back to Toby and said, "Come on buddy, don't be shy. This is Kim."

Toby didn't allow the encouragement to dispel his cautiousness and continued to move toward them at a slow, careful pace.

"Don't tell the landlord, but I used to let him down here when the place was empty just to explore a bit. He's not used to seeing furniture and stuff."

"I won't," she said. "Wait, do you have a key?"

"What?"

"For the stairway door."

"Oh, no. It was unlocked when no one was here so I could check it every now and then and make sure things were okay."

Kimberly nodded.

At the same moment Toby jumped up on the couch next to her and sniffed her leg. She looked down at him with surprise.

"So, do you want me to go get the number for the police department? I have it on my phone upstairs. I don't think this is a nine one one situation."

"Jeez, I don't really know," Kimberly said while reaching a hand to pet Toby. "Do you really think it's necessary?"

"Honestly, I think it's in your best interest just so there is a report on file."

"Kind of like going to the doctor after a car accident even if you feel okay," she said.

Bill thought about that for a second and then nodded, "Yeah, exactly."

Without warning Toby stepped up onto Kimberly's lap and laid down on her leg, the sound of his purrs loud enough to reach Bill's ears.

"Awww," she said.

"He's very people friendly," Bill said. "Aren't you Toby?"

In reply, Toby rubbed the side of his face against Kimberly's knee.

"He was born on my parent's front porch. Took me like six months to tame him. It was funny because we had a blizzard one day and he was out on the porch shivering in the corner so I just opened the door and left it open and he slowly came inside into the warm air and never left."

"Wow," Kimberly said. "He seems so sweet."

"He is. Hey, let me run up and get that number for you."

"Okay."

Toby lifted his head from the lap as Bill stood up and started for the stairs. "It's okay buddy, I'll be back," he said. With that he went up to his apartment, looked around for a moment, found his phone sitting on his side table, and returned to the first floor. "Here's the number. You can use my phone if you want."

"What do I tell them?" she asked.

"Um, that someone is harassing you and that they actually came to the house and made a physical presence." He shrugged. "Seems fitting."

She looked at the phone while still petting Toby with her free hand and said, "I don't know why but I'm nervous."

"I know. I was the same way a few months ago when the phone line fell off the side of the house and was on the street. Don't worry though; they're very nice out here."

He thought back to that moment and remembered wondering whether or not the police were somehow aware of his online activities and if calling them would lead to them realizing he was wanted for something -- maybe like accidentally visiting an illegal porn site or for creating a fake web presence. Of course nothing like that had happened, but the fact that the fear had been present had startled him.

"Yes, hello," Kimberly said into the phone. "Um, I'm calling to report that someone is harassing me." She listened. "No, they actually came to the house and left pictures of me on the front door." She listened some more. "Oh . . ." she looked up at the ceiling for a moment and then rattled off the house address, listened for a moment, and then nodded. "Okay, thanks." With that she closed the phone.

"Someone on their way?" Bill asked while taking the phone back.

"Yeah."

"Good. They'll be here pretty quickly too unless they have a dozen calls or something. The station is like a mile that way."

He pointed to the north. "Next to the library actually."

12

"How're your friends doing?" his mother asked as Mark stepped inside the house around ten thirty.

"They're good," he lied, her presence in the kitchen surprising him since she had to be out the door at eight fifteen in the morning for work.

"What's wrong?"

"Nothing," he said with a shake of the head. "Just tired. I forgot how long of a drive that is and how crazy people get on ninety."

"You weren't drinking, were you?"

"No, of course not."

"It's okay if you were, just remember not to drive home if you've had any even if it means you need to call a cab and then have us run you out in the morning to get your car," she said. "Your father and I would rather have you -- "

"Mom, I know. I wasn't drinking, and if I had been I wouldn't have been driving. Honestly, I'm just tired."

She looked at him for several seconds and then nodded. "Okay. Well . . . good night then."

"Good night," he replied and started toward his bedroom. He made it halfway there before turning around and going back into the kitchen to get a soda, his mind not caring about the caffeine because chances were he wouldn't get any sleep that night. Not when his thoughts were so focused on Nikki and the torment she had caused him.

13

"So at no point today did you notice anyone following you or maybe just consistently being around you," the officer asked. She seemed a nice lady and quickly put to rest the fear Kimberly had of this situation not being serious enough to warrant a call to the police.

"No," Kimberly said after trying really hard to picture some-one. "Maybe if I had been paying attention and looking for someone I would have noticed, but I never even considered someone could be following me."

"And nothing like this has happened before?"

She shook her head.

"Okay," the officer said. She took a moment to read over her notes and then looked up at Bill. "You said you saw someone running through the backyard. Any more details about them come to light in the last few minutes?"

"Not really," Bill said. "I did see someone earlier, though, at the front door. It completely slipped my mind. It was a young guy with flowers who asked me if you'd be home soon." He nodded toward Kimberly during the last part of this statement.

"He actually wasn't looking for me," Kimberly said before the officer could ask for more details on that. "He thought someone named Nikki lived here and -- "

"Nikki?" Bill blurted.

Both turned toward him.

"Yeah, Nikki," Kimberly said. "I figured she must've lived here at some point before me because I also got some mail for her a while back. I was going to ask the landlord about that tomor-row."

The officer considered this for a moment while looking at Bill and asked, "Did the name spark something?"

"No," Bill said. "Nothing. I just, well, I didn't realize the guy had the wrong person. He never told me a name."

Kimberly stared at Bill, who then looked back at her for a sec-ond and then looked down at his feet. *He's lying,* Kimberly said to herself. *And he knows I know he's lying.* She wasn't so sure about this last part, but the way he looked away from her made it seem likely.

"Is there any reason to think this guy with the flowers -- did he give you a name?" the officer asked.

"Yeah, um . . . Mark?" Kimberly said. She thought about the name and added, "Yeah, I'm pretty sure it was Mark."

"Last name?"

"No, sorry."

"It's okay. Any reason to suspect he may have had anything to do with the pictures?"

"I really don't know." Kimberly pictured the moment when Mark had realized she wasn't Nikki and how the flowers had slowly lowered until they pointed toward the ground. "He seemed pretty . . . I don't know, confused by the whole thing."

The officer wrote this down.

Kimberly looked at Bill again, and again he looked away. Silence settled.

"Anything else you think might have bearing on this?" the officer asked after nearly a minute. She was looking at Kimberly.

"No," Kimberly said.

The officer turned to Bill. "Anything?"

He shook his head.

"Okay. As it stands now I'm going to file a report and bring those pictures in. A case is going to be opened on this, but I will tell you there probably isn't anything the investigator can do at this point. However, if anything else happens you make sure to call and an officer will be out here to make a report and gather any evidence that is left. Every incident, if more occur, will be filed with this one and if the person harassing you is eventually identified we will have a pretty good case built up."

Kimberly nodded. She had known there probably wasn't anything they could do about it, but even so hearing it now from the officer felt like a let down. It also was a bit disconcerting to know that the person would have to do more in order to be caught, kind of like those crimes shows were the detectives were forced to wait for a serial killer to strike again because they simply didn't have enough evidence to get anywhere.

"And if you see anything out of the ordinary please call as well," she said to Bill. "Is it just the two of you or is there a third apartment?"

"There's a basement apartment too, but the guy that lives down there is rarely home," Bill said. "He travels for business I believe."

"Okay, well, if you get a chance to speak with him let him

know about all this."

Bill nodded. "I will."

"Very good," the officer said. Less than a minute later she was gone.

Kimberly turned to Bill. "So?" she asked.

"What?" Bill asked.

"Who's Nikki?"

"I don't really -- "

"Yes you do," she insisted before he could finish the denial, arms crossed.

He didn't reply.

"Who is she?" Kimberly asked again.

Bill sighed. "She's nobody."

"What?"

"I made her up. It's just a name I wrote under for a while to make extra money before my real novels started to pay the bills."

"What? Like a pen name?"

"Yeah, and that's why the name caught me off guard. There's no way it could have anything to do with this though, and given the popularity the books under my name are starting to achieve I would really prefer that the connection between those books, which don't even exist anymore, and myself, isn't revealed."

A realization dawned on her. "Those books weren't horror, were they?"

"No," Bill said. "And like I said there is absolutely no way anyone could make a connection between them and this place."

"But then how do you explain someone asking for Nikki, and the mail I got?" Kimberly asked.

Bill thought about this for a while and said, "Maybe someone named Nikki did live here before the Roberts. Actually, that might be why the name appeared in my mind when I was think-ing of one to use, because I may have heard the name at some point and it stuck in my head."

"Oh," Kimberly said. She thought about this for nearly a minute and realized it made sense. *Besides, why would someone show up with flowers unless they had actually made plans to see that person, something that couldn't possibly have happened without Bill knowing about it?* "I suppose you're right."

"Thanks. I think I'm going to call it a night. Do you need anything before I head up?"

She shook her head. "Did Toby go back up?"

"Yeah, the knock on the door spooked him."

"Oh yeah." Kimberly remembered seeing him flying toward the stairs.

"Well, good night," Bill said. He waited for her reply and then started up the stairs and closed his door.

Kimberly did the same with her door and then quickly double checked to make sure the front door was locked. After that came the kitchen door, followed by the windows. Everything seemed secure. Sadly she didn't feel safe.

14

Tales of a Sex Crazed College Student. The carefully designed title stood against an erotic backdrop that displayed a naughty looking schoolgirl kneeling provocatively before a laptop on the floor, the letters arching over her so as not to mar the focus of the image. The image itself was a real photo rather than something an artist had created, yet even so, it was evident to Mark that quite a bit of thought had gone into it in order to maximize the seductive power it would have on guys like him. It wasn't until he had started to notice certain trends in the timing of Nikki's emails on the Adult Friend Finder site last spring, however, when he began to suspect a lack of genuineness to the girl and her blog. The question was would a company like Adult Friend Finder really create a completely different web page that was updated constantly just to steer visitors to the main Adult Friend Finder dating site? For some reason his mind had always leaned toward an answer of no when contemplating this. Using staff to pose as girls on the main site who would email guys shortly before their monthly membership was set to expire so they would renew was one thing, but creating an entirely new site that had no income potential itself and had to be maintained seemed too much -- especially considering the size of the Adult Friend Finder enterprise. A blog like Nikki's, even if it directed half its new daily visitors to the Adult Friend Finder site, would be like the equivalent of adding coins to a millionaire's bank account. It just didn't seem worth their time. Plus the link to Nikki's Adult Friend Finder profile, which was promptly displayed on the upper right corner of the blog, wasn't the only link to an adult site. Almost daily (until the site had stopped being updated) new video trailers for different porn sites would appear beneath the profile badge. Book cover images were there as well, most belonging to the erotic category, but some just to the standard genres of horror, mystery and fantasy. One author in particular -- William something -- had always had a book cover image displayed on the blog, and while Mark didn't know for sure, he often had wondered if authors (and the porn sites) had paid for those ads. If so, then the traffic to the William guy's book must have been pretty good given the consistency of his covers appearing on the site.

Another element that had always swayed Mark to thinking Nikki was real, aside from the content of the posts, was the wish list that had a permanent spot above the posts themselves. Why would the Adult Friend Finder site want guys like him sending them sexy garments and sex toys? It didn't make sense.

Forget that, Mark told himself. *What doesn't make sense is this girl emailing you and suggesting you come to her place and fuck her so she could write about it on the new blog she was creating.*

Why go so far when nothing was really going to happen?

If the email had required him to once again sign up for the Adult Friend Finder site he would have finally concluded she was an employee of it, but this time around the message had been sent to him on the OK Cupid site, which was free. Getting him to sign up served no purpose. In fact, it was this sudden switch, after months of silence from Nikki that had convinced him to give her a second try; convinced him she was real.

All because you stupidly looked at the blog again after five months, he scolded himself.

It had occurred two weeks earlier. Facebook had gotten dull, and the basic cable at his parent's house sucked, so without really thinking about it he started browsing some adult sites and eventually went to the Nikki blog out of curiosity (and because the stories and pictures had the ability to get him off). As expected nothing had been updated, the last post still bearing the April date upon it, but Nikki had made her presence known. It was in the comment section beneath the final post on the site, and was in response to twelve comments that had asked her where she went.

My email account was hacked!!! Nikki wrote, the comment being a guest comment rather than from her standard blogger profile. *I can't log in to the site anymore! I'm now on OK Cupid! Click my name to see my profile!*

Normally Mark would never have clicked on such a link within a blog, past experiences having taught him that it would either take him to some pyramid building scheme or put some Trojan virus on his laptop. This time, however, while hovering his mouse icon over the name, he saw that it really was a link to the OK Cupid profile and clicked it. After that he set up his own profile and sent her a *Remember Me?* email and waited. The reply came three hours later.

He looked at that reply now and followed the thread of their conversations to his last message, which had been sent this morning and told Nikki how excited he was about getting to see her later. Nikki had not replied.

Don't even bother, he told himself as his mind contemplated sending a new message. *Just leave it alone.*

The advice was probably good, but Mark ignored it and quickly wrote and sent an angry message. A demand to know why she had lied to him was present as well, one that he wasn't really expecting to get a reply to but sent nonetheless.

After that he contemplated posting a message on her blog that warned people of what she had just done to him, but in the end was able to hold back. Public shouting matches always made both parties look like idiots, and such a shouting match would probably develop electronically if he posted something.

15

Guilt followed Bill up the stairs. Concern was present as well. He had lied about having used the name Nikki to sell certain novels on Amazon, and about the possibility that someone named Nikki had once lived downstairs. His assurance to Kimberly that the Nikki connection had been a coincidence wasn't a lie, however, and had been the reason he felt it was okay to keep the truth of the situation to himself. There just was no way that his use of the name Nikki could be connected with that young man thinking Kimberly was Nikki. It wasn't possible, not when he would have been the one setting everything up.

"I'm not doing anything like that in my sleep, am I buddy?" he asked Toby who was sitting atop his TV room perch.

Toby didn't reply.

Thankfully, Bill didn't need any reassurance that he wasn't signing online in his sleep because he would need a web connection to do that.

Unless you're driving to Panera in your sleep, he said to himself even though he knew such an excursion wasn't possible. Sleep walking was extremely rare. Hell, just moving in general while sleeping was rare given that the body paralyzed itself while in the dream state so it wouldn't actually hurt itself in the midst of a dream. Most people didn't know this, though, which was why movies and TV shows were frequently allowed to get away with scenes where people tossed and turned while suffering a bad dream.

Just a coincidence, he concluded. *An eerie one that no one would believe if you used it in a novel, but a coincidence all the same.*

And the situation with the pictures probably isn't related at all, he added several seconds later. *That's a whole other issue, and really is the only thing Kimberly should be worried about.*

Satisfaction with his conclusion arrived, and for a moment all was well. He then made the mistake of thinking about Kimberly's statement about receiving mail addressed to Nikki.

What kind of mail?

It was a question he wished he knew the answer too, yet was one he hadn't asked because it could have led to other questions about why it mattered, which in turn would have forced him to explain everything.

Had it been a letter or some sort of bill then it wouldn't mean a thing, but if it had been a risqué garment or sex toy that would mean someone had actually purchased something through the wish list link he had posted on the blog; one that his friend and model had suggested he put up as part of her payment for the continued pictures and videos he occasionally embedded within the posts and used on the Adult Friend Finder profile. The agreement had been easy to make because the two had needed various outfits and toys for the pictures and videos, and since the expense of such things was his responsibility, he preferred to get the stuff free of charge. Being able to then hand the items over to Nicole as a deduction to the agreed upon payments for her modeling services had been perfect. Plus it had been fun to see her wearing the items and using the toys. A lot of fun.

What a mess, he concluded. *You should have deleted the blog once the books started selling.*

If he had done that there would have been no possibility of a connection, which would have been great because then he would have felt better about lying to Kimberly. Such a step had never occurred, though, because he had been proud of the success the site had achieved, and had always wanted to keep it up and running just in case his books stopped selling one day due to the traffic the site still earned and the income potential it still had.

You need a fallback plan, his family had always insisted and despite his denial of the necessity he had actually created one. He just would never reveal what it was to them.

Don't worry about it, he finally said to himself. *It's a coincidence and will blow over. The guy with the flowers now knows Kimberly isn't Nikki and will move on, and whoever is leaving the pictures will display a motive soon enough if they continue.*

Unfortunately, the concern would not fade and made for a sleepless night, his mind too worked up to allow itself to drift away.

Even watching some of the videos he and Nicole had made, sound muted so Kimberly wouldn't hear, didn't help, though the eventual ejaculation and hot shower did feel good. It wasn't enough. Back in bed his mind went about speculating on the strange situation as the hours ticked by until he eventually gave up on sleep and watched four episodes of *The X-Files* back to back, unconsciousness finally arriving during the fourth episode.

His alarm clock went off an hour later.

Friday, August 19, 2011

1

Dear Horny4you!

I'm going to play hard to get and will probably act confused when you come to the door. PLEASE DON'T GIVE UP! If I slam the door in your face it is all an act. Come back over again and again. If you have persistence I will give in and suck your dick and let you fuck me in the ass. If not, someone else will eventually do things correctly and I will have sex with them. I hope you make the cut because I'm looking forward to seeing you and that thick hard cock. Nikki. PS: Make sure you only knock on the first floor door or else you'll get my neighbor who lives upstairs.

2

Confusion followed by pain ushered Kimberly into the day-light hours, her body having mistakenly spent the remainder of the night sleeping on the couch rather than her bed. The TV was the reason for this. Unable to stay in the dark silent bedroom she had moved to the couch to be near the TV, her finger not really caring what program she selected just as long as it cushioned her with sound. The National Geographic Channel ended up being her destination, a program on something called String Theory helping guide her mind into a state of sleep.

A large kitchen knife had also added to her comfort, its blade tucked beneath a cushion so all she had to do was reach down and grab the handle if someone tried to get inside.

Thankfully it had not been needed.

But will it later?

She thought about the pictures that had been taken and Bill's statement about how whoever had left them probably would not stop with just them, not when it was such a bold move, filled her mind. *How far would they take this? Would it reach a point where the knife was truly needed? If so, would it be enough?*

No answers arrived. Instead she simply asked herself why someone would do this. Unfortunately the answer to that question was a mystery as well.

Nikki.

The name sat in her head for several seconds, but didn't really guide her mind anywhere. Bill had said he had used the name for some 'non-horror' titles he had sold on Amazon, the connotation being that they were porn novels.

He also said they don't exist anymore, her mind quickly added, which; she had to admit, made it seem very unlikely that the two incidents could be connected. Instead she thought about his suggestion that someone named Nikki had lived there before the Roberts and that hearing about her had sparked the use of the name for those books. Such a situation would explain the mail. *But would it really explain why someone would suddenly start leaving pictures?*

And if Nikki did something so horrible to make someone leave pictures like that wouldn't they know enough about her to realize you're not her?

This thought made so much sense that it put an end to all the speculation, though not in a way that brought relief because if such a situation went unrealized by whoever was doing this then that meant their ability to rationalize things was lacking.

A chill slithered through her.

She pulled the knife from the couch.

If things got out of control she would help whoever was behind this understand the consequences of their failure to comprehend reality.

A memory appeared, the thought of stabbing the blade into some one's flesh sparking it. Blood filled her mind. She then thought about the cat she had loved and that horrible moment of insanity.

NO!

She tried to push the thought away, but it resisted. Tears arrived. She couldn't help them. Reliving the terror she had faced last night when seeing the pictures would be better than visualizing the moment in the bathroom back in Champaign, but the recent memory wouldn't replace the old familiar one. Chances were nothing short of being killed, or maybe some form of brain injury (electroshock therapy?) would ever rid her of it.

Maybe not even death? If Hell existed and she went there she could think of nothing more fitting than being forced to relive that awful day over and over again.

She shivered, and then wiped the tears from her face and forced herself into the kitchen where she set the knife on the counter and contemplated some breakfast.

In the end she didn't relish the thought of making anything and decided to head out and see what types of breakfast joints were in the DeKalb area.

Need to call the landlord at some point too and ask about Nikki, she told herself.

Ideally she would have taken care of that before heading out, but knew he worked during the day with a temp agency called Manpower, one she had actually submitted info to before getting a job with Steak and Shake, her thinking being that working a temp job would be perfect for a college student. The agency, however, hadn't thought so, not when she told them school would come first.

Upstairs she heard footsteps.

You could ask him about breakfast places, maybe even invite him along?

In the end she vetoed the idea and headed to her car, a quick detour to the front of the house to check and see if anything had been left on the door.

All clear.

Relief arrived, but didn't last long. More would come. She knew it to be true. Even if Bill hadn't stressed it last night she would have eventually realized it herself. Whoever was behind this had only just gotten started.

I won't let them get the better of me, she insisted.

Yeah, we'll see, the cynical part of her mind replied.

3

Oh cry yourself to sleep, why don't you? You weren't for me. I realized it the moment I answered the door. WTF made you think I'm a flowers type of girl? Did you ever really look at my website? I just want a good hard fucking from the guys I talk to, no strings, no drama. Men should think of themselves as a self operating vibrator when they come to see me, nothing else. If you think you can get this through your head maybe I will let you try again. Swing by tomorrow afternoon to find out. The best you will ever have, if you're lucky, Nikki.

Mark stared at the reply on the OK Cupid website, his mind unsure what to think.

A part of him was actually considering heading back to the house again, the promise of sex difficult to resist despite the doubt that was present.

She's teasing you again, he told himself. *And you already decided that the girl last night wasn't her.*

But then how did she know about the flowers?

She could have been watching!

Really?

Mark had to admit that going to all the trouble of getting him to knock on someone else's door so Nikki could watch him humiliate himself seemed a little over the top. It wasn't out of the question though. The variety of people populating the planet was so great one would never be able to fully document all the different types of craziness out there. Now that he knew the motive wasn't so he would continue to subscribe to a dating site that required a membership fee there had to be a different reason for her continued teasing.

But what could that reason be?

No answer.

And what if there is no reason? What if she really did get pissed off by the flowers last night and put on an 'I have no idea who you are' act? Do you really want to miss out on another opportunity for sex due to your own 'over the top' theory?

Do you really want to humiliate yourself again with that girl who had no idea who Nikki was? Fuck, she didn't even look like Nikki.

But maybe that's because the pictures were dated. The blog was almost two years old, and since many of the pictures on the profile had been the same ones as the blog they too were probably older.

Ask her about this, he told himself and see what she says.

And risk pissing her off to the point where she gives up on you completely?

The debate went on and on, his mind completely and hopelessly divided.

4

Bill stared at the laptop screen for a long time before the words began to flow, but even then the rhythm he was used to didn't take hold. The sleepless night was to blame. Being creative required quite a bit from the brain, so failing to get any rest one night made it nearly impossible to get going the next day. The twenty-two pages he had completed the day before probably played a part as well. A normal writing period saw him producing ten pages of fresh manuscript. Doubling that had sucked him dry. It was like doing the same type of workout everyday at the gym and then, for no reason, doing a second workout one day when the urge struck. Trying to get back into the routine the next day wouldn't be easy, not after having fully exhausted oneself.

In the end he managed four pages of new writing, the total taking him to page three hundred and one. Normally crossing into a new hundred page threshold was cause for some simple celebration. Today, however, it didn't feel all that spectacular. Nothing ever did when he failed to hit his ten page daily total.

Some satisfaction did come his way when he knocked out the rest of the movie review he had been working on the day before. It was funny too because he hadn't really planned on trying to add anything to it until after lunch -- he didn't want to break his routine -- but then, after realizing his work on the new novel wasn't going anywhere, he decided to take a look at what he already had and the rest just came out.

"What do you think?" he asked Toby who was lying next to the printer. "Knock out another six pages this afternoon?"

Toby lifted his head, and then, realizing Bill was getting up, got up as well and hurried into the kitchen, a loud meow leaving his lips.

Bill shook his head and then headed into the kitchen to dump some cat treats on the floor. After that, he added some fresh coffee and cream to his mug and then, unsure what to do, headed into his "library" (front room with bookshelves) and stared at the various authors he had read over the years. Disappointment that printed copies of his novels weren't sitting on the shelf arrived. He knew being able to make a living from his writing was no small feat, and was proud of the success his Kindle uploads were achieving, but it wasn't enough. Ever since he had been a kid his dream had been to see his novels on a bookstore shelf, a publisher logo and author blurbs decorating the cover. For years it had been his driving force; his motivation for waking up everyday at five to begin his writing before school or his shift at the different manual labor and fast food jobs he had worked, yet it still hadn't happened.

Toby came into the room, looked at him for a moment, and then began to clean himself.

Bill watched for several seconds before heading back into the main room to sit on the couch by the window, his hand flicking on the radio as he walked by so he could catch the second half of the Eric and Kathy show on 101.9.

Nothing interesting was being talked about, but just hearing the voices felt good. Listening to Melissa's traffic report and visualizing what the daily commuters were facing on the various roadways leading into the downtown Chicago area also felt good and knocked down the disappointment he was feeling about his writing career.

Seeing he was on the couch, Toby hurried into the room and jumped up on his lap, paws kneading his chosen area into submission before settling his body down. After that it wasn't long before Bill fell asleep, the coziness of having the cat on top of him coupled with the total exhaustion he felt from the sleepless night making it impossible to keep his eyes open.

5

Kimberly half expected to find a new envelope taped to her front door, or another package for Nikki sitting in the mailbox, the time away at breakfast having provided ample opportunity to place something, but nothing was there. The relief this created was short lived, not because something occurred after she got home, but because she knew something would occur in the near future.

Such thoughts had made it impossible to enjoy her breakfast. She also had caught herself constantly scanning the people around her to see if they were eyeing her or taking pictures of her. Eye contact was made on a few occasions, but she couldn't figure out if it was just due to her frequent glances their way or had a more sinister purpose. She also never caught anyone taking her picture.

A question on why someone had taken pictures of her yesterday appeared, but then faded away without an answer. *Don't dwell on it,* she told herself.

Naturally the suggestion was easy to make, but hard to follow. She would do her best, however, the systematic flipping through channels while also going over her upcoming class schedule seeming to work . . . for a while.

6

Why are you doing this? Mark asked himself as the sign for Route 47 appeared on the right hand side of I-90. *You know it isn't going to end well.*

The answer was simple. If he didn't try his mind would quickly convince itself that he had made a mistake and that if he had just gone back to Nikki's place and given her a second chance he would have finally gotten sex. It was a 'better to try, fail and feel sorry for yourself then think you missed out on a sure thing' attitude, one that hopefully would go away once the virgin version of him was finally laid to rest.

And if she laughs at you again?

No answer arrived.

He did know one thing. Those profiles he had seen on some of the escort service websites he had been visiting every couple of nights for the last several months were growing more and more enticing. The trouble was he couldn't break the fear that he would hesitate in making his interest in paying for sex known to the girl, concern over the possibility that she would be one of those escorts who really didn't prostitute herself getting the better of him. Plus, with his luck, he would get a cop.

Safer to head out to the Bunny Ranch in Nevada, he told himself. Looking at the profiles on that site was another activity that was seeing more frequency during the nighttime hours, thoughts on maybe scheduling a trip to the Bunny Ranch, or some other legal brothel, during his spring break earning some serious consideration. It was an option he had first started to consider last year, but hadn't really taken all that seriously, especially once his conversations with Nikki had begun. Had it not been for those emailed messages he very well may have scheduled an appointment and bought a plane ticket, his need for sex making the exorbitant cost of the trip seem superficial -- at least when heading out there. On the way home he probably would have kicked himself over and over again for spending so much money on something that he should have been able to get for free.

If only I could pay for it here without fear -- and without the travel expenses. Sadly, the moral police would never allow such a situation to develop, the idea of paying for sex somehow wrong in their eyes.__

But I wouldn't be paying for the sex; I would be paying them to

leave afterward. Mark had come across the statement when reading opinions on a news story about the legalization of prostitu-
tion a few months earlier. It was one he knew many men agreed
with, the attraction of being able to have sex without all the other
relationship necessities hard to pass up. In the future, if he ever
found himself having sex more often, he might have been able to
claim the same sort of statement, but now he knew he wouldn't
care what type of relationship activities followed. If it meant
having sex he would happily do whatever the woman wanted
afterward, no questions asked. *Cuddle for an hour? No problem.
Buy her dinner? Of course, I'm a gentleman. Clean her toilets? If she
asked I'd probably say yes.*

He considered several more extreme examples of things he
would probably agree too while turning onto Route 47 and heading toward Plank Road. Concern came with the thoughts because he suddenly wondered if he would put his better judgment
on hold in order to get it.

Oh, you want sex, the lady says while taking off her respectable
business attire to reveal a tight leather garment complete with a
belt for holding nasty stinging punishment tools. *Well, you can
only have sex if you're a good little boy, and first things first, a good
little boy has to do whatever --*

He cut the thought off and focused on the road ahead, hands
guiding the car to the right lane as he crossed the intersection
where a BP Station stood, and then merging back into the only
lane as the left lane split off into Route 20. From there he eyed
the upcoming turn onto Plank Road, a strange type of Hindu (or
some other Indian religion) temple sitting on the corner. The
building always caused Mark to wonder when the change from
farmland Christian church to temple had occurred since the
building obviously had been a simple community built church at
some point.

Of course the thoughts on this faded as he neared Burlington,
his car forced to slow to a measly thirty miles an hour as he
passed through the small little community.

Blink and you might miss it, he had told his parents two years
earlier when telling them about the drive between their Barring-

ton home and his DeKalb dorm. *And I once saw a horse hitched up at the gas station.*

No horse stood hitched up today as he drove by. He also didn't have to wait for any chickens to cross the road from the nearby farm where they occasionally broke free. Because of this nothing but thoughts on Nikki filled his head as he got closer and closer to her place, images of her in one of the sexy outfits from the profile and ready for him forcing out the ones of him standing like a fool before her door.

Behind him a car tried to kiss his bumper.

Mark was already going fifteen over the speed limit on the twisty roads, his hands forced to grip the wheel tightly, yet the driver still wanted him to go faster. Instead, Mark took his foot off the gas and let the car slow as he came to another huge bend.

Within seconds a horn was blasting at him as the car sped by in the oncoming traffic lane, and then cut across before the oncoming traffic caught up with him. Another couple of seconds and the road would probably have been shut down for hours as the police tried to separate the dead bodies from the wrecked cars.

An NIU sticker was stuck to the back window.

Figures, Mark said to himself. He then smiled as he thought about that winter, one which the weather people were saying would be incredibly snowy, and how he would probably see this car and a dozen others in the ditch when he drove home for the holidays. It never failed. The people he went to school with never could get it through their heads that the brand new modern cars their parents had given them still couldn't drive in defiance of Mother Nature. It was great.

Almost there, he told the excited part of his mind as the intersection of Plank Road and Route 23 appeared. *It won't be long before you know whether or not you're finally going to get to know what a warm pussy feels like around your pulsating cock.*

Not long before you start driving home again, Nikki's laughter ringing in your ears as your pulsating cock shrivels from embarrassment.

The second thought caused his fingers to tighten around the wheel as he came to a stop at the light. They did not loosen for ten minutes, not until he was sitting outside of Nikki's place.

He took several deep breaths before he stepped out of the car and walked up to the front door.

7

Kimberly paused as she dug through one of her few unpacked boxes that was sitting on the floor of the unused bedroom, and listened to see if someone actually was knocking on the door or if her mind had just played a trick on her.

It took a second, but sure enough another knock echoed, the sound barely reaching her ear thanks to the TV that was still turned up so she could have sound filing her ears while needlessly going through the box (why she kept so many CDs when all her favorite songs were now saved on her phone puzzled her).

Probably too loud for Bill, she thought (hoped?) as she pushed herself up from the floor and hurried to the door.

It wasn't Bill.

Instead a peek through the window revealed the young man from the night before standing on the small concrete landing, his hands fidgeting as he waited, eyes looking down at his shoes.

He didn't notice her looking through the window.

Why is he back? she demanded to herself while contemplating her next step.

Open the door and ask him, a confident voice said.

She considered this, but didn't know if it truly was a good idea.

Do it, but unlock the door to Bill's apartment so he can help you if needed.

The suggestion emboldened her and she quickly flipped the lock to the open position on the stairway door and then opened the front door, the force of which startled the young man.

"Yes?" she asked, arms quickly crossing over her chest.

"Um, hello again," he said.

"Hello," she replied. "What are you doing here?"

His smile faded a bit. "I thought . . . I thought this time you would . . ." he shook his head.

"Thought what?" she asked, her confidence at her own power within this situation growing.

"You told me I might have a chance if I didn't bring the flowers this time because you weren't a flower type of girl," he said. "But I suppose the idea that you would want to see me if I didn't bring flowers today was still just wishful thinking on my part."

"Who told you this?" she demanded.

Suspicion unfolded in his eyes.

"I'm not her," she added. "Honest."

"You didn't email me last night and tell me that the reason you decided not to see me was because I had brought flowers?" he asked.

"No, I didn't," she said, then, after some hesitation, "were you the one that left a bunch of pictures with slut and whore written on the back on my window last night?"

"What?" he asked. "No!"

The disbelief that appeared on his face was genuine. *Or he is a really good actor.*

She waited.

He didn't say anything for several seconds.

A part of her wanted to tell him to get lost so she could close the door, but another wanted to know who had told him she really was the girl he was looking for. Had he not seemed so innocent and gentle this second course of action would never have been contemplated. "Who keeps telling you I'm this girl?"

"I don't know," he said. "But I promise I won't bother you again."

"Wait," she said as he turned to leave.

The young man stopped; a hopeful look suddenly on his face.

"Where do you keep hearing that I'm this girl, this Nikki?" she asked.

"Um . . . online," he said, face turning red.

She gave a *go on* look, one that was emphasized with a *give me more* motion of her hands.

His face got even redder. "The OK Cupid dating site," he said.

"OK Cupid?" she asked. It was one she had never heard of before.

"Yeah," he muttered. "A girl on that site who I've been talking too for quite a while says that she lives here and told me the reason she didn't want to see me last night was because of the flowers."

"Why?"

"Why what?"

"Why would she keep telling you she lives here?"

"I wish I knew." A small hint of accusation was present in his voice.

"It's not me," she said. "I'm being perfectly honest with you. I don't use dating sites and even if I did I would never give out my address to anyone without first meeting them somewhere in public."

He shrugged.

Something he had said a moment earlier suddenly caused a chill to caress her bowels. "Did you tell this person online that you brought flowers?"

"No, and that's why I figured it really was you when she told me the flowers were the reason she didn't want to see me."

"But that means -- " she started, but couldn't finish.

" -- that she's watching," he completed with a nod and a quick glance toward the road. "Or at least she was watching last night."

Kimberly crossed her arms again, only this time it wasn't so she would look confident. "Why?"

"Probably because she gets off on making guys like me look like fools," he said, his eyes continuing to scan the cars parked on South Avenue.

Kimberly followed his study of the cars on the street to see if anyone was watching, her hope being he was right and that it was his foolishness that was the appeal. Unfortunately the pictures last night made her think it probably had more to do with her than him.

But why? she demanded to herself. It was a question she would probably be growing familiar with in the days to come, unless, of course, the person behind this did something to reveal themselves. If not she would . . .

"Hey, what was the girl's profile name on this, what was it, OK Cupid?" Kimberly asked.

"NIU Nikki," he said.

"NIU Nikki," she repeated. "As in Northern Illinois University?"

"Yeah, and there is a bottom line dash thingy between the NIU and NIKKI."

"So she claims to be a college student," Kimberly noted. "How long have you been talking to her?"

"Since the spring," he said.

"Really? Has she been telling you this was her address the entire time?" *If so then maybe she wasn't the one that was being targeted in this strange series of events.*

"Oh, no," he said with a shake of the head. "I only learned her address the other day, once she came back online. Before that she always hinted at wanting to meet but never really provided that final bit of necessary information."

Yet you kept talking to her week after week, Kimberly thought. But then, *you kept going out with Kyle week after week,* followed. Then, *Is it Kyle?*

"In fact," he continued, his voice pulling her back from the thoughts of Kyle. "I started to wonder if she was real, or just one of those girls who works for the site to keep guys like me paying members -- this was when she had the Adult Friend Finder profile -- but then she popped up on OK Cupid which is free so . . ." he left it at that.

An idea appeared in her head. "Hey, do you think you could do me a favor?

"What?"

"If I gave you my email address could you talk to this girl and find out how long she claims to have lived here?"

"Um . . . I suppose," he said after some thought. He then asked, "Why?"

"Because I moved in on the first of this month, you know, to start school out here, so if she claims to have lived her for as long as she has been talking to you then it will be a huge lie, one that you can maybe tell to the people who run the site so they take down her profile or something. And then, after that, you can email me and let me know what's going on and everything."

"I see, and you know, you could always set up a profile and talk to her and see what she tells you," he suggested.

"Oh, is she bi?" Kimberly asked.

"Actually, yeah . . . well, she claims to be. But I was thinking you could set it up as, you know, a guy and see if she tells you to meet here. Then you could also tell the administrators of the site what she is doing."

"I see, but couldn't I get in trouble for putting up a fake profile?"

"They'll just kick you off the site and if you don't use dating sites anyway what's the problem?"

"Oh, good point."

He gave her a brief smile.

Silence followed.

"So," he said after several seconds. "You're a student at Northern?"

"Yeah," she confirmed. "Start on Monday."

"First year here?"

"Uh-huh."

He nodded. "This'll be my junior year. I'll be moving back to the area in September and was thinking, instead of just giving you email updates I could, well, we could get together somewhere and I'll tell you what's going on that way."

"Oh . . . I . . . hmmm, I suppose that will work," she said.

"Great. How about I swing by after classes on Monday and we can go from there."

"Okay."

He smiled. "And if anything major happens in the next day or two that you need to know about I'll swing by then. My parents place is in Barrington, so it isn't too terrible a drive. We could get lunch or something."

"Okay," she said again. A realization struck. *Is he trying to work his way into a relationship type of situation with me?*

"Well, I guess I'll see you on Monday then," he said. "And, sorry for all the confusion last night and today. Hopefully we get this all straightened out."

"Hopefully," she agreed.

He waited for more and then started down the steps, a slight wave signaling his departure.

Kimberly acknowledged the wave with a nod, closed the door, and then watched as he headed to his car to drive away. Before getting in he looked down the street. Nothing seemed to catch his attention, however, and soon he was gone.

With that Kimberly headed to her computer to check out the profile he had given her, a nervous anticipation building as she waited for the Internet connection to be made and did a search for the OK Cupid website.

8

"Ah, fuck!" Bill cried as pain ripped him from his dream, the source being Toby's back claws as the cat used his chest as a springboard. Adding to the intense sting was the sweat that soaked into the torn flesh, the moisture having oozed from his pores as he slept in the ever-warming apartment.

A knock on the stairway door shifted his focus, though it did little to dull the pain. Having lived with Toby for a long time now, he knew the hot sting of the scratches would be there for quite some time. He also knew that dabbing it with disinfectant in the near future was a must given that those claws had been frequent visitors to the litter box.

For now, however, that could wait as he found out what Kimberly wanted.

He opened the door.

"Sorry if I'm bothering you, but can you come down and look at something real fast?" Kimberly said. "I found out who has been telling people I'm this girl Nikki."

"Oh, no problem," he said and started following her down the steps. "How'd you figure all this out?"

"That guy from yesterday stopped by again and told me that

this Nikki person had told him if he came by again without the flowers this time that he would get lucky. Can you believe that?"

"Wow, weird."

"Anyway, he told me where I could find this girl's profile on a dating site -- that's how he's been talking to her by the way, so you're right about your previous books having nothing to do with it."

"Oh good," Bill said, concern over what he was about to see upon her computer screen making it difficult to talk.

"Have you ever heard of the site called OK Cupid?" she asked as they stepped up to her computer. It sat on an oddly constructed glass desk in the corner of her family room.

"No," he said, a bit of relief appearing.

"I hadn't either." She reached for the mouse. "But it was pretty easy to find. So was her profile once I was on the site." She moved the mouse to knock out the screen-saver.

Oh shit! Bill's mind cried, the relief he had felt a moment earlier fading fast as he saw the profile picture.

"Now, I have to ask, does that really look like me?"

Bill didn't reply.

"And what about these?" Kimberly continued while using the mouse to scroll through the profile pictures.

Again, Bill didn't reply. How could he when he was looking at a dozen pictures he had taken of Nicole back when the two had started the process of setting up the blog and the Adult Friend Finder profile?

"Bill?" she asked.

"Oh, um -- " he looked at her and then back at the screen and then at her again " -- maybe a slight resemblance."

"Really?"

"Yeah, not one where I'd be like 'that's that girl from the profile' if I looked at these, then at you without already believing there was a connection."

Kimberly didn't reply to this.

Damn, even her profile name is the same, Bill realized. His mind then tried to tell itself that it was all a huge coincidence, but then dismissed the possibility before it really took hold. *Having the same name, maybe, but having the same name and all the same pictures, not a chance.*

"You know what I'm going to do," Kimberly said.

"What?" Bill asked.

"I'm going to set up my own profile on here, as a guy, and message her and see what she does."

"Why?"

"Because what if she gives me this address. I can then contact the administration people and inform them of what she's doing. If they don't care I'll then tell the police about it because I'm sure this is somehow illegal. Even if it isn't I'm sure whoever is doing this will get scared off if the police tell her to stop." Kimberly seemed really pleased with herself.

Bill on the other hand was a bit concerned because if the police did get involved it would probably lead back to him, and while he knew he hadn't done anything wrong, he still didn't want it all coming to light.

Then again, it's not like you're a famous horror author who is going to be dragged through the media spotlight if this information comes to light.

Still, he didn't want the attention.

He then realized something. Only one person could be behind this, because only one person knew the truth behind the NIU Nikki profile on the Adult Friend Finder site, which had pretty much been reproduced here, and the blog. The question was why would Nicole do something like this? If she had found a way of making money from it okay, but having guys show up here, that didn't make any sense.

"So, what do you think?" Kimberly asked. "Is it a good plan?"

"Seems like it could work?"

Kimberly smiled. "I hope so. The last thing I want is for more guys to show up thinking I'm her."

"I bet."

"Now the only thing I'm confused about are the pictures from last night. Do you think that has anything to do with all this?"

"Honestly, I can't say for sure." Had he been more focused on her question he would have added a statement on how it seemed a little far-fetched that two completely separate incidents would begin occurring within hours of each other. Instead all he could really think about was why Nicole would leave pictures like that. No sensible answer arrived. Just figuring out why she would send guys here through the profile was a mystery.

Is it really her?

Who else could it be?

9

Kimberly stared at a picture of Kyle she still had on her phone and debated on whether or not to use it for the OK Cupid profile she was creating. Nothing but disgust was present when thinking about him these days, yet still the right and wrong aspects of posting such a picture fueled her indecision.

He wouldn't think twice about using your pictures for something, she told herself. *Hell, he probably is using your pictures.*

Thankfully, he didn't have anything explicit, though he had often tried to get her to agree to take pictures and video of such things – *for my private collection since you don't put out nearly as much as you should.*

She shook her head at the memory, and then grew frustrated with herself for often hesitating in her rejection of the idea.

You almost gave in once just to please him.

Actually, she had given in, her lips uttering an agreement to suck his dick while he filmed it, but then, as he got the camera ready, she came to her senses and reversed her decision.

'You can't do that!' he had cried. *'You already said yes!'*

'I changed my mind.' Then, to appease him, *'I'll still give you a blowjob though and let you cum in my mouth.'*

Being a guy, he had accepted this, and, naturally, being herself, she had later regretted it, her conscious telling her she should have said no and not offered the blowjob as compensation.

Now, looking back, she was just glad she had put the kibosh on the videotaping because if she hadn't she was sure the video would be up on porn sites right now for guys to download and enjoy.

See, he wouldn't think twice about using pictures and videos of you, so why are you so concerned with using one of him. And it's not like you're trying to hurt him with this picture. You just want to try and learn something about someone who may be trying to hurt you.

Then you should just call the police and show them the profile, she argued with herself.

No, not yet.

Once she had emails from the NIU Nikki profile telling her to meet at this address, then she would alert the police (well, maybe), but until then all she really had was a young man's word, a young man who had actually tried snagging a semi-date out of all this – or so it had seemed.

She shook her head and then looked at the picture again. Indecision still gripped her, however, so she turned her attention to the *About Me* box. *Well hung and fit twenty one year old with an unquenchable thirst for sex.*

The statement caused her to grimace, yet it seemed to fit perfectly with what other men on the site were saying about themselves, so she left it alone.

Does it actually work? she wondered. *Do other girls see something like this and think, 'oh yeah, that's the guy I want to start talking to?'* If she were one of those girls, the answer would be a huge NO, but maybe she was the odd one out. Maybe girls who used sites like this to find men were the type to enjoy such statements.

A thought about the type of guys who had been 'significant' to her suddenly entered her mind followed by the realization that she wasn't really one to talk about anyone else's choice in men.

Memories of the bathroom and the blood and her beloved cat began to arrive.

No! No! No!

She did everything she could to keep the memories from filling her head, but the harder she tried the more forceful they became. Thankfully, they didn't overwhelm her this time, all because she started searching profiles in the DeKalb and Sycamore area, her bare arm constantly wiping away the tears that were falling so she could see the screen.

You should talk to someone, Melissa had told her a while back. *Even if you think you can handle it on your own you'd be surprised how much talking about it with a professional will help.*

But I can't afford it, she had replied. *And I don't want Mom and Dad to know why, and they'll pester me and pester me until I tell them.*

Then I will help you cover the cost.

Kimberly had almost given in at that point, but then said no. She knew her sister was well off, but not well off enough where she could simply lay down that kind of money without having to shift some things around. She also knew that if she really needed it there would be people she could talk to at NIU, people who were free.

Should have done that back at U of I, she now told herself. *Might have been able to finish school, or at least gotten some sympathy on why your grades slipped and not been tossed out on your ass.*

She shook her head.

What's done is done.

On screen she noticed something in a profile that she needed to add to hers, one that made her *About Me* section read: *Well hung and fit twenty one year old college student with an unquenchable thirst for sex.*

Once added she went back to looking at the picture of Kyle. She then thought about all the times she had given in to his demands, and all the times she had allowed him to make her feel insignificant, and thought, *Ah, fuck it.*

A minute later the picture was up on the profile.

He'll never even see it, she told herself. *And it will be taken down in no time anyway.*

Well, if NIU Nikki actually responds to it.

Concern on whether or not NIU Nikki would think the profile a trick filled her head, and she wondered if there was anything she could do, aside from answering all the questions, to make it look more realistic.

Searching the OK Cupid site filled her with ideas, but she then wondered if seeing all the sudden activity would make NIU

Nikki think the profile was trying too hard to look real.

Can she even see your activity?

If we favorite each other what does that mean?

Is it like Facebook?

She sighed.

You're over thinking this.

You can always set up another profile if this doesn't work.

Of course, that would require finding a different picture to use, which could start to become tricky.

Unless Bill would agree?

Actually, Bill could probably do a nice job with something like this. After all, creating characters that seemed real was how he earned a living, and with this he wouldn't even have to keep them seeming real over several hundred pages. Instead, he would just need to create one and then speak for it whenever NIU Nikki messaged him.

With these thoughts on her mind, Kimberly nearly headed upstairs to ask Bill's opinion, but then caught herself moments before making the actions a reality.

Don't want to make a nuisance of yourself.

Instead, she would wait and see what happened with the profile she had created, and, if it failed, she would see what Bill's thoughts were on creating his own.

You might want to ask his help in sending her a message, though, her mind suggested.

Doing a simple 'I have a big dick and want to fuck you' message didn't seem like it would get her anywhere. It would need substance.

She also wanted to wait a while. Creating a profile and sending a message right away wouldn't look right, almost like she had simply created it to target NIU Nikki.

That is what you're doing.

Waiting would be good. Unfortunately, it would also be difficult. She wanted to send and receive a message from NIU Nikki right now, one that came out and boldly said to head to this address.

Naturally, this brought up the question of *then what?*

Kimberly had no idea.

10

"Hey Nicole, it's Bill. Can you please give me a call? It's important. Thanks."

Bill closed the phone and looked over at his laptop, sudden uncertainty flowing through him. Questions were present as well, mainly ones that asked why Nicole would do this. A debate on whether or not it really was her always followed. When asking himself these questions downstairs he had settled on a statement of *who else could it be*. This time around was no different. He couldn't think of anyone else that would do this, at least not when factoring in the address being used.

But why torment Kimberly?

Asking this brought him full circle.

Once again no answer arrived, nor would one until he was able to talk to Nicole.

He looked at his phone, his mind willing it to ring.

No call arrived.

She might not call at all, he realized. *Not if she suspects it has something to do with whatever game she is playing.*

Doubt arrived with this thought. Directing it was the familiar question on why Nicole would do this, only this time he wasn't asking it in hopes of bringing about an answer, but more with a sense of disbelief because the idea that she would be behind something like this was seeming less plausible the more he contemplated it.

But if not her then who?

Nothing followed.

You're missing something; something important.

What?

Again, nothing.

He thought about all the times he had been stuck when working on a story, the sudden halt in narrative flow the result of his mind being unable to come up with a realistic reason for the crazy events that were taking place. Whenever this happened he didn't force the issue because he knew an answer would eventually arrive, the sudden *click* usually occurring when he was thinking about or working on something else. Once this happened everything would fall together in his mind and the rest of the story would flow from his fingertips without much trouble.

Nothing like that would happen this time.

Several *clicks* might occur, but whether or not they truly provided an answer would be a mystery until he was able to talk to the person involved, be it Nicole or whoever else was behind it. Without such action he would be in the dark, his mind unable to figure out who the person was that was using the pictures he had taken, and why they were using them to lure men to the house.

He looked over at his phone, a demand for it to ring echoing in his head once again.

If it is Nicole she might not call.

If she doesn't you can go to her apartment, and if she doesn't answer the door just go to her work and make sure you get seated in her section.

Give her a reasonable chance first.

He sighed and took a seat, his mind unable to focus on anything but the need to speak with her. Attempting to sidetrack his mind would meet with failure. Adding to the turmoil he felt was the lack of progress he had made with his writing this morning. Had he completed the daily goal of ten pages he wouldn't have minded sitting and staring at his cell phone, just like he wouldn't have minded sitting and staring at the TV (if he had cable), or watching porn (if he had Internet), but having failed in his goal left him on edge. In fact he felt downright lazy.

Nothing, not even the knowledge that he was paying all his bills and slowly but surely knocking down the credit card debt with his writing, could dispel this feeling of inadequacy.

He shook his head and stood up from the couch, his mind now unable to stand the thought of just sitting there. Pacing was better. Back and forth he went, eyes constantly glaring at the phone.

Ten minutes came and went without him even realizing it. He didn't pace the entire time. Sometimes he stared out the front window at the street, or went to the back window and looked at the yard. During this latter staring moment he realized it was time to cut the grass again, but decided against using it as a distraction. Later, once he had the Nicole issue figured out he would take care of that.

11

Bill saw the flashing blue light on the phone as he walked back in from the kitchen where he had grabbed a soda, his ear having never heard the single buzz as the message arrived.

1 NEW MESSAGE was centered on the screen when he opened the phone. Beneath that was the word NICOLE.

Finally, he said to himself.

JUST GOT YOUR MESSAGE. WORKING DOUBLE SHIFT TODAY. NEED ALL THE HOURS I CAN GET BEFORE CLASSES START. WHAT'S UP? I HAVE ABOUT TWENTY MINUTES TO EAT SOMETHING. I CAN TEXT BUT WON'T BE ABLE TO CALL UNTIL I GET OFF TONIGHT AT NINE. TTYL.

Bill thought for a moment on whether or not he wanted to ask the question he needed to ask through a text, and then decided, *what the hell,* and typed up a message that read: DID YOU SET UP YOUR OWN NIKKI PROFILE LIKE THE ONE I USED TO HAVE?

He didn't send it right away, concern that she would simply say NO even if it was a lie stalling his finger.

The fact that she replied at all is a sign that she probably isn't behind this, he silently noted.

The hesitation didn't disappear and lasted so long that the phone screen turned black. A simple press of an arrow key brightened it once again. He then hit SEND.

WHAT? was Nicole's reply.

SOMEONE SET UP A PROFILE USING THE PICTURES WE TOOK AND IS SENDING GUYS TO THE HOUSE. ANY IDEA WHO IT COULD BE? WE WERE THE ONLY ONES THAT KNEW ABOUT WHAT I WAS DOING.

I DON'T KNOW, Nicole sent back. BUT IT ISN'T ME IF THAT IS WHAT YOU ARE IMPLYING.

OK, Bill typed, mind unsure whether or not to believe her. Then, ANY IDEA WHO IT COULD BE?

NO.

WHAT ABOUT YOUR ROOMMATE? The two had once discussed the possibility of taking pictures with the roommate as an added lure, but in the end Nicole had never been able to convince the girl to go ahead with it. Even the suggestion of wearing sunglasses and a wig so that her identity wouldn't be known had been vetoed. The girl just had not been interested.

I DOUBT IT.

AN ANGRY BOYFRIEND?

ARE YOU KIDDING?

NO! Then, after a few minutes passed, he added, THIS IS PRETTY SERIOUS. PLEASE TRY TO THINK OF WHO IT COULD BE.

Nothing.

Bill waited and waited, his hand holding the phone so he would feel the buzz, even when he walked in to use the bathroom, but Nicole never replied.

Frustrated, he went to the window and stared out at the road. Nothing was going on out there. Several different cars were sitting empty, but that was typical for the area given that most of the houses had been divided into apartments and had more renters with vehicles than driveway space. Why no one was ever out and about was a mystery to him, but one that he figured had something to do with the fact that most of the people were college students, and thus they had odd schedules. Then again, the ones who weren't college students, the ones who had families, were rarely out, their kids always kept indoors for some reason. He often had wondered about this, but figured maybe it had something to do with all the perceived threats the media instilled in parents these days.

Or maybe it's the graveyard?

Bill walked to the back window while thinking this and looked out between the two houses that butted up against the backyard. Beyond them, on the opposite side of the street, was the graveyard, one that stretched further than the eye could see from the road it stood against. Last year on Halloween, while waiting for the series premier of *The Walking Dead*, he had strolled along the fence that partially enclosed the graveyard, his mind trying, but failing, to get a spooky vibe from it. Nothing it seemed could freak him these days, his decade long immersion into the horror genre having completely desensitized him to fear.

Time drifted away while he stared, his eyes no longer seeing anything beyond the window. Instead, he was looking into his thoughts, his inner eye replaying various moments from his life.

The phone buzzed.

He looked at the message that read: SORRY, BUT I DON'T THINK THIS IS COMING FROM MY END.

He sighed.

If not from her end then from where?

Who would start messing with the girl down there and why?

No answer arrived.

A new question did though. Maybe it had nothing to do with the girl downstairs. Unfortunately this still left him with the questions of *who* and *why*.

What would the purpose of sending guys to the house be? And the pictures? Who took those and what was the reason for leaving them?

He considered the possibility that the two weren't connected and coincidentally happened upon the same day.

Readers would never buy it, he told himself. In real life, however, things like this did happen.

Of course thinking this just added a second *who* and *why* to the question, and once again he had no way of putting a face or reason to them.

Wait, she just went through a breakup. He knew this because he often heard her talking on the phone, the floor / ceiling that separated the two of them doing little to buffer the sounds each one made.

And if the guy she broke up with was the same guy who came over and fucked her silly that one night, then he obviously knew where she lived.

Memories of that night and the different sounds he had heard while his ear was pressed to the floor filled his head. Images of what he imagined Kimberly looked like when in such moments of sexual ecstasy appeared as well.

Urges within himself began to develop while thinking about this, ones that he somehow pushed away. Thoughts on the guy and whether or not he would start to torment her with pictures didn't disappear, however, and for several minutes he played around with the ideas as if it were a storyline, his mind trying to figure out how likely it was. One thing he couldn't do was attach the boyfriend to the new Nikki profile and the guy who had showed up because of the address he was given. Nope. The odds that the angry boyfriend would find the profile he had created and then recreate it so that he could use it against his ex-girlfriend were just too great.

Unfortunately, this brought him back around to the idea that whoever had created that profile had known the original profile was linked to this address. How someone could figure that out was a mystery, as was the motive behind their actions. It just didn't make any sense to him.

Frustration arrived.

He didn't know what to do. Hell, he didn't even know if there was anything he could do.

Such a thought would not shut off his mind, however. Nothing would.

12

Why are you teasing me? Why do you keep sending me to that house when it isn't really you who lives there?

Mark stared at the two sentences, finger hesitating over the SEND button, the anger he felt toward this Nikki girl almost getting the better of him. He then got control of himself and deleted the message, his mind glad he hadn't simply hit SEND once the two sentences had been typed.

Be cool, he told himself. *Play along and try to figure out something about this person so you can share it with the girl at the house.*

Future moments of pride for helping the poor girl put an end to whatever torment she was experiencing filled his head.

She'll be so very thankful for what you did, he told himself. *You'll be her hero.*

Yeah, keep dreaming.

Still, trying to learn a thing or two about the real person behind the NIU Nikki profile would be better than just typing up a few sentences calling her out, especially when those sentences would probably just cause her to stop talking to him.

Play along. Tease her just like she teased you.

But how?

Being easily teased by girls like this didn't mean he was good at giving it back.

He also knew that lying to her about how wonderful the sex was that they shared might not be the best idea because if she had been watching she would know he hadn't gotten beyond the front door.

Maybe you should just report it to the administrators and be done with it?

The trouble was he knew the administrators would want to keep a girl profile like Nikki's around. Even if this wasn't a paid site that used women like that to lure in men and get them to pay for a membership, it still was a site that earned income through advertisers (he assumed) and therefore they would want to keep as many women on as possible. His complaints would be viewed as nothing more than a disgruntled male who couldn't get the pussy he wanted.

And in the end, even if he did manage to get her kicked off, she'd probably just start up a new profile somewhere else, one that he wouldn't be able to help the girl at the house with. Dating sites were not in short supply when it came to the Internet. Hell, new ones seemed to pop up everyday.

What to say? What to say? What to say?

He thought about this for a long time, his mind so focused that he never left the email page he was on to browse other girls in the area, which was unusual for him.

Then again, why browse for girls who would probably never respond to him when he kept picturing one in his head, one who needed his help and might possibly fall head over heels for him if he managed to save her.

A scene of her answering the door and instantly pulling him inside by his belt buckle arrived, her lips quickly locking upon his before the door was even shut, her hands working to remove all the different layers of fabric that stood between them.

You wish, he silently said with a shake of the head. *Even if you do help her she'll never --*

An idea arrived and killed the thought.

His fingers began typing:

Many thanks for giving me a second chance and once again I'm sorry about bringing the flowers the other night. What can I say, I'm a bit old fashioned. I have now realized the error of my ways and am looking forward to the blowjob and sex you have promised me. Please let me know if anything changes in the location we agreed to meet in. If not, I will see you at The Junction for dinner tomorrow night and –

He stopped typing, a thought occurring.

If she isn't a 'bring me flowers' type of girl then why would you be taking her out to dinner beforehand?

He then reminded himself that he wasn't actually trying to convince Nikki that the girl he had seen was Nikki. She obviously already knew the truth of that situation. Instead, he was trying to convince her that he believed the girl at the house was she, and that she had agreed to see him again.

And, being a normal girl, she wants to go to dinner first.

But, would you have bought that after the whole flower thing? If so, Nikki might find that odd and grow suspicious.

Keep it simple.

He did and allowed the email to end with: *Please let me know if anything changes in location. See you soon, Mark.*

Hesitation arrived again, but didn't last very long.

He hit SEND.

Satisfaction followed.

Then concern.

You should have just walked away from all this.

You should have recognized the fact that Nikki was still a fake and moved on.

Of course if he had done that he would never have been able

to talk to the girl today, and while he knew that probably wouldn't end the way he hoped (his mind flashed to an image of her pulling him down onto the bed, her shirt now removed and the beautiful nipples he had seen poking through the thin fabric this morning finally exposed and ready for his touch), it would still feel good to help her.

If you really are helping her.

The thoughts of sex with her were pushed away by an image of him showing her what he had uncovered on this Nikki girl, information that he had spent countless sleepless nights trying to achieve, only to realize she had figured it out several days earlier. Not just figured it out, but figured it out, put a stop to it, and moved on, her lips asking, *'Nikki? Nikki who? Oh that! Were you still poking around? Wow! My bad, I should have told you it was all over.'* The thought brought up a memory of playing Ghost in the Graveyard when he was younger and realizing that everyone had gone home while he was hiding.

Images of the concern he had seen on the girl's face when she answered the door pushed the Ghost in the Graveyard memories away, and also put a damper on the idea that she wouldn't be appreciative of his help.

Maybe she won't go so far as to have sex with you, he admitted, *but that still doesn't mean your work won't be appreciated.*

Plus, despite how much he wanted that sex, he also didn't want to be known as a guy who would only help a girl if such an outcome were promised. No. Even if he was the only one that knew the motive for his actions, or lack of actions if he refused to help, it would be enough to view himself in a negative light for the rest of his life.

You're stuck.

You have no choice but to help her.

13

Even though it was a Friday night, working her evening shift at Steak and Shake didn't seem as crazy as other nights had been. The reason for this was simple: more employees. The only downside was her exhaustion, which most likely stemmed from her decision to sleep on the couch. Having done that seemed silly to her now, but then the fear she had felt at the time was far from her mind. Later, once it was time to go to bed again, she was sure some of that sensation would return. *Or would it?* Having set up a profile and then sending NIU Nikki a message before heading to work made her feel almost as if she were taking control over the situation. The question was would it accomplish anything? Would she really get a response that helped her put an end to whatever it was this person was trying to achieve, or would it prove to be a useless endeavor?

Thinking about this and wondering whether or not she had gotten a response caused her to watch the clock a bit as the end of her shift drew near. This, coupled with her exhaustion, resulted in an order mix-up for a young girl who was eating alone at one of the small tables near the window. Thankfully, the girl didn't make a big deal out of it, though the same couldn't be said about the other customer. He wasn't in her section though so she didn't get the brunt of his disgruntlement. Max, who was waiting that table, also didn't say anything to her, though she did apologize to him once the two were back near the expo counter.

"Blah, when you've been waiting tables as long as I have stuff like that doesn't even register. His food was like, what, three minutes late? If that's the biggest problem he faces today then I wish I had his life."

He added a wave of dismissal to the statement and grabbed a plate that was ready to go out.

Kimberly watched him for a moment and then, realizing the food she needed would be a couple minutes still, headed back out in the dining area to check on her tables. With the exception of two drink refills, everyone was doing okay. Drinks replenished, she headed back to the expo counter to grab the food that was up. While there, Max, who was working on a shake, said, "Might want to bus some of those tables in your section. Believe it or not they say dirty tables will reduce tipping in the surrounding area regardless of how good the service is."

"Given the tips I've been getting I don't think they could go any lower," Kimberly said, food tray ready to be hoisted up. "In fact, any lower and I'd be paying them."

Max laughed.

Tray balanced, Kimberly brought the food to the waiting table – a family of four -- and then headed over to the first table that needed cleaning, eyes zeroing in on the folded dollar bills that were waiting.

She didn't pick them up.

She didn't clean the table either.

Instead, she fought back a startled gasp as her eyes settled upon a picture of herself sitting beneath the bills, and then scanned the restaurant.

No one was paying any attention to her.

She looked back at the picture. Someone had snapped it as she stepped out of her car before her shift, the cars location in the parking lot and her Steak and Shake uniform making the moment easy to identify. Equally easy to identify was the word SLUT scribbled all over in red marker.

Don't freak out, she told herself and then nearly shouted as Max came up behind her and asked if everything was okay.

"What do you mean?" she demanded, hand slipping the picture into her large apron pocket.

"You were standing here for like a minute staring at the table," he said.

"Oh, just drifted off I guess." She snatched up her tip. "Had a rough night."

"Ah, well, it happens I guess," he said. "Want some help with these?"

"Nah, I got it." To prove this she quickly gathered up all the garbage from the table and dumped it. She then moved onto the next table and did the same, relief that nothing had been left beneath the three-dollar tip filling her mind. The same was true with the third table: nothing but a tip and garbage.

Max watched for a moment, eyes following her to the second table, and then moved back to his section and his customers. Once there Kimberly started to wonder about him and his suggestion that she go bus her tables.

Was it because he wanted you to find the picture, or had he been generally concerned about the potential for low tips?

More questions followed, questions that she couldn't answer, questions on why he would choose to torment her.

And why would he pose as a girl to do this?

He seemed too nice and straightforward to do something like that.

But then that's what everyone says when they learn someone is truly a psycho.

"Excuse me," a voice said.

Kimberly turned and saw the girl whose order she had mixed up earlier staring at her. "Yes?" she asked.

"I'm ready for my check, now," the girl said.

"Oh, okay." Kimberly began rummaging through her apron for it, her hand bumping the photograph several times while searching for the elusive slip of paper that she had printed up twenty minutes earlier in anticipation of the girl's request. Little had she known the tiny girl, whose body looked as if it had never even come within range of anything fattening, let alone eaten anything, would down every last bite of her cheeseburger and fries, and then take her time and finish the entire shake. "Here you go, and again, I'm sorry for the mix up earlier."

"No problem," she said and then pulled out two fives. "Can I just give this to you?"

"Um . . . sure," she said. "Let me go get some change."

"Nah, keep it."

"You sure?" *That's almost a six-dollar tip!*

"Yep, maybe you can split it with that other guy since the fat guy that complained didn't leave anything." She shrugged. "I feel bad about that."

Kimberly didn't know what to say.

The girl smiled and then left.

Once gone Kimberly realized she should have asked the girl if she had seen someone leave the picture on the table. Given her observation of the tip-less table earlier there was a chance she would have noticed other things as well. Then again, several people had watched the mini confrontation that had taken place with the disgruntled customer who had not been shy about voicing his opinion of Max's waiter skills, or the establishment, so that everyone within could hear.

Having not asked, Kimberly was stuck with her own observations of the people who had been in the restaurant, which did little to help her pinpoint a possible suspect – other than Max, though, the more she thought about that the more far-fetched it seemed. Making this attempt even more frustrating was that she couldn't even picture the people who had been sitting at the table where the picture had been left, their faces all a blur to her.

Adding to the torment of the picture were the three others that had been stuck beneath her windshield wiper, two of them showing her by herself at various points during the day, the other showing her standing at the door with Mark. On this later one a statement had been written that read: *You'll fuck anything with a dick won't you! SLUT! SLUT! SLUT!*

14

"Honestly, I don't think this is connected to me at all," Nicole said.

"You could be right," Bill admitted even though he wasn't ready to close this line of thinking just yet. "At the same time I just don't understand how someone could connect the dots like this unless they knew about what we were doing. It doesn't make any sense."

"True, but then you'd think they'd be sending me stuff too, right? But I haven't gotten anything."

"Yeah, but it seems like they think the girl downstairs is you. At least that is the impression I've gotten."

"Does she look like me?"

"Not really, but I can see how someone could draw a connection if they thought one was already there."

Bill heard Nicole sigh on the other end of the phone and then, "Why didn't you shut the site down?"

"I don't know," he said, frustration building. "I've been thinking about that a lot today." He shook his head even though she couldn't see it. "I think the fact that so much work went into it, and that it had become so popular, I didn't really want to just end it, you know."

"Yeah, but maybe this wouldn't have happened if you did."

"Well, that could be said about a lot of things and if I had even suspected something like this I would never have let the site stay up."

"Of course you've taken it down now, right?"

"Um . . ." he hadn't even thought about it.

"Are you fucking kidding me," she said, his hesitation telling her all she needed to know. "Here you're asking me all these questions as if I had something to do with all this and you haven't even taken any steps to put a stop to it yourself?"

"Getting rid of the site won't put a stop to it. Whoever is doing this has already set up another dating site profile and has told a guy the house address. Plus I can't exactly access the Internet from my place, as you already know." Despite the statements, Bill knew her anger was valid. He also knew that shutting down the site was probably a good idea, not because it would put a stop to anything, but because it wouldn't give anyone anything to look at and connect to him if an investigation unfolded.

"Don't tell me you can't drive out to a hotspot and get online. I've done that hundreds of times. Head over to the college if you have too. They have Wifi."

"I do it all the time," Bill said. "The trouble is I can't access the blog from any of those places because it's blocked." Actually, he probably could access the blog dashboard, which would be all he needed. A few simple clicks and goodbye blog. "Plus my computer is so old I barely have any reach. I have to be right up next to the Wifi, which isn't always easy."

"Whatever, I just think it's crazy that you're jumping all over me about this as if something I did caused all this, yet you haven't really done much about it yourself," Nicole said.

"Okay, I'm sorry about that. I'm just a little freaked out by what happened."

"And I guess I'm exhausted and moody from working all day,

so . . ." she let the statement hang.

Bill wasn't sure what to say.

Nicole stayed silent as well.

Finally, he asked, "So, nothing out of the ordinary has happened at all?"

"I told you, NO."

"Maybe it was something you didn't really associate with all this at the time."

"Bill, nothing has happened. I would know because I think about what we did quite a bit."

"You do?" This caught him off guard because he had figured she had put this all behind her.

"Yeah. I hate to say this, as much fun as all that was, a part of me wishes I had never actually done it because I worry that it might come back to haunt me later on when I try to get a job."

"Oh." That hadn't been the statement he was hoping for.

"And now that I know someone has actually tracked down your address, I'm even more concerned about that. How would anyone do that, anyway?"

"I don't know," Bill admitted. "I'm not really knowledgeable when it comes to tech stuff."

"Well maybe you should look into that. I'm sure someone at Northern could give you info."

"Good idea."

"And keep me posted on what you find out."

"Okay, I will."

"Anything else before I head in – I've been sitting in the car in my parking lot for almost ten minutes since I didn't want my roommate to hear and freak out about all this."

"No, I don't think so. I guess just let me know if anything does start to happen. I don't think it will, but . . . well, if it does. The police have opened an investigation into it as well, so hopefully it will be resolved soon."

"Oh, I didn't know that," Nicole said, a positive ring suddenly present. "Maybe they'll be able to track down the tech stuff then."

"Maybe," he agreed even though this didn't seem likely since he hadn't told them anything about the blog or his connection.

"Do they know about me, like my address and name and stuff?"

"No, they just were more interested in the pictures that had been left and whether or not Kimberly – the girl downstairs – had any enemies. But I'm sure they'll look into everything."

"Okay."

The call ended after that.

Unsure what to do, Bill stood in his apartment for a couple minutes contemplating things. The window then brightened as Kimberly pulled her car into the driveway – motion sensor again – and finally into the garage.

Will anything happen tonight? he wondered.

A few seconds later, he learned that something already had.

15

"I couldn't even drive," Kimberly said. "I was so shaken I just sat there in the dark with my hands on the steering wheel for almost ten minutes." She shook her head and wiped at her eyes, which were wet with emotion, eyes that had made driving difficult once she had gotten some control of herself and started heading home.

"You didn't see anyone taking these?" Bill asked after examining the pictures.

"No," she admitted, a sense of failure descending upon her. After last night, she should have been more aware of everything. She should have known that things like this could happen anywhere and at anytime, not just while she was at home.

"And you really have no idea who this could be?"

"No!" she snapped, and then, "I'm sorry. This whole thing . . ." she felt her lips start to quiver and clamped down with them.

"It's okay," he said, voice calm. "I'd be pretty flustered too if someone were leaving pictures of me all over the place. It's scary."

Unsure how to reply, and fearing her emotions would get the better of her if she tried, she simply nodded.

Bill flipped over the picture that had captured her and Mark talking at the front door. He then looked up at her and asked, "Any idea why this was written?"

Kimberly shook her head.

"Is there anyone from your . . ."

Kimberly waited, but when he didn't finish, she asked, "Anyone from my what?"

Bill sighed. "I was going to ask if there was anyone from your past that may have been upset with you and with the idea that you might be seeing someone, but then realized that probably isn't the case since it seems like it's more the apartment and your location that's to blame." He shrugged. "Someone thinks you're someone you're not."

"But why?"

He didn't reply.

Kimberly stared at him for a moment, her mind thinking – knowing – there was something more within his head, something he wasn't saying, but she couldn't figure out how to get at it. She also didn't know why she knew this, or if her thoughts on the subject could be entirely trusted. Everything that had occurred was threatening to overwhelm her. It was all too much.

He handed back the pictures, which she took and stuck inside her apron, her mind realizing for the first time that she had failed to take it off before getting into the car. Noting this somehow added another layer of turmoil to her mind. It was just too much. She had moved out here and signed up for classes so she could get a fresh start, a second chance almost, and already someone was ruining it. It wasn't fair.

"Do you want something to drink or anything, something to take your mind off all this?" Bill asked.

The question caught her off guard and took a moment to process. "I don't usually drink, but yeah, I could probably use it right now."

"Oh, um . . ." embarrassment appeared ". . . I don't actually have anything like that, just soda, tea, juice." He twisted his palms upward in a helpless 'that's all' gesture.

"A writer without liquor," she said and attempted a smile.

"Yeah, doesn't seem right, does it, but . . ." nothing else followed.

"I'm okay. I'll probably just head down and try to get some rest." Once she put some thought into it, she was glad he didn't have any liquor. Getting shit-faced, while appealing, had bad idea written all over it.

"That's probably best. Did you call the police about this yet?"

She shook her head.

"Will you?"

"In the morning," she said, though she hadn't really decided yet. It was one of those things she knew she had to do, but didn't necessarily want to do. "I just can't handle that added level of stress right now."

"I hear ya."

She nodded.

"If you need anything please don't hesitate, okay, even if it's the middle of the night," he added and then reached for the handle of the stairway door so he could open it for her.

"Thanks," she said to the first part. Then, seeing his gesture, added, "Oh, my door's locked. I'll have to go out and around." Rather than going to her own place once she was home she had come straight up here, the idea of being alone, even if it was just for a few seconds, something she didn't want to experience at that time. Hell, she didn't really want to experience it now, but there was nothing she really could do about that, not unless she invited Bill down.

If only Kyle were here, she started to think, but then shot down the thought. Having him here wouldn't be much comfort, and really, given the situation, she didn't trust herself. Feeling vulnerable would make it too easy to give into any of his wants, which in turn would make her feel sick later. No. Being alone, but knowing someone like Bill was only a scream away, was better – *but only if you unlock the stairway door.*

"Uh, do you want me to walk you down to your door?" Bill asked.

"No, I'll be fine."

"You sure?"

She nodded.

"Okay." He walked her to his front door. "Well, I hope your night is peaceful. And really, if you need anything, please, please, please, don't worry about asking."

"I won't."

He smiled and then opened the door for her.

She stepped out and at first felt fine walking down, but then, once she rounded the corner of the stairway and was on the backside of the house, the darkness got the better of her.

You should have had him walk down with you.

No, no, no, you can do this.

Taking a deep breath, she hurried off the creaky stairway and started toward the side of the house where her own steps were, but then stopped when she realized the motion sensor light didn't turn on. Her eyes were then drawn to the abandoned house beyond the backyard, one that must have been empty for years given how decrepit and rotten it looked.

So many dark windows –

Light engulfed her from behind.

She gasped.

Up above Bill's porch squealed as he stepped out upon it. "Kim?" he asked.

Eyeing the porch, she stepped around where the garbage cans stood, and came into view.

"You okay?" he asked.

"Yeah," she called. "The light startled me."

"Sorry. I just now realized the switch was flipped off and figured it'd be best to have it on once again."

"You know the light over by the garage is out."

"Really?"

"Yeah, does it take batteries or something?"

"No, all these, mine up here, the one down by you, and that one over the garage all plug in so . . . um . . . does the one by your door work?"

Kimberly looked at the small light attached to the post just below where the underside of Bill's porch began. Anytime any-one pulled into the driveway it would go on, therefore if she got just a little bit closer . . .

"Anything?" Bill asked.

"No, it's not working," Kimberly said, fear once again creeping in. "What does that mean?"

"Hang on, I'm coming down."

More boards squealed as Bill hurried down the steps, the entire stairway shaking with each foot placement.

"Okay, let's see what's going on with this," he said, his feet not stopping once he was next to her, but instead continuing around until he was up her steps.

In order to get at the small square flood light he had to climb up onto the railing, an act that required quite a bit of courage given how rotted everything was.

Realizing her exposure, Kimberly followed him up the steps and started to ask, "Is there anything I can – "

"It was cut," he said.

"What?"

"Look."

It took a second given how little light made it through the cracks of the porch above, but then, as her eyes focused in on where he was pointing, she saw it.

"But how would someone do that without electrocuting themselves?" she asked.

"I don't know," Bill said while examining the small metal pipe that ran along the underside of the porch and connected with the house. "But whoever did it must know a few little tricks when it comes to wires, because as far as I can tell there is nowhere to unplug this thing out here."

"And what about the one on the garage?"

"Same sort of setup I'm guessing, though given how high up it is, it seems really far fetched that someone would be able to lean a ladder up against the house and climb up without someone seeing -- me in particular since I've been here all day." He jumped down from the railing. "My guess would be that the door was unlocked – it always is when I go to grab the lawnmower – and that whoever did this just walked inside, found where the cord came in and snipped it as well."

Kimberly didn't know what to say to this. It seemed incredible to her that someone would risk so much to cut wires like this. Then again, it seemed incredible that someone would go to all this trouble to torment her.

"You know what is really creepy? Whoever did this must have done it sometime today, in broad daylight, because if it had been after dark I would have noticed the lights going on as they neared it. I always do."

"Yeah, me too," Kimberly muttered. She remembered the first time it had happened right after moving in. She had been lying in bed, the room pitch black, when suddenly the entire window erupted with light. Had the shades been open she would have been able to see within the room as if the inside light was on.

"I'm sure, both our bedroom windows face the stupid thing and it's so sensitive that even if the wind blows some leaves across the driveway it switches on for two minutes." He took a breath. "I once suggested the landlord remove it because it drove me crazy during the fall, but he always felt it was a good safety device."

"Will he be able to fix it?"

"I'm sure he could, but actually having him get to it is another thing all together. It can take a while for things like that around here."

Kimberly didn't know what to say and simply muttered, "Why is someone doing this to me?" She wasn't really expecting an answer, but that didn't stop Bill from making a statement.

"Even if you heard why from the person chances are you'll never understand it. People that do this type of thing, they aren't right. They – woah!"

"What?"

Bill took a deep breath. "Nothing. A cat went through the backyard. Kind of spooked me."

Kimberly looked in that direction and sure enough watched as a cat easily hopped the fence. With that her eyes were once again drawn to the abandoned house and its windows. A shudder passed through her. "Do you think it's possible someone could be inside there watching us?"

Bill followed her gaze to the house and said, "Possible, but not likely."

"How come?"

"I just can't picture someone sitting in the dark for hours just staring at the house, even if they are crazy. In movies stuff like that happens, but that's because no one actually takes the time to sit there for hours. If they did they'd realize that no one would do it unless they were one of those brain-dead slasher movie villains."

"Oh."

"Plus the owner keeps the place locked up nice and tight. I know because I was curious what it looked like inside and tried the door last year."

Kimberly didn't reply.

"Slowly the owner is remodeling it so it can be separated into apartments like this place, but at the rate they're going it won't be ready for another five years."

Again, Kimberly didn't reply, not because she wasn't interested, but because she just couldn't focus on such information at that moment.

Bill looked as if he was going to say something else about the house, but then hesitated. A few seconds later he said, "Why don't we get you inside and make sure everything is locked up nice and tight."

"Oh, I'm sure it's fine," she said.

"Same here, but why chance it. Besides, you know you'll feel better if I took a look around."

He was right; she would feel better. Still, she felt kind of silly having him look around, almost like a kid that wanted her mother to look under the bed.

So what!

With this final thought she led the way inside and then followed him around as he checked every little potential hiding spot. At one point, she even let out a small chuckle at a comment he made about the previous tenants and how he had often had to come down here to help them find their python who was a good escape artist. "Thankfully, there are fewer places to hide for a person," he added.

"Sadly, my imagination won't think that later on when I'm woken from an odd sound at three in the morning."

"I know what you mean. My mind will – " he stopped and twisted around toward the kitchen.

"What?" she asked.

He held up a finger and then slowly headed into the second bedroom, eyes looking up at the ceiling.

Kimberly followed, heart racing.

The silence grew heavy.

"What is it?" Kimberly whispered after nearly a minute.

"Thought I heard something on the stairway and my door isn't locked, but it must have been -- "

A footstep, or something similar, echoed from the floor above.

"Shit," Bill hissed. He started to move toward the inner stairway door, but then stopped and quickly said, "Watch from the window and see if anyone runs down the steps."

Kimberly nodded and then listened as Bill headed upstairs, his own footsteps echoing across the floor.

No one came down the steps.

"See anything?" Bill called down.

"No," Kimberly replied.

Nothing but the sounds of him walking back and forth up there followed. She then heard him coming back down.

"Anything?" she asked.

He shook his head. "Must've been the house or maybe Toby walking around."

"It sounded like a person," Kimberly insisted, her heart still racing despite his 'all clear' attitude.

"I know, but . . ." he shrugged ". . . nowhere to really hide up there."

She didn't reply.

"Look, we're both probably letting our imaginations get the better of us."

"And it's not even the middle of the night yet." She attempted a smile with the statement, but couldn't manage it.

"Yeah."

Silence settled and lasted for nearly two minutes at which point Bill said, "Well, I suppose I should head back up."

Kimberly nodded.

"Remember, if you need anything, or if anything happens, come get me. My stairway door will be unlocked."

"Thank you."

An awkward smile crossed his face. "No problem."

I'd rather he stay, Kimberly admitted to herself as he headed up. Making such a request would be too much, however, so she kept the thought to herself and, once his door was closed, went to her computer to see if any replies to her message had arrived.

16

Despite his statement to Kimberly that no one was in his apartment, Bill spent the next several minutes doing a thorough search of the place before attempting to call it a night. During this search he held a knife from the kitchen. It wasn't a big knife by any means (he never bought any when moving in), but it would still do the job if wielded properly. He also figured a person's natural fear of blades would give him the upper hand, thereby allowing him to run the person into a corner and subdue them rather than actually having to kill them.

Then again, you have always wondered what it would be like to end a person's life, and right now, if someone is in the apartment, it will probably be the best opportunity you'll ever have.

He let the thought fade as he peeked into one of the three closets his apartment sported, his rational mind knowing that subduing and questioning the person (with the help of the police) would be better than killing them since it would help uncover the why of everything.

No one was in the closet.

No one was in the apartment.

And you knew that would be the case, but . . .

It was always best to make sure of something. When running upstairs earlier he had been certain that if someone were in the apartment he would see them, their unfamiliarity with the place and sudden realization that he was coming up the stairs making it almost impossible for them to successfully duck into a good hiding spot. Yet such an encounter hadn't happened. When downstairs he had been certain the sound had been a person, therefore he had been certain of seeing them attempting to flee. Without confirmation of his suspicion, he had been left with a nagging doubt, one that he couldn't just brush aside – especially not when that meant stripping down into his underwear and climbing into bed. No. Such an act would have been an invitation to disaster and once the horrible events unfolded (in his mind he saw his throat being cut or something while he slept), he would have no one to blame but himself.

17

Thanks for the heads up and the link. I will check it out. Kimberly.

Though short, the praise within the message was enough for Mark to breathe a heavy sigh. He would also be able to go to sleep now, the anxiety over waiting for a reply, or, more accurately, waiting to see if she would reply, having been sated.

Muscles moaned and joints popped as he stood up from his desk chair, which, given how old it now was, probably needed to be replaced.

Being able to go an hour, two, or three without checking his email would have helped as well, but despite his determination to not hover when waiting for a response from whatever female he was in contact with, he just couldn't break himself away from the repeated checks. It was ridiculous. All evening long he had been within reach of the computer, a finger constantly refreshing his email inbox to see if he had a new message, heart racing every time he saw (1) rather than (0). It had begun around five, an email to Kimberly about his message to NIU_Nikki and a link to her original blog having gone out around four thirty. In the first draft of his email he hadn't included the link, but then, after reading the message over and over again, felt as if there wasn't enough to warrant a message, and added some fluff about the start of their fall semester and where he was going to be living.

Fifteen minutes later, he took the fluff out, a couple rereads proving to him that the information given in that short paragraph was pointless. A decision to send the message in its first form followed, but never was enacted, his finger unable to hit the send button due to his original fear that he hadn't put enough into the email. *She'll read it and start to think you're one of those guys that just messages a girl every thought that comes about.* Such actions, which he had done in the early days of his Internet dating experience, had ruined several relationships before they had even reached the 'first meeting' stage. Because of this, he was now very careful of what he sent and when he sent it.

Not that it really matters, he told himself. *You still haven't hooked up with anyone.*

But at least I'm not to blame for that, he countered.

Realizing this had taken quite a bit of time, his mind often thinking and worrying that he was somehow at fault for the frequent rejections he suffered. Now he knew differently. The women were at fault. He could be a perfect gentleman when messaging them back and forth, but that didn't mean they had to keep talking to him, or agree to meet him, or actually show up at the agreed upon meeting spot. Nope. The decision was in their hands. All he could do was keep his fingers crossed.

And make sure there is a point to your messages.

Having added the link to Nikki's blog, the one that had been the reason for his contact with her, helped him meet the self-imposed standard of having a point. Unfortunately, doubt had followed as time without a reply had grown longer and longer and longer. During the nine o'clock hour he even turned off his computer in frustration after getting his hopes up when seeing a (2) on his email screen, his mind thinking one of those messages had to be from her. Wrong. Both were spam. Fifteen minutes later, he turned the computer back on, a sense that a message had arrived during that off time having hit him while flipping through the channels. Nope. Well, at least not one from Kimberly. NIU_Nikki had replied. It was funny too because in the past receiving a message from her would have been cause for celebration, especially if it told him she would be on the instant messenger for a while and wanted to discuss what they would do when they eventually met for the first time. Now that wasn't the case. Instead, he felt a small bit of dread mixed with curiosity. Excitement was present as well, the knowledge that he was the one pulling a fast one on her adding this unexpected emotion.

I just hope I'm not wasting my time, her message read. *Having your cock in my mouth, pussy, and ass better be worth sitting across the table from you for an hour. To add a little thrill I might be hesitant about letting you inside my place afterward, but that is just to see how much you really want it. Don't take NO for an answer if you hear it and show me what a man you are. Nikki.*

The feelings the message induced in him were hard to explain, as was the fact that they turned him on a bit. A debate on whether he should send the message to Kimberly followed, but then he decided to wait for a reply to his first message since he knew that most women hated being bombarded.

But this is different!

Still, he held back. If no reply came by morning he would go ahead and send this along, a statement about it having come overnight with it just in case she grew irritated that he didn't send it right away.

Of course, since a reply did come a new debate developed. *Should I send it now or still wait?* The last thing he wanted was for her to think he hovered over the computer waiting for messages.

In the end he decided to wait.

Sadly, despite having received the message he had been hoping to receive, sleep did not come easily to him. Making it even worst he couldn't find anything on TV to ease him into it.

18

You sound interesting. I would like to meet up with you and see how 'well hung' you really are. I work at the Steak and Shake in DeKalb off of Route 23 and Barber Green so I would need some notice of when you will want to come fuck me. Actually, if you want to come see me at work and then follow me home that is sweet too. Nikki.

Though she shouldn't have been startled by the fact that this person knew where she worked, not after having gotten the pictures on the table and on her car earlier in the evening, Kimberly still felt her heart start to race after reading the suggestion. Adding to it was the possibility that this NIU_Nikki would tell other guys to meet her at work as well, which would be a nightmare because she would never know who was there to meet her and who was there just to eat.

Even the knowledge that the guys who were coming to meet her would probably be by themselves didn't help much because she got five or six of those every shift.

Why, why, why?

Knowing she wouldn't be able to come up with an answer, she pushed her mind away from the contemplative process and instead decided to focus on coming up with a reply to NIU_Nikki. Nothing but anger appeared, however, so she distracted herself by browsing the web a bit and checking her regular email, which was when she discovered the message waiting from Mark.

Confusion as to what he was trying to accomplish by telling NIU_Nikki that they were getting together at The Junction soon filled her mind, but then she figured he had needed to say something to explain what had occurred at the front door earlier in the day. She then saw the link he had sent her and clicked it.

A Blogger content warning appeared.

She clicked the YES button to let them know she was an adult and then watched as a page loaded, one that had quite a few explicit pictures on it, most being links to porn sites.

While browsing through that an idea for a reply to NIU_Nikki popped into her head. She had no clue where it had come from or what might have sparked it, but once it played out in her mind, she knew it was perfect.

Not wanting to close the blog she opened a new window and signed back into the dating site and her email. A blank space beneath NIU_Nikki's message was waiting. In it she typed: *That sounds great. What hours do you work so I know when to be there?*

Try to answer that one, bitch, she said to herself while hitting

SEND. Then, *What if she does know your schedule?*

Then you'll know it is someone who works there because they are the only ones who can see it.

Thinking this brought about a positive vibe.

Unfortunately, it didn't last long, not after she returned to the blog page Mark had sent her and really started to explore it.

19

Bill wasn't exactly asleep, but was far from being awake, when the pounding on the door erupted, and for a moment he didn't know what to make of it. He then heard Kimberly calling his name through the door and bolted upright, his mind thinking something must have happened.

"What is it?" he asked once the door was open, a brief battle with his pants having delayed his ability to let her in right away.

"Who's Nikki?" she demanded, arm crossed.

"I told you, I don't – "

"Don't bullshit me!" she warned. "I saw her blog."

"Her blog?" he questioned.

"Yes! Her blog. *Tales of a Sex Crazed College Student.* The one that for some reason has links to all your books on it."

"A lot of sites link to my books," he said and instantly regretted it. *You need to tell her the truth.*

"Really?" she asked before he could continue. "And how many of those sites just happen to be all about a girl named Nikki? And how many of them link to an Adult Friend Finder profile with the name NIU_Nikki, one that – " she stopped, eyes going wide. "One that has a picture of her kneeling right there!" Spittle flew from her lips while shouting this last part, it, and a pointed finger, indicating the area of his apartment she recognized.

Bill, of course, didn't have to follow the finger to see the spot she was talking about. Instead, his mind simply replayed the day he and Nicole had taken the picture. Many others had followed; both of them coming up with different ideas left and right, the scenes depicted quickly going from tastefully erotic to downright explicit.

"Well?" she asked.

"Okay, fine, I built the site. So what?"

This seemed to catch her off guard, almost like an unexpected speed bump to slow her anger.

Bill waited.

"Why?" she finally asked.

"I needed some money." He shrugged. "That's all."

"And this girl paid you to build her a site?"

"No, I paid her to use her pictures on my site, you know, so guys would think it really was being run by a girl."

Confusion hit, then disgust. "Wait! You're Nikki?"

"Well, for the writing portions and the networking, yeah, I was. Not anymore, though. I stopped updating the site last spring."

"But . . . but . . . you pretended to be a girl online?"

He nodded.

"Why?"

"Like I said, I needed the money. Back in 2010 Dorchester Publishing started to fall apart and I had to pull my first novel from them. I had no job and couldn't seem to get one, and didn't yet know about the success I could expect by uploading their books to Amazon. I figured I would have to be waiting six or seven months to hear from another publisher whether or not they were even interested in taking a look at my book, so in the meantime I created that blog to make some money."

"I don't follow," she said, exhaustion staining her words now that her anger had dissipated.

He sighed. "Do you have the site up right now? Down on your computer?"

"Yeah."

"Okay, I'll just show you." He motioned toward the stairs.

She hesitated, and then led the way.

A few seconds later he was leaning over her computer, hand working the mouse to get to the area of the page he wanted to show her, that area being a link to the Adult Friend Finder profile he had created with the pictures from Nicole. In the link was another picture of Nicole, one that showed her leaning toward the camera, hands pressing the sides of her breasts so that the cleavage displayed by her partially opened blouse would catch the eye. "This is it; this is why I created the site. At one time I had the link near the top of the page -- above the fold as web developers would say -- but then realized that was too obvious so I pushed it down a bit."

Kimberly shook her head. "I don't understand."

"Don't understand what?"

"This." She pointed at the link. "Why try to drive traffic to the site?"

"Because the Adult Friend Finder affiliate program pays me fifty percent of the sign up fee every time someone pays for a membership though this link. They then continue to pay me fifty percent every month that the member renews their membership."

"I still don't get it. How do they know someone joined through this link?"

"There's special programming code in the link that tells them it was my account. Same with the porn sites that are linked below it, only I don't know why I bothered with those because no one seems to pay for porn anymore."

"So you did all of this just so people would join Adult Friend Finder through that link. Why would people do that?"

"Because I told them over and over again in posts that the only way they could ever have sex with me . . . well, with Nikki, was to join the site and talk to me about their interests. After a while most realized nothing would ever happen and they either sought out other girls to talk to or just ended their account, but with new people always coming in, that never really made much of a difference."

Kimberly stared at the screen for quite some time before finally looking at him and saying, "You're sick."

It was his turn to ask, "Why?"

"Because, you pretended to be a girl online. You talked to guys about having sex with you while they thought you were a girl all so you could get money. You – "

"So what, thousands of girls make a living doing this. Why can't I do the same?"

"But . . ." she started. Nothing followed, probably because she realized the truth of what he said.

"In fact, if you think about it, the only difference between me and them is that I had to hire someone so I could have pictures. They just use their own body."

"I don't even know what to say. How would you even think something like this up?"

"It just kind of hit me one day after I clicked on a Join Our Affiliate Program link at the bottom of a site. At first I figured I could create a blog as if it were a character from one of my books and share made up sex stories in hopes that people would join the porn sites. A few days later I discovered the Adult Friend Finder affiliate program. It all kind of came together after that."

"And this girl?" Kimberly asked. "What's her story?"

"Nicole? I went out to eat one night and she was the waitress. I thought she was really pretty and simply asked if she would be interested in modeling for me for extra money."

"Just like that? You just randomly asked a stranger if she would take off her clothes for you and she said yes?"

"Yep. Believe it or not finding girls to do this isn't that hard, especially in a college town. I could probably make a killing in the amateur porn field here. All I'd have to do is walk by Northern everyday asking girls if they wanted to make a couple hundred bucks."

"Unbelievable."

Bill didn't know what else to say, nor did he know how to answer the next question that left Kimberly's lips, one that asked if he knew who was responsible for her harassment.

"And don't tell me it isn't connected to this," she warned after he stayed silent.

"Okay, I'll admit, I don't see how it couldn't be connected. That said, I honestly don't know how someone could have made a connection between the blog and you, especially after all this time."

"Nothing like this ever happened before?"

"No, never."

"You still should have told me about this. After last night, once you realized someone thought I was this Nikki girl you created, you should have said something."

"I know, but . . . well . . . what's done is done." *And it's not like it would have made much of a difference,* he silently added, but didn't dare say, not when he knew he was in the wrong.

"So you really don't have any idea who it could be that's doing this?"

"No," he said. "And believe me; I've been thinking about that quite a bit today. I even called Nicole to see if she had any idea, which she didn't. It just . . . I don't know, it doesn't make any sense really because if someone was able to figure out the address you'd think they would have also figured out it was me."

"Unless they figured out the address, but not a name to go with it and then after seeing me around just assumed I was Nikki."

"Maybe," he admitted. "But . . ." he started. Nothing followed.

"But what?" she asked.

"Oh, nothing." Her suggestion made sense, yet for some reason he didn't think it fit. More was going on here than met the eye. Unfortunately, simply thinking about it and talking about it wouldn't produce an answer. Nope. In order to understand this situation they were going to have to confront the person responsible and hear what they had to say. Of course, once that point was reached it would most likely also mark the end of this entire ordeal. The question was *what would happen between now and then?* Though he didn't want to say it to her, he had a feeling things were going to get ugly. People didn't knock out motion sensor lights just so they could leave pictures on doors without being noticed. Hell, just leaving the type of pictures that had been left was extreme and meant things would probably escalate. Had it only happened once, then maybe that would have been it – a statement someone wanted to get off their chest. But leaving some on the door, and at the restaurant, and on the car . . . that meant someone was going to a lot of trouble; more than was needed for a simple message.

20

Anger laced frustration made it impossible for Kimberly to even contemplate sleep, so rather than attempting it she stayed at her computer exploring the blog that Bill had created, her mind still barely able to comprehend the fact that he would do something like this. It seemed too perverted; too twisted. Even for someone who made a living writing horror tales. Adding to her mental dilemma was how normal he had seemed once she had interacted with him a few times. *A little quiet, but still normal.* Also, why would a girl go along with doing this? Had it been purely for money or had she enjoyed herself? Kimberly was looking at an explicit picture of Nicole giving a blowjob while wondering about this, a blog post titled "The Joys of Sucking Cock" having been written with it. A smiling face covered in semen ended the blog post, along with a statement that read: *If you would like to help me with another post like this please follow the link below and send me an email.* Naturally, the link below was to the NIU_Nikki profile on Adult Friend Finder.

Sex sells, she silently muttered.

She then wondered how many guys had followed the link and signed up with hopes of actually getting to be in a picture like this.

And how many of them would be angry after learning they had been tricked into laying down thirty bucks for a membership once it became clear that Nikki wasn't going to reply?

Guys like Mark.

Guys who are now being told you are her and how to find you.

The thought made her shiver.

Disgust then followed as she suddenly acknowledged that the penis in the picture probably belonged to Bill. Of course, deep down she had known this all along when seeing the picture -- and others like it on the blog -- but hadn't really thought about it until now.

It wasn't an image she wanted to possess, yet sadly, she knew she would probably see it in her mind every time she talked to him now. And talk to him she would because despite her anger toward him for not sharing information about this blog earlier, she knew she would still have to interact with him in the coming days as more events unfolded.

A yawn struck.

Though tired, going to bed was still not an option. If anything, she would spend another night on the couch watching TV, her mind needing the distraction from her thoughts.

On cue, she heard the theme for *The X-Files* upstairs. Bill seemed to watch it every night.

Has she replied?

The question was directed toward the NIU_Nikki profile. Earlier she had asked about her own schedule at Steak and Shake. A good chunk of time had passed since then, though not as much as it felt like should have passed – it wasn't even midnight yet. Enough for the person to have replied with something if she (or he) was the type that lived on their computer when at home.

Keeping the blog in one tab since she would be looking at it some more, she opened the OK Cupid site in a new tab and logged in. A message was waiting. It was from NIU_Nikki. In it, her work schedule for the next week was laid out.

Saturday, August 20, 2011

1

Staring at the laptop screen, exhausted and unable to write for the second day in a row, Bill feared a case of writer's block was setting in. The Nikki situation was to blame. The stress from that, brought about by the constant thoughts and concerns that would not go away, made it so his mind couldn't focus on anything. Even reading, once he gave up on his writing, seemed a challenge. His eyes would see the words on the page, and would send the meaning of their layout to his brain, but after that nothing would be retained. A scene would come and go without leaving any impression on him and finally, after about ten pages, he gave up.

Without reading and writing, his apartment was pretty dull. Sure, he had a DVD player, but nothing that he owned was appealing, especially not during the morning hours. Just sitting down to watch a movie while his laptop was in his peripheral vision would be too much for him to deal with, the knowledge that he had failed in his writing that day a constant layer of guilt.

He had to get out.

He also desperately wanted to talk to Kimberly and reassure her that his creation of the Nikki blog had been for money and nothing else. Some of this had been conveyed to her the night before, but given everything that had occurred between her finding the pictures at work and discovering the blog, he doubted she had processed much of what he had said.

Why do you care what she thinks?

No answer followed.

With the exception of his junior high school years, Bill had never put much concern into the impression others had of him, mostly because he doubted there were many that spent much time even thinking about him. With Kimberly, however, he really didn't like the idea that she might see him as a pervert that got off on making guys think he was a girl. If she thought he was a creep for setting up the blog that was fine, he could live with that. But thinking he actually enjoyed what he had done, that was a whole other thing.

Well, you enjoyed taking the pictures and making the videos with Nicole.

Yeah, but what guy wouldn't?

You also enjoyed some of the conversations you had with the guys.

Yeah, but only because I pictured myself doing the things we were talking about to Nikki.

Yeah, well –

He forced his mind to focus itself elsewhere, a final inner statement on how, if he truly enjoyed teasing men online as if he were a girl, he would have still been doing it regardless of how much money he was making with his novels.

After that, a debate on whether or not it would be a good idea to ask Kimberly if she wanted to get some breakfast and talk appeared. Naturally, doubts followed, most of them spewed forth by the part of his mind that loved to torment him with all his shortcomings and failures – especially those that revolved around the female side of humanity. Maintaining a relationship with a girl had never been a strong skill with him. Getting sex from women wasn't a problem; he almost never failed at that when the desire struck him, but the entire dating thing, nope. When in such a situation he became as pathetic as the men that usually wanted to fuck Nikki, his insecurities plastered all over his statements and actions. It was sad.

Go on, just ask her.

Bill nodded his head as if it was needed to make the voice inside understand that he would do as suggested, and then, after changing out of his pajama pants and into some jeans, headed down and around to the front door.

Not long after that, Kimberly and he were in his car heading toward The Junction for breakfast. Neither said much during the ride, and, knowing it would probably be annoying, Bill resisted pointing out interesting things along the way.

2

"Okay, I see now," Kimberly said while looking up at the electric train that circled the establishment near the ceiling. "This place used to be a railroad junction and now it is a restaurant, right?"

"Um, it may have been," Bill said. "Or they just called it The Junction because it sits next to the tracks. I don't know, I never really looked into it."

"Oh."

"I just like the atmosphere and the food. Beats sitting down in an Ihop or Denny's. It doesn't matter what part of the country you're in, you sit down in one of those and it will pretty much be the same as whichever one is closest to your home."

"Hmm, I never really thought about that." A yawn followed, her hand automatically going up to block it from view.

"You get any sleep last night?" Bill asked.

"Some," she said.

"Yeah, same here." He hesitated. "I felt bad about not telling you about the blog and it made me toss and turn all night."

"Water under the bridge," she said with a wave of the hand.

"I guess I was kind of in denial that the two could even be connected, but then when I saw the pictures on the profile you showed me, I should have said something."

"Well, what's done is done." She really didn't want to talk about this, not when the anger about his deception was still smoldering beneath the surface. "Let's focus on figuring out what the next step should be. I've made contact with the Nikki profile on the OK Cupid site and Mark, the guy with the flowers the other day, he has made it look like him and I are getting together tonight."

"Why'd he do that?"

"I'm not really sure," she admitted. "I guess he's trying to gage her reaction and maybe see if she does something irrational because of it."

"Um . . . okay."

The waitress came by to fill their coffee cups and then promised to come back for their meal orders shortly.

"I just wish he had told me he was going to do this because he has now told Nikki that we are getting together tonight at . . . well, here actually."

"Are you?" he asked while adding sugar to his cup. "Meeting him tonight, I mean."

"No, I can't." She added her own sugar. "I have to . . . oh crap!"

"What?"

"Last night she sent me my work schedule for the next week in hopes that I would start hanging out there and freaking myself out – you know, because she thinks I'm a guy on OK Cupid."

"Okay . . ." he carefully sipped some coffee while waiting for more.

"But Mark told her that I told him we could get together tonight."

Bill nodded, but didn't reply.

"She'll know he's lying about us getting together if she knows my schedule." She expected to see a 'holy crap, that's not good' look appear on his face, but it went unchanged.

"So?"

"She'll get suspicious and realize he is jerking her around, won't she?"

"Not necessarily," Bill said. "She might just think you're jerking him around and then will somehow play it up if he messages her about it. After all, that's what my Nikki would have done to someone like him, and I'm guessing this person is doing all this because they are pissed about it having happened to them."

"Would someone really do that?" she asked. "After already knowing how much it hurts to be teased and jerked around like that?"

"Happens all the time; the abused become the abusers." He shrugged. "There is a mindset among some that having been on the receiving end of something justifies them being able to then dish it out in return. Kind of like a spouse that feels it's okay to cheat since they caught the other doing it, or something to that extent."

"Did something like that happen to you? Is that why you felt it okay to jerk guys around with your own female character?"

"What, me?" He shook his head. "No, not at all. Like I said last night, I just needed money. Also, it took a while before it turned into what you saw. At first, I just started the blog as a female character. I put up all the ads and links to the different sites I could make money from, and just hoped that by writing sex stories from Nikki's point of view that men would then be drawn to those sites and sign up. As money grew tighter and tighter I started trying to subtly direct them that way and then, when things got really tight and it looked like I might lose my apartment, I started telling guys to join the site so they could talk to me and try to hook up for sex."

"Why didn't you just try and get a real job?" She knew the question was leading down a path that could cause some un-wanted tension, but asked it anyway.

"In my opinion I had a real job. I mean, I was making money and when the time comes I will be paying taxes on it, so . . . " he held his hands up ". . . but to answer your question the way you'd like, I actually did try to get a 'real job' and must have filled out a hundred applications. Every day I would walk around all the different business areas in Sycamore and DeKalb seeing if I could get an interview without any luck. I even paid entry fees for job fairs at NIU and went to the free ones at Kish and never even got a bite. No callbacks, no interviews sched-uled, nothing. It was very frustrating."

Kimberly couldn't relate to that, which led to some disbelief on how hard he had tried. After all, she had gotten a job without much trouble once she started looking. "You ever apply at Steak and Shake? I pretty much walked in and got the job."

"Four times; twice when they had a Now Hiring display too."

He sighed. "I don't know, there must be a mark against me or something that I don't know about, because even I find it difficult to think that no one would even ask for an interview."

With that the waitress came by to take their order, which, naturally, made Kimberly aware of the fact that she hadn't even opened the menu. "You go first," she suggested to Bill.

He ordered a standard 'two eggs over easy' breakfast with hash browns, bacon, and toast.

"I'll have the same, but with pancakes if that's okay," Kimberly said and handed the menu over.

"Okay, one with toast, one with pancakes," the waitress said while looking at her order pad. She then looked up at them and smiled and, before heading to the kitchen, added, "I'll have that out in a jiffy and some fresh coffee."

At the table silence settled.

Unsure what to say, Kimberly once again looked up at the electric train and watched as it went through a small cutout in the wall. She then looked back at Bill, a question having occurred. "So, do you really think this could be someone who you talked to that got pissed off that you, as Nikki, never followed through with what was talked about?"

"I can't really think of anything else it could be. My only question now is how in the world did they learn the address?" He took a large swig of coffee after that, probably because he eyed the waitress returning with the pot.

"You don't think someone could have hacked the site and learned the address that way, do you -- like through the IP address or something?" She choked down some of her own coffee as well, and vowed to add a bit more cream to it on the next pass. "After all, wasn't everyone in the house using the same Internet when you were doing all this, therefore the main house address would have been uncovered?

"Huh, I never really considered that."

"And then maybe whoever found out the address came and watched the place and saw me and just assumed I was Nikki."

"Wow, seems logical to me."

His statement brought her a sense of satisfaction.

"Now we just need to find out if it's plausible. Know any tech heads at NIU who could help out with this?"

The satisfaction faded. "Not really, but I could ask around."

"Good idea. There has to be someone there that knows a thing or two about this stuff." For a moment it looked as if he was going to say more, but then the food arrived and his focus shifted to that.

"Can I bring you anything else?" the waitress asked.

Bill looked at Kimberly who shook her head and then said, "Just more coffee when you get a chance." With that the two dug in, the sounds of their chewing the only thing that broke the silence in their little area of the restaurant.

3

Hey. I'm new in DeKalb and was wondering if you would like to get together one day for drinks or something. Like many others, I'm here for school and while that will be my main focus, I would like to find a nice guy to hang out with and maybe more if things take that route. Please let me know if you are interested. BTW, I don't always have good access to the web, so my number is below if you want to call or text me. Looking forward to hearing from you. Amy.

Mark stared at the message for a long time, his mind completely caught off guard by the fact that a girl had messaged him. Normally things went the other way. He would message a girl and eagerly await a response, the days growing longer and more agonizing as time without one grew. Hope was what caused him to send the messages, hope that the girl would see it and then visit his profile and realize he was just what she was looking for. Countless hours of sex would follow. It was a fool's dream, he knew, but one he couldn't get away from. Who in his situation could?

This time, however, he didn't have to hope that a message would instill interest because it seemed interest was already there. She had messaged him. She was now the one waiting for a response. Everything was up to him.

Just don't screw this up, he warned.

To help prevent such a screw up he did not reply right away despite a deep desire to send off a message letting her know he was very interested. Instead, he headed into the kitchen to eat some breakfast and drink some coffee, and then, once his mind had calmed down enough, went back to the computer to send a reply. Before doing that, though, he looked at her profile to see if there was anything written in the About Me area that would help him think up a response. Nothing. That was okay though. Some chose to go this route from time to time. Or maybe she wanted to write something but couldn't find the words. Whatever the case he didn't let it bother him and moved on to the pictures she had uploaded to see what she looked like.

Wow, was all his mind could think. To say she was hot was an understatement.

And she contacted you!

The inner statement caused his heart to race once again. He also started to worry that he might not have been the only guy she messaged and if so what if someone else had already re-sponded. After all the message had been sent several hours ear-lier, before midnight actually, so during that time she might have already agreed to hook up with someone else who was quicker on the reply.

With this on his mind, Mark typed up a response and hit SEND, his fear of missing out making it so he didn't spend much time on the actual wording or content. Naturally, concern about this followed, especially when he went and re-read what he had written and realized it sounded desperate.

You also forgot to give her your phone number.

This thought led him to wonder whether or not it would be okay to send her an introduction text.

What if she is reading your message right now and then gets the text.

Such a moment might make him seem even more needy, which wasn't good. Girls didn't like guys like that.

But she sent you her number.

She had also said something about not being online all the time.

What if someone calls her first?

Being the first to reply to the message might be voided out if others had her number, especially if she didn't sign online again until tonight.

Send her the text. It will help her see that you truly are interested.

After that he would be cool and wouldn't overload her with messages, which would help her realize he was not an obsessive guy who would overburden her with need.

Phone in hand Mark typed up a message that read: HI. THIS IS MARK FROM OK CUPID. JUST WANTED TO INTRODUCE MYSELF AND GET MY NUMBER TO YOU. FEEL FREE TO CALL OR TEXT ANYTIME.

Afterward he realized he should have sent her the name he went by on OK CUPID as well, but then figured it wasn't a horrible mistake. If she wanted to know, she could always ask.

Don't hover, he told himself a minute later after realizing he was going back and forth from staring at his phone to staring at the email icon on the OK Cupid site. *And don't forget to send Kimberly that latest message from Nikki.*

Once sent, he decided to withdraw himself from his room and computer. Sadly, he couldn't really withdraw himself from his phone, which was in his pocket, and kept waiting for it to buzz with a message. Sometimes he even checked it to see if he had failed to feel the buzz, past moments of not realizing a message or call had come through guiding his actions. No messages were ever waiting during these checks. Even worse, once a message finally did come through it was from his mother asking if he would be home for dinner that night.

Anger at her developed even though he knew it was silly. Her question was valid and it wasn't her fault the buzz had induced excitement followed by a serious let down.

Hmm, will I? he wondered, his mind thinking of the lie he had told Nikki the day before about going to dinner with Kimberly. It seemed the best way to add realism to the deception he was trying to pull would be to actually go to dinner with her and then make it look like they went back to her place. That way if Nikki was watching, which he was sure she was it would look genuine.

But will Kimberly go for it?

The answer to that would not come while wandering the mall, so rather than continue that he headed home to send her a message. While doing that his phone buzzed. It was a message from Amy.

I'M SO HAPPY YOU REPLIED! I HOPE WE CAN GET TO-GETHER SOON! MAYBE SOMETIME TODAY OR TOMOR-ROW IF YOU AREN'T BUSY? LET ME KNOW.

Within seconds another message came.

PS: WHAT IS WITH ALL THE GUYS ON THIS SITE SEND-ING ME MESSAGES EVERY TEN MINUTES? IT'S CRAZY!!!

Not wanting to leave her hanging, Mark pulled into a parking lot and typed up a message.

I HOPE WE CAN GET TOGETHER SOON TOO. THAT WILL BE FUN. TODAY IS GREAT IF THAT WORKS FOR YOU. WHEN AND WHERE? BTW, SORRY ABOUT ALL THE GUYS ON THE SITE. IT'S AMAZING HOW DESPERATE FOR SEX MANY OF THEM CAN BE. DON'T LET IT GET TO YOU.

Message sent, he continued toward his parents' house, his mind trying to figure out whether or not he would even try to get together with Kimberly tonight or just leave that all alone for a while now that he could focus on Amy.

4

"You know, since we're right here, do you just want to head over to NIU and see if anyone can help with our IP address question?" Bill suggested as the two left The Junction.

Kimberly seemed to consider this for a few seconds and then said, "Okay why not. Might do me some good to get familiar with the place a bit too since I start on Monday."

"Oh yeah, good idea."

"I kinda meant to do that during the week but totally dropped the ball." She then shifted gears. "Do you think anyone will be there that can actually help us?"

"I really can't say. If nothing else we can at least get some

names on people to contact and make an appointment or something." Truth was he had no clue. When he had suggested she
contact someone at NIU earlier he hadn't really pictured himself
with her and instead he just saw her going to some computer lab
or department between classes. Now, however, he figured it was
important that he be a part of this as well. "It will be a good way
to get the ball rolling so to speak."

Kimberly nodded.

Less than a minute later the two were in the car waiting to
turn onto Lincoln Highway, a seemingly endless line of cars
coming from the Annie Glidden direction making it look like
they would be there a while.

"Do you have any idea where we need to go?" Kimberly
asked.

"Not really," Bill admitted. "I figured we'd just head to the
main entrance and go from there."

"Oh . . . hmmm."

"What?" he asked, sensing something in her tone.

"Nothing," she said. "For some reason I was under the impression that you had gone here, that's all."

"Ah, no, sorry. I did my time at a community college for a
couple years while waiting for my novels to take off and then
moved out here due to the low rent when it seemed like I had
finally made it into the big leagues."

"What happened?"

Bill saw a small opening in the traffic and took it, his hands
fighting the wheel so that he didn't throw the back of the car into
the second lane where cars were present. "I spent all summer
doing rewrites on a novel for Dorchester Publishing and then
one day learned from Facebook that the entire editing staff had
been let go. After that I figured that publishing with them would
be a bad idea given how shaky they seemed, and given the growing statements by authors that they hadn't received any payments for quite some time, and took my novel elsewhere. Sadly,
no one was interested in it, which is why I set up that blog and
then eventually self-published."

"Wow, that really sucks."

"Yeah, but I'm just glad I learned of how poorly the company was doing before I signed anything." He couldn't even begin to imagine how awful and stressful it would have been having had his first novel with them while they were in such a situation.

"True. Why didn't anyone else want to publish it?"

Bill shrugged. "That is a question I will never know the answer too. It was funny though because one publisher did tell me there was no market for my fiction. Guess I proved them wrong on that front." He shifted into the left lane and got ready to turn into the main area of NIU. "I do hope that I can make a deal with one of them one of these days though. I hate doing everything myself."

"I bet that is a pain, especially without having good access to the Internet."

"Yeah, but I manage." He thought about sharing with her the fact that he was getting more work done now without it and how he planned on never hooking it up again no matter what, but then realized this was all stuff she didn't really need to know. Plus, he had no idea where the two were going and needed to focus his attention on finding a parking spot. "Do they have like a visitor lot or anything?"

"Yeah, but you have to pay for it."

"Really?"

"Yeah, sorry, I completely forgot about that until just now. I looked at their website about two weeks ago while trying to figure out if I could come visit and see the layout and everything, but then, like I mentioned earlier, didn't follow through with anything."

"Is that common for universities like this?" At the community school he had gone to everything had been free. Of course, during the winter he would have gladly paid for a parking spot if it meant not having to walk a mile through the snow piles and slush to get into the building.

"Um, I don't know. I didn't have a car when I went to U of I. Once I moved out of the dorms I took a bus to the campus."

"I didn't know you went to U of I," Bill said. "Why'd you change schools?"

"Um . . ." she started, then ". . . there's the parking garage if you want to use that, or we can pass that and hit the visitor lot. I'll cover the fee."

Hmm, sore spot? Bill silently questioned. He was no detective, nor could he write detective characters very well, but that didn't mean he hadn't easily spotted that topic shift. Hell, even the dumbed down bumbling idiot version of Watson that TV shows and movies had frequently produced before the respectable Judd Law version had come about would have been able to spot such a misdirection without Holmes pointing it out to him.

Leave it alone, his mind urged. *It's none of your business.*

As curious as he was to know what had happened, he decided to listen to the rational part of his mind. In time, if she wanted to, she would share her experience with him.

Why? the rational part asked. *You think something is brewing between you two?*

Rather than debate this within his head, Bill focused on finding a spot within the visitor lot. While doing this Kimberly said something about needing to pay with a credit card since she didn't have any cash on her.

"You know what, I've got plenty in the armrest," Bill said, his right elbow tapping the lid. "Grab what we need."

"You sure?" she asked.

"Yeah. If it wasn't for my blog we wouldn't have to be doing any of this, so . . ."

"But you just paid for breakfast."

He shrugged.

Kimberly didn't say anything more and reached inside the armrest between the seats. Though he didn't know how much was in there he guessed it had to be around twenty to thirty dollars, all because he used to stockpile singles in it before he had gotten an I-Pass. Now he used them for coffee at Dunkin' Donuts whenever he felt like an extra cup while writing or for the occasional hot dog when he didn't feel like cooking.

"Well," Bill said once the two were standing on a sidewalk. "Let the search for some sort of computer science department -- " a thought suddenly arrived, one that would have been even more helpful if it had made itself known about ten minutes earlier. He pulled out his phone.

"What're you doing?" Kimberly asked.

"You know the girl in the pictures on the Nikki blog," he said.

"Yeah?"

"She's a senior here. I don't know why I didn't think of it earlier. I'm going to call and see if she can help."

"Gee, that might be helpful."

"Tell me about it. I can't believe I -- "

"Hello?" Nicole said in his ear.

"Hi, Nicole. I got a favor to ask. You busy right now?"

"No, not really."

"Great. I'm at NIU looking for the computer science department in hopes of seeing if anyone there can help me find out how someone learned my address through the Nikki blog. Do you have any idea where it's located or who I should talk too?"

"Yikes, that isn't really my area. Hang on a sec. My roommate's boyfriend will probably know. He's does web design. In fact, he might be able to answer your question for you."

"Really, that would be great."

"Okay, let me go get her."

Bill felt the phone being carried into the next room, his mind creating all the necessary sensations from the visuals he already had from past visits to the apartment she lived in, and then heard Nicole talking with her roommate Tammy. A moment later her voice appeared in his ear again. "She's calling him right now."

"Okay."

Nothing else was said between them as Nicole waited for her roommate to reach her boyfriend. During this Kimberly quietly asked, "Anything helpful?"

Bill nodded and then whispered back, "Her roommate is calling her boyfriend."

"Okay?" Kimberly asked, voice making it known that she wanted more information on how this would help.

Bill would have filled her in but Nicole came back and said, "Okay, he's on the phone. What do you want her to ask him exactly?"

"Can you find out if it's possible for someone to find out my address through my blog, like through the IP address or something?"

Nicole repeated this to her friend.

Several seconds passed.

"He says the only thing they could learn would be your city, and that's if they were pretty sophisticated. It would take a court order to learn your name and address."

"Really?"

"That's what he says."

"What about hacking the site to find out information about me? Is there any way someone could learn my address that way?"

Kimberly took a seat while he waited for an answer to this and pulled out her phone. Bill would have joined her, but couldn't hold still when talking on the phone. Instead, he paced. It was something he couldn't help.

"He says it's possible but very unlikely and that chances are they learned your address another way, like through a phishing scheme or email fraud or something. You didn't give any information out in an email, did you?"

"Of course not," he said, frustration rising.

"Hey, what about through the wish list we had?"

"I don't think so. That company is very secure and wouldn't have sent out the address to anyone." He sighed. "It had to be through the IP address. It's the only thing I can think off."

"NO!" Kimberly snapped catching Bill off guard. She was talking on the phone, anger spreading across her face. "I don't care if you came out here, we're through. You should have called before making the trip."

"Bill?" Nicole asked. "You still there?"

"Yeah," he said, turning away from Kimberly. "Sorry. What'd you say?"

"I said that he says that unless someone got a court order there is no way they could find out your address, especially if it was a Google blog, which I told him it was." She hesitated. "It was Google, right?"

"Yeah," he said. "And he's positive about this?"

"Yep. He said chances are you accidentally gave out your address to someone. Did anyone ever ask for it?"

"Tons of people did. Everyone wanted to hook up with you, well, with Nikki. But I never gave it out to -- " he stopped, a sudden memory from a few weeks earlier occurring. "Oh shit."

"What?" Nicole asked.

"Tell the guy he may be right, I may have sent the address out to whoever this is. I can't believe it."

"Can't believe what?"

"Remember the forms I had you sign when we first started taking the pictures and videos and the copies I made of your driver's license and birth certificate?"

"Yeah?"

"A few weeks ago I got an email request to provide that info to someone that checks up on stuff like that, an investigator of sorts."

"You didn't give them my name and address, did you?"

"No, I gave them my address so he could come and inspect the paperwork. Only no one has ever showed up. They say to keep that paperwork for up to seven years though, so I just figured . . . God dammit!"

"Do you still have the email?"

"Yeah, it's sitting in the Nikki account I made."

"You should give it to the police and find out if it was legit. If not maybe they could use it to track down the person who sent it to you."

"Yeah," he said, his mind barely even acknowledging what she had said, its focus having shifted to that panic-stricken moment in the library when he had first opened the email from the investigator. The panic hadn't been due to his fear that he had done something wrong. Instead, it was just the typical panic everyone gets when confronted with a law enforcement official who is looking into something, panic that makes one hope to God that they doted every 'I' and crossed every 'T'.

"You still there?" Nicole asked.

"Yeah, my mind is just all over the place now."

"Hey, you still don't know whether or not that email is legit. This could still be something else."

"Maybe." Given the timing and the lack of any other explanation, he was almost positive this was the answer. He also felt foolish for falling for it, yet at the same time knew he didn't really have a choice. Not providing the information when requested could mean jail time. All over the web one could read stories about amateur porn creators who hadn't had the proper paperwork filled out when the government came calling and suffered serious consequences for it.

"Well, I guess you'll know soon enough. At least you now have a path to explore, right?"

"Yeah." It was all he could manage.

5

"No!" Kimberly snapped, anger rising. "I don't care if you came out here, we're through. You should have called before making the trip."

"But that's not fair," Kyle whined. "You never even gave me a chance to apologize that night, and you stopped answering your phone when I called."

"Something I should have continued doing."

"But – "

"Bye Kyle. Stop calling and leave me alone. I have enough to worry about right now without you stressing me out too." With that she disconnected the call, her mind scolding herself for answering it in the first place.

She looked over at Bill. Had he not still been on the phone when Kyle had called she would have ignored it, but given the wait and her need to do something while sitting there, she had answered it.

And he's still talking!

The original purpose of the call had been to locate the Computer Science area, a location they could have probably walked to by now had he simply gotten the info on where it was right away. It wasn't just a simple chitchat conversation, however, not

if the look on Bill's face was any indication. Something important was being discussed; something that could possibly shed
light on what was happening. *A discussion that you should be a
part of.*

Though true, she stamped out the frustration that began to
grow because she knew that the conversation hadn't been
planned. If it had, she would have been a part of it. The three
(or four?) would have sat down and talked things over and come
up with a plan on how to deal with the unfolding scenario.

BUZZ!

She looked down at her phone, her eyes not needing to see the
name Kyle to know the message was from him.

WE'LL TALK WHEN YOU GET HOME. IF YOU'RE HUN-
GRY WE CAN GET SOMETHING TO EAT.

Anger returned.

She typed, I JUST HAD BREAKFAST WITH A NICE YOUNG
MAN. GO HOME. I DON'T WANT TO TALK TO YOU EVER
AGAIN.

Once sent she stared at the phone waiting for a reply, but
none arrived. Unfortunately, she didn't know what to make of
the silence. If luck was on her side he would have read the message as 'I have a new boyfriend, thus there is no chance for us to
get together again' and would leave. If not, he would have read
it as 'I'm not interested in getting anything to eat since I just ate,
but will gladly talk to you when I get back.'

You know how he thinks, she warned herself. *He will be waiting
when you get back. He might even get –*

"I don't think we need to bother with visiting the computer
area," Bill said.

"What? How come?" she asked, staring up at him, his statement catching her off guard. She was startled by how distraught
he looked.

He shook his head. "I fucked up."

"What do you mean?"

"I'll tell you in the car. Oh, unless you still want to walk
around and get familiar with the place."

"Um . . ." she looked toward the main building and then

scanned a couple others in the surrounding area " . . . no, I'll come by later. Tell me what you think you did."

Bill told her, frustration clinging to every word that left his lips while driving.

At Peace Road, after turning off from Barber Green, she said, "I wouldn't be too hard on yourself for that. Sounds like you could have gotten in a lot of trouble if it was legit and you didn't respond."

"Yeah, I suppose," he said.

Kimberly looked out at the farm fields for a moment, their crops stretching beyond the curve of the horizon, and then asked, "Wait a sec, if you sent them the address why would they still be tormenting me, and why wouldn't they have realized you were the one behind the blog?"

"I just put the house address down since most places don't recognize my address," he admitted. "I didn't want them thinking I was fucking with them. And my name wasn't on it, just the title of Record Keeping since that's what most of these sites always say. You hadn't moved in at the time and I figured anyone who came by would get the idea once they looked around."

"Well they got the idea all right. They got the idea that since I was living at the address you gave them I must be the one that fucked with them. Thanks." She knew her anger wasn't necessary, he hadn't purposely done this to her, but couldn't help it.

Bill didn't reply.

Silence stuck with them as they made the turn from Peace Road onto Prairie Street.

BEEP!

Kyle Cell

"Shit!" she snapped.

"What is it?"

"My ex-boyfriend. He won't leave me alone. I think he's waiting at the house for me to get back too which is something I just don't want to deal with."

"Oh, that sucks." Then, after a few seconds he laughed and said, "What's he going to think when he sees us together?"

"I have no idea. I gave up trying to figure out his thought

process several months ago."

"That's comforting."

"Well, maybe he got the message and left."

"You don't think that at all."

You're right, I don't.

"Is that him?" Bill asked as they turned onto South Street.

It was, sitting on her front steps, staring at his phone. Even worse, he had parked in the driveway making it impossible for Bill to pull in.

Or me to pull out.

Chances were he hadn't intended for this to be the case. He just never was the type to think about how his actions would inconvenience the people around him.

"I'm going to pull around and park on the street," Bill said.

"Okay."

The roundabout maneuver didn't take long and soon he was easing the car to a stop alongside the curb, the house on their right.

Seeing this, Kyle came off the steps and walked into the yard, eyes studying them.

"I told you I didn't want you here when I got back!" Kimberly shouted. Though forceful, her words were offset by a misstep on the curve that sent her to her knees in the grass, right forearm breaking her fall.

"You okay?" Bill asked while stepping around and helping her back up.

"Yeah," she mumbled.

"Kim, I just want to talk," Kyle said. "We can work through –"

"I don't think she wants to talk to you," Bill said before Kimberly could reply, his body positioning itself between the two of them.

"And who might you be?" Kyle asked.

"I might be Bill, and I might live upstairs, and, if you don't leave right now, I might be the one that calls the police."

"I see. And I might be the guy that tells you to fuck off." He motioned to Kimberly. "Come on, let's go talk. I promise, if you still don't want to have anything to do with me once we finish I'll leave."

"I don't want anything to do with you period, so let's cut out the middle part," Kimberly said. With that she walked around Bill and started toward the driveway, keys in hand.

"Kimberly, don't be like – "

"Get your hand off me!" Kimberly shouted as his fingers closed around her upper arm, her body instinctively twisting away from him.

"Hey!" Bill snapped and stepped forward.

A sudden look of horror came over Kyle and he stepped back.

Kimberly looked at Bill, but couldn't see what it was that had caused Kyle to go so pale. When she looked back, however, anger was present, as was a fading look of shame. Things were about to get ugly.

"Bill," she said quickly. "Why don't you go in and call the police because I don't think he's going to leave."

"I'd rather do it right here," Bill said and pulled out his phone. It was the wrong thing to do.

Kyle sprang forward in what appeared to be an attempt to grab Bill's phone, an act that was most likely instinctive rather than fully thought out. Instead of grabbing the phone, however, he missed and hit Bill in the face. It wasn't a punch or even really a slap, more of a forceful finger poke, but even so, it was enough for Bill to react with his own punch, one that landed right below Kyle's left eye.

"Motherfucker," Kyle shouted.

With that the fight was on, the display easily one of the most pathetic things Kimberly had ever seen. No skill was displayed in the blows that were exchanged, each one hurting the thrower as much as the receiver, and soon the two were rolling on the ground, their bodies taking on the image of two kids wrestling over a ball.

"Stop it," Kimberly cried. She thought about kicking them, her mind not caring who she hit, but then held back as Bill suddenly got the upper hand and twisted himself around so he was on top of Kyle, a knee in his lower back and a hand holding his head face down in the grass.

Several deep breaths followed, then, "Unless you want to spend a night in jail I suggest you leave right now." Another deep breath, and then an unintelligible muffled reply from Kyle. "You should also get it through your dumb little head that Kimberly doesn't want anything to do with you anymore, so just relish what you had if you can and move on."

Bill eased up on his head.

"Fuck you!" Kyle shouted once his mouth was away from the ground.

Bill pushed the face back down and glanced at Kimberly, a look of hopelessness appearing amid the redness and heavy breathing.

Kyle began to squirm.

Bill eased up again and then pushed himself off Kyle and onto his feet.

Kyle, face and body covered in grass stains, struggled to stand, the words, "We're through," echoing from his lips.

"Are you fucking kidding me?" Kimberly asked.

"Yeah," he said while wiping away tears that had appeared beneath his eyes. "I mean, no, we're finished!"

"You are something else, you know that." That's all she could think to say, her mind completely blown away by his thinking.

"And you better watch your back," Kyle shouted at Bill, a pointed finger jerking toward him as if he were trying to puncture the air with it. "Because I'll be gunning for you."

Bill didn't reply.

Several seconds drifted away and for a moment Kimberly was worried a second fight would ensue. Kyle then turned and walked toward his car.

Thank god – her mind started.

Kyle then turned back and said, "I dropped my keys."

Bill looked down for several seconds, eyes glancing up a few times to make sure it wasn't some sort of ploy, and then found them sitting about a foot from the sidewalk.

Kyle didn't make any moves toward them during this, a look of embarrassment growing more and more pronounced.

"Here," Bill said and tossed the keys toward him. They went nowhere near Kyle, who still made a pathetic attempt to grab them, and landed on the driveway.

Once secure, Kyle went to his car, opened the door, and then looked back at the two of them. Thankfully, nothing else was said. He then got in, slammed the door and started the engine.

"Are you okay?" Bill asked.

She sighed, nodded, and said, "I'm going inside. Thanks for breakfast and helping with Kyle and . . ." she let that fade. "I need to be alone for a while."

Bill nodded. "I'm just going to put my car back, then. If you need anything, well . . . you know."

Kimberly didn't reply and then headed inside, her mind too distraught by everything to do anything but sit and watch TV. There she stayed until it was time to get ready for work, a shift she did not look forward to being a part of.

6

The Ollie's Frozen Custard stand in Sycamore was crowded, the line stretching all the way to the backside of the building. This wasn't unusual, though, at least not during the visits Mark had made in the past. What was unusual, at least for him, was sitting around and watching the line rather than getting in it right away.

What if she doesn't show?

What if you wait here for an hour or two like a fool?

The fact that she had contacted him, and had suggested this as a good meeting place, did offset the fear of the two questions a bit, but not enough for him to relax. Nothing but having her arrive, walk up to him and introduce herself would. Too many bad experiences made this need inevitable; too many times of waiting at a Borders, or Barnes and Noble, or a bar, or the NIU Library, or Starbucks, or Caribou Coffee without the interested girl showing up.

They all always show interest and then –

A car pulled into the lot, a young looking female in the driver seat.

Heart racing and breath held, Mark watched as the girl found a parking spot and got out of the car. His hope then faded as she went right to the end of the line without looking for him.

It's okay, he said to himself, chest tight with anxiety. *Two minutes late is not a big deal.*

Unfortunately, given his past, and the fact that he had arrived fifteen minutes early – just in case she was early too – it felt like she was later than she actually was. Two minutes was nothing. A stoplight or two could cause it, especially coming down Route 23.

Another car pulled in, but two people were within, so he doubted it was her.

Unless she brought a friend as backup just to make sure you aren't –

His phone buzzed.

He looked at it and saw the message was from her.

SORRY. RUNNING A BIT LATE. SHOULD BE THERE IN TEN MINUTES.

Relief flowed through him. Fear that he would leave had most likely fueled the message, which meant she was serious. She wanted to see him and was anxious about accidentally making a bad impression.

OKAY. NO PROBLEM. I'M HERE AND AM SITTING NEAR ONE OF THE SMALL SHADE TREES BY THE FRONT. ALL THE TABLES WERE FULL. SEE YOU SOON.

He considered adding a smiley face, but then realized she had not sent any to him which could be a sign that she was disgusted by how frequently things like that were passed back and forth, and simply sent the message as it was.

A few minutes later, he signed online with his phone and started browsing things, just to pass the time. He checked his email while doing this to see if Kimberly had said anything, but no new messages from her had arrived. From there he looked at his OK Cupid profile and saw a message from Nikki, one that claimed excitement about seeing him that evening.

I can't believe I fell for this shit, he told himself. *Girls just don't talk like this when they're real.*

Actually, he was sure some did, but not the ones who contacted him. Those always seemed to be fake. Focusing on this and his frustration for falling for it so many times did not follow, not when he caught sight of a car making a right turn from Route 23 and slowing to make the right into the Ollie's parking lot. A female in sunglasses was behind the wheel. She was the only person in the car from what he could see, and somehow he just knew in his gut that it was her. Seeing her quickly check her face in her mirror while still in the car added confirmation to his theory because it didn't seem like something a girl would do before heading over to wait in line for ten to twenty minutes, at least not when they were alone. Nope. It was her.

He returned his phone to his pocket and waited.

She stepped out of the car and turned toward his area rather than toward the line, scanned it, and then seemed to focus in on him.

He acknowledged her glance with a smile and stood up, the latter action probably being the only thing she could see from that distance.

"Amy?" he asked once she was within speaking distance, a smile still on his face.

"Yes," she said, shyness present. "Um, Mark?"

"Yes," Mark replied. He held out his arms for a quick, 'nice to meet you' hug, which she accepted, bodies lightly touching, and then motioned toward the line. "Shall we?"

"Okay."

With that, they headed toward the end of the line, a nervous silence settling between them.

A minute passed, then two.

Mark kept looking around, his mind demanding that he say something to spark a conversation. *Take charge, don't make her initiate anything. She's already done enough in that department. Show her you're a man and up to the task of being a good choice for a future get together once this one concludes.*

"So," he asked, voice catching for a second. "Have you been in the area long, or did you just move here for school?"

"Just moved here a few days ago," she said. "I'm so nervous;

I've never been away from home and on my own before. It's kind of scary."

"I know what you mean. The first time I was away from home was quite an experience. You'll get used to it pretty fast though, and then, when you go home for the summer or holidays, you'll wonder how you could ever live with your parents again because they'll drive you nuts. It's funny."

"Hmm."

The silence that followed caught him off guard and made him worry that he had hit a sore spot without meaning too. Such a mistake was never good, especially this early in the initial conversation.

"So, what kind of yummy custard treat are you going to try?" he asked in an attempt to get things moving again.

"I don't know. Last time I was here I got something that was great, but can't remember what it was called. Some kind of Sunday thing."

"Ah, well maybe you'll recognize it when we get closer to the menu."

Knowing the line would be long the place not only had a menu on the inside behind the registers, but also one displayed on the sidewall where people waiting in line could see it. A few more steps and it would be in view.

"I hope so. It was delicious." Then, a few seconds later, "So, where do you live?"

"Right now I'm back at my parents place, but starting in September I'll be in an apartment off of Annie Glidden. I would be in my own place now, but my stupid roommate got us evicted while he was living there himself during the summer."

"Oh, that sucks."

"Yeah, but this new place is cheaper, so maybe it was all for the better."

"You never know," she said.

Silence returned as they were finally able to study the menu, each one carefully scanning the selections while continuing to move forward in line.

"Know what you're going to get?" Mark asked as their time in front of the first menu ended, their bodies rounding the corner.

"Yep. Same thing I always get. Strawberry Hill Sunday."

"Oooo, that sounds interesting. I'm going with the Black Forest Sunday."

"Black Forest? Isn't that usually a kind of ham?" She chuckled

"Hopefully not in this case," Mark replied. The levity made him feel good. It meant they were already growing comfortable with each other.

The space in front of the register opened.

Mark and Amy moved in and placed their order. Less than three minutes later the two were looking for a spot to sit, their custard treats ready to be eaten.

"I guess we'll have to curb it," Mark said.

"Looks that way. Wish they could get more tables."

"Yeah." *Only they'd have nowhere to put them.* He kept this second part to himself, his mind thinking he didn't need to point out the obvious.

The two took a seat, their bodies almost in the shade.

"So, why NIU?" Mark asked.

Amy spooned a mouthful of her dessert into her mouth, and allowed it to start the journey to her stomach before saying, "No real reason."

"Really?"

"Yeah. I need a college degree to go into my field of study and this place was the closest and the most attractive of all the schools I got accepted into, so it was the one I chose." She took another spoonful. "You?"

"Pretty much the same I guess. I still don't really know what I'm going to do as far as a career goes but figured having a bachelor degree in something would be helpful."

"What are you studying?"

"Economics."

She gave him a 'yuck' look.

He shrugged. "I figure there will always be room somewhere for someone that understands how the economy works and hell, if the world ends next year like so many people think, maybe I can help rebuild a financial structure with whatever new society grows out of the rubble."

"You don't actually believe all that stuff, do you?" she asked.

"Not really," he admitted. "But it doesn't hurt to be prepared."

"Hmm."

The two took several more bites of their desserts, their spoons seemingly in a race against the heat. While in the midst of this, a couple a few feet down on the curb finished their own items and got up to leave. Without a word, Mark and Amy moved in and took their spot, the shade giving them a wonderful reprieve from the glaring sun.

"So, if you don't mind my asking," Mark started. "What was it that drew you to my profile?"

Amy blushed. "Do I have to say?"

"No," Mark said, mind scolding himself for making her uncomfortable. "Not at all."

"But you want to know."

"I was just curious, that's all. If it embarrasses you or makes you uneasy, that's okay; you don't have to tell me."

"No, no, it doesn't." She waved a hand. "I'm just being silly I guess. Your profile seemed more real than everyone else's, like you weren't just out there to get under a girls skirt or something."

"Really?"

"Don't get me wrong, I enjoy a good romp as much as the next girl, but there has to be substance beforehand. I'm not looking for a flesh and blood vibrator. If I was I'd have no trouble finding one."

The comment caught him off guard.

"Sorry, that was crude," she said.

"No, don't worry. I prefer people that are up front about things and I know exactly what you're saying. Most of the guys out there only want one thing. They see sites like this as a place to cast out many lines like they're fishing and will reel in the easiest catch." He popped a fudge covered cherry into his mouth.

"But not you," she said.

"Well," he said once the cherry was down. "I have to admit, I've cast out lines too, but my goal isn't just sex. I want a relationship with a person. In the end that makes sex more appealing anyway." He couldn't believe they were talking about this. "I also know that what they're doing doesn't work, at least most girls don't go for it."

"And the ones who do?"

"I don't know. The only ones I've ever run into were fakes. For some reason they get off on teasing guys like me. Doesn't make much sense really, but they do it anyway."

"Wow, that's just weird. I don't get why someone would go to all that trouble to waste someone else's time – and their own." She shook her head. "And just think if they did it to the wrong person. That could cause some serious trouble."

"Yeah."

"But at least you know I'm not like that, and I know you're not just working to get under my skirt so you can move onto the next girl that comes your way."

He smiled.

After that the rest of their desserts were eaten in silence, one that didn't seem uncomfortable at all.

7

Bill couldn't help but feel a sense of pride at his fighting abilities after the small confrontation in the front yard, and wanted to post about it to the world via his blog and Facebook. At the same time, he knew the encounter had upset Kimberly, and that a part of her frustration was directed his way. Why exactly he wasn't sure, he had simply defended himself (and her), but he could tell this was the case. Thankfully, knowing this didn't dampen the overall gratification he felt. It did, however, make him feel odd being up in his apartment, especially knowing she was down there. In fact, given the layout, he almost felt as if the two were living together but had separated themselves on opposite sides of the house. With this feeling came an urge to go down and work things out with her, something he wouldn't even have contemplated if the two weren't within walking distance of each other.

And why do you even care? he asked. *It's not like you two are dating or anything.*

This troubled him because he knew what it was pointing toward, which was something he didn't want. At least he told himself he didn't want it. One serious relationship early in his adult life had been enough for him to realize he didn't want a woman in his life. Sex from time to time, yes, who didn't, but a relationship, nope. Yet here he was growing more and more attracted to her, and not just on a physical level. If it had been just that, he wouldn't be worried about her being upset with him, nor would he have the helpful protective desire he was displaying. This wasn't to say he wouldn't stand up for her or anyone that needed help, he just wouldn't be this focused on it.

Even knowing he was partially to blame for the trouble she was facing wouldn't have really fueled any need to be part of the solution, not without the foolish desires that were growing.

And now, because of all this nonsense, you're taking her to breakfast, paying for parking spots at the college, and growing worried about the possibility of upsetting her.

He didn't even realize it until that moment, but he was trying to be as quiet as possible while moving around, his hope being he didn't aggravate her any further with his pacing.

Just relax.

Following this advice was easy, but only after he heard her leaving for work. Once that happened he almost felt like a guy who had the house to himself for a while, a house that had had an unbearable amount of tension within it.

It was ridiculous, he knew, yet something that he couldn't help.

Boredom followed.

Making it worse, he couldn't read. His mind was just too preoccupied. He also didn't want to pop in a movie, not when his mind wouldn't be able to focus on it. What he needed was TV, some mindless show to eat away time.

Eat up time until what?

The question went unanswered; at least, that's what he told himself. Deep down inside he knew what he was waiting for. He wanted Kimberly to come home from work. He wanted to hear the car out by the garage and then, by design, happen to be taking down some garbage as she walked to her side door so he could casually ask if anything had happened.

You're hopeless, he said.

Admitting this didn't change anything.

He walked to the window and looked out at the street.

Ten minutes came and went, his eyes not really focusing on anything in particular, his mind pretty much shut off.

Then, without warning, *go to the library you idiot and access that email.*

Earlier, while driving back from the NIU campus, he had planned to ask Kimberly if they could open the Nikki email address from her computer, his thinking being they could start working toward finding out if the person who had sent it was also responsible for everything that had followed. Being confronted by Kyle had knocked the idea aside. Now that it was back, he knew he had to act upon it. Unfortunately, he also knew that he had no idea where to go from there.

Once you have the address, then what? Email the guy and ask if he was for real?

Obviously, the answer to that was no, yet at the same time it was the only thing he could really think of, unless . . .

The possibility that Nicole's roommate's boyfriend could somehow help entered his mind, and for a moment he considered calling her to find out. He then realized that she was probably working, and figured it would be better to have the email in his possession first.

And if nothing else you can always just give it to the police.

Fear of getting in trouble for the things he had done with the blog last spring followed, but only lasted a second. Nothing he had done had been illegal. In fact, given how many of those men Nikki had promised to meet with at the Sleepy Time Motel out on Route 64, he had probably helped boost the economy a bit. If nothing else, the motel owner was probably happy during that two-month period when he had really put the screws to the men, his goal of earning enough money from the renewed subscriptions to pay his rent for at least three months having been met. He (or she) had probably been a bit confused too as to why so many lone men had stopped in to get a room during the first week of March and then again in April.

Confused, but happy. In fact, if he knew the why of everything he probably would have started his own Nikki-like profile and lured men in himself.

That might be illegal, though.

It was one thing for him to send guys to a random motel as if he (Nikki) would be arriving shortly after they paid for the room. It would be another for the motel itself to do it in hopes of just getting guys to pay for a room. Chances were good that there was some type of business law against such actions.

But if the right precautions were taken . . .

He shook the thought away since it didn't really matter. Maybe in the future, if he used this situation as the basis for some horror tale focusing in on a motel and the things the owner would do to acquire guests, he might look into it more, but now all he needed to focus in on was getting the email.

After that . . .

His mind once again drew a blank, but that was okay. He had his next step planned out. Once it was achieved he would send Nicole a text asking for her to call him once she got off work, if he was right about her working tonight, and would find out if her roommate's boyfriend could help.

Laptop in hand, he left the apartment and headed toward the library.

8

Mark had hoped he and Amy could spend more time together once the desserts were finished, and kind of figured she was going to suggest something more they could do after asking him if he had any fun plans for the rest of the day, but nothing had followed. His answer of no had simply earned a skeptical look, and then a comment that that said, "I don't want to get in the way of anything."

"You're not," he said. "Trust me."

She studied him for several seconds, an odd smile in place, and then shook her head, "No, you had something planned, I can tell."

"Okay, I did tell a friend I might get together with them, but that was only if nothing else came up. If you want to do something, they'll understand completely."

"You say that now, but it won't be long before me getting between you and your friends would be a burden that caused conflict."

"No, really, I'd rather – " he started.

She laughed. "Don't worry; I'm not bailing or anything. I think this was fun and we'll get together again soon. I like you and given that we've been sitting here talking for nearly an hour even though we finished our treats I think it's safe to say you like me too."

"I do," he said. "And I'm glad you messaged me. Any idea when you want to get together again?"

"Is it a long drive out here for you right now?"

"A bit, but I don't mind."

"I'd say tomorrow, but then you're going to have to go back and forth between here and your house again the next day for class, and that just seems like so much driving, so – "

"I could get a motel room tomorrow night," he blurted before she could finish. "That way we could get together for dinner or something, and then I'll stay here so I can go to class the next day and we could get together again afterward or something."

"If that is what you want to do. Are there many motels in the area that don't cost much?"

"Oh yeah, tons. I've even – " he stopped himself from blurting out that he had stayed at one all day once waiting for Nikki to show up last spring after the two had agreed to have sex.

"You've even what?" she asked.

"Oh, nothing. For some reason I add in pointless little tidbits from time to time when talking."

"I don't mind. Pointless little tidbits are how people get to know each other. Share away – unless you're itching to get home and away from me." She gave a fake pouty look.

"Not a chance. We could sit here all day talking and I wouldn't mind."

"Awww." She leaned over and hugged him. "You're so sweet."

He smiled.

"How is it that such a sweet charming guy is still single?" she asked.

The question caught him completely off guard. He also knew that answering it could be dangerous, though given their conversation thus far he doubted she would suddenly decide not to see him again if he said the wrong thing. The fear didn't completely disappear, however, so he simply said, "I really don't know."

"Me either," she said and smiled.

Mark had no idea what to say after that.

Silence arrived.

Inside he screamed at himself to think of something so that they didn't have to end their time together. *Get another topic going,* he said. *Suggest you two go do something that makes her realize it's okay that you had 'plans' with a friend, that you'd rather spend time with her. Do something!*

Nothing.

The two sat there in silence, one that grew a bit awkward, for nearly five minutes before she suggested they go their separate ways.

"You have fun with your friend," she said during their drawn out goodbye.

"I will, and tomorrow, what time did you want to get together?"

"I don't know. Maybe give me a text in the morning and let me know if you still want to come out here and we'll go from there."

"Okay, I will." *Should I kiss her?*

She hesitated a moment, then said, "Well, thanks for the ice cream."

He almost corrected her by saying it had been custard, but caught himself. "You're welcome." *Do it.*

"Well . . ."

"Let me walk you to your car," he said, an inner statement about kissing her there rather than right here following.

In the end no kiss happened, his sudden reasoning being this wasn't really a date, more of a just meet and greet, and that a hug would be more appropriate. Naturally, concern about this arrived shortly after she left, his mind pretty sure she had wanted a kiss.

Now she's probably second guessing getting together with you again, he said. Tomorrow he would message her and she would tell him something had come up. The simple excuse could be genuine, so he wouldn't panic right away, but then, as the excuses continued day after day, he would realize the reality of the situation. After that . . . *Hello Bunny Ranch.*

No, she won't do that, he said to himself, his confidence overpowering the concern. It didn't do away with it completely, nothing ever would, but it did dispel enough of it so that it didn't dominate his mind. *Tomorrow we will get together and have a great time, and, if things work out . . .* images from several different porn films followed, his mind attempting to superimpose the two of them upon the people within them.

Maybe.

He knew pushing for sex could prove disastrous, so he would do his best to control himself and let the mood guide things. *If you can even read it.*

Interpreting signals from women wasn't really up there among his talents. Even worse was his ability to act upon those interpretations once he did have them figured out.

But at least the opportunity will be there.

This thought put a smile on his face. It also once again brought to light the realization that one never truly knew what each day would bring. At this time yesterday, he had no idea a message would be coming his way. Instead, his thoughts had centered on Nikki and Kimberly and how he might go about helping one and ruining the other. Now . . . well, he didn't really care all that much about it, though he did think it would probably be in his best interest to continue helping Kimberly.

Who knows, you could go from suddenly having one girl who wants you, to having two girls.

He felt a tingle at the thought, and once again pictured scenes from some of the porn films he had watched, scenes that involved two girls and a guy rather than just one girl and guy.

Yeah, right, in your dreams.

But, you never know . . .

With that he took one last look at the area where Amy and he had been sitting, his mind savoring the time they had shared, and then got into his car.

Now what?

The question stuck in his head for a good minute, a debate on whether he should go home or stay in town appearing.

Eventually the debate led him to his phone where he signed online to see if Kimberly had said anything.

Nothing.

Nikki had stayed silent too.

Go by her house and see if she's home.

But she might not like that.

In fact, she might find that downright creepy given that she knows you don't live out here right now.

On Monday, after class, such an impromptu visit could be easily explained and probably accepted. Now, not so much.

Go home.

BEEP!

He looked down at his phone and saw that it was Amy.

THANK YOU FOR SUCH A WONDERFUL TIME THIS AFTERNOON. I CAN'T WAIT TO DO IT AGAIN TOMORROW. SEE YA SOON!

A warm feeling of happiness filled him and stayed with him all the way back home. It apparently was showing itself because at dinner that night his mother asked him about it. He didn't share any details, though, not when he knew it would just lead to an endless round of questions about Amy, as well as comments from them that would make him feel like a little kid with his first girlfriend.

9

HE SAYS TO FORWARD HIM THE EMAIL AND HE WILL SEE WHAT HE CAN DO. NO PROMISES THOUGH.

An email address followed.

OK, THANKS, Bill replied.

He waited a few minutes before heading back out, but nothing else arrived, so he grabbed his laptop and started toward Panera. Once there he forwarded the email as Nicole instructed, his phone number included in the message with a note that said he didn't have easy access to the web. After that a debate on what to do next began, one that involved food. Given the money he had spent earlier he didn't really want to spend anything else, but at the same time going back home and making some quick noodle dish or a frozen pizza didn't seem all that appealing.

You could go see Kimberly.

No, that'll probably just piss her off.

An idea arrived.

What the hell, why not.

Rather than make an instant noodle dish he would have the people at Noodles and Company do it for him. The eating establishment was across the street from Panera. Inside, he ordered a regular bowl of the Pesto Cavatappi to go.

Ten minutes later he was sitting in the parking lot of Steak and Shake, his car positioned so he could see the front door and Kimberly's car.

Now if only you'd thought of this last night.

If he had chances were he would have been able to see whoever it was that put the pictures on Kimberly's car, and while it might not have been enough to make a positive ID, he still would have had some idea of who the person was behind all this. If positioned properly he might have even been able to follow the person.

And of course your skills at this would be incredible given how often you, as a writer, have penned scenes detailing such events, his mind chided. *That's always the case when writers get involved in situations like this, right.*

He sighed.

In his mind he saw himself following the perpetrator all over the DeKalb area, and maybe even beyond, as they headed back to their lair for the night. In reality he would probably lose them after the second stoplight.

Still, just getting to attempt such action would be better than sitting at home pondering the situation. Add in the chance that the email he had forwarded to Nicole's roommate's boyfriend might uncover something useful and it suddenly felt as if progress were being made.

With this thought he opened his noodle dish and began to eat, his eyes constantly scanning the area around Kimberly's car after each forkful.

No one stirred.

Ten minutes turned to twenty minutes and then to thirty minutes and then . . .

Movement!

Someone cut through the bushes that edged the parking lot and separated it from the Ruby Tuesday establishment, their path choice putting them right up against Kimberly's car.

Only they continued forward, feet taking them across the parking lot and around the building to the front door, an apron held in one hand, a cell phone in the other.

Bill took a deep breath in an attempt to calm himself, his adrenaline having spiked. He then told himself that several employees would probably come walking from that direction given that a bus stop was situated just beyond the abandoned bank on the far side of Ruby Tuesdays.

Plus, the perpetrator probably won't try anything until its dark out, so you might as well get comfortable.

A part of getting comfortable involved repositioning his car so that he didn't have to constantly look to the right to see Kimberly's car. Unfortunately doing this made him stand out a bit more since he chose to back into a spot on the opposite side of

Kimberly's car so that he could simply look forward and see it across the lot. Hopefully once darkness fell he would be shielded a bit. Now, however, anyone looking at his car would see him sitting there. This included people inside looking out the windows, though given the position of the sun, he doubted they could see much beyond the glass.

10

Kimberly was having an off evening, her mind too focused on everything that had occurred in the last few days to be able to handle the orders and demands of the customers. Thankfully, she would have a break after tonight, one that would extend until Tuesday evening. It was something she had orchestrated during her first week of work, her thinking being that not having to work on her first day of school would be a blessing so she could focus on getting settled and wouldn't feel overwhelmed. Ideally, she wouldn't have worked at all that entire week, but that wasn't possible.

Only three more hours to go, she said to herself, eyes having settled on the clock. *Only three more hours and then . . . what, go out to find a stack of pictures on your car, go home to find your door wide open and a note inside, go home to find Kyle waiting on the front step.*

Or maybe nothing will happen, maybe –

"Kim, wake up."

Kimberly looked at a co-worker named Dale who was working the grill.

"Customers," Dale said with a nod toward the entrance.

Kimberly turned and sure enough a group of young adults were waiting to be seated. After them was a young woman by herself, and then another couple.

Once they were all settled, Kimberly hurried back toward the expo area where food was waiting, served it, and then got the drinks for the customers who had ended up in her section. Orders were then placed that she took to Dale. A family then entered that needed to be seated. She took the family to her section since she had the tables for them and took their drink orders.

While filling those she caught a glance of a young man staring at her from the doorway. He smiled.

A chill gripped her.

Soda ran over her hand.

Crap! She silently cried while pulling the glass away from the fountain trigger. She then grabbed some napkins to wipe her hands and then the glass before setting it on the tray.

She looked up toward the entrance.

The young man was no longer standing there. He was now sitting in her section, watching her.

Sam, a fellow waiter who only seemed to come in during the weekends, came to the expo area to fill some drinks.

"I have a silly question," Kimberly said.

"Oh?" he asked.

"That guy that you just seated, why'd you put him in my section?"

"He requested it," Sam said.

"What?"

"He specifically asked to sit in your section."

Kimberly didn't reply.

"What's wrong?" Sam asked. "He's not like stalking you or anything, is he?"

You have no idea, Kimberly said to herself. In reply she simply smiled and said, "Who knows?"

"Wait a sec, do you know him?" Concern was now present in Sam's voice.

"No."

"Wow, that's kind of creepy. Let me know if he gives you any trouble."

"Okay." She lifted the drink tray. "Thanks."

If he replied she did not hear it as she brought the drinks to the waiting family. She then took their orders, her mind growing impatient as one of the kids demanded French Fries but his mother said no. While listening to this she glanced at the young man and tried to figure out if he was the one behind all this, or if he had simply been told to come here to see her.

You'll know soon enough, she told herself and focused back on the family.

"You got all that?" the mother asked.

"Yes," Kimberly said.

"Read it back, please."

Kimberly did and the orders were correct, yet this didn't bring a satisfied look to the mother's face. Nothing would have. She had run into this type many times while working food service jobs. The look the husband gave her confirmed it; she was the type that enjoyed correcting people. She also would have a complaint once the food was out. Of this, Kimberly was certain. It wouldn't matter if everything was correct, some error would be found.

Order in hand, Kimberly headed back to the grill area to place it, and then headed over to the young man at the table, her mind trying to figure out how she was going to greet him.

Just be normal as if he is a typical customer.

"Hi, my name is Kimberly. Are you ready to order?"

"Um . . . I'm actually waiting for someone, but, well, could I get a Coke?"

"Oh?" This caught her completely off guard. "Sure."

Back at the fountain machine she asked Sam, "What did the guy say when he asked to sit in my section?"

"I don't know, he just asked to sit in your section." He shrugged.

"Did he ask by name?" She filled the Coke.

"Yeah."

"Huh."

"He's a creep, isn't he?"

"No, I don't think so. Just . . ." rather than finish she simply shook her head and headed back to the young man with the Coke.

"Thanks," he said and took a nervous sip.

Kimberly hesitated and then asked, "Why did you ask to sit in my section?"

"What, oh, um, the girl I'm meeting told me to. She's a friend of yours actually."

Kimberly didn't need to ask to know what the name would be

and said, "Let me guess, Nikki?"

"Yes," he said with a smile. "I'm Malcolm." Relief appeared. "I have to admit, I thought this all sounded too good to be true, but now, well, I'm really excited. Do you and Nikki do this often?"

"Do what often?" Kimberly asked. She didn't like where this was going, if it was going in the direction she thought it was.

"You know, take guys like me back to your place after you get off work and . . . well, you know." His voice had fallen to a soft whisper that she could barely hear, yet that was okay because she knew exactly what was being implied.

"I'm sorry. Malcolm, right?"

He nodded.

"I hate to break it to you, but Nikki isn't real. Someone has been telling guys stuff like this quite a bit lately and causing me all kinds of trouble."

His face sank.

"Was it on OK Cupid?"

"No, um, Plenty of Fish."

Jesus Christ, how many sites are there?

"I – I – " he shook his head.

"Sorry," she said again, mind unable to think of anything else to say.

He didn't reply.

She turned to see if there was food up near the expo area, which there was and quickly said, "I'll be right back, okay."

Five minutes passed before she was able to return, the control freak mother having had several issues with the food that she brought, the biggest being that fries had been put on the child's plate by mistake.

"I'm sorry about that," Kimberly said with as much sincerity as she could muster. "You won't be charged for it."

"We better not be," the mother said. "Now you take this back and prepare the meal correctly."

Kimberly agreed even though the burger was fine.

"What's wrong with it?" Dale asked.

"Wasn't supposed to have fries," Kimberly said. "They want

an entirely new plate."

"Are you serious?"

She nodded and then dumped the plate in the trash and then returned to the table and told them it would be a few minutes.

"I knew this would happen," the mother said. "Every time we come here you screw up our order."

As far as she could tell Kimberly had never served this family before. She also wanted to know why, if the orders were frequently wrong, they kept coming back. A nod and an apology was all she let leave her lips, however, and then returned to Malcolm's table. "Did you still want to order something?" she asked.

He shook his head.

"Okay. I'm really sorry about all this."

"Why? It's not your fault."

"Yeah, well . . ." it was all she could say.

"Can I get my check?"

"Don't worry about it, it was just a Coke."

"You sure?"

"Yeah. It's fine."

"Thanks," he muttered while standing, the word sounding stale.

Kimberly nodded and watched as he left the restaurant an inner statement on how this really needed to end flowing through her head. The familiar question of WHY appeared as well, but like all the times she had asked it since this had started, no solid answer arrived.

11

As expected the envelopment of darkness brought about a sense of relief as Bill sat and watched Kimberly's car, his mind feeling less exposed than it had during the first half of his watch. Not that anyone had probably even noticed him. People always felt as if they were the focus of everyone around them, but the truth was that they probably didn't make much of an impact at all. In fact, if asked, most would have a difficult time describing anything beyond the gender of the people they had met during the day, unless something significant had occurred during that meeting. Even then, the details surrounding the event would probably be a bit fuzzy.

Still, the darkness brought comfort and a more relaxed atmosphere to what he was doing, as well as a certainty that the time of something occurring was near.

If something is going to happen.

Given the frequency of the torments he was sure something would, the only problem was he didn't know if he was in the right location to witness it. Just because pictures were left on the car the other night didn't necessarily mean pictures would be left tonight. Something else could unfold, something involving the house.

You might have been better off sitting in the bushes.

Actually, he wouldn't have lasted twenty minutes out there, not with all the mosquitoes and slithery creatures that liked to prowl the area. Hell, just cutting the grass was sometimes a spooky ordeal given the snakes. In fact, after stepping on one during his first lawn mowing adventure he had started leaving the mower running in the middle of the yard for five minutes before cutting it, just so all the creatures would scatter from the noise. Every now and then he still would encounter a snake, though, and while they weren't poisonous given their type, they still freaked him out.

Besides, if the person behind all this enjoyed watching Kimberly whenever a torment unfolded, then following Kimberly was the best chance at catching them in the act. And since the person had told Kimberly to meet Nikki here at her own work via the fake profile Kimberly had set up, chances were they would be watching.

But how will you know it's them?

What if they don't do anything to the car and simply leave?

No answers arrived.

All he could do was wait and see.

He looked at his laptop while doing this and considered turning it on to see if he could hook into any free wireless services offered by the local businesses, but then vetoed the idea for two reasons. First, he knew he would get completely hooked and would probably miss anything that unfolded with Kimberly's car. Second, given the darkness the light from the screen would illuminate the inside of the car, and would be hard for people to ignore, especially if they were the type that looked around the parking lot first to see if anyone was watching what they did to a certain car.

Nope. Sit and stare. It was the only course of action. In time he added peeing into an empty cup as a third option, a slight pressure in his bladder having slowly grown to a level of intensity that could not be ignored. While taking care of that he caught sight of a young man leaving the restaurant by himself, one who had entered by himself only ten or fifteen minutes earlier. Adding to Bill's suspicion of him was what he had witnessed inside the restaurant, the light within making it easy to see everything that happened through the windows. Upon entering the young man had sat in Kimberly's section and then, after waiting a bit, talked to her briefly. After that he simply left. The question was what had they talked about? Had he been a guy sent to see Kimberly by the Nikki fake, one whom Kimberly had set straight, or had he been the Nikki fake himself acting as if he had been sent there? If the latter he apparently didn't want to mess with Kimberly's car tonight. Instead, he got into his own car and drove away.

But maybe that's because he wants to hurry and do something at the house while she is still working?

If that had been the case, however, why go the trouble of coming here? He knew her work schedule and could have done the stuff at the house without making this trip.

More people left the restaurant.

He waited for them to get in their cars before attempting to dump the pee cup. Naturally, more people filtered out just as he started to open the door, his hand having taken a moment to shut off the overhead light, so he waited again. Once that second group was gone he reached for the door handle, but then stopped as movement by Kimberly's car caught his eye.

It was a person and they were doing something that was taking a few moments.

Putting the cup in the cup holder, Bill switched on his car and pulled to the left, his hope being that the building would shield his actions from the Nikki impersonator. Sadly, this also would shield them from him for several seconds. To his relief, they didn't slip away during that opportunity and he was able to get himself into a position that allowed for him to watch as the figure went through the bushes onto the Ruby Tuesday side of the parking lot and walked to a car.

Bill followed, his hope being they would think he was simply a customer leaving Ruby Tuesday now, one who waited for them to pull out of their spot and just happened to take a similar route out of the large shopping center parking lot.

It worked.

Keeping to a standard parking lot speed, the dark -- possibly blue – car eased itself out of the Ruby Tuesday lot and turned right onto a strip of road that cut between two other parking lots and ended at another road that would lead out onto Route 23. Once on that they got into the left hand turn lane and waited at the light.

Anxiety crept into Bill's system as he contemplated his car position in the waiting turn lane, his familiarity with this light letting him know that he probably wouldn't make the arrow. He also worried about his car being recognized, the fake Nikki person having probably seen it many times sitting behind the house in his portion of the driveway. Then again, given the darkness, the chances of them recognizing it in a rear view mirror were probably slim. Still, the fear was there and wouldn't budge.

The light changed.

The lead car hesitated and then slowly made the turn. Other cars did the same, each one seeming to contemplate the necessity of the turn rather than just hitting the gas and going for it.

Come on! Come on! Come on!

Green went to yellow before the Nikki imposter's car even made it into the intersection.

They didn't stop.

Bill didn't either, his car crossing the line seconds after the yellow went to red.

To his left he saw a squad car waiting for their light to turn green. It was three cars behind the lead car.

Please, Bill's mind pleaded, his heart racing. *Don't come after me –*

Up ahead near the Jewel the light changed to red.

Bill pulled to a stop behind the Nikki imposter and then stared at his rear view mirror. No emergency lights appeared. The cop was not coming after him.

The light changed.

The Nikki imposter continued forward, car following the curve of the road as it headed toward the more residential areas of DeKalb. They also stayed in the right lane, which, as anyone who was familiar with this stretch of road knew, meant they planned on cutting across to First Street when the lane ended. Such a route would take them to some of the popular college housing areas, the low rent and short walking distance to the college and all the businesses located on Lincoln Highway making it an ideal choice. Most were houses similar to the one he lived in that had been converted into apartments. If one wanted an apartment in a real apartment building they had to pay more and head further west toward Annie Glidden, or north along First Street toward Harrison.

Anticipating the turn and thinking the person must be heading toward one of those converted houses, Bill started to let his mind speculate on who they were, a theory on them being a college student who got pissed off by his Nikki character seeming to be the best option.

How far are they planning on going with this?

Will it just be pictures and frequent encounters with men sent to the house and work, or will there be –

His mind stopped as the Nikki-imposter went to make the turn but then quickly cut back across onto Route 23.

Fuck! Bill silently cried while swerving over as well.

Had there been traffic in the lane cutting over would have resulted in a wreck. Thankfully, all the other cars had turned off by now, making it just the two of them. Unfortunately, it also meant his cut over had probably been witnessed, and, if planned out, had been a great way for the Nikki imposter to find out if he truly was following them.

And you fell for it.

Up ahead the car made a right onto Locus Street and then, after passing two intersections, a left onto First Street, followed by a right onto Lincoln Highway.

Bill followed all of this.

The driver then pulled into a parking spot alongside the businesses and waited.

Bill pulled in behind them.

There the two cars sat.

If they didn't know before, they certainly do now, Bill told himself. He then contemplated getting out and rushing the driver door, but then figured they would just lock it and pull away.

You really fucked this up.

The car pulled out.

Bill followed.

They went all the way to Annie Glidden and then beyond it, which really surprised him since things would change over to farm fields quickly and stay that way until Malta.

Once in that farm area the car signaled for a turn on the first road.

They're just randomly driving now, Bill thought, his mind trying to pinpoint where this road would take them. If he wasn't mistaken it would turn off at Twombly before wrapping around and turning into Bethany, which, if taken, would lead them fairly close to his own apartment, after about fifteen minutes of driving. *Actually, they are probably starting to panic and will –*

A crash echoed throughout the car as his windshield shattered, his hands quickly spinning the wheel to the right in an attempt to take himself out of the line of fire.

Tall corn crops met his car, the remains hitting him in the face and filling the front seats as the front bumper decapitated them.

His foot slammed down on the brake.

The car dug into the dirt and halted.

Ignoring the glass and the corn guts that covered him, Bill tried opening the driver side door, but couldn't move it, and then, without really thinking, quickly scrambled out through the broken windshield, body rolling across the hot hood into the corn where he maneuvered himself into a row. Breathing heavily, and holding a nasty cut on his arm, he watched the short narrow path his car had created, his eyes expecting to see a figure with a gun coming his way.

Nothing.

The quiet night air was still, the sounds from the city of DeKalb unable to reach out to this area and the road free of traffic.

No one's coming.

He didn't budge.

Time drifted by, each minute bringing about a new source of pain as the adrenalin faded. None of the wounds were serious, but they all stung like hell.

And they could become infected if you don't tend to them soon.

Still, he didn't break his cover, not when it could cost him his life.

They might not have been trying to kill you, just stop you from following them, in which case they will be long gone by now.

He allowed several more minutes to pass before taking this thought into consideration and moving toward the road, his body walking between two cornrows rather than attempting to use the path his car had created.

Sure enough, the road was empty.

Whoever it was had simply wanted to shake him off their tail.

And they were quite successful.

They were –

Headlights appeared in the distance for several seconds, but then disappeared down Twombly.

Bill sighed.

He then reached for his phone to call the police, but found his pocket empty, his hand having placed the phone in the cup holder while watching Steak and Shake a few hours earlier.

His eyes shifted to the car.

Mature corn stalks stood tall along the sides, almost as if it had been perfectly slotted within. Opening the doors would be impossible. He would have to crawl through the windshield once again.

12

Aside from having to tell the young man that Nikki's threesome idea was not going to happen, Kimberly's shift was mostly Nikki-free. It also ended well, her last hour having seen an above average total to her tips for a Steak and Shake shift, which was nice. She then went out to her car.

A single picture was waiting, only this time it wasn't an image of her. In fact, no one was pictured. Instead, all that was displayed was a door that had a crooked 6 on it. Once she had the light on she could see that paint was peeling as well.

YOUR FAULT was written on the back.

What is? Kimberly's mind shouted.

Frustration, fear, and anger started to mix within her mind. She wanted to scream at whoever was doing this and tell them it wasn't her. She wanted Bill with her while doing it so she could point to him. She wanted –

You should leave a note for them to find that shows a picture of Nicole and lets them know it was she, not you, pictured on the blog.

Details on how and why Bill had created the blog could be within the note, along with a statement telling whomever this was to torment those two instead.

Of course, nothing good would come of it.

Even if the person believed the note and left her alone she would have to live with the guilt of putting them upon someone else, which was something she didn't need, not after what had happened in the bathroom all those years ago.

Memories started to flow.

She tried holding them back but couldn't and saw her foot kicking Misty, the sensation of the impact and the image of the cat bouncing with a squeal still fresh in her mind. It had been a moment of insanity, one that she knew could be rationalized by others. She, however, could not rationalize it. She had kicked her best friend, had kicked her in a way that caused her to retreat under the bed where she died from a collapsed lung.

It was the fear and confusion Misty had probably suffered during those last hours of her life that really got to Kimberly. Nothing she could have done would have made Misty understand what had occurred. A lifetime of love had been shattered by a single, nearly involuntary action, one that would forever mark the final memories they both had shared of each other.

Tears fell.

A silent apology followed, one that she hoped Misty could understand up there in kitty heaven. She hoped that given whatever afterlife was available for cats, and other beloved pets, that Misty was now fully able to understand what had happened and knew Kimberly hadn't meant to hurt her. This was the only constant wish she had in life. Nothing else was more important.

Thunk! Thunk!

Kimberly twisted toward the window.

"You okay?" Sam asked.

Heart racing, Kimberly rolled down the window with one hand while wiping away tears with the other. "Yeah, I'm fine."

"You sure?" he pressed.

"Yeah, just was . . . I'm fine."

"Okay. Have a safe drive home."

"Thanks, you too." She rolled up the window as he walked away and then shifted the car to reverse. Not long after that she was home, her eyes startled to see Bill's car missing.

You'll have the entire place to yourself, she noted.

The thought brought an odd sense of fear, though it didn't last long, not when the door upstairs opened and Bill stepped onto his porch.

13

"A Snapple Bottle?" Kimberly said in disbelief. "Seriously?"

"Yeah," Bill said. "And boy did it do the trick. Shattered my entire windshield. I then added to the damage by driving into a cornfield."

He left out the part about spilling a cup of pee all over the car. Some details just didn't need to be shared.

"Wow, I'll have to start carrying some of those."

Bill didn't reply to that.

The bottle had been sitting in his front passenger seat when he got back in the car, though he didn't notice it until the police arrived and did a search through the car to see if the bullet he had told them about had gotten lodged anywhere. Once they pointed out the bottle and asked him if it was his, he had realized what had happened.

"They might have thrown a couple of them too before hitting you and you would never have known it," the officer had said. *"You're lucky. At these speeds that could have been just as lethal as a gunshot."*

"They say anything else?" Kimberly asked.

"Not really. They're filing a report and all that and they took the Snapple bottle for fingerprints, though I'm guessing a good defense attorney could probably get that dismissed." All they would have to say was that anyone could have touched it while it was on the shelf at the store, and voila, reasonable doubt.

"And are they adding it to my case?" she asked.

"Um . . ." he hesitated ". . . I didn't tell them I was following them, or about the stuff that was going on."

"What?"

"I got worried they would think I was the aggressor and that they threw the bottle because they feared I was coming after them, or something."

"But you watched them put the picture on my car!"

"I know, but you know how things like this unfold."

"What are you talking about?"

"All they'd have to do is think I followed the wrong person and suddenly I was the instigator and the police report won't help me and I'll get stuck having to pay for a new windshield and all the damage I did to the underside of my car."

"Bullshit."

"Huh?"

"If you were the instigator why did you, and not they, call the police?"

Bill hadn't really thought about that.

"And even if you were provoking them, they would still have the issue of the other person using excessive force rather than calling the police themselves. Stuff like that doesn't bode well in this day and age."

She's right, Bill admitted to himself. The words, "Okay, I fucked up," followed, along with a shrug.

Kimberly shook her head.

"So, what did they leave on your car?" Bill asked. This wasn't the first response to her head shake that he had thought up, but it was the better of the two. Suggesting she should thank him for putting his life on the line to try to uncover who was doing this probably wouldn't have gone well.

"Oh, just a picture of a door."

"What?"

She fumbled in her purse for a moment and then reached into her apron.

Bill waited but no picture emerged. "Did you leave it in the car?"

"Oh crap, I think I did." She looked toward one of the dark windows, concern appearing on her face.

"You want me to go grab it?" Bill asked.

"What? No, I can do it. I just -- " she looked at the window again " -- can you come with?"

"Yeah, let's go get it."

The two stood up, Bill leading the way from her family room to the kitchen door. Once there he hesitated a moment, mind wondering if he should grab something that could be used as a weapon, or if that would be overkill. They were, after all, just walking fifteen feet to the garage.

"What is it?" Kimberly asked, her body close as she tried to peer over his shoulder.

"Nothing." He opened the door. "Do you have the garage key?"

"Yeah."

"Okay."

The two stepped out of the house, Bill still leading the way.

"You know," he said while coming upon the back corner of the house. "It's almost better without the motion sensor lights because I don't feel like we're being spotlighted by -- " he stopped.

The garage door was wide open.

Behind him he heard Kimberly's breath catch.

"Did you lock it on the way out?" Bill whispered.

"Yeah."

Maybe the guy downstairs came home?

The thought did little to reassure him, especially since he would have heard him.

"Wait here," Bill said and then began moving toward the door, mind once again thinking about the idea of grabbing a weapon. Nothing within the vicinity seemed adequate, and the last thing he wanted to do was waste time running back up to his apartment to grab something.

At the door he waited, listening.

Nothing seemed to move within.

Given the noise they'd made before seeing the door was open, however, could have silenced whoever was inside.

And someone is inside.

How he knew this was a mystery, but know it he did.

He looked back at Kimberly and made a phone out of his hand that he pressed to his ear.

She shook her head.

His was inside too.

Okay, just step inside and demand to know who's in there.

He took a deep breath and stepped in, his hand flipping the light switch while shouting, "Hey!"

The word faded in the darkness, the light having failed to turn on.

He flipped the switch back and forth a few times while staring into the darkness.

Nothing.

He then considered hitting the button to open the garage door, which would let some light in, but then vetoed the idea.

Whoever was in here would have to confront him if they wanted out and once that happened –

Something crashed to the right and then a figure was rushing toward him.

Startled, Bill stepped back through the doorway while bracing himself for the impact that was coming, his heel catching on the bottom part of the door frame just as the figure slammed a shoulder into his gut.

14

Kimberly let out a surprised yelp as the figure crashed into Bill, his slow movements up to this point and her feeling of exposure having caused the tension within her to grow with each passing second. She also took several steps backward, her body acting as if distance were needed to prevent some kind of collateral damage from occurring.

Bill then did something unexpected.

Rather than fall back with the impact, he somehow twisted himself with it and grabbed the hooded figure, his arms attempting to lock themselves around their chest in an unbreakable bear hug.

Unfortunately, the culprit was pretty fluid as well and squirmed free before the arms could lock.

Both then went to the ground, Bill having been on his way down due to the impact, and the figure having been snagged by his right hand after breaking free of the hug.

A loud, almost feminine cry escaped the figure as they hit the ground. *"Fucker!"* followed, a kick to Bill's face emphasizing the anger they felt.

It was then that Kimberly found the courage to make a move and charged forward. Had she not backed up several steps in the beginning she probably would have been able to tackle them, but the small bit of distance her body had created was enough to allow the figure to stand and bolt.

Kimberly gave chase.

The figure went to the right between the two houses and then took a left toward the neighbor's front yard.

Kimberly followed, her foot slipping once on the grass, which cost her several more feet, but not enough to make the chase seem futile.

From there the figure followed the sidewalk until they had gone halfway down the street and cut left into a yard where they disappeared from view.

Pushing herself, Kimberly increased her speed and managed to enter the yard just as the figure took a right in front of the house opposite of the yard Kimberly was in, the direction taking them toward the far side of the graveyard, which they entered just as Kimberly emerged from the houses.

Far to her left Bill appeared, his route having taken him through a different set of yards. He would never be able to close the distance between him and the figure. Kimberly thought she still had a chance though and continued to push herself, her body rounding the large stonework of the graveyard entrance just seconds after the figure had.

Crack!

The sound actually echoed in her head before she felt the impact, along with several yellow spots that danced before her eyes against a black backdrop.

The ground then hit, her knees having disappeared.

"You okay?" It was Bill. How much time had passed was a mystery. It felt like none, but she knew that couldn't be right.

Pain arrived.

It felt like her nose had been smashed with a brick. Memories of cracking her face on a diving board as a kid came to her. The sudden shock of the impact followed by a dark splash into the water was all that had registered back then, and now she felt a similar lack of detail in everything surrounding her.

"She hit you with her arm," Bill said. "You ran right into it. I don't think your nose is broken though. Can you stand?"

All the words were there but the meaning was a bit fuzzy.

"Here, try to sit up."

Kimberly felt his arms lifting her.

Dizziness arrived.

She closed her eyes.

Her stomach squeezed.

She gagged, but nothing came up.

Blood!

It was in her mouth.

"Easy does it, you're all right."

"Everything okay?" someone asked.

"Yeah, she's fine. She tripped while jogging."

Liar!

"Need any help?"

"No, we got it."

"Okay."

"Think you can stand up?"

"Uh-huh," she mumbled, the taste of blood mixing with mucus. She then felt his hands on her arms, and up she went, his body pressing against her from behind to help her keep her balance.

The dizziness returned, but wasn't as bad as before. She then opened her eyes. Things wobbled for a moment before firming up.

"You okay?" Bill asked.

"Yes."

"Can you walk?"

In reply, she took a step and nearly fell down.

"Woah, easy does it," Bill warned. His hands were the only thing keeping her upright. "Take it slow and lean on me."

She did, the first steps feeling as if she had never walked before. By the time they crossed the street, however, she was able to stand on her own, not that Bill would let her. He held her arm all the way back to the house and grew very protective of her as she went up the stairs, and then into the house.

"Here, I don't think they'll do much good for your shirt, but you'll be able to get some of the blood off your face."

For a moment she didn't know what he was talking about, but then saw the handful of paper towels he had grabbed from the kitchen.

She took them and dabbed at her lower face.

Blood soaked into the towel.

She pressed it to her nose and started leaning back, but then remembered someone somewhere saying that doing so was actually bad, so she just looked forward instead, fingers pinching the nostrils shut.

"Do you have a flashlight in here?" Bill asked.

Kimberly let go of her nostrils and asked, "What?"

"A flashlight." He seemed full of energy all the sudden. "I want to see what they did in the garage, if anything."

"Um, I don't know." She knew she had at least one, but couldn't focus her mind on where it would be. "Maybe in the kitchen somewhere?"

"I got one upstairs," he said and quickly turned. "You okay here for a second?"

She nodded.

With that he was gone, first going up the inner stairs to his door, which apparently wasn't locked -- *I could have searched his place if I wanted to* -- and then down the outside stairs to the garage, his steps vibrating through the wall.

Fear did not arrive with his departure. In fact, despite having been knocked on her ass, she felt an odd sense of optimism. They had caught her tormentor off guard. They had put them on the defensive and made them flee. They had –

Bill returned, the sound of him locking the door reaching her from the kitchen. He then entered the room.

"Find anything?" she asked.

He shook his head. "We probably caught her before she did what she wanted."

"Wait, *her*?" Kimberly asked. She had caught him using this description a few times since the confrontation, but this was the first time it really registered.

"Yeah, it was a woman," Bill said.

"How do you know?" Even as she asked this she could now see it, especially in the way the figure had been running and the cry of 'fucker' that had left her lips when Bill knocked her down.

"Easy, I grabbed her boobs when tackling her."

15

The handful of boob had actually startled him; so much so, that he had unconsciously tried to shift his hand placement to a more appropriate spot while grabbing her, which had then allowed her to squirm free, all while falling to the ground. The action, while odd given the situation, was probably one most men could identify with. Unintentionally touching a girl's boob usually caused a reflexive pull back. Somehow, it was ingrained into the muscle and nerves of the body, along with the ability to suddenly recognize what was being touched.

"Why would a woman be doing this?" Kimberly asked.

Bill shrugged.

"I mean, I can understand a guy getting upset over your Nikki character teasing him for several weeks, but a girl?" She dabbed at some blood near her lips. "Did you ever tease any girls?"

"No. All guys." Pain from the sweat dripping into all the tiny cuts he had sustained that evening, some from the windshield and some from the driveway surface, began to appear. "That I'm aware of," he added. "Hey, you need any fresh paper towels. I'm going to grab some for these." He held up his forearms to display his wounds.

Kimberly looked at the bloodied up paper towels she held, and then touched at her nose again. Nothing fresh dripped onto it. "I'm okay."

Bill nodded and went to grab the towels. He then dampened them a bit at the sink.

"Did you ever work with any girls other than Nicole?" she asked upon his return.

"No, just her."

"Did any other girls know about what you were doing?"

"A few, but I'm certain that wasn't any of them." He would have recognized them; even without getting a good look at their face, he would have still felt a familiarity about the person.

"Jealous girlfriend?"

"Yeah, but that's very old news and she wouldn't --
" he stopped and actually considered it. *Could she be behind this? No, I would have known it was her.* "I'm pretty certain it isn't her."

"You should still check."

"Hmmm." *Um . . . yeah, that's not going to happen.* Getting into the why of this wouldn't produce anything but a conflict, so he kept this decision to himself.

"I don't know any of the details, but if someone who had feelings for you somehow connected you to your Nikki site and then decided I was the girl you were using for it, I could see them going after me."

"I'll look into it," Bill lied. Hopefully that would change the direction of the discussion. To help this he then asked, "Were there any suspicious females in Steak and Shake tonight? Maybe one who seems to show up in your section a lot?"

Kimberly shook her head. "None that I can really pinpoint, but I haven't been paying much attention to them since I just figured it was a guy."

"Yeah, same here," Bill said. Then again, he hadn't really been paying attention to the people around him at all. Up until tonight his focus had been mostly inward as he tried to mentally process everything to a point where he could point at someone with confidence. The only exception to this was the email he had forwarded earlier in the day, one that he really hoped would prove to be the address source for the person (or people) behind all this.

"And why are they so adamant about getting guys to come here and torment me?" she asked.

Bill didn't have an answer.

"And why put a picture of a door on my car?" she added.

"Well, obviously they blame you, well, Nikki, for something, the question is, what?" *And how is the door connected.*

The picture in question was sitting on the sofa.

Bill walked over and picked it up.

Why is this significant? he asked while looking at the door number. *What would have –*

"Do you think you could sit down?" Kimberly asked.

Bill looked at her, not understanding at first, but then realized he had been pacing. "Oh, sorry, I do that when thinking."

"I know, I hear it upstairs all the time. Right now it's just a bit unnerving."

"Okay." Bill took a seat on the floor. "Better?"

She nodded.

He considered telling her that talking to someone with a bloodstained outfit and face was unnerving as well, but decided against it. A thought did occur, though. "Do you need an ice pack or anything? I didn't think of it until now."

"Is my face swollen?" She carefully touched herself while asking, a wince appearing as her finger pressed against a part of her nose.

"No, not really," Bill said. "I just – " he waved a hand " – ah, never mind." He looked at the picture again. "I can't figure out what this means or why it's significant."

"Me either."

"You sure?"

"Yeah." A new, exhausted ring was present in her voice.

"I almost wish we hadn't interrupted her while in the garage, at least not before she could place something else – or do whatever it was she was planning on doing. It might have given us more insight."

Kimberly nodded and yawned.

"You going to be okay down here by yourself?" he asked, his mind thinking it was time to call it a night.

She thought about this for a second and then nodded again.

"Okay. I think I'm going to head up. My door will be unlocked if you need anything."

She smiled.

"And please don't hesitate to get me if something comes up, or if you suddenly feel the need to stay up there for the night with the door locked -- " *Okay, too far,* he silently admitted.

If so, she didn't seem to take offense to the suggestion and simply said, "Thanks."

"Mind if I hang onto this?" He lifted the picture.

She shook her head.

"Okay. Something might come to me in the middle of the night and I'd hate to have to wake you to get it."

She yawned again.

Bill took the hint and headed up. Toby was waiting, a curious look on his face. He then jumped up onto the coffee table to sniff the picture after he set it down, but then, seeing where Bill was headed, quickly joined him in the kitchen.

"Fine," Bill said in response to a meow and grabbed the treat bag. Once a couple were dished out he started looking around for something to indulge in himself, but nothing jumped out at him.

In the end he settled on a soda since he needed something and took it to the couch, his mind once again wishing he had a TV connection so he could just turn it on and zone out for a while.

You'd probably figure out quite a bit about all this stuff too since you wouldn't be thinking about it intensely.

Naturally, this shifted his focus back to the picture, which he looked at for another fifteen minutes before forcing himself to go take a shower. After that, he took a seat on the couch again, where Toby joined him, and before he could even pick up the picture, fell asleep.

Sunday, August 21, 2011

1

Mark had two emails waiting for him that morning on the OK Cupid site, one from Amy and one from Nikki. He read the Amy one first, a nervous excitement making it impossible to wait.

I had so much fun yesterday. I couldn't do anything but think about you all night long. I wanted to call you to just talk but wasn't sure if you'd be sleeping. I hope you had fun with your friend last night. I can't wait to see you today. Could we meet again at like noon? Maybe at Tom and Jerry's or something? I'll make your drive worthwhile.

A huge smile arrived, along with an erection as he thought about the final statement.

It probably doesn't mean what you think it means.

But what else could it mean?

He gave the question some serious thought, but nothing came to mind. He then moved on to Nikki's email.

I don't think I'm interested in you anymore. You just aren't my type and I'm pissed that I wasted so much time waiting to see if you would be a good fuck. By the way, I got an interesting email from a young lady asking about you. What should I tell her? Any suggestions? I'm too tired to think of something now, but maybe in the morn-

ing I will know what to say.

Panic hit.

Was it Amy? Had she messaged Nikki? If so, why? Did she know about the two of them communicating? If so, how? Unlike some sites he had been on Ok Cupid didn't broadcast to the world who you were interacting with, so it wasn't like she could have sent questions out to people on a friends list or anything.

Is Nikki just messing with you?

Could the message have been sent without any knowledge of another girl entering his life?

It seemed too coincidental.

Unless she is just trying to make you think that another girl is interested, one that doesn't really exist.

Mark wouldn't put it past whoever was behind this. After all, they had been jerking guys like him around for over six months, so starting in on him from another angle after this one got old was very plausible. Why exactly they were doing it was a mystery, especially given the lack of any monetary gain from the website itself, but that didn't change the fact that they were doing it.

And what if she really is in contact with Amy?

The fear such a situation brought about was not easily subdued.

Send her a message asking for details on who this girl is? Find out if she really knows her or is just bullshitting you.

He considered this option for several minutes, and then, when no decision arrived, took a trip up to the kitchen to get some coffee. This added another five minutes to his indecision given how unappealing the last inch of coffee at the bottom of the carafe was. Once a fresh pot was brewed and a mug filled, he returned to his room in the basement and typed up a message. It said: *A girl asked you about me? Really? How exciting. What's her name? Hope she isn't a tease like you.*

He hit SEND.

Satisfaction arrived.

Unfortunately, fear was still present as well.

He went and looked at the message from Amy again and

typed up a response telling her that meeting at Tom and Jerry's at noon was perfect. He then asked if she meant the one on Lincoln Highway near the school or the one on Route 23 over in Sycamore. Hopefully the former. That one was his favorite. It had more personality than the one in Sycamore given that it was older. The new one seemed too modern to him; too much like the other dozen fast food places one could visit while driving down the road. The one by the school, however, didn't have that feel. It felt original. It felt –

A new message was waiting, the screen having refreshed itself.

He opened his email.

It was from Nikki.

Her name is Amy. She seems sweet. Do you think she'll be interested in hearing about some of the fantasies we talked about? Maybe it will give her some ideas on things you two can do when alone.

Mark stared at the message in disbelief, his mind unable to register anything beyond terror.

Here he had finally met a girl that was interested in him, one who actually showed up at a first get together and had enjoyed herself so much that she was hinting at sex, and this Nikki bitch was going to ruin it. It wasn't fair.

Another message arrived.

Once again, it was from Nikki.

Instead of the fantasies maybe I should tell her about our time together last night. Do you think she would be interested in that? I'll tell her how you filled my mouth with cum and then pinched my nose until I swallowed it all. Yep. I think she'll like that story better.

Mark hit the reply button and typed: *We didn't get together last night and you know it. Nothing happened.*

It took Nikki three minutes to reply.

I know that, silly boy, but will she? Did you stand me up so that you two could be together? If that's the case I guess she has nothing to worry about, but if you simply went home and were by yourself I think this could be quite an eye opener for her on what you're really like, especially once I send her the messages you sent me about getting together. Women typically like to be aware of these things from the start so they don't waste time with perverts like you.

Mark didn't know what to say to this.

Who would?

Less than an hour earlier he had been overcome with joy about getting together with Amy for a second time that afternoon (and, of course, the possibility that sexual things would occur), and now he was worried that he would never see her again. And this time it wasn't his usual insecurity creating this fear. Nope. The threat was real. If Nikki sent a message like that Amy would bail on him. He knew it to be true.

You should call her before any messages arrive and let her know someone is harassing you.

He stared at his phone while thinking this, finger ready to push the AMY entry in his address book.

But will she believe me?

If he had told her about Nikki before she herself had contacted her then things would probably be okay, but suddenly getting concerned after contact had been made, well, that might just seem like he was trying to cover his tracks. Such panic wouldn't look good.

He closed the phone.

A new message arrived.

Please be from Amy, he pleaded, his eyes hoping to see a message confirming the Tom and Jerry's location.

It was from Nikki.

I'll tell you what. I won't tell Amy about how sick and twisted you are if you buy me some items from my wish list on my blog. I want you to have a gift note sent with each. The first will be the large black dildo on page two of the wish list. I want you to write a note with it that says: I CAN'T WAIT TO SHOVE THIS UP YOUR BUTT WHILE YOU BEG FOR MERCY! The second item will be the standard police issue handcuffs on page three. With those I want you to write: AND TO MAKE SURE YOU CAN'T GET AWAY WHILE I HAVE MY WAY WITH YOU. The third item is the Tantalizing Lace Up Teddy on page four. With that you will write: FOR YOU TO WEAR TO SHOW EVERYONE WHAT A WHORE YOU ARE. Ship it all next day. Do that now and then save and send a screen shot of your order confirmation to me. If it arrives before ten thirty this morning I will not send a message, if it doesn't . . .

Mark felt his jaw drop while reading the message.

Why in the world would Nikki want him to send this stuff to Kimberly? What possible good could come from it, especially since Nikki had to know that he knew Kimberly was not her.

Or does she?

The idea that this Nikki person had the same abilities to deduce things that would be obvious to people like him was probably a mistake. Now, he wasn't saying Nikki was stupid. In order to orchestrate something like this one had to have a good chunk of intelligence. High intelligence, however, didn't necessarily mean a good ability to understand reality.

Send her a message about this and see what happens.

Or just do what she says and warn Kimberly that items will be headed her way.

Though he didn't like it, the second option seemed the safest. Going the first route could be interpreted as him provoking her, which could cause all kinds of trouble. Best to play it safe, especially if it meant making sure his chances with Amy weren't threatened.

But what if she still threatens to send the message?

Maybe you should put some of your own terms down.

He could send two items but hold back on the third until after his date today. Of course, just suggesting that could fall under the provocation category.

Indecision gripped him.

He honestly didn't know what to do.

Oddly enough the money he would need to spend on the three items wasn't even coming to mind with this dilemma, not when he would gladly spend twice that much if it meant things would be okay between him and Amy (or any other girl he wanted to try and have sex with). Nope. His indecision was based on the fact that he was pretty much being blackmailed, and whether or not he wanted to give in to it. After all, what else would Nikki instruct him to do after this?

It won't matter because after today Amy will know about Nikki and understand the problems she has caused you. It will be a one-time thing.

He just had to remember not to spill all the Nikki stuff to Amy right away. The last thing he wanted to do was upset her with information that could ruin the potential for sex. That, and nothing else, was the most important factor right now.

2

The girl who called herself NIU_Nikki sat at her laptop waiting for the message from Mark, her fingers crossed that he would be frightened enough about his true nature being revealed to Amy that he would give in to the demands she had made. If not, she did have a plan B that was probably just as good as this one (plan A?), one that involved buying the items with a Visa gift card, but figured things would be so much easier if the items were bought under his credit card.

Unless that looks too obvious?

Would he use his own credit cards knowing the purchases could eventually be traced back to him?

The thought was unsettling, but didn't ruin the pleasure she felt at everything she had accomplished thus far – and, with the exception of last night, almost completely without a glitch. And even if it looked too obvious and brought suspicion upon itself for that very reason, at least it would still focus attention away from what had truly happened. Add in all the DNA that would be left upon the scene of the eventual crime and it would be hard for the police to look elsewhere.

Satisfaction arrived.

It got even sweeter when the message from Mark appeared, one that had the screen shots of the receipts just as she had instructed.

Amazing.

Nothing else could describe it. Men were so weak when it came to issues involving women that is was no wonder the girl named Kimberly had been able to manipulate them so easily.

And now you are doing the same.

NOPE!

This was different. This had a purpose. If she could have put an end to Kimberly's ways without having to manipulate so many men she would have, but no workable options had presented themselves. Plus, she wasn't manipulating any guy who didn't deserve to be manipulated.

Well . . .

Memories of her interaction with a young man named Dominick started to arrive. Guilt tagged along. He hadn't been like the men she was using to torment Kimberly, at least not to the same degree. She couldn't dismiss that he had agreed to help her in exchange for sex, so the potential to be like all these other guys was there. Still, if given the chance and not forced into situations of temptation, he seemed like a nice guy. Sadly, leaving him alive would have been disastrous for her, so she had killed him.

More memories filled her head, specifically those that saw her playing with his penis with one hand while pulling the knife from behind her back with the other. One quick slice and his throat had been open, blood from the severed jugular spraying upon a tree that stood next to them. Interestingly that hadn't been the only thing that spurted. She would never forget the feel of his penis actually bulging in her hand as the blade opened his throat and the powerful ejaculation that had followed.

Experiencing such an event had been so unexpected that she almost wanted to try it again, her mind and body actually craving the moment when such an opportunity would present itself. At one point she had almost considered attempting it with a total stranger, but then thought better of it. Kimberly came first. Once that situation was taken care of she could experiment with this new found sexual interest. First, she would use her hand again just to see if it happened a second time. After that she would see how it felt once that penis was inside her, an image of her riding the guy to the point of near ejaculation and then grabbing the knife and quickly cutting his throat playing out in her mind's eye.

3

As expected, an idea about the picture arrived early that morning, one that he couldn't shake or push far enough from his mind to allow for the desired sleep to arrive once again. Unfortunately having the picture within his hand didn't really help confirm his theory on what it represented. Then again, confirmation wasn't all that necessary since he was almost positive it was what he thought it was.

But why leave a picture of the motel room door?

And is the actual room number significant, or was it just chosen at random?

These thoughts plagued him for most of the morning, his sore exhausted body able to do little else but dwell on the unanswerable questions. As always, he did make an attempt at writing, but nothing flowed.

And nothing will until you fix this situation.

The optimistic part of his brain didn't even try to argue this statement. The reality of it was too strong to attempt contesting it.

So, now what?

Only one answer arrived. He couldn't put it into action right away, however, not when he was certain that Kimberly would want to join him in his little trip to the Sleepy Time Motel.

Plus you need a car.

This realization didn't come to him immediately, the lack of transportation so unfamiliar that he probably would have headed out to his car without even thinking about it if it hadn't been for a trip to the bathroom to check on his cuts.

4

Kimberly felt worse than she looked, which was probably fairly typical after a night like the one she had endured. Most of it was good old fashion exhaustion from staying up late; something she still remembered quite well from her freshman year party nights down at the University of Illinois. Pain was present too, however, which wasn't as familiar. Actually, being hit in the face was a new experience all together, one that she hoped would never happen again.

I would gladly dish it out if that bitch ever wants a rematch, though.

God, she hoped for just such an event soon.

Careful what you wish for, there is no telling what type of weapon this girl may bring next time.

This thought brought to mind the question on what the girl hoped to achieve. Was she just tormenting her because she was a bitch with a bug up her ass, or was this all just setting the stage for something bigger? Something carefully calculated?

A knock on the inner stairway door cut off the line of thought.

"Just a second," she called and hurried back into the bedroom to grab some clothes, her hand first reaching for her work shirt from the night before, but then stopping when she caught sight of the blood. A College of DuPage t-shirt was next in line, followed by a pair of sweatpants.

Both items in place, she went to the door.

"I didn't wake you, did I?" Bill asked.

"Nah, I was up," she said, her mind doubtful that he hadn't already known this.

"Okay, good." He yawned. "Sorry, didn't get much sleep." He smiled. "I think I figured out where that picture was taken."

"Oh?"

"Out on Route 64 heading toward St. Charles there is a small rundown motel called the Sleepy Time Motel. It looks like something right out of a horror flick; cheap little forty dollar a night dump."

"Okay?" she questioned.

"Anyhow, I used to send men there with the Nikki profile."

"What . . . why?"

Teasing men to earn a membership referral fee was one thing, and while she couldn't condone it, she could at least understand the motivation behind it. But sending men to a motel?

"Money was growing really tight and I wanted to make sure I would have enough to cover the rent for the summer, so I promised two dozen men that I would meet them for sex at the motel.

It was toward the end of March, and I made all the 'dates' for the first and second week in April."

If he thought this had explained anything he was wrong. "I still don't understand."

"You pay by the month on Adult Friend Finder, so by making the date the following month it pretty much sealed the deal on them allowing their memberships to renew one more time." He shrugged.

"How much did you make per renewal?" she asked.

"Like thirty bucks."

So, roughly thirty times twenty, she said to herself while calculating. "You did that for six hundred bucks?"

"Well, plus the money coming in from all the new subscriptions."

"How many did you typically get when doing this?"

"Three to five a week."

"You did all this just to get a hundred bucks a week!" Back at her parents place she knew neighborhood kids that made that much cutting grass during the summer.

"Hey, it kept a roof over my head."

"How?"

"My rent isn't much and I used credit cards for everything until my novels started to sell."

She wanted to argue with him on how ridiculous this was, a simple part-time job would have netted him more and most likely wouldn't have resulted in her being tormented, but then realized how pointless it would be. *Plus he probably would have kept doing the blog anyway for the extra income.*

"It was a good thing I did it too because after April the Internet was gone and I couldn't get online to talk to the men through the Instant Messenger, so my renewal rates plummeted. The money I made from sending guys to the hotel in April and May was enough to keep me going for a while."

"Wait, you did it twice?"

"Yeah, but the second time around wasn't as effective. I promised ten guys to meet at the hotel come the first week of May. I would have done more, but like I said, the Internet was taken away during the last week of April and I couldn't get Comcast to figure out the situation."

Kimberly shook her head.

Bill didn't say anything more.

"So, you think the door in the picture is from this motel?"

He nodded.

"But why would she want to direct my attention toward it?"

"I don't know, but it seems like she does, which means it's important -- at least to her -- and we should find out why."

Driving all over the place was the last thing she wanted to do today, especially considering she started school tomorrow and wanted to be nice and rested for that. On the flip side, she knew that she probably would never feel rested until all this shit was finished, and if he thought going to the motel could help, then maybe that was the best bet. "I suppose you're right. I'll meet you by your car in a few minutes, I just want to grab some – "

"Oh, my car was trashed last night, remember," he said before she could finish.

"Wow, you're right, I completely forgot about that." *And that explains why he didn't just go check out the motel on his own.* Then again, even with access to a car he probably would have wanted her to come along. "Let me just get some juice or something."

"Okay." With that, he headed back up.

She watched him go, then closed the door, and went to get the juice she required, followed by her purse since she would be the one driving.

Both tasks completed she headed outside.

Bill was waiting by the garage door.

"Anything new left for me?" she asked.

"Not that I saw. I don't think she came back."

"Maybe we scared her off for good by catching her in the act."

"Hmm, maybe."

He didn't believe it. She could tell by his tone. Of course, she felt the same way and wasn't sure why she had even suggested it. This wasn't going to end that easily.

"You said Route 64, right?" she asked once they were on the

road.

"Yep, you know how to get there from here?"

"Not really."

"Okay, just head toward downtown Sycamore. Route 64 is also the main street through the town."

"Oh, that's easy."

Three turns and they were on it, heading east, Bill randomly pointing out things on the route that he thought was interesting as if he were a tour guide.

Kimberly never replied, though she did tuck away the information about the good Chinese place called Rens.

In time his voice stopped. Kimberly didn't know if it was due to her lack of replies, or because they had entered a sea of corn. Whatever the reason she welcomed it.

5

"Should be coming up," Bill said. They had been driving through nothing but farm fields for twenty minutes, the sheer expanse of crops between Sycamore and the next area of civilization always instilled a sense of awe within him. The fact that they really weren't that far from Chicago, about an hour and a half when taking I-88 added to his amazement. Growing up near the city, he had always felt as if the world had been paved over. Driving west proved this to be false. Once beyond Route 47 nothing but the city of DeKalb really made a dent within the landscape. After that, it was the Mississippi river. "On the left."

"Okay."

On that side a field came to an end against a wall of trees. Thirty seconds later the trees ended and the motel came into view.

Kimberly slowed the car for the turn, which took them onto a gravel driveway that eventually became cracked pavement as they entered an opening between the motel office and the three sided box setup for the motel rooms. Grass poked through the pavement in several places, and one area had been so badly damaged that it had been replaced with gravel.

Only two vehicles were parked in front of the rooms, which, given the looks of it, were separated into five for each row of the room portion of the box, totaling fifteen rooms.

"Wow, you couldn't pay me to stay here," Kimberly muttered while coming to a halt in the middle of the courtyard-like square of pavement.

"Same here," Bill said. "The place is a dump." He scanned the area. "I think that is room 6 over there."

Kimberly pulled up to where he was pointing.

Bill didn't even need to leave the car to know this was the door in the picture left last night.

"You were right," Kimberly said, which meant she didn't need to vacate the vehicle for a closer look either. "So, what does it mean? Whoever is doing this is somehow connected to one of the men you lured to this room?"

"I guess, but . . ." he didn't know how a woman would fit into that.

Kimberly, either thinking the same question, or having read his mind, said, "I wonder if you ruined a relationship and now the girl who was scorned is pissed and seeking revenge on Nikki?"

Bill considered this.

"I know I'd be pretty upset if I found out my boyfriend was online talking to someone like Nikki and planning to meet them for sex," she added.

"Would you start stalking the girl he had planned on meeting?" Bill asked.

She replied with a glare.

Bill brushed that off and said, "I still don't get why she would leave this picture though. Is it really that important to point out this place to Nikki?"

Kimberly didn't reply.

"Something just isn't clicking with me."

"It seems pretty straight forward to me. She's pissed that you ruined her relationship and wants you to know the reason she is seeking revenge."

"Hmm."

"It might even be more for her than it is for you."

"What do you mean?"

"Maybe she needs you to know why she is doing this as a sort of justification for herself. It's not enough that she just torments you . . . well me . . . she wants the reason for the torment to be known. Make it understood."

Bill thought about this for several seconds and said, "I know what you're saying, but I still think there is more to it than just that."

"Like what?"

"I really don't -- "

THUNK! THUNK!

Kimberly shouted, which caused Bill to jump. He then twisted toward the window, eyes startled to see a man looking in at them.

"What are you two doing here?" the man demanded, his words loud enough to make it through the glass.

Bill went to open his door, but Kimberly clicked the automatic locks before his hand found the latch.

"Don't go out there," she hissed.

"Why?" Bill asked.

"We don't know who he is."

"It's probably just the manager." He searched for his own lock release while saying this and pressed it.

Kimberly locked it again.

"Come on," Bill snapped. "He might know something about the room."

"Like what, that husbands use it to get laid while their wives are at home?"

Bill hit the lock release again, only this time he had his other hand on the door handle and opened it before she could re-lock it.

The man was still standing there, a puzzled look on his face.

"Excuse me, sir?" Bill said. "We had a question about that room over there, number six."

The man studied him across the car roof, a quizzical look upon his face, and then asked, "Why?"

"Why?" Bill repeated. It wasn't the word he had been expecting from the man, especially not when paired with caution, which was now present upon the man's face. "Did something happen here a while back?"

"You a reporter?"

This really got his attention. "No."

"Then why are you here?"

"Because someone keeps sending her pictures of this room, along with other upsetting things, and we'd like to know why."

"Pictures of the murder?"

That caught him off guard. "Murder? No. Just the room."

"Then I don't know what to tell you, and unless you two want a room I'm going to ask you to leave." He turned to head back to the office.

"Wait!" Bill called. "Who was murdered here?"

"Look it up if you want to know. It was in the papers." He stopped and twisted back. "Just keep in mind they left out some details, ones they thought would be too much for their readers."

"Like what?" Bill asked, feet closing some of the distance the man had created.

"Like the guy having his penis cut off and stuffed in his mouth."

Bill felt the blood drain from his face. "When did this happen?"

The man stared at him for what had to be thirty seconds and then asked, "You really want to know all this?"

"Yes."

"All because you got some pictures of the room?"

"And threats, and statements about it being her fault. Someone has mistaken her – " he nodded toward the car " – for someone she isn't, someone involved in whatever happened here, and we would like to find out who it is so we can set them straight."

The man didn't reply.

Bill, unsure what to do, simply waited.

"You're really not a reporter?" he asked.

"I'm not, honest to god."

"Business is bad enough without people fearing for their

lives."

"I completely understand." Truth was he didn't think a newspaper story would do much damage to this place, not when the only people reading it would be locals, and the only people staying here weary travelers who most likely hadn't read the local paper. Unless Kimberly was right and the typical client was one cheating on a significant other? Knowing a man was killed here while involved in such infidelity could put a dent in others selecting this local for such practices.

"Fine, come on in back and I'll tell you all about it. Bring your girlfriend too. No sense leaving her out all by her lonesome. I get some odd folks here. Just last week I found a ball gag left in the sheets of a bed."

Bill nodded and hurried over to the driver side door to get Kimberly.

"What?" she asked while rolling down the window.

"Pull around to the office. He's going to let us in and tell us about the murder."

"Murder?"

"Yeah. Nasty one by the sounds of it. Come on."

"Maybe I should stay here. He seems like a creep."

"Um, I'd be more worried about the clientele. Besides, two sets of ears are better than one. Something may click with you that doesn't with me."

"Fine," she said and shifted to reverse.

Bill walked over and rejoined the man who was waiting, hands in his pocket, an odd look of disinterest on his face.

"Here okay?" Kimberly asked as she pulled in front of the office. If parking spots had ever been marked out, they had long since faded away.

"Anywhere" the man said with a wave of the hand, and then started into the office.

Bill and Kimberly followed.

6

Nothing from Amy arrived before it was time for Mark to start heading toward DeKalb, which, naturally, caused him to worry. A debate on whether his decision to buy everything Nikki had told him to buy had been the right thing to do also began to unfold.

If we get together and everything is fine, then it would have been worth it. If we don't get together and I never hear from her again, then I'll be pissed.

He checked his phone before starting the car just to see if any messages had come in unannounced.

Nothing.

Should I send one?

Concern on appearing insecure arrived. But then would she really think him insecure if he sent a simple 'I'm on my way' text?

Just do it and move your ass.

Chances were, if everything was okay between them, a reply would arrive at some point while on the road, which would help calm him down while driving.

But if one doesn't . . .

He tried shaking the thought away, but it would not fade.

Type it up and get moving.

HEY! ON MY WAY. SHOULD BE THERE IN AN HOUR. LOOKING FORWARD TO SEEING YOU AGAIN :) MARK.

After a few seconds he removed the smiley face -- just text would be best – and hit SEND. Not long after that he was maneuvering the car onto I-90 and heading west.

The phone buzzed ten minutes into the ride.

It was Amy.

He looked at the message while keeping an eye on traffic. It said. SWEET! I'M LOOKING FORWARD TO IT TOO. LET ME KNOW WHEN YOU GET HERE. MY PLACE IS WITHIN WALKING DISTANCE OF TOM AND JERRY'S, SO I WILL HEAD ON OVER ONCE I GET THE MESSAGE.

Mark sighed with relief.

A moment later he flipped on the radio, his mind knowing he would be able to enjoy whatever was playing rather than be stressed out by it as his concern over the possibility of being stood up continued to pester him.

But what if Nikki sends her a message between now and then?

He tried not to think about the possibility or the feared out-come of such a message, but couldn't hold it back and soon found himself growing worried all over again. Thankfully, it wasn't an all-consuming worry because he did have Amy's reply text to focus on. Having talked to Amy quite a bit the day before he also figured she was the type that would ask him about Nikki's message rather than just bail on him. Sadly, this wasn't enough to keep all his worries at bay. Nothing but watching as Amy arrived at the Hot Dog place and happily joined him for lunch would. And once that happened he knew his concern would then shift over toward making sure he didn't say some-thing that unintentionally upset her. The possibility that the two might have sex, based on what she had said in her email, would also be a constant thought, one that would bring a level of stress into things.

Are all guys like this? he wondered as the car passed Medieval Times. *Do we all worry to the point of madness before meeting a girl, or is it just me?*

Just you, his mind said.

If this was true he hoped it would come to an end soon. Once he and Amy had sex – *if we do!* – maybe he would be able to re-lax. If not . . . well, he couldn't imagine going his entire life this stressed out all the time over girls. It just wouldn't work.

7

The living quarters behind the front desk was pretty much on par with what Bill had expected to see, which was a bit unset-tling since all the back office living quarters he had ever seen had been within horror flicks centering on out of the way motels. Nothing good ever happened at those motels, and from what the man had hinted at moments earlier in the parking lot, something similar to what was witnessed in those movies had happened here.

"If the bell rings I'll have to go up front for a bit, but chances are that won't happen," the man said. "Things are pretty slow."

"Is that a recent thing or has it been slow for a while?" Bill asked.

The man shrugged. "In my father's day the place did pretty well, but now we survive on couples that need a place to stay for a while who aren't interested in just parking the car and hopping into the backseat."

"You welcome that kind of business?" Kimberly asked, a note of disgust present in her voice.

"I welcome business, period. If not here, they will go somewhere else."

Kimberly didn't reply, which, given the look on her face, was probably for the best.

"You do what you have to do to survive," Bill said.

"Yep," the man agreed with a nod.

Silence descended.

"So, what happened in room six?" Bill asked.

"And when?" Kimberly quickly added.

He looked back and forth between the two for a moment and then said, "It happened in early May. I remember that because my wife and I had been talking a lot about the expected boost in customers we usually saw thanks to the different prom events going on in the surrounding areas.   Plus, with all the police questions and then the reporter stuff, you just don't forget much even when you want to because it just gets pounded into your brain." He was quiet a moment. "It was a happy time, that first week in May. Business had been great in April and looked like it was going to be good again. I don't rightly know why but we were seeing quite a few men during that time who were hooking up for a few hours. It was so sudden and unexpected that I started wondering if maybe some site had recommended us, you know, a site that maybe caters to those who are looking for one night stands or something."

Bill caught a look from Kimberly.

"It's funny; you can always tell when a man is planning on cheating because the first thing they always ask is if they can pay in cash. It makes you think that maybe part of the problem in their marriage is the lack of personal privacy. I mean, why should she be questioning him on what appears on a credit card statement? Most women would balk over a man asking them about a charge that appears on theirs, but then they feel it's okay to just look over everything he is involved with?" He held up a finger. "One of the reasons my wife and I stayed together as long as we did was because we respected each other's space."

'*As long as we did*,' Bill noted. Did that mean they were separated now? He tucked the question away.

"The man that came in that day, his name was Martin Moore. Normally I wouldn't have remembered it, but, like I said, it has been drilled into my brain so well that I will never forget it now. I remember he seemed more nervous than most. Excited too. Guess he was expecting quite the experience."

The name didn't ring any bells, but then most of the men who he had talked with when taking on the role of Nikki had never revealed their full names. He also never really cared enough about them to remember their first names when given.

"I have to admit, I was kind of curious to see what the girl would be like, so I watched from my seat here which gives a pretty good view of things."

Bill and Kimberly both twisted around to look, as if it needed to be confirmed.

"The lady that eventually arrived, however, well . . . let's just say I didn't want to picture the two having sex and actually started calculating the costs in my head on replacing the bed springs because they probably wouldn't be able to handle her weight. I know that's mean, but boy was she fat. Even from this distance I could just sense a grossness about her that I'd never want to experience." He shuddered. "Anyway, I went back to my normal business and didn't give them much thought until later that night when I noticed his car was still here. Most of these guys don't stay beyond four or five, not when they have a wife to get home too. Technically the room was booked for the night though so I didn't go check on him until the next morning after he failed to check out. That was when I knew something was wrong. Sadly, I went to check it myself rather than just calling the police like I should have. That would have saved me seeing what I saw."

"You said his penis was cut off," Bill said when the man didn't continue.

He nodded. "Not just cut off though. She spent a good amount of time mutilating that entire area. Police found a bloody nail file, you know, one of those long ones that women will sometimes carry in their purse. It had a point on it that they say she used to stab him over and over again in the . . . well, you know."

"God," Kimberly grimaced.

Bill didn't know what to say, his mind unable to contemplate how horrible something like that would be.

"I was in Vietnam," he said. "During the battle of Hue we had a civilian population trying to flee the city that came under mortar fire. The road had been mined too it seemed. The worst thing I ever saw was a pregnant lady who had caught a mortar blast. The fragments had ripped her belly open and the baby had fallen halfway out onto the –

"Excuse me!" Kimberly said suddenly. *"Bathroom?"*

"Um . . . over there," he said while pointing.

Kimberly hurried that way, door slamming behind her once she was within. A horrible retching sound echoed.

"Ah jeez, I'm sorry," the man said. "I didn't mean to upset her like that. I just wanted to mention how this was worse than that."

Bill wasn't sure how to reply, which was probably for the best since he didn't want to open his mouth, not when the sounds he was hearing was making his own stomach turn over. Next would be that horrible pre-vomit sensation building in the back of his throat and then . . .

The toilet flushed, followed by the sound of the sink faucet going. A minute later Kimberly came out of the bathroom, looked at them, and without a word left the office.

Bill watched this, a debate growing, and then turned to the man and said, "I'll be right back. I just want to make sure she's okay."

The man nodded.

Bill headed out; his eyes squinted due to the sudden brightness, and scanned the area.

Kimberly was not at the car. Instead, she was leaning against the wall by the ice machine, crying. Not sobbing by any means, but tears were certainly running down her cheeks.

"Are you okay?" Bill asked.

She nodded.

"You sure?"

"Just leave me alone, okay?" It was a plea rather than a demand, one that he heeded by heading back inside.

"Your girlfriend okay?" the manager asked.

"Yeah," Bill said. He thought about correcting the girlfriend statement, but then let it pass. "So, this lady that came in and killed the guy, is it possible she was wearing some kind of fat bodysuit disguise?" He was thinking about the girl he had confronted last night when asking this. She had not been fat. Not skinny either, just that comfortable middle zone that always seemed perfect to him, but not to the women he had been with.

"Body suit? Not a chance. I saw footage of the arrest. It's all real. Fitting her in a jail cell was probably a trick." He grinned. "Okay, that's a bit of an exaggeration."

"Wait, so the police caught the person who did it?"

"Yeah," the man said, a 'weren't you listening' tone present. "That night. Once I gave them a description it wasn't too difficult for them. All they had to do was go to his home and see his wife. I hear she didn't even bother to deny anything. Whenever she was on the news, she almost seemed proud of what she had done. The only thing she regretted, according to a statement in the paper, was that she hadn't been able to catch the whore he was seeing. Guess she had wanted to kill them both."

Bill didn't know what to say.

"Whoever the girl was, she's lucky she didn't show up before the wife did."

"Yeah," Bill muttered. "She is."

"Makes you wonder though, she must have been planning on calling him or something when she got here because how would she know what room he had. It's not like he requested room six. Poor thing probably thought she'd been stood up when he never answered the phone."

"Or maybe she stood him up," Bill said. The words appeared without any real thought.

"What?"

"Never mind. You said the story has been in the papers? Do you have any copies I can see?"

"Gee, I don't think I kept any of them," he said and stood up to look around as if they could be lying in plain view without him having realized it. "It wasn't exactly something I wanted to keep thinking about on a daily basis."

"That's understandable," Bill said. He thought for a second, mind trying to connect the recent events to what had occurred. "So, has anyone else come by to ask about the room, almost as if they were overly curious about it?"

"Nope, not really. Earlier when the summer first started there were some folks that wanted to look at it. Morbid fellows who enjoyed visiting murder scenes and taking pictures for websites and stuff." He shook his head. "Half the time they didn't even want to rent the room, but just have me let them in to see it. At first I thought the publicity might be good, but it wasn't so I stopped letting people like that go in."

"And you never saw someone taking the picture of the door?"

"No, and they must have been quick about it because most things don't go unnoticed around here, not when I can see everything."

Though he didn't think it would help, Bill persisted and asked, "Not even a young woman? Maybe she didn't take any pictures when you were looking, but asked about the room?"

The man shook his head. "Nope, no one like that, and no one recently either if that makes a difference."

"Hmm, okay." Bill didn't know what else to ask, shrugged, and then said, "I suppose that's all I need to know. Thanks so much for talking to me about it."

"Yep," the man said and shook his hand. "Hope it helps with your problem, and I hope I didn't upset her too much."

Bill looked back toward the door to the office and said, "I think she's fine."

"Hope so."

Me too, Bill silently said. *Me too.*

8

The stoplights and then the train on Route 38, or Lincoln Highway as it was known in DeKalb, got the better of Mark. He wanted to get to Tom and Jerry's; wanted to get there and text Amy and have her text him back. He wanted to be reassured that everything was okay.

And you would know by now if it wasn't for the god damn train stopping you!

He slammed a fist against the steering wheel in frustration. No relief came from the act. If anything, the slight pain that vibrated through his wrist from the impact aggravated him even more.

You should have taken Route 23.

Having come from I-90 he originally had been on Route 23 for his journey through Sycamore and could have simply stayed on it all the way to Route 38. If he had done that, he would have been ahead of the train, especially if he cut over toward First Street, which would have put him a block away from Tom and Jerry's. Instead, thinking the lunchtime traffic would be a pain in the ass along Route 23, he had cut over to Peace Road, his plan being to follow it until Pleasant Street and cut across toward Route 38 on Seventh Street. It was a good plan, the only danger being the possibility of a train.

You should have known there would be one.

Anything that could happen to make his trip more stressful would happen. That was how things worked in his life. If he was smart he would start –

BUZZ.

He looked down at his phone, his eyes hoping to see AMY written on the screen. Instead, there was just a number, which meant it wasn't someone he knew.

Or someone who got a new phone, he silently added.

He looked at the message.

HAVE FUN WITH AMY TODAY. I'LL BE WATCHING.
NIKKI

What the fuck!

Nothing else came to mind.

Up ahead the end of the train came into view.

How did she get my – the thought stopped when he realized he had messaged it to her on OK Cupid back when they had agreed to meet, back when he had thought things were really going to happen between them.

Ignore it.

He put the phone down and got ready to move forward as the train cleared the intersection.

A new thought arrived: *How does she know where we are getting together?*

She doesn't and is just trying to spook you.

Either that or she and Amy really were friends, Amy having gotten in contact with her in an attempt to make more contacts within the DeKalb area. Such a situation would be unthinkable in anyone else's life, but not his. Nope. With him things like that always unfolded and eventually screwed him over. It was just the way things worked. He had a target on his back it seemed. Whenever a higher power was pissed it used Mark to relieve the stress of the situation.

The train finished crossing the intersection.

Mark sighed and shifted to drive

After that his luck changed a bit and he managed to make every light but one.

I'M HERE, he typed into a message for Amy. AT TOM AND JERRY'S, he added a few seconds later to clarify what HERE meant.

Naturally, concern over this second message arrived. Had he thought about it before quickly typing it he would have realized it wasn't necessary. She knew what HERE meant. But his excitement-laced concern had once again gotten the better of him.

No reply.

Now what?

He was sick of being in his car, especially in the heat of today, but wasn't sure if going inside and sitting in a booth without ordering anything would be okay. Standing out here in the parking lot didn't seem that appealing either, especially if it took her some time to get here. Too many memories of standing around places waiting for a girl to show up who never did were caught in his mind.

You can always go in and order a soda.

Fear that she would think it rude of him to order before she arrived was pushed aside. All he had to do was tell her the drive had made him incredibly thirsty. She would understand.

Wait!

From the corner of his eye he saw a girl headed his way. The distance made it impossible to tell if it was Amy though.

A few seconds later he realized it wasn't her. She was headed in the same direction however and eventually walked into Tom and Jerry's.

Could that have been Nikki?

Could she be positioning herself to watch the two?

The thought was cut off as a text arrived, this one from Amy.
BE THERE SOON :)

A huge sigh of relief arrived.

9

"So basically some guy's wife got pissed that he was going to see your Nikki and killed him," Kimberly said as they headed west on Route 64.

"It seems so," Bill said.

Bet that makes you feel good, Kimberly silently prodded, then, "And that's the only thing that happened in Room 6?"

"Uh-huh."

Kimberly considered this for a while and said, "Still no closer to knowing who this is and why they're doing it."

"Well we know it's connected to the murder."

"But if the wife is in jail and he is dead who else is there?"

Kimberly asked.

Bill apparently didn't have an answer.

"Maybe it isn't connected," Kimberly suggested. "Maybe whoever is doing this knows about the murder and simply wants us to think it's significant."

"You could be right. If everything she is doing is meant to scare you, then pointing you at this would be a good idea even if it has nothing to do with us."

Kimberly sensed a 'but' coming.

Bill didn't continue.

"You don't really think that," she pressed.

He shrugged. "I don't know. I suppose it seems just as plausible as anything else, but my gut says it's all connected. I think the guy that was killed was one of the men that talked to me online and that his wife somehow found out all about it and went a little crazy."

A little crazy? Try, a lot crazy.

Rather than voice this she said, "Which once again brings us to asking who is doing this? We know it isn't the wife because she is in jail, so who else is there?"

"Don't forget that just because the murder is probably connected to the Nikki thing doesn't mean the person involved now has to be connected to that murder."

"But you just said you think it's all connected," Kimberly snapped.

"To Nikki," Bill said, voice calm. "I don't think the murder was a separate incident that someone just pointed at to scare you, but that doesn't mean whoever is doing this now has to be connected to that murder."

Kimberly shook her head.

"I can understand your confusion though; I didn't make my thoughts all that clear."

Kimberly didn't reply to that statement and instead decided to change their focus a bit by asking, "Why now?"

"What do you mean?"

"Why now?" Kimberly repeated and then added, "You stopped talking to these guys last spring and now summer is winding down. Why wait this long?"

"That I don't know."

Kimberly sighed.

"Maybe she wanted to start sooner but it took this long to fig-ure out the address. We've already verified that all this started shortly after I got that email asking for model age statements."

"Yeah," Kimberly acknowledged. She felt her frustration starting to get the better of her, all because she knew that if the address had been figured out sooner the girl behind this would have come upon an empty apartment. *But no.* Fate had decided to make it take just long enough so that she was in the apartment once the address was uncovered, almost as if . . .

She tried cutting her mind off from the possibility that some higher power was screwing with her, but couldn't dam up the thought process. Thinking this also made things easier, excuse wise. She could see it now: *Why didn't you ever finish your bache-lor degree?*

Um, because God made it pretty clear that he didn't want me too, so why fight Him.

She wouldn't be the first person to use the God excuse on why something hadn't been achieved, nor would she be the last. Be-ing able to fall behind such an excuse was great because it was something others couldn't successfully argue against since there would never be any proof one way or the other. Even the person using the excuse couldn't fully argue against it.

But you aren't the type that would allow such a thing to stand in your way, she said to herself.

Or am I?

Though she wanted the answer to be yes, there was still doubt within her mind; doubt that said *you have no idea what will unfold in the next few days.*

10

Mark caught a glance from the lone girl on the far side of the sitting area while carrying the tray of food over to the booth Amy had chosen for them, and decided he had to ask about Nikki.

And you have to do it now. If he didn't, his mind would drive him crazy with anticipation of asking the question and receiving an answer. Better to just get it out of the way.

"Ah, excellent," Amy said as he set down the tray. "I'm starving." She grabbed her hot dog.

"Me too," Mark said. He removed his own hot dog from the tray and then his Coke, which he took several sips from in order to clear his throat. Then, "Can I ask you a question?"

"Oh, sure," she said, mouth getting ready to take a chunk out of the hot dog.

"Okay, don't look at her, but you see that girl sitting by herself off to my left?"

Amy's eyes darted to his left and then back. "Yeah?"

"Do you know her?"

Amy gave him a puzzled look and said, "No . . . why?"

Mark wasn't sure how to answer this and bought himself time with a bite of his own hot dog. Several sips of Coke followed.

"I got a weird message today from someone on OK Cupid who said they knew you and that we were planning on getting together today. They also said they would be here watching us."

Amy smiled. "You're joking right?"

"No."

The smile faded. "How would anyone know about you and me? I didn't tell anyone. I haven't even talked to anyone else on OK Cupid since we got together."

"Really?"

"Honest to god." She held up her right hand. "I swear."

"Okay, I believe you. Must be someone just messing with me then. I don't know why people do that, but it happens from time to time, especially when I stop talking to some girls."

"What do you mean?"

"Oh, every now and then I run into someone who is a tease and they just message me over and over again as if they want to get to know me, but then stand me up over and over again. In the end, you realize they are just messing with you and that the best thing to do is cut them off. Sometimes they keep pestering you though. There was a girl named Nikki who did that to me last year."

Nothing about the name Nikki seemed to register with her, and while he might not have been an expert at reading people, he was sure he would have been able to tell with this situation.

"We talked about this a bit yesterday, didn't we?" Amy asked.

"Yeah, I think we did," he said and added a smile.

She took a bite of her hot dog, chewed it, swallowed it, and said, "Were you a bit worried that I was going to end up being one of those girls?"

Mark didn't know how to reply to that, but finally just said, "A little. It has happened so many times in recent months, so it's hard not to wonder about it in the beginning."

"I can understand that," she said. "I will also say this, after today you won't have to worry about me being a fake and leading you on."

He jumped as her foot touched his groin beneath the table, his right knee slamming into the plastic underside of the table. Embarrassment followed, especially when he saw the look of surprise on Amy's face.

"I'm sorry," Amy said, a hand going to her mouth to hide a smile. "I shouldn't have done that."

"No, no," Mark said. "I liked it. You just really caught me off guard."

"Oh, well, in that case." The foot was back, the toes pressing into his jeans with a firmness that was just right.

A shiver ran through his system, one that he knew she saw.

"It's okay, just relax," she said. Then, "Hmm, I can feel something in there waking up."

Mark wanted to reply, but nothing would come. He then looked around the sitting area to see if anyone was watching.

"Don't worry, no one can see," Amy said. "And if this Nikki person is watching from some undisclosed location let her see what it is she is missing out on."

"Oh . . . kay." It was all he could manage.

Amy grinned.

Down below the foot continued to toy with him.

11

"Do you mind if I use your computer really quick, or hook up mine to it?" Bill asked as they pulled into the garage.

"What for?" Kimberly asked.

"To look up news stories on the murder and see if anything jumps out."

"Oh, sure."

"Okay, great.

She shifted to PARK and asked, "Do you think anything will?"

He shrugged. "Won't know until we look."

"Good point." She opened her door and stepped out.

Bill did the same.

The sound of locks being engaged echoed. The two then left the garage, Kimberly testing the door to see if the lock would hold this time. It did, but given the noticeable gap between the wood of the door and the frame, it was probably easy to pop it free.

Bill pointed this out.

"You think so?" Kimberly asked.

"Let's see." He pulled out his house key and, while holding the knob, slid the key into the gap and attempted to push the latch back toward the door. It didn't take much effort at all. "See."

Kimberly just stared at the door for several seconds and then shook her head. "So, locking it is pointless."

"With the wood warped like that, yeah," Bill said.

"Anything we can do to fix it?"

"Short of buying a new door and building a new frame, I don't think so."

"Fuck it," she said and turned toward the house.

"I'll be down in a second with my computer," Bill said.

She waved a hand in acknowledgement and disappeared around the corner.

Bill pulled the door shut and checked the knob to see that it was still locked -- why make it easy for the Nikki imposter -- and headed up his own stairs. Inside all was well, a fact Toby emphasized by heading right to the treat drawer after greeting him.

"Fine," Bill said and dished out a handful. A few seconds later he had his laptop and the old internet cord he had used when the Roberts lived below, and was heading down the steps.

Kimberly opened the door after a quick knock.

"Long enough cord?" she asked as he started to hook his laptop up to her modem.

He smiled. "It's the only cord I have. It's what we used to use when the Roberts lived down here. We simply threaded it beneath the two doors and shared the cost of the connection."

"Yeah, that's what the landlord said, but then there was a dispute or something about an adult video that had been ordered on the cable."

"There was. We have no idea who ordered it, but no one would ever admit to it. My guess was either one of the Roberts kids or the guy downstairs, because it wasn't me."

"Really?" she asked, arms crossed. "The guy who used to make a living sending people to porn sites?"

"Why would I buy it when I get all these videos sent to me for free? That's the great thing about signing up to be an affiliate for those sites; you have access to all their promo videos." He had also had his second laptop that he had used to download things from the free sites. The stuff had been full of viruses and spyware but when using a crap computer that had no personal information on it, he didn't care.

Kimberly shook her head and said, "I'll never understand a guy's fascination with porn."

"Mars and Venus," Bill muttered.

"What?"

"Oh, nothing. Men and women are just wired differently, that's all. We're stimulated visually, women aren't. It's as simple as that. You can go deeper into it and do all these studies, but in the end, that's what it's always going to boil down too."

Kimberly didn't reply.

"Okay." He looked around for a place to sit with the laptop and elected to head to the couch, cord uncoiling behind him. "Let's see what we can find."

Kimberly started to follow him, but then stopped and asked, "I'm going to grab a soda, you want anything?"

"Nah, I'm good," he said. "Thanks though."

By the time Kimberly returned he had plugged a search string into Google, one that had generated quite a few hits. "Gotta love the internet age," he said while selecting the first one. "Not too long ago we would have had to go to a library and look at microfiche copies of the newspaper, if they had even saved them, and flip through page after page looking for the right headline."

"Oh god, I had to do that for an anthropology class at C.O.D last year," Kimberly said.

"Really?" Bill asked, his eyes scanning over the text on the link he had pulled up.

"Yeah. It was a pain in the ass, but, thankfully, didn't take too long since it was just old anthropological studies we were looking at. I think the professor just wanted us to realize what it was like for him when he was a student because we were allowed to use other sources too. He just wanted one from the microfiche."

"I guess they do stuff like that a lot in college; you know, getting students familiar with all different types of research and classes. That's one of things that always drove me crazy. All the general education crap. College should be for learning a career or trade and then you're done. High school was the general education." He paused and took a breath. "I could start a rant about that though, so I'll stop right there."

"I know what you mean," Kimberly said and sipped her soda. "All this time at school already just to get my Associates Degree and I still probably have two years to go if I want anything worthwhile for a career. It's stupid."

"Yep," Bill acknowledged. "Hey, here's a picture of the wife that killed the husband."

"Oh?" She looked at the screen as he twisted it her way, her body getting close enough to his for him to feel a tingle. "Wow, she looks crazy."

"Seriously, right." Looking at it was enough to cause a chill to creep down his spine.

"Do you think she always looks like this or that the photographer chose the best of the bunch in what was taken?"

"I'm sure they took some time in choosing a good one, but at the same time you can tell it goes deeper than just a facial expression. This lady is wacked."

"Does it say anything about her being in jail, or still being in jail that is?" She was still close to him, her eyes scanning the page.

"It just says she is awaiting trial. My guess is she's doing that waiting in jail given the brutality of the crime. Plus she is quoted as saying she wished she had killed the girl he was seeing too, so they wouldn't want her out on the street."

"Whose identity is still unknown," Kimberly read.

Thank god, Bill thought.

"Do you find it odd that the police never made a connection between you and Nikki?" Kimberly asked. Then, before he could answer, added, "I mean, I know they didn't really have to 'solve' the crime, but you'd think they would still have looked into things a bit and tried to find out who Nikki was so that she could be a witness or something."

Bill thought about this and nodded, "Does seem a little strange. Maybe given the size of the town, which means a small police force, they just didn't have the man power or time to pursue everything, especially if it was already solved."

"I guess."

Though the answer was his, it didn't sit well in his system. He wouldn't admit it, though, mostly because he didn't really know all that much about police procedures.

"Any others?" she asked.

"Yeah, tons." Bill backed out of this newspaper article and clicked on the next one. Everything within was pretty much the same.

Once that one was read they moved onto the next one, and then the one after that as well. Each story was a near clone of the first one they had read, which, initially, confused Bill. He then realized each paper was an online affiliate of a larger paper and that the story had been 'reprinted' with each outlet.

"Hey look at this," Kimberly said and put a finger on the

screen.

Inside Bill winced at the fingerprint that would be left behind, but didn't say anything. *"The couple had been separated for six months,"* he read. "That's new."

"Yeah, and look at this." She touched the screen again. *"Daughter, who is currently a student at NIU, could not be reached for comment."* She looked at him. "You don't think . . ."

". . . that it could have been her last night?" Bill finished.

Kimberly nodded.

A memory of pulling the girl to the ground filled his head. Though it was hard to say for sure based on that simple touch, it did seem possible that she would have been the right age and build for a typical female college student.

"It could be," he said. "Does it give a name anywhere?" He asked this as if she had the computer all to herself when really he was in the better position to scan the article.

"Nope," she said.

He came to the same conclusion.

Neither spoke for several seconds and then, without saying anything, Kimberly stood up and walked over to her computer.

From where he sat, Bill watched as she double clicked the Internet icon and asked, "What are you looking for?"

"I just want to check something." On her screen, he saw part of the NIU page, but could not tell what item she clicked on, or what the next page that opened was. "What was the last name of the guy that was killed?"

"Um . . . Moore."

"With an 'e'?" she asked.

"Yep."

"Okay." She clicked something with her mouse and then, after waiting several seconds, said, "Tada."

Curious, Bill set the laptop aside and came over. What he saw was a listing of names, a header in red displaying the words LAST NAME, FIRST NAME, TELEPHONE NUMBER, EMAIL ALIAS, DIRECTORY TITLE, and DEPARTMENT. "What is this?"

"The NIU Directory." She touched her own screen. "Look,

out of eight Moore last names three are female students."

"Emily, Katie, and Rachel," Bill read.

Kimberly repeated the names and then said, "It could be one of them."

"Or none if they chose not to add their name to the directory." He paused. "Unless you're automatically added when you register? Did you ever add yourself to it?"

"No."

"Put your name in and see what happens."

Kimberly did and sure enough her name appeared as a student.

"Can you opt out of it?"

"I don't know. I didn't even think I'd be in here until I thought about checking the directory for her name."

"Wow, do all colleges have something like this?"

"Yeah, and at some they used to be called Face Books."

"Wait, what, like the website?"

"Yep. Didn't you see the movie about it?"

He shook his head. "Haven't gotten to that one yet."

"Oh, well, never mind. Most colleges have a directory of some sort. In fact, I wonder if . . ." she started typing a new web address in, but then stopped before she hit ENTER. "Never mind, we'll just stick with this."

"What were you thinking?"

"Oh, I was just going to see if I was still in the U of I directory, but . . ." she shrugged ". . . kind of pointless. We should just focus on these three names and see if one of them is the daughter."

"What made you change schools?" Bill asked.

"Oh . . . um . . . I flunked out during my freshman year."

"Ah, I've heard it's a tough school."

"It wasn't that," she said, voice barely audible. "It . . . it doesn't matter. Any idea how we go about connecting any of these girls to what's been going on?"

"No," he admitted. "That doesn't give a living address, does it?"

"No."

"Didn't think so. We can try to Google each one of their

names and see if it comes up in any newspaper articles about the murder."

"Think that'll work?"

"Don't know, but it's something. Open up a new window and do a search."

12

"I hope you don't mind, but I kind of live in a dump," Amy said as they pulled up outside of the house she lived in.

"I don't mind," Mark said.

"Last year I had a better place, but it required a co-signer and my parents weren't willing to sign anything this time around, so I had to settle on this."

"Oh, that sucks." Simple statements like this were all he could manage at the moment, his mind too preoccupied with what he was certain was about to occur.

"Yep," she said and then stepped out of the car.

Mark pulled the keys and stepped around to join her, goose-flesh appearing as she took hold of his hand.

"I can feel you trembling," she said, a bit of amusement in her voice.

"Sorry," he muttered.

"No, it's okay. I like it."

A smile was all he could muster.

With that, she led him across the yard and up the front steps. More steps followed as they headed up to the second and then third floor. "I got what was once an attic," she said.

Mark looked around. "I like it. Very cozy." This was stretching the truth quite a bit, but the last thing he wanted to do was tell her the place seemed off, especially considering the lack of personal belongings. From what he saw, aside from a laptop that sat atop an old child school desk, she hadn't brought anything when moving in. *But then maybe that was because she had had some kind of falling out with her parents?* She had just mentioned them refusing to co-sign her apartment. *Wait, wasn't this her first year here?* He thought she had said that at some point; something about being new in town and a first year student and --

"What is it?" Amy asked.

"What?"

"It's my place, isn't it? I'm sorry, I wish it were nicer."

"No, no, it's fine. I just realized that . . . well, I feel kind of foolish, but I don't have any, um, protection."

"And here I thought all men carried condoms because thanks to porn they learn fairly quickly that women almost always want to have sex in the most random situations."

"That is – " he started to say, but found his throat caught as she playfully grabbed him by the groin.

"No worries, I planned ahead," she said and then, without missing a beat, unzipped his pants and pulled him free.

The touch of her fingers to his bare flesh was unlike anything he had ever felt before. Pure bliss. Nothing but the sensations he was experiencing registered, and even those he was barely able to comprehend. And then she knelt down before him and took him in her mouth.

13

"There it is," Kimberly said, satisfaction brewing. "Emily Moore was the daughter of Martin and Olivia Moore."

A simple search on the name Emily Moore had brought about the newspaper article they were looking for. "Olivia Moore. You know, that name just doesn't sound like it belongs to a crazy person."

"Yeah, well, neither does Ted, or Dennis, or Jimmy. Names don't make one psychotic," Bill said. "The inability to sympathize with others and associate within the normal rules of society does."

"Unless it's so bad that kids never stop picking on them and scar them for life and make them think of nothing but revenge." She said this in an attempt to lighten the mood, but failed.

"Okay, that might do it too," he conceded. No amusement was present. "Now the question is, is the daughter Emily following in the mother's footsteps and if so, why and how? If revenge

is all she wanted then simply killing you at an opportune moment would have been the best option. Obviously, that hasn't
happened so it seems like something bigger is unfolding. Of
course, this is assuming the daughter Emily is responsible for
this. We really should try to lock that down."

"Did you learn anything about the email address you sent
out?" Kimberly asked.

"No, not yet."

"Well, if it turns out to be linked to her, there is your 'how' as
we have already established. Maybe the 'why' is her simply trying to point the finger at Nikki and show the world what she did
with her parents? It isn't like she actually has tried to harm me
or anything?"

"What about the Snapple bottle thrown at my car? The police
said that could have killed me."

"Yeah, but was that her intent or did she just want you to stop
following her? She might not even have thought about it much,
just grabbed the bottle that she had been drinking from and
threw it."

A simple nod was his only reply, one that morphed into an
odd half shrug.

"Of course," she added. "I'm not justifying her actions or anything, and won't let it all blow over if she is just simply trying to
point a finger at me."

"Good," Bill said. "Because this is serious stuff she's doing.
What if one of the guys she gave your address to turned out to be
a psycho themselves and tried to rape you or worse?"

Kimberly hadn't really thought about that, nor did she want
to now.

"Actually," he continued. "What if that was her hope all
along, only the guys she's contacting aren't really as psychotic as
they seem. If that's the case this could get really bad as she
grows more and more frustrated by the lack of results."

"God, that's not a very comforting thought."

"It isn't meant to be."

"Yeah, I know," she muttered.

Nothing else was said.

Kimberly twisted back to her computer and attempted to find a picture of Emily Moore. Hundreds of different girls appeared when she clicked the IMAGE tab in the Google search. Nothing about any of them jumped out at her as being the Emily they were interested in, though she was able to eliminate some based on age, race and gender. This still left hundreds, the SHOW MORE RESULTS button at the bottom of the page always doubling the length of the page. Even so, she began to go through them, her mouse icon hovering over each picture one by one until the website location appeared in a small pop-up window that enlarged the photo a bit and gave all the details beneath it. Most were from Facebook. Others carried site addresses or names that she was unfamiliar with and wouldn't click on for fear of viruses. None seemed to be from newspapers, which is what she was looking for.

"What're you doing?" Bill asked.

Kimberly nearly jumped, her ears having failed to catch him approaching from behind.

"I Googled 'Emily Moore' and these are all the pictures from the web it found." She hovered over one and sure enough a Facebook address appeared. "As you can imagine most are from Facebook."

"With a billion members -- or whatever it is they claim to have -- I'm not surprised they have a few Emily Moore's in there."

"Yeah."

"Hey, did you try 'Emily Moore' and 'DeKalb' in the search?"

"Oh, no, didn't think of that." Silently she wondered if the girl would have changed her Facebook location upon moving to the college town, but then thought about her own actions. She had changed it before she even had the key to her place, her excitement of moving from her parents place again, and her desire to start connecting with other students, having spurred her into action. And she wasn't even a Facebook addict. Kyle had been, as was her mother and sister, but not her. She only went on four or five times a day to check things.

A new idea appeared.

Rather than search 'Emily Moore' and 'DeKalb' she typed in

'Emily Moore' with 'NIU' and hit ENTER. Unfortunately, the results were not helpful – or too helpful if one was looking for quantity.

"Hmm," came from Bill. Then, "Is there any type of Facebook page dedicated to NIU that would show the people who are networked into it?"

"Um . . . I think there are several different types of NIU pages," she said and brought one up. "Can't really see who likes it though, just the friends I have that like it."

"Any Emily Moore's in there?"

Even though she doubted he was serious, she checked anyway. Stranger things had happened. The answer, however, was no.

"There has got to be a way to use Facebook to find her," Bill said, frustration evident in his voice. "With all the uproar over privacy issues and whatnot you'd think we would have been able to pull her up and know everything about her within a minute or two."

"Maybe we could, we just don't know how. I've never been one to really use Facebook that way."

"Me either."

Stumped, the two stared at the screen.

Then, Kimberly had an idea. "The person you sent the email address too. Do you think he could find all the Emily's in the DeKalb area and send us links so we can check out their profiles?" Truth was, she didn't really know what could be gained from seeing the profiles, but figured it might be nice to have a picture of her if possible.

"I can always ask. He might say *no* though since it does sound a bit like something a stalker would do."

"Even if you explained it to him?"

"I don't know. Like I said, I can ask, but that's about it. If I knew him personally I'd be a bit more optimistic, but . . ." he left it at that.

"What about the police? Should I call them and tell them about all this and what we suspect?"

"It couldn't hurt, but I don't think they will be able to do much with it since we don't really have anything actually point-ing at this Emily Moore as being responsible. Plus . . ." he didn't continue.

"Plus what?" she asked.

"I was going to say they might come after me for doing what I did with the blog, but in reality I don't think there is anything they can do. I didn't break any laws and certainly didn't insti-gate the murder."

Despite his statement, she could still sense a bit of worry pre-sent in his voice. Had she done what he had done, she would be worried too. In this day and age there was no telling what the law could do to a person who did what he had done, especially if the media got hold of it and turned it into a moral issue.

14

Amy actually had an orgasm from the sex, which she hadn't been expecting. It was a powerful one too, one that made her cry out in ecstasy as all the muscles within tightened into a nearly un-bearable squeeze and then released itself.

Of course, Mark had very little to do with this. Sure, his penis was there and it filled her nicely (he wasn't lying online when he said he was big), but it might as well have been a dildo that she had strapped to the bed beneath her for all the skill he dis-played. Instead, the orgasm was mostly brought about by her mind as she replayed a wonderful moment from her past, one that involved her and a college professor she had loved. The wonderful friction she was creating inside herself by thrusting her hips up and down upon his erection helped as well.

"Oh, Jesus," she said once the orgasm had finished, her body collapsing down upon his so that her head rested on his chest. "Wow."

"Did . . . did you just cum?"

The question, and the innocence within it, caused her to laugh against his bare flesh. "I did." She then realized something, his penis, which was still inside her, had remained firm. "Did you?"

"Um, no, not yet," he admitted.

"Really?" *After all that?* Most virgins, and she was sure he was one, would have exploded just from her lips being on them, which was why she had only sucked on him for a little while as a sort of tease before the main event. After that, she had just assumed he would cum quickly once she unrolled the condom onto him and slipped the covered organ inside herself.

"I was holding back waiting for you."

"Oh." She smiled. "How sweet." In her mind she said, *bullshit.* Men couldn't hold back like that. It just wasn't possible. She had been taught this at a young age just so she would never fall for the 'I will pull out in time' claim that all men made, a claim that had resulted in her being born.

Frustration was present as well, but she hid it as she began to rock her hips back and forth once again, her movements slow due to her own exhaustion.

"You like that?" she asked.

"Uh-huh," he muttered.

"Are you close to coming?"

"I think so."

What? You think? How was that even possible? "And when I do this?" She reached down with her right hand and grabbed the base of his penis while still rocking her hips.

"Oooo," he moaned.

She took that as a good sign and then, in hopes of having another orgasm herself, started thinking about her professor and all the wonderful moments they had shared together last year. Sadness and anger came with the thoughts, but didn't dampen the pleasure she felt. Instead, the emotions seemed to enhance everything, almost as if --

"Ahh," she gasped as pain shot through her breast.

Surprised, Mark pulled his hand away from the boob he had grabbed, a look of horror and embarrassment appearing on his face. "Sorry, I just thought – "

"Shhh," she interrupted, putting a finger to his lips. "It's okay. I tripped coming out of the shower the other day and crashed into the sink." She slipped her shirt off to reveal the bruise he had grabbed. "See? I should have said something, but thought you might find it a turnoff."

"Oh, no, I don't," he said while lightly touching the battered flesh.

Amy shivered, which startled him, the slight buck of his body actually feeling good since it forced his penis to pull forward a bit.

"Do that again," she moaned, her own body still rocking back and forth on top of him.

"What?" he asked.

"Pull it forward like that again."

Puzzled, he just stared at her, then understanding seemed to arrive and he said, "Like this?"

"Ohhhh, God, YES!" she cried.

He grinned.

Down below his penis kept making a pulling forward motion, the head pushing right into that ultra sensitive circle of nerves that some liked to call the G spot every time. This, coupled with the fingers of her right hand rubbing her own clit, caused an explosive orgasm, her cry echoing throughout the house.

"Wow," was all she could say while rolling off him, her body too weary to do anything else at that moment.

They were not finished though, her eyes easily able to see that the condom was still nice and tight against his firm erection.

"Do you always last this long?" she asked, lungs struggling to find enough air to create the necessary words.

"I – I – um, sometimes," he said.

"Well," she just took a deep breath. "We'll just have to keep going then, only this time you take charge."

"Oh, um, what do you mean?"

She laughed and shook her head. "I mean get on top and fuck me."

"Oh, okay." He shifted around and rolled over, his movements awkward.

Once he was in position, she opened her legs for him. To her surprise, however, he didn't thrust himself inside right away. Instead, he leaned his face forward and started probing her with his tongue and fingers.

"What're . . . ooooo!"

For someone who probably had never laid a girl before, he somehow knew what he was doing with his fingers and tongue and managed to pull forth a third orgasm from her.

"You like that?" he asked. Unlike his previous statements there didn't seem to be any hesitation in his voice.

"Yes," she moaned.

"And how about this?" he demanded while sliding his penis into her.

"YES!"

He grinned and started moving his hips. At first, the thrusts were awkward, but then, as his body got used to the unusual movements, he seemed to find a rhythm that worked. An aggressive side also appeared, one that saw him grabbing hold of her hips and lifting them so that he could thrust from his knees rather than while laying on top.

Knowing he might grow tired quickly while in this position, and fearing it might end too quickly, she clasped her hands beneath her butt and helped keep herself lifted.

His thrusts grew more forceful, each one punctuated by the lifting motion of his penis, which, while enjoyable, was torturous given the amount of pleasure that had already been pulled from her.

And then it happened, her mind knowing it was coming due to the sounds he was suddenly making and that added pressure she felt within as his own muscles clenched.

"Oh yes," she cried. "Give it to me! YES! YES!"

A serious groan escaped him followed by a heavy grunt and a long sigh.

During this, she felt warmth through the condom and, though it might have been her imagination, thought she could feel each spurt as more fluid erupted from him.

"Ohh," he gasped and gave one final thrust. "Yeah."

He then slowly pulled out of her, the gentle withdrawal causing a subtle pleasure as each nerve seemed to send one final signal of ecstasy racing to the brain.

"Oh, wow," she said while looking at the condom, cum visible

within. So much had been ejaculated that it had actually drib-
bled out beneath the bottom ring. "I don't think I have to ask
this time."

"Not this time," he agreed. His hand then moved toward the
base of his penis, fingers ready to pull it free. "Um, what should
I – "

"Here, let me get that for you," she said and shifted herself so
that she was between his legs. "There we go," as it slipped free,
"and – " she leaned in and put her mouth on his penis and
sucked as hard as she could, the salty flavor instantly assaulting
her taste buds.

"Ahhhh," he cried and tried to pull out, his nerve ending obviously too sensitive for any contact.

"Yum, yum," she said once her hold was broken. "Didn't
want you feeling all sticky." She grinned. "Be right back."

"Oh . . . kay."

With that she got up from the bed and headed into her bathroom where she took a much needed pee while her hands tied a
knot in the condom, and then hurried out into the kitchen.
"Want some water or a soda?" she asked.

"Oh, sure," he called back. "Soda's good."

"Okay." She grabbed two Cokes and walked back to the bed
where Mark was sitting up, naked body on full display.

"You can get under the covers if you like," she said and
handed him the soda. "That's what I'm going to do."

"Oh, I wasn't sure if that was okay without first – "

"Shhh," she said and motioned for him to lift himself so she
could pull back the sheets, his movements awkward due to his
nakedness.

Once settled she crawled in as well, took several sips of soda,
and then snuggled up against him, her body savoring the comfort the intimate position provided. In return he put his arms
around her, his muscles pulling her close with a gentle firmness
that she loved. It had been a long time since she had been in
such a position with anyone -- a long time since the nights when
she and her former professor would curl up together after a night
of strenuous lovemaking.

15

A terrible sense of boredom arrived once Bill was back in his own place, one that could not be broken by his normal everyday activities. The fact that he hadn't written anything of note for a while made it even worse, especially when in view of his laptop sitting upon his desk. Attempting to add pages to his latest novel would be fruitless, however, so he wouldn't even try it. Some writers could sit down and produce words no matter the time and location. He couldn't. If he didn't start writing during the early morning hours, fingers typing before the sun crested the horizon, a cup of fresh coffee at his side, then he didn't get any writing done that day. The only exception to this was his blog posts. He could pen those without much trouble, just as long as he actually sat down to do it and wasn't facing a moment of mental exhaustion.

And just as long as you had a topic to write about, he said to himself.

Nothing within his head seemed interesting enough to share with the visitors to his blog, though. In fact, nothing but the events concerning Emily and her parents could hold his attention for long. It was all so surreal. Unbelievable too. If someone had warned him a year ago that he should hold off on trying to get men to sign up for the Adult Friend Finder dating site because it would one day lead to a girl in the apartment below him being threatened by the daughter of a man who was killed by his estranged wife, he wouldn't even have known what to say. Yet here he was now living that situation.

And if given the chance, I wouldn't change what I did.

Admitting this to Kimberly, or anyone else that asked, wouldn't be good, and therefore was something he would lie about. When talking with himself, though, he couldn't deny it. He also wasn't ashamed of it. How could he be when the money had been like a life raft in a storm? Without it he and Toby would not have been able to stay in the apartment, which meant . . . well, he didn't even like to contemplate what the consequences of that would have been.

His lack of shame didn't equal a lack of feeling somewhat

responsible for what had happened, though, but not in a 'You're to blame for this' kind of way. Mrs. Moore had made a choice to kill her husband, thus the responsibility for that act rested with her. His responsibility lay within the realm of knowing he had created a situation that had helped push a crazy lady over the edge. For this he was sorry, and wished it hadn't happened. At the same time he knew that if not for his actions, something else would have probably produced the spark that eventually led to the same outcome. That was the trouble with crazy people.

And she passed it down to her daughter.

Or did she?

Though slim, doubt about the identity of the harasser was still present so he couldn't say for sure that the daughter was to blame. It did feel right, though. Laying out that possibility with Kimberly earlier had produced a 'click' within his mind that he could not ignore. He had a feeling Kimberly felt the same way. If he wasn't mistaken, there had also been a change in her ever since they had realized the perpetrator was female, yet he couldn't pinpoint what that change had been exactly. It was there though.

Downstairs the sound of the kitchen door slamming shut echoed, the needlessly tight hinges always producing a *crack* when released.

Bill went to the window and watched as Kimberly went into the garage and then, after a minute, drove away. He had no idea where she was going, and for a moment felt an odd sense of rejection that she hadn't asked him to tag along.

Don't be silly, he scolded himself.

The inner comment should have put the feeling of rejection out of his mind, yet it didn't. Knowing it was ridiculous made it worse too, because it brought about a sense of foolishness that he couldn't shake.

You're falling for her.

Normally such a realization wouldn't have been a problem, but this time around it was because he had a feeling she would not see him as the type she would want a relationship with.

What was strange was that for several years now he hadn't

wanted a relationship with anyone and would quickly sever ties if one began to loom. Sex, yes, he always craved that, but relationships, no. That was why his partnership with Nicole had been so wonderful. When sex was a part of a business deal it didn't create that awkwardness of having to enjoy each other's company when not taking part in the physical act. Now, however, he found himself not just enjoying the time spent in the company of Kimberly, but craving more. It was weird. Just sitting downstairs with her had been nice and something he could have spent all day doing. Driving to the motel had been fun too, despite the situation requiring it.

And now, sitting here, you're obsessing over her rather than focusing on other things that could be more productive.

I can't help it.

It kind of reminded him of the feelings he had experienced after a nasty breakup several years ago, one that had put an end to what he had felt was a perfect relationship -- though one that looking back upon he knew was far from it. During that time he had not been able to stop thinking about what he had lost and wondering how he would ever move on with his life. Nothing he could do would shake the thoughts of her from his mind. Now, the same thing was happening, only from the opposite side of the spectrum. Because of this sadness was not a constant companion.

But it might be soon if you push too hard and she ends up wanting nothing to do with you.

This, coupled with the fear that the only reason Kimberly was even spending time with him was because of his connection with the situation, brought about an unwanted worry that he could not shake.

You're being pathetic, he said to himself.

No rebuttal followed. How could one when every ounce of his being knew the statement to be true?

16

Is it possible to think about nothing? Two years earlier a philosophy instructor had asked this question of Mark's class, which, of course, was an attempt to spark a discussion on the concept of nothing. It also had been an introduction of sorts to what the class would be like given that it had been the first day, though of all the discussions and debates that had followed throughout the semester; this was the only one he really remembered.

You were thinking about 'nothing' but now you're not, he said to himself, his mind having been completely blank for an unrecognizable amount of time following the sex. At one point he might have even lost consciousness, though not in an 'I'm asleep now' way. Instead, it had been as if his mind had simply shut down for a brief period, its satisfaction with the events that had taken place enough for it to disappear into some unknown region for a while since it knew the body was content and could be left alone. Now, however, it was back and letting him know he needed to use the bathroom. In fact, it was insisting. The only problem was that Amy was completely snuggled up against him, her arms actually having threaded themselves so that she was holding him.

You have no choice.

He had to untangle himself from her grip and get to the toilet. If not, well, the term 'move it or lose it' would take on a whole new meaning, the second half probably signifying two future events: losing the fill within his bladder, and losing Amy because she didn't seem the type that liked to be peed on.

Breaking free of her grip was not easy, especially when not wanting to wake her. He also knew she had that bruise upon her breast and didn't want to accidentally bump it – a task made difficult given that it was pressing up against him.

A few days ago you would have wanted to stay like this forever just because of that boob, he told himself with a smile. *Now you're trying to get away from it.*

Disbelief at what had unfolded this afternoon struck. He was no longer a virgin.

And you were good.

From his readings and media watching experiences Mark knew that most guys thought they were good, and would claim perfection after the act even when the evidence showed otherwise. In this case, however, Mark knew the evidence didn't point toward a different conclusion. Amy's reactions had made this clear. She had had an orgasm, and not just one, but several. That was huge. He had also lasted a long time, which seemed unusual for a first timer. Actually, according to popular culture it was unusual for men in general, the joke always being that they came in two or three minutes. Why this hadn't happened with him he didn't know, but he didn't mind. Lasting a long time like that had been great, except when he had started to worry that he wouldn't come at all. That would have been humiliating.

Nothing to worry about now though, nor did he have anything to worry about in the future because even if he had an off night (or day) in bed Amy could remember how amazing this time around had been. Because of that, she would know the potential was there and would crave such future moments.

He managed to slip free of her arms while thinking this, his body sliding under the covers completely and then popping free in the foot of space between her arms and the wall.

"No," Amy mumbled during this, startling him. Nothing else followed, however, and it seemed she was still asleep.

Being careful not to rock the bed too much, Mark crawled to the edge and stood up, gooseflesh rising upon his naked body despite the heat within the attic room.

Knowing he would just take them off in a minute or two so he could crawl back into bed, he dismissed the urge to put his pants on and headed into the bathroom, his hand easing the door shut so as not to disturb Amy's sleep.

Relief arrived.

Never before had peeing felt so good; it was almost like another ejaculation, though he wasn't sure why.

Once finished he decided to clean himself off a bit, both because he didn't like the odd feeling the condom had left upon him and also because he thought there might be a good chance that Amy would suck him off again if he hinted at it once she woke up.

A few seconds later, with a wad of crumbling toilet paper in his hand, he discovered the bathroom was lacking a garbage can, and, not wanting to flush the toilet a second time for fear of waking Amy, he headed into the kitchen area where he knew there had to be a garbage can.

With that taken care of, he went to the fridge to grab a bottle of water, and then returned to the bed, his body failing to ease himself in without waking Amy this time.

"Sorry," he muttered. "Had to use the bathroom."

"It's okay," she said with a smile and then snuggled up against him once again. "I'd hate to spend all my time with you sleeping, though it is nice to have someone in bed with me. I get so lonely sometimes."

He smiled. "Me too."

"Then you'll just have to come keep me company whenever possible," she said. "That way no more lonely nights for the two of us."

"It's a deal."

"And make sure you always bring this guy with," she said, her hand slipping down between his legs and gripping his penis, which, naturally, began to grow.

"Ha, no worries there," he said and then, as her hand started stroking him, "Oooo, I like that."

"I know you do."

After that it wasn't long before a new condom had been opened so that he could start fucking her once again, this time with her bent over on the bed, while he came at her from behind.

17

Amy had to admit, she was pleasantly surprised by the pleasure Mark was able to pull from her that afternoon. Never before had a guy brought forth so many orgasms from her in one event, professor included. He also was the first guy that ever managed to give her a clitoral orgasm, his focus on that area after fucking her doggy style for a while unlike anything she had ever experienced. Even her own masturbation moments couldn't compare, which just completely blew her away. It was also the reason he was going to have a huge bruise on the side of his face come the first day of class, her knee having jerked inward as the orgasm arrived.

"You sure you're okay?" she asked for the third time once the second round was complete.

"I'm fine," he said and smiled. "It'll be like a badge of honor. I can't wait to tell people how I got it."

"You wouldn't!" she cried and gently hit him with a pillow.

"Hmm, sounds like me keeping this secret is worth something to you, so what will you do to keep this information secure?"

"What would you like me to do, sir?" she asked, her voice taking on the innocence of a schoolgirl, a roll her professor had always enjoyed. He had even bought her outfits to wear to enhance the fantasy.

"I'll let you know tomorrow after class when we get together again. Just so you know it will involve your lips."

"Oh, that sounds naughty."

He grinned and then lifted his arm so that she could curl up against him again, a wonderful sense of comfort arriving as he pulled her close. Pain followed as her bruised breast was pressed into his chest and caused her to wince slightly.

"You okay?" he asked.

"Yes," she said. "We both have our bruises."

"We do, but I think mine was more fun to get."

She smiled and then rested her head on his chest once again.

He tightened his own hold on her and said, "I really like this."

"Me too," she replied. *And I'm not just saying it,* she realized. The thought both thrilled and chilled her. "I wish you didn't have to go."

"Aww, but I won't be leaving anytime soon and once I do go it won't be long before I'm back." He ran a hand through her hair while saying this.

Leaving for the day hadn't been what she meant by her statement, but she didn't correct him.

"By the way," he asked. "What time are your classes tomorrow?"

"Oh . . . um," she started, her mind quickly trying to think up a time that would sound legitimate. "Wow, see what you did to me, my mind is too exhausted to pull it up right now. I'll have to look at my schedule."

He chuckled. "Okay. I was thinking we could get together between classes or something, or just afterward if nothing matches up."

"Send me your class list tonight once you're home and I'll let you know. And of course afterward is good, unless you think I'd be a distraction from your homework or something."

"If you are I won't complain," he said and smiled. "Especially if that distraction involves activities similar to those we did to-day."

"Hehe, oh they will. I promise." Once that was said she rested her cheek on his chest again, and, like before, found her-self drifting away.

18

Kimberly didn't accomplish anything of note that afternoon, though this was to be expected given that she had no real goal when leaving the apartment. All she did was explore the city of DeKalb, her feet taking her up and down the sidewalks of Lin-coln Highway and, occasionally, up and down some side streets if the areas looked interesting. One of these side trips brought her to the Confectionery, which Bill had mentioned to her at some point during their time together. It was located a few doors down from a famous local landmark called the Egyptian Theater, and pretty much consisted of every homemade choco-late treat one could want to eat. Willpower did not make itself known during her time inside, her stressed out mind deciding she could have anything she wanted. Because of this she bought thirty dollars' worth of chocolate, some dark, some milk, and systematically put items in her mouth as she walked the rest of the street, her hand crumbling up the top of the large white bag anytime she entered a store for fear of access restrictions due to food.

Her thoughts were few and far between, and when they did appear, they mostly focused on how unfair everything was. Thankfully, putting a piece of chocolate in her mouth would dispel these thoughts, though it didn't clear them away completely. And then it happened. She was near a small park to the south of Lincoln Highway and caught sight of a mother pushing a stroller. Memories flooded her mind and no amount of chocolate would help dispel them. Tears came too, along with a weakness in her knees that forced her to sit down on a bench.

Looking down at her feet she saw a pool of blood upon the tile floor rather than the concrete sidewalk, and felt the chocolate in her stomach turn sour.

Not again! her mind pleaded.

The image would not go away.

When she did vomit, she did it into a bush behind the bench so that people wouldn't have to come upon it unexpectedly when taking a seat.

She then left the playground area, her mind vowing never to return. Unfortunately, she knew it was just one of many things that could spark a memory of her miscarriage and that more incidents like this would occur without warning in the days ahead.

Back at her car exhaustion struck and she knew that even though it was only a fifteen-minute drive she couldn't make it just yet. At the same time she didn't want to simply sit there for fear that her thoughts would turn to the miscarriage again and the horror that followed.

Call Melissa, her mind suggested. *Call her and tell her everything that has been going on.*

A discussion on this idea was not necessary. Instead, her hand simply pulled out the phone, found her name in the address book, and hit CALL.

Voicemail.

Go figure.

She left a message asking Melissa to call her back and then dropped the phone in her cup holder. She then risked another piece of chocolate, her hope being to remove the taste of stomach acid from her mouth. It worked. Even better, Melissa called her back as she swallowed the chewed up sweet.

"What's wrong?" she asked, concern dominating her voice.

For the second time that hour, Kimberly broke down in tears; her voice making this condition known as she told her little sister about everything that had occurred since their last talk a few weeks ago.

"My God, why didn't you tell me about this sooner?" Melissa asked.

"I don't know," she admitted. Though it had taken days to unfold, it had felt like it had happened quickly and without pause. One thing had led to another thing and another and another until this moment. "At first it didn't even seem real, but now . . ." she didn't know what to say.

"Did you tell Mom and Dad about all this?"

Kimberly knew her sister already knew the answer, but didn't chide her for asking and simply said, "No."

"And is Kyle helping you at all?"

"Oh, I didn't even tell you about that. I broke up with him right before all this really got going."

"Well . . . that's good I guess."

"Yeah," Kimberly agreed. Kyle would not have been much help during any of this.

The two were silent for a moment, then, "So, you know who this girl is, the one who is leaving the notes and everything?"

"Kind of," Kimberly said. She wanted to explain how it was nothing more than a theory at this point, though one that seemed incredibly likely, but it all seemed too exhausting to relay, so she left it at that.

"Well, my suggestion would be to find her and make sure she realizes that it isn't you. I know this might sound silly given everything she has done already, but honestly, if she isn't a full-blown wacko, she might realize her mistake and back off."

"And if she doesn't?" Kimberly asked.

Melissa didn't reply, which, in itself, was an answer.

"Yeah," Kimberly said after a moment.

"There is something else you could do, though I know you won't like it."

"What?"

"Give all this information to the police, which you should have done right away anyway, and then go back to Mom and Dad's place for a little while."

"I — " she started.

"I know you wouldn't like that, but it would just be for a little while. The police should have no problem tracking this girl down now that you think you know who it is, and once that happens I can't imagine it going any further than it has."

Kimberly didn't reply.

"And if this is all a mistake like you say then chances are she'll have no idea where you are."

"I don't know," Kimberly said.

"Just think about it, okay?"

"Okay."

"And keep me posted on what's going on. I don't care what time it is, if you need to talk to me give me a call. If I'm busy I'll get back to you as soon as I'm finished."

"Okay, thanks."

19

"Hey Mark, wake up," a voice called.

Startled, Mark opened his eyes and looked around, confusion filling his head. Amy's face then appeared which sparked relief. *It wasn't a dream.* Lord knows he had had enough of them in the past, ones that always left him disappointed upon waking, yet also turned on to the point that he had no choice but to look at some porn and play with himself.

"Wow, I fell asleep," he muttered.

"We both did, actually," she said. A smile then appeared. "I was going to wake you by playing with your penis a bit, but then thought it might be worn out from everything."

"It's never *that* worn out." He grinned and pushed himself into a sitting position.

Amy laughed. "Men. The whole building could be burning down and yet you'd all still consider sex if it was an option."

"Well, at least you always know the answer is yes. It's not so easy when the tables are turned."

"Really? Maybe that's just because most women haven't experienced what I just experienced. If they did then the answer would always be yes as well."

"Oh? Good to know." An unexpected yawn hit. "Wow, you wore me out. What time is it?"

"Almost seven."

"Are you serious?"

"Yeah, we slept for quite a while it seems."

"I'll say." *And I could have slept longer if you hadn't woken me.* This, added to the fact that he had finally had sex, left him in awe.

"By the way, the reason I woke you, aside from my being really REALLY hungry, is that your phone buzzed several times.

"It did?"

"Yeah, and I think one of them was a call."

"Probably my Mom," he said with a sigh. "I forgot to tell her I wouldn't be home for dinner. She worries."

"Oh, in that case you should probably let her know what's going on," Amy said. "Well, maybe not everything that's going on." With that she got up from the bed and retrieved his pants for him.

The phone was in the right front pocket.

"Let's see," he said while opening the phone to check the missed call. "Yep, my mother. Looks like I got some texts as -- " *shit!*

"What is it?" Amy asked.

Mark shook his head. "Remember I told you that girl was harassing me?"

"Yeah?"

"Well, she's still at it." He turned the phone screen toward her. "See."

"Wow, why's she doing that?"

"I don't know, but it's really annoying. Did you know she sent me to a completely random address?"

"Wait, what?"

"Not too long ago actually, she told me she wanted to get together but rather than meeting someone in public like we did yesterday she wanted to meet at her place, only it wasn't really her place. Some poor girl who had just moved in lived there." He stopped, his mind debating how much he should tell her. The last thing he wanted was for her to think she was a fall back girl or something, especially after what they had just done.

But she likes you, a voice said. *What you just did is proof of it so relax.*

"What happened?" Amy said, unknowingly adding pressure.

"Well, I looked like a fool. Brought flowers and everything only to learn the girl had no idea what was going on. At first I figured she just didn't like what she saw, but then I kept getting messages and soon realized the person claiming to be this Nikki was just fucking with me the entire time." He shook his head. "The worst is what that poor girl is going through though. Can you imagine moving to a new place for the first time and being pummeled like this from guys who all think you're someone else?"

Amy didn't reply right away.

Mark shifted his attention to the text, which read: HOPE YOU AND AMY ARE HAVING A GOOD TIME. Several others followed, the next of which read: HAVE YOU SHARED WITH HER SOME OF THE FANTASIES YOU SHARED WITH ME YET?

"How do you know it isn't really her?"

Mark looked over at Amy and said, "Sorry, what do you mean?"

"That girl at the house," Amy said. "How do you know it isn't really this Nikki girl?"

"Um . . . I could just tell when talking to her. She is so distraught about all this and concerned. I showed her the blog that the Nikki girl used to have and the profile online. It's really weird."

"I don't understand why this person would send you to her house if it isn't really her. And you said you're not the only one. There has to be a reason for it, right?"

"Whatever it is, I can't figure it out." He shrugged. "Neither can she it seems. I feel bad too because I told her I would help, but there isn't really anything I can do. Plus I don't want to keep encouraging this Nikki person. It's bad enough she won't leave me alone when I'm not even sending her messages or trying to mess with her."

"Yeah, probably best not to poke around, unless of course she forces your hand." She reached around him for a hug. "Don't want anything to happen to you."

"Awwww," he said. "Don't worry."

"Plus I'd be worried about this other girl. It seems the possibility that she might be this Nikki girl herself still exists. People can be pretty convincing in person."

"True," Mark said. He didn't really think this was the case, but didn't want to argue. Who would after everything that had just occurred?

"So, what'd she say in her texts?" Amy asked.

"Oh, um . . ." he hesitated ". . . nothing important. She's just taunting me."

"How so?" she urged.

"Well . . ." he really didn't want to frighten her. At the same time he didn't want to make her think he was hiding something because that could make her feel as if he might not be trustworthy enough to keep doing what they had just begun. Plus, he had told her a bit about Nikki earlier and how she had messaged him about her, so it wasn't like this was a huge surprise or anything. "I can't figure out how it's possible, but like I said earlier, she seems to know you, and now was asking if we are having a good time."

"Hmm." It wasn't the reaction he was expecting. What followed was even more unexpected. "Tell her YES."

"What?"

"Wait, are you not enjoying yourself?" She pretended to pout.

He laughed. "If I wasn't then there would be something seriously wrong with me."

She smiled.

He typed up the suggested reply and hit SEND.

Didn't she just seconds ago agree that poking at Nikki would be bad? It was funny how people could suggest something and then disregard it in a matter of minutes.

"Hehe, and now, rather than wait and see if she replies, let's go get something to eat. I'm starving."

"Good idea. Where should we go?"

"Huh, I have no idea."

With that they began discussing their options, each one throwing out restaurant names until they finally settled upon Los Rancheros on Route 23.

20

Bill waited a long time to see if Kimberly would come up and talk with him, but it never happened. Surprise wasn't present with this, though disappointment was. Frustration toward himself for feeling this way also appeared. Nothing he could do about it. One couldn't control their desires. Things like this just happened.

And don't instigate any contact!

This, more than anything else, was the hardest aspect of this entire situation. It was also probably the most important. The last thing he wanted to do was to pester her. Running down there if something happened was one thing. Constantly going down there just to talk with her and be with her was another.

Plus you would hate it after a while if things did develop because chances are she would come up here all the time, and when, not up here, would expect you to be down there.

As hard as it was to imagine feeling like this toward Kimberly, he knew from past experience that it would happen. Whenever he entered a relationship he loved it in the beginning, but then quickly grew to hate it in the end. With this one it would almost be like they were living together right from the start since no driving was required when visiting. That wouldn't be good.

Nope. The best thing right now was to keep things just the way they were, despite how much he wished otherwise.

To help stick with this plan he popped in the latest DVD that

Netflix had shipped to him and, with Toby on his lap and a glass of Coke at his side, began watching it. Of course, while doing this, he hoped for contact by Kimberly; or, at the very least, an incident that would bring him running down the stairs to her rescue.

Nothing happened.

21

NIU_Nikki sat outside Kimberly's place for quite some time that night, but never made a move toward the house. Nor would she. Instead, she just stayed in the car thinking, her mind trying to decide what the next course of action would be. She also debated on whether or not she should keep attempting to send men to the house via the dating sites she had joined. In the beginning, she had pictured hundreds of men converging upon the house, their frequent visits driving Kimberly mad. She had also hoped some would refuse to take 'no' for an answer – if the whore even said no that was – and forced the issue. Such an event would have been incredible, though only if it didn't go too far because in the end she wanted to be the one administering the killing stroke. She wanted to be there and watch as those final pleas for mercy were made. Watch as her lips gasped for air that would not help her. Watch as her eyes glazed over.

Unless you are then caught and put in jail.

If that happened she would look back fondly at what she had done, but would also always have the nagging wish that one of the men had completed the deed for her instead.

But why?

It's not like you have much of a future beyond this.

This thought had been a constant companion for several months now. In fact, it had been a companion for years, but had been temporarily smothered out as everything in her life became bright and happy. But then . . .

She shuddered at the memories, most of which dealt with what had occurred last May, but also those that had happened earlier. March and April had not been good months for her, the former marking the moment when the brightness in her life began to fade.

Fear had been a constant companion. As always, it had started small, but then, as more and more evidence began to appear, it grew until it reached an unbearable level. Soon nothing but it was present in her life; her mind frantically trying to do everything it could to halt its progress and find a solution despite knowing it would be fruitless. And then, Nikki had appeared.

The anger that this memory brought forth was so strong that she almost had to drive herself away from the house just so she wouldn't go in and kill the girl.

In fact, the only thing preventing such a brash act was her sense of accomplishment in what she had achieved thus far in her revenge.

And soon it will be complete.

But then what?

In her mind, she viewed one of the final scenes of *The Princess Bride*, which, coincidentally, was her favorite movie. In the scene Inigo Montoya mentioned to Westley that he didn't know what to do with his life now that his revenge for his father had been fulfilled. Soon she would be in the same dilemma, only no one would offer her command of a pirate ship.

No one will offer you anything.

The reason: she had no one. Everyone who had ever cared for her, or pretended to care for her, was gone. She was alone.

Well, there is someone . . .

She didn't want to think about that though and pushed the thought away.

The sudden presence of a figure walking toward her car helped with this, concern that they would confront her removing everything else from her mind.

The figure walked by the car without even looking her way and eventually disappeared around the corner, feet taking whoever it was toward the cemetery.

She sighed and then told herself to go home. Nothing good would come of her sitting out here.

Unfortunately, sitting out here, though nerve-racking, felt

better than sitting at home due to the emptiness that always filled her soul.

And that emptiness will always be there so who cares if you manage to convince the police that some sex addicted pervert was to blame for –

Oh shit! her mind cried as the driver side door was yanked open.

"Get out!" a voice demanded.

It was the guy from last night, the guy who lived above Kimberly, the one she had been unaware of due to the piss poor information Dominick had given her about the type of place the 'Nikki' girl was living in.

A hand reached in and attempted to help ensure that she complied with his command.

She replied by grabbing hold of that hand and biting down.

"Jesus Christ!" he cried. "Let go!"

She tasted blood as her teeth punctured his flesh, her jaws putting down as much pressure as possible to achieve the best results.

He tried pulling away, her teeth feeling the tug as he tried to free himself.

She would not let go, however, and started to grind her teeth back and forth, her hope being to sever some important artery so that he would bleed to death.

He grabbed her throat and squeezed.

Panic arrived.

She had no choice but to release him, her jaws unable to maintain their hold as the blood flow to her brain was cut off. He did not do the same, though, his hand seemingly tightening with each second that passed.

Do something!

Her right hand fumbled for the key, which was sticking out of the ignition, while her left tried to pry his hand free, all while her body did everything it could to prevent him from pulling her out the door, which he was trying to do.

His right hand, despite the injuries she had inflicted with her teeth, grabbed her by the hair.

She gasped, the lack of air making it more of a dry squawk

than a scream.

Twist it! NOW!

The engine came to life.

She hit the gas.

The engine revved up, but the car didn't move.

SHIFT TO DRIVE!

Knowing what she was trying to do, the guy gave one last pull with both hands, her throat feeling crushed while her scalp felt on the verge of ripping.

And then the car leaped forward as she got it into drive and hit the gas, his holds on her broken as he dove away from the car.

DOOR AJAR.

The light was present on the dashboard as she maneuvered the car out of the neighborhood and onto Peace Road, the force of hitting the gas having closed it, but not enough for the car to recognize it as being latched.

Also present was a heart that felt as if it would burst free from her chest, one that would not slow and forced her into a parking lot rather than heading all the way home.

Several minutes passed before she could even contemplate completing the drive, her mind thinking of little during this time. And then, once thoughts did start to reappear, they all focused on the guy from upstairs and the realization that he needed to be removed from the picture.

But not tonight.

Unless . . .

Rubbing her throat, which still felt like it was being squeezed, she thought about how unsuspected it would be for her to make a move against him this evening. Given everything that had just occurred he probably figured she would rest and recover, thus it would be safe for him to do the same.

But you don't know enough about him yet.

And killing him could bring way too much attention upon the house, which in turn could prevent you from enacting your revenge upon Kimberly.

These thoughts frustrated her, as did her lack of awareness

while sitting outside of Kimberly's place.

He could have ruined everything.

Worse, he could have killed you!

This thought stuck with her for several minutes, an odd realization appearing as she contemplated it.

Death did not frighten her.

Failure did, but once all was said and done she would not be upset if the revenge resulted in her death as well.

Even odder, she felt comforted by this, almost as if she welcomed such an outcome.

22

Bill winced as the peroxide landed upon the teeth tears in his skin, his own jaws clenched tight in hopes that he didn't cry out.

A demand to know why he had done what he did followed. He should have called the police. Seeing the car during his walk, which he had taken due to his boredom halfway through the movie (not because the movie was bad, but because his mind couldn't focus on it), and realizing the girl was inside should have prompted him to pull out his phone and report it. Instead, he had attempted to subdue the girl himself. What exactly he would have done after that he did not know, and now, thinking more clearly about it, he knew he probably could have gotten in legal trouble for his actions.

And you didn't even take down the license plate number, he noted to himself, frustration growing.

Next time.

If there is one.

Twice now he had almost gotten a jump on her, and twice she had gotten the better of him.

No, three times, he corrected, his mind picturing the moment outside the garage last night.

That was more of a draw, another part countered.

No such thing in this game.

These thoughts ceased as he dumped more peroxide on the wound and watched it fizz, the fear of infection from her teeth a worthwhile worry given how bacteria ridden mouths generally were.

After that, he tried to figure out what he would do for a bandage, the wound too big for the simple Band-Aids he owned.

Go to Walgreens?

Without a car the trip would take him about an hour, which, at the moment, didn't seem worth it. At the same time he knew he needed to cover it somehow, especially given that Toby would probably rub up against it many times once he finally went to bed.

Gas station?

That was only a ten-minute walk. Unfortunately, he didn't know if they carried what he needed, or if they would even be open at this time of night – out here, many of the gas stations closed at ten and it was now almost midnight.

Then again, if that didn't work there was a 7-11 just down the street from the gas station and that, he knew, would be open. They also probably carried what he needed.

So . . . his mind started; a debate on whether or not he really wanted to venture out once again arriving.

Five minutes later, he was on the sidewalk again, legs re-walking the steps he had taken a short while ago as he tried to burn off the energy that was keeping him from being able to re-lax.

And it was right here when you saw the car.

At first he hadn't really believed it was her, but then, as he got closer and closer and realized someone was sitting inside it, knew that it was. Seeing it from the back had cemented this.

Should have called the police.

Should have gotten the license plate number.

Should have, should have, should have . . .

He pushed the thoughts from his mind since there was nothing he could do about it now. Instead, he would simply focus on getting what he needed to cover the wound and go to bed. Tomorrow, once he was rested and thinking more clearly, he would do whatever he could to figure out where the daughter of Martin and Olivia Moore lived and see if he couldn't put an end to this horrible situation once and for all.

Until then . . .

Buy some bandages, patch up the wound, and then go to bed.

And forget about getting up early to try to do some writing because it just won't work.

Nothing would until this was over.

Monday, August 22, 2011

1

I had such a wonderful time yesterday, as you probably guessed based on all the noises I made, hehe. I hope you did too. I'm pretty sure you did. I can't wait to see you again today. Let me know what time you'll be in town. Oh, by the way, that weird girl somehow got my number and sent me some texts. I'm not sure what she is trying to accomplish. I'm not going to respond, so hopefully she will get bored and leave me alone. Anyway, see you soon. Hugs and kisses. Amy.

Mark read the message five times before even contemplating a reply, a smile growing larger and larger each time he got to the 'hugs and kisses' statement. The only downside to the message was the part about Nikki, but, thankfully, it sounded like Amy wasn't letting that get to her. Nor would she allow it to ruin what the two shared, which was great.

Oddly enough, he hadn't received any messages from Nikki, which led him to wonder why she would contact Amy. Was she trying to ruin his chances with her? If so, why? What possible purpose could it serve? Was there even a purpose?

It doesn't make sense.

Well, not to you. To Nikki it probably all seems reasonable, even necessary.

Thinking about this would get him nowhere, however, so he decided to let it go and focus on sending a reply to Amy and then getting ready to head out to DeKalb.

I'm so glad you had a good time. I did too. In fact, yesterday was one of the best days of my life and now I can't wait to see what else is in store for us. My first class today is at ten, but I plan on being on campus around nine given how crazy everything will be. I then have a break at eleven thirty that lasts until two thirty. If you are free let's get together during that time. That class ends at five and then I'm done for the day. We can get together afterward if that works better. What is your schedule like? Oh, and I'm really sorry that Nikki girl is bugging you. I don't know why she's doing that. I'm thinking that just ignoring her would be best. That's what I'm going to do. Hugs and kisses to you as well. Mark.

As usual, a bit of worry entered his mind once the message had been sent, the focus of it being the 'best day of my life' statement. It wasn't overwhelming, however, and by the time he was finished with his shower he was able to push it from his mind.

2

Kimberly was in a bit of a panic that morning, which was pretty typical for her when it came to first day events. And nothing but going to class (or the new job if that was the case) would calm her down. It was kind of like waiting to be called upon to give a speech. The anticipation of getting up there in front of the class was torture, but the actual event not so bad, and before she knew it, she would be finished.

Soon you will be pulling back into the garage.

And what will be waiting?

The thought brought a chill, though one that wasn't as bad as it would have been a few days earlier given that her fears of the situation had lessened somewhat with the realization that a girl her own age was behind it. Why exactly this was the case she didn't know, especially given the knowledge that a woman could be just as lethal as a man, but the fact remained that it didn't frighten her as much.

Yeah, well, you're still sleeping on the couch.

Understandably, her fears did increase a bit with nightfall. Plus having the TV on seemed to help keep her thoughts free of the situation.

The question was would she still be wanting the TV on once this situation had resolved itself, or would she be able to go to lay down in the dark bedroom and drift away without it?

If not, you'll just have to buy a second TV for the bedroom, she told herself while stepping into the shower.

Twelve minutes later she emerged, body clad in her bathrobe, feet taking her into the kitchen to freshen her coffee.

THUNK! THUNK!

God, what does he want? she asked herself while walking to the inner stairway door, a somewhat creepy realization that he had probably been listening for the shower to cease before coming down filling her mind.

"Good morning," Bill said once the door was open.

"Morning," she said back, his worn look catching her off guard. "You okay?"

"What?" he asked with a yawn, then, before she could reply, "Oh, couldn't sleep."

Kimberly nodded.

"You start class soon?"

She nodded again and said, "Will be leaving around nine."

"Ah, nice. Not so early that it's a pain to get up every morning, but not so late that you spend half your day just waiting for class to start."

Impatience gripped her.

"Anyhow," he said. "I was thinking, while you're gone today I could spend time trying to figure out who this Emily Moore is and possibly where she lives."

"Great. Sounds like a good plan."

"The thing is I think I need to go online to do that."

"So . . . what, you want me to drop you at the library on my way to class or something?"

"Well, see, they have a two hour limit on the internet there and I have a feeling this might take longer than that, so I was thinking that maybe I could just run my cord down here like I used to do when the Roberts lived here?"

She didn't like this idea, but --

"And I could give you some cash to pay for the day if you like," he quickly added. "Or we could even arrange to split the bill if you want to share it with me like I used to do with them."

"Um . . ." she stalled while thinking about this. "Would we have to keep the doors open for the cord?"

"No, not at all." He shook his head. "We actually cut a notch in each, see."

She followed his finger and to her surprise saw a good-sized notch cut out of the bottom of the door. "Wow, I never noticed that."

"There's one on the basement door as well," Bill said.

"Really?" she questioned and then to herself wondered, *What else is there in here I'm unaware of? Peepholes in the shower? One in my bedroom?*

"Yep." He nodded. "Places like this get quite a few modifications from the tenants and most of the time the landlord isn't even aware of them."

"Well . . . I suppose if you think you might be able to figure out more about her and need more time than the library will give you, we can run the cord through."

"Wonderful." He smiled.

"As for doing some kind of permanent split, let me think about that, okay?"

"No problem." He motioned up to his own apartment. "I'll get everything hooked up if you want to continue getting ready for class."

"Okay." She turned to head back to kitchen where her coffee was waiting but then stopped and asked, "Oh, by the way, don't let me forget to give you my cell number before I leave so you can let me know if anything happens."

"Ah, good idea," Bill called down. "Will do."

With that, Kimberly headed back into the bathroom to finish getting ready, the steam from the shower having dissipated enough for her to see what she was doing.

Meanwhile Bill went about hooking up his laptop to her router, which, of course, didn't take long at all, his steps up and down the stairway only echoing twice.

Then again, given her hair dryer, he could have run up and down them several times and she probably wouldn't have heard a thing.

Finished, she headed into her bedroom to get dressed, and then returned to the front of her apartment to check the connection.

"Hey, I'm all done," she called up to him through the open doorways.

Up in his apartment she heard a squeak of a desk chair and then footsteps as he came toward the door. "Okay," he said. "Let me grab my phone."

"Of course, I won't be able to talk today, so let's just keep it to texts," Kimberly said once the numbers had been exchanged.

"Oh yeah, no problem. I prefer texting anyway."

"Great." She pocketed her phone. "Well, I gotta run."

"When will you be back?"

"Um, probably around four." She paused. "Why do you ask?"

"Just curious."

"Okay then. Let me know if anything crazy happens."

"Will do. Have a good day."

"Yep, thanks."

He started back up the stairs, which she watched for a second before closing the door. Hesitation on whether or not to lock it followed.

Do you trust him?

The fact that she couldn't answer YES right away caused her to press in the little lock tab. At the same time she didn't not trust him. It fell somewhere in-between.

And it leans toward the YES more than the NO, she admitted.

He's still a creep, though. And that was enough for her to be a bit weary of him.

3

Knowing it was probably fruitless at the moment given that nothing would have been delivered yet, but unable to help herself, NIU_Nikki paid a visit to the mailboxes at Kimberly's place to see if she could figure out who the guy living upstairs was. To her surprise the trip was not fruitless at all, not when the guy upstairs had printed his name in big bold letters on a piece of paper that was secured to the front of the box with long strips of shipping tape – probably to waterproof it, if that was even possible.

A sense of familiarity about the name hit, though she couldn't place it. Rather than dwell on this, she quickly snapped a photo of the name with her camera, and then headed back to her car, feet walking at a normal, nothing wrong here, pace.

Where have I seen it before? she asked herself once she was behind the wheel.

Nothing jumped out at her, and for all she knew her mind could have seen the name printed on the box a dozen times without even realizing it, which was why it seemed familiar now. The brain did odd things like that from time to time. She had learned this during her freshman year at college; during the happy time last year before everything once again crumbled around her.

Before Nikki ruined everything.

But was it really her fault?

The thought, which came out of nowhere, completely caught her off guard.

Devastation followed.

What if he was getting ready to dump me anyway? What if Nikki came around simply because he was looking for someone else? What if –

NO!

Teeth clenched, she tried keeping her mind focused on Nikki. Without her, things would have been fine. Without her, the two would have continued to be happy. Without her . . . happy pictures of a momma with her newborn baby appeared and brought tears to her eyes. Anger too.

Without Nikki . . .

You can't change what happened so don't dwell on it!

But at least I can make it so no one else ever goes through what I did.

This brought a smile to her face.

It didn't last long.

How could it when so many horrible memories were constantly floating around inside her head, all thanks to people like Nikki.

It's your fault.

NO!

Yes, it is.

The calmness of her inner voice was no match for the protests that came from elsewhere in her mind, protests that were fruitless given that she knew the truth.

You can't lie to yourself.

The words were his and had been spoken to her as a way of softening the blow she had known was coming, a blow that had forced her hand in going through with a decision that had been plaguing her for several days at that point. Only things hadn't quite worked out the way she thought they would have. If they had . . .

Happily ever after, she said to herself.

A new sad smile appeared on her face.

It would never have taken that direction.

Realizations like this only ever arrived after things had taken an ugly turn. Why she could never see such outcomes beforehand was a mystery.

If you had known what would you have done?

She had been thinking about this a lot lately, her mind not wanting to admit what she knew to be fact. She also didn't want to admit that things had probably worked out better this way, because it allowed her to be free. Had she acted on her initial rage that probably wouldn't have been the case.

But you never really wanted him dead so you never would have gone through with it.

As much as she wanted to believe this, she wasn't sure if she could. The hurt she had felt back then had created a volatile mix of anger and sadness that had left her mind in a state where things couldn't be fully processed to the point of making rational decisions. Thankfully, things were better now.

And because of this everything is working.

For the most part.

Her run-ins with this William guy from upstairs were proving disastrous, but thankfully, she would fix that.

And once he is gone . . .

Well, she wasn't really sure what it would be like, though her mind kept seeing the 'shields are down' moment from *Independence Day*. The comparison was so ridiculous, however, that she didn't want to focus on it. Instead, she wanted to try and figure out a way of removing the guy from the picture in a way that wouldn't draw attention to the house and Kimberly.

Could you make it so it looks like he was the one that killed her?

Is that even possible?

She thought about that odd kinky murder thing that had taken place with that college student in Italy a few years back, the one that had gotten quite a bit of news coverage. If possible, she could create something similar, something that looked as if Mark, Nikki and the guy upstairs were all part of something twisted that exploded in their faces and resulted in a bloody disaster.

First, though, she had to learn a thing or two about this upstairs guy; find out if he was vulnerable enough for her to get at. Just thinking about it already seemed tricky given his location on the second floor. She also didn't think she would be able to watch him that easily.

You should have seen if you could finish him off after you hit the car with the Snapple bottle, she told herself.

At the time, she had just been hoping to get away from him, her panic so great she didn't know what to do. Looking back, however, she now realized the opportunity to get rid of him had been perfect. No one would have ever known what happened to him. It would have looked like some bizarre random incident out in the middle of nowhere – an attempted car jacking maybe, or a drug deal gone wrong. Things like that happened from time to time out here, especially now that so many low-income families had been moved out from Chicago to DeKalb. Why the government had thought such actions would be beneficial to society was a mystery, one that she remembered her class talking about last year. The goal had been to end the families involvement in gangs, their thinking being if they moved the families out into areas with non-gang families they would be influenced by them to become normal productive citizens. In reality, all the government did was move the gangs out into a new area, one that was actually a decent market place for the drug sales given the college. Even worse, according to some of the students that had been in the class, many of the kids from those families would get money from the government to go to college, but never would actually attend classes. And the money never went toward the books and class supplies like it was supposed to.

Frustration at this situation momentarily pushed away the feelings she had toward everything else that had been going on in recent days, mostly because of the money she had spent on that first year of college. No one had helped her.

And no one will if you start going again.

Will I go again?

She considered this for several minutes as she maneuvered her car back through the twisty streets of DeKalb, her mind eventually settling on the 'wait and see' approach since she had no idea what the outcome of her current path would be. At the moment things seemed to be working, but that didn't mean they would continue to do so. Plus she had another factor to work into the equation now, one that she was going to focus on a bit.

Hopefully a solution would present itself.

Hopefully –

Her phone buzzed.

She looked down at the name on the screen and smiled.

A moment later, she pulled her car into her parking spot outside of her apartment and read the message, her mind taking a moment to think up a reply.

Once that was taken care of she stepped out of her car and headed into her place, her mind hoping she would have a decent wireless connection today and that she would be able to use it find out information about the guy upstairs.

Too bad Dominick isn't around still.

The boy had been a computer wiz and could have found out everything there was to know about him.

But he had to go.

Of this, there was no question. Leaving him alive would have been a mistake.

But so soon?

This thought did leave room for some speculation. Had she known she might need his expertise again then leaving him alive might have been a good idea? At the same time the longer he was left alive the greater the chances were that he would spill something about what he had done for her, or, accidentally leave a trail pointing toward her.

And you would have needed to keep him interested.

Of everything, that would have been the most difficult because she had not really been attracted to him at all. Sure, she had thought it cool that he had ejaculated upon his death, but that had been more of a 'wow, that was unexpected' moment than a 'this guy was great' moment.

Her phone buzzed a second time.

Once again, she smiled.

Sadness followed.

You have no choice, she reminded herself. *It has to be done.*

I know, another part of her mind said, the part that was mourning some of the events to come.

Why did life always have to get so complicated?

Nothing was ever simple.

All she wanted to do was make Kimberly pay for what she had done; make her pay for ruining one of the happiest moments of her life. While a bit tricky due to the desire to get away with everything, it still should have been pretty straightforward. All she had to do was follow the plan she had laid out, one that had left room for some alternative steps just in case certain things didn't pan out the way she had hoped they would.

But you didn't plan for this.

Hell, she hadn't even considered anything like this happening. Who would have? It was unreal. It was –

Don't dwell on it!

Easier said than done!

Thankfully, she had some work to do, which would be a bit of a distraction. If, that was, the wireless from the college reached her. Most of the time it did, but sometimes it didn't. Whenever this happened she was forced to head out into areas that had unsecured wireless connections. Not difficult to find, but still a pain since she preferred doing everything from the comfort of her own home.

Home?

The word brought about some dismay because this crappy little place was not what she had envisioned herself living in as a child. Nope. And unlike most children, her dreams of her future hadn't been unrealistic fantasies that only occurred to Disney characters. Everything had been simple and down to earth; she would grow up, fall in love with a charming man, get married, have kids and live in a house with a yard perfect for the children and whatever pets they owned to play in.

Instead . . .

She looked around at the dump she was in, the dump that didn't even have all its windows because the last tenant had ripped out the air conditioner rather than taking the time to un-screw it, which had shattered the window. Not that she would have ever used the window, not when it simply looked out at a gravel driveway and dumpster. Still, it would have been nice to have the option to view such things if she wanted.

All because some idiot was in a hurry and because the landlord is too cheap to fix anything.

But at least you talked the rent down because of it.

This latter was a plus, especially since money had grown tight. What had once been a pretty impressive savings account was now in danger of drawing fees due to the lack of money within. College was to blame. Not just the classes, but every-thing that encompassed one's life when going to school, which was probably why her family had refused to pay for it.

'A waste of time,' her father had said.

'And money,' his girlfriend had added.

'And money,' her father had agreed with a nod. He then

added, *'It's better to find a job and stick with it until you rise to the top.'*

'And then get fired when the company moves to Mexico?' she had said, the words leaving before she could contemplate the wisdom of such a statement.

Unpleasant memories followed, not because she had taken a beating that night or anything – her father wasn't the type to ever lay a hand on her in that way – but because after the argument that took place, her father had agreed with the girlfriend that they should kick her out for a few days so she could see what living like a bum would be like. How this would teach her anything was lost on her, but since the girlfriend thought it was a good idea her father had as well, thus she had been forced to leave. Adding to the dilemma of what she would do was that she knew her mother wouldn't take her in, not after she had made it clear all those years earlier that she never wanted to see her daughter again after she had chosen to live with her father after the divorce. Nature had decided to fuck with her that night as well by drenching her in rain, almost as if it remembered a statement she had once made about how being homeless wouldn't be bad during the summer months.

Distracted by her memories, she failed to realize that her computer had not just finished opening but had also automatically connected to the NIU wireless network. Once she did finally notice this she shifted her focus from those horrible days on the streets back to the present and typed the upstairs guy's name into Google.

Surprise at the sheer number of hits arrived.

Apparently the guy was a writer, and one that was doing pretty well given the amount of talk that seemed to be taking place all over the web.

One link brought her to his Amazon page where all his books were listed.

She scrolled through them, an unplaced recognition entering her mind.

Bookstore? she asked herself while trying to place them, her mind thinking that maybe some of his paperbacks had been on a stand or something when she entered one day.

Though plausible, the connection didn't seem correct. Dwelling on it wasn't going to get her anywhere, however, so she continued to follow links. She also sent him a friend request on Facebook, a message about enjoying his books accompanying it.

On a whim, she checked his friends list to see if he was friends with Kimberly. Her profile didn't appear anywhere. After that, she did a search of Kimberly's profile. Sadly, everything on it but her profile picture was blocked.

Friend request her as well?

The temptation was strong, but in the end she decided against it due to the connection factor and the possibility that the police might grow interested in her friends list at some point.

And what about the writer's profile? a part of her mind taunted her. *Won't they grow interested in that as well?*

Unlikely, she countered. *He's a public figure who is bound to have a lot of random friend requests.*

No other comments arrived.

Not wanting to be sucked into Facebook, she backed out until she was once again on the Google results page. While continuing with those results she opened a second window to check some of the dating site profiles she had just to see if any men would be paying Kimberly a visit in the near future. As usual, dozens of requests had been made to see her, and, on the sites that were setup like Facebook, friend requests were waiting.

She accepted them all and then, after some debate, went ahead and gave them Kimberly's address.

4

It was everything Kimberly could do not to check her phone during her first class, the sound of its buzz having reached her ears halfway through the opening lecture.

Was it Bill? Did something happen? Did he find out information on the girl? Or is it Kyle trying to get back together with you? What if it is Bill telling you that Kyle came by the house and wouldn't leave?

On and on the questions went, their frequency overwhelming

her to the point where the professor's lecture was barely audible.

Stick it out she did, however, and then, once the class was over, quickly checked her phone while everyone else was filtering toward the exits.

It was from Bill.

I THINK I'VE FOUND HER.

That was it.

REALLY? HOW? she asked and then grabbed her things to leave.

Her phone buzzed.

FACEBOOK, was his reply.

Typing and walking wasn't going to work given the sheer volume of people crowding the hallway, so she waited until she found a spot where she could stop without becoming a road-block to everyone else. Not that she would be the only one caus-ing such a blockage if she stopped. It was amazing how clueless many of these people were. Still, she wouldn't allow herself to do such a thing.

HOW? she asked. WE SEARCHED HER NAME THE OTHER DAY.

A few minutes passed.

EASY. I SEARCHED HER FATHER'S NAME AND SHE WAS LISTED AS HIS DAUGHTER.

BUT HE'S DEAD.

GUESS NO ONE BOTHERED TO TAKE DOWN HIS PRO-FILE.

Huh, her mind muttered. She had never before thought about what would happen to her profile if she died.

She shifted her thoughts back to the daughter and asked, DID YOU FIND OUT WHERE SHE LIVES?

NOT YET. BUT I KNOW WHERE THE FATHER LIVED. WE COULD GO ASK AROUND AND SEE IF WE CAN LEARN ANYTHING.

Kimberly thought about that and started to type up a message voicing her doubt that anyone would talk to them when the phone buzzed again.

Keep typing and send this, or check and see what else he said? It was moments like this that she wished she could view a message while typing one up with this phone.

Are there phones that allow that? she wondered.

The question faded without an answer as she ended her message and checked his newest one.

HIS PROFILE WAS COMPLETELY PUBLIC.

Gah, you could have kept typing.

DO YOU REALLY THINK PEOPLE WILL TALK TO US? she asked.

WON'T KNOW UNTIL WE TRY.

He has a point.

OKAY. A second later she added. WHERE DOES HE LIVE? GENOA.

WHERE'S THAT? She had heard of it before, but had never really bothered to see where the town was located.

LIKE FIFTEEN MINUTES NORTH OF HERE. STRAIGHT UP 23.

Oh, that's not too bad. Even if the trip proved to be fruitless, at least they wouldn't have wasted too much time driving back and forth.

IF THAT'S ALL THEN WE COULD GO BETWEEN MY CLASSES, she said. Hell, she wouldn't mind being late to her next class if it meant finding out where this bitch lived and confronting her.

BETTER TO WAIT UNTIL AFTER YOUR CLASS, Bill wrote. LESS CHANCE PEOPLE WILL BE AT WORK WHEN WE RING DOORBELLS.

Kimberly hadn't thought about that.

Another message arrived.

IN THE MEANTIME, I'M GOING TO ATTEMPT TO FRIEND HER AND SEE WHAT HAPPENS. DOUBT SHE WILL ACCEPT, BUT YOU NEVER KNOW.

DO YOU HAVE A FACE PIC AS YOUR PROFILE IMAGE? Kimberly asked.

WHY? was his reply.

CHANGE IT SO SHE DOESN'T RECOGNIZE YOU WHEN THE FRIEND REQUEST ARRIVES.

OH, GOOD IDEA.

Satisfaction arrived. Still, she doubted his attempt would work. She also doubted she would be able to focus in her next class, not when the possibility of confronting the girl seemed within their reach.

And if this doesn't work, give her information to the police.

Kimberly shook her head, not because it was a bad idea, but because she knew she should have contacted them as soon as she knew the name and suspected the daughter of being the one behind everything.

No time like the present.

She stared at her phone while thinking about this, fingers ready to make the call, but then decided to wait. The reason for this was simple. She knew they would want to talk to her face to face, which meant she would probably have to miss her class, and while she wouldn't mind doing that, she didn't think a few hours would make much of a difference.

You shouldn't put this off, she told herself. *You've already done that enough.*

The police lady had told her to contact them if anything else happened, which, obviously, stuff had.

You were assaulted too.

But you were chasing her.

After she broke into the garage.

Kimberly sighed.

Once she called she was going to be in for a lecture, of this she was certain.

And you deserve it for being an idiot.

It's Bill's fault.

Though this last part made her feel better, she knew it wasn't really a good excuse. In fact, giving in to his wishes on this had been ridiculous; another sign that she was still a pushover despite the stance she had made with Kevin.

But would they draw the same conclusions you and Bill have? Is there enough evidence to connect the daughter to this?

Who else could it be?

Who else would send you to the motel room where that guy was killed?

She looked around at all the other college students while thinking about this, a sense of envy at how 'normal' their current life probably was developing within her. Chances were none of them had a stalker tormenting them, nor did they have to frequently relive the horrible images of a miscarriage or the knowledge that they had accidentally killed their own cat during that moment of horror. None of them lived below a writer who had set up a fake blog in order to sell porn and dating site subscriptions. None of them . . .

On and on it went, her mind coming up with dozens upon dozens of things that these students didn't have to experience. It would have continued too if she didn't spot a young lady walking to class while carrying an oxygen pack over her shoulder, one who stopped every ten feet or so to catch her breath. Seeing that put an end to the silent 'feel sorry for me' rant and spurred her onward toward her next class, one that wouldn't be starting for a while still. Once located she would go get some lunch, her mind knowing that eating was a must because the last thing she wanted was for her stomach to start rumbling in class.

In her head, the debate on calling the police began once again, and this time around, she actually thought long and hard about skipping class so that she could fill them in on everything that had happened since the last visit.

5

Two hours. That was the amount of time Bill managed before casually checking some of the webmaster programs he still belonged with to see what kind of new promo material they were offering for people like him to advertise the sites with. It was just supposed to be a quick peek; a reward for locating the address of Mr. Moore and, potentially, his daughter, but quickly turned into an all out download frenzy. Thirty promo videos later he went ahead and pulled out his old porn laptop, the desire to see what had been added to all the free 'spyware and virus ridden' sites too much to resist.

And it's not like this is going to turn into an everyday thing, he told himself. *Not when she will probably say no to you two sharing the connection.*

But what if she says yes?

Bill thought about this while the old laptop was booting up, its progress slow due to some of the viruses that probably roamed it, and decided he would worry about that if it became a reality. In the meantime, he was going to enjoy the time he had with the web while waiting for Kimberly to come home so they could go check out the address and see if they couldn't get someone to share with them where Emily Moore currently lived.

7

Mark tried getting in touch with Amy after his first class ended, but never got a reply to his text, which asked if she wanted to do lunch with him. Naturally, concern followed, but then faded as he realized she might be in her own class and couldn't reply. That was the problem with not having her schedule. He didn't know at what points during the day she was free.

And what if your text made her phone ring in the middle of class?

He knew such an outcome wouldn't really be his fault, not when it was her responsibility to silence her phone so things like that didn't happen, but still didn't like the idea that his actions could have potentially caused her embarrassment. He also didn't like the dilemma he now faced due to the lack of a response and knowledge about her schedule, one that focused on whether or not he should go ahead and grab some lunch himself or wait and see if she did reply in the near future. Again, finishing a meal moments before she replied with a 'yes, let's grab lunch' wouldn't be his fault, especially since he had asked her what her class schedule was, but it would be disappointing. After all, the reason he was asking if she wanted to have lunch was because he wanted to have lunch with her. The actual eating of a meal wasn't important beyond the fact that it would provide some needed sustenance.

Wait a little longer and see if she replies, his mind suggested. He did have a decent chunk of time before the next class, so it wasn't like he was in any kind of rush. Also, given the hour, any place he went would probably be packed, so waiting a bit just to let the rush die down wasn't a bad idea.

You could also go see if she's home.

The house she lived in wasn't far. He could actually see if from the main area of campus. And if she wasn't home he could just cut over to Tom and Jerry's again and grab something.

And if she asks why you walked over here, you could just say you thought her phone might be dead.

Such a gesture could be interpreted in two ways. One: that he was sweet for double checking and seeing if she wanted to get some lunch before going by himself. Two: he was too needy, had a habit of over thinking things, and would probably constantly harass her anytime she didn't reply to a message.

Throw in a third option, one that combines both of those.

It took some time, but in the end he decided that walking to her place to ask in person if she wanted to do lunch was going a bit too far. Walking to her place, however, wasn't. He still did that, but only because it was on the way to Tom and Jerry's. Plus, he was curious on whether or not her car was at the house she lived in. It was this curiosity that actually sealed the deal on his going to Tom and Jerry's, because, truth be told, he didn't really feel like eating there again, not if it was just him. At the same time he couldn't shake that curiosity and knew that if he did get caught walking by her place (caught as in 'hey, what are you doing here?' or, if she saw him and asked him later why he had been outside her place) he could always claim the 'I was simply going to Tom and Jerry's for lunch' excuse. He would even have a receipt to show her.

And if her car is there?

The temptation to head up to her apartment and find out if she wanted to go to lunch would be strong.

Maybe you should hold off on that.

He had already started walking toward her place when this thought hit and quickly halted himself. Indecision gripped him. He didn't know what to do. The curiosity on whether or not she was home was huge, as was his desire to get a reply to his inquiry about lunch. The fear of looking like a creep was present as well, however, and was something he didn't want to instill in her.

Probably best to hold off.

Probably best to —

His phone buzzed.

Excitement echoed throughout his body as he looked at his phone. Disappointment followed. Amy couldn't do lunch today.

Another text arrived.

BUT COME ON BY AFTER CLASS.

He smiled. I WILL.

AND CHECK YOUR FACEBOOK. YOU MIGHT HAVE A FRIEND REQUEST WAITING.

OH REALLY! I WONDER WHO THAT COULD BE FROM?

HMMM, I WONDER :)

Feeling good, Mark headed toward the computer lab so he could log onto Facebook to accept her friend request and see what her profile was like, his thoughts on eating lunch temporarily put on hold.

8

Bill was surprised by Kimberly's early return and wondered if something had happened between her classes. Concerned, he considered going downstairs to ask, but then held back and sent a text instead.

YOU'RE BACK EARLY. IS EVERYTHING OKAY?

Several minutes passed before a reply came, one that simple read: YOU SHOULD COME DOWN.

Go figure, he said to himself and started toward the stairway door.

Hesitation hit.

Having spent the last two hours looking at and downloading porn he probably wasn't in the best state for social interaction, especially with the pre-cum soaked underwear he was currently wearing.

A quick trip to the dresser helped the situation a bit, though he still felt somewhat soiled. Nothing short of a shower would rectify that, however, one that would see him first releasing the sexual build up that currently plagued him, followed by a good scrubbing away of the fluids that would be clinging to him. Given the trip Kimberly and he were scheduled to take later on, this was something he had planned on taking care of before her return home from class, but now . . . well, he would just have to risk going down there in his current state.

9

"I want to go to the police and tell them everything that has happened," Kimberly said.

"Oh, um . . . okay," Bill said.

This reply caught her off guard. She had been expecting some protest from him; maybe even a well thought up reason why they shouldn't go, one that would nearly persuade her to rethink the decision.

"And by everything I mean everything," she added. "Including your website and how we think it's connected."

He didn't reply to that right away.

Kimberly waited.

Finally, he nodded.

"You're okay with that?" Kimberly asked.

"It's not really a matter of me being okay with it," Bill said. "It's more I've come to terms with the realization that the police would know about it eventually."

Kimberly expected more, a 'but, I also think . . .' of some kind that would tell her how fruitless going to the police would be.

Nothing else followed.

"You said you know where the police station is?" Kimberly questioned.

"Yeah, it's right next to the library. You want to go there or have them come here?"

"Which do you think is better?"

He shrugged.

"I suppose if they come here they could dust for prints on the lights that she destroyed," Kimberly added after some thought.

"Maybe? Some time has passed, so I don't know if they would be able to get anything, plus I'm guessing she wore gloves, but . . ." he shrugged again ". . . I'm no expert."

Should have called them that night, Kimberly scolded herself. *And every other time something happened.*

Kicking herself over this wouldn't change anything, however, so she attempted to look beyond it. She also knew that blaming Bill, though easy to do, wasn't really a good way of nullifying her own responsibility for not calling the police. She was a big girl and should have made the decision herself.

"You know, they probably won't want us looking into things ourselves," Bill said.

"Yeah, but that wouldn't be necessary if the police were doing it."

"True, but only if they are actually following up on the information we give them."

"Why wouldn't they?"

"It's hard to say. All I know is that sometimes things that seem pretty straightforward to people like us, aren't as straightforward when the law is concerned given all the investigative protocol they have to follow."

Kimberly didn't know how to reply to this.

"Chances are good they may look at everything, make a note of it all, and then simply tell us that we will just have to wait and see what else happens, just like the officer did the other night."

Kimberly shook her head. "I find it really hard to believe that they would say that after everything that has happened. With all the information we give them they will have to do something."

"Maybe," he said again. "Let me just tell you, when I was in grade school our garage was broken into and a lot of stuff was taken. Something was also left behind, an employee name tag. My mother found it that morning before the police showed up and pointed it out to them, yet they never followed up on it and later when confronted about this simply said that the nametag alone wasn't enough for them to go question the person."

"I don't buy that for a second," Kimberly said. Oddly enough, she was pretty sure he was telling the truth about this, but she wouldn't admit to that, not when it would help his argument about going to the police.

"Nothing I can do to prove it to you, but it happened," he said. "Anyway, I'm just sharing my thoughts on this with you. If you want to go to the police I will go with and help explain everything that has happened."

"That's what I want to do."

"Okay then, let's go do it." He paused and looked down at himself. "Let me just go change first."

Kimberly nodded and then went about collecting everything they would need for the trip to the police station. After that, while still waiting for Bill, she started to go over the timeline of events, starting with the lingerie she had gotten earlier in the month.

You'll have to tell them about uploading Kyle's picture to the dating site, she warned herself.

Or will I?

Just telling them she had created a profile and gotten in touch with the NIU_Nikki girl would probably be enough.

Yet you're expecting Bill to share everything he did.

That's because he's responsible.

Her little dating site activity couldn't even compare to what he had done.

A thought struck.

"Hey Bill," she called up.

"Yeah?"

"Do you think I should contact Mark and have him come with us?"

"Who?"

"The guy with the flowers."

"Oh, I don't know. What do you think?"

She sighed. She had been hoping he would make the decision. "I guess I'll give him a call and find out where he is and what his thoughts on this are."

Bill appeared at the top of the stairs. "Sounds good to me."

10

Friend request accepted, Mark began going through Amy's photo albums, his curiosity on what her life was like momentarily pushing aside his desire for lunch.

Has she looked at mine?

His profile didn't have many restrictions so if she wanted she could have spent quite a bit of time exploring things, her eyes getting to see much of his existence thanks to his mother having uploaded and tagged him in just about every picture she had ever taken. The same could not be said about Amy's profile. Few pictures had been uploaded and those that were looked mostly like they had been self-shot. In the ones that did show other people, no tags had been added, which, naturally, left him wondering quite a bit on who the other people were – especially in one that showed her with her arms around an older gentleman.

Her father?

The question hung in the air for several seconds, an odd anxiety building as the likelihood of his mind's suggestion crumbled. It was the way Amy was holding the man and the look of happiness on her face that did it. This was not a father / daughter picture.

Fortunately the picture had been uploaded several months earlier, thus it obviously wasn't someone he needed to worry about. Unfortunately, he knew the question on who the man was would be hard to dismiss and that at some point he would like to know.

You want to know if there is a lingering threat.

You want to know if –

His phone began to vibrate.

Hope that it was Amy took over his thoughts; a scenario of her having decided lunch would be a good idea playing out before his mind.

Kimberly.

Surprised, he quietly answered the call while exiting the computer lab, guilt at not learning anything that would really help
the poor girl building.

"Hey, we think we might know who the Nikki girl is and
were going to go to the police," Kimberly said after an introduc-
tory reply to his greeting.

"Really?" Mark asked. "That's great."

"Yeah," Kimberly agreed. "Anyhow, we were thinking it
might be a good idea if you came along as well so you could tell
them about how she kept trying to make you think I was the girl
you were talking with."

"Oh . . . um . . ." this completely caught him off guard. "I
suppose that makes sense."

"Great, are you free right now?"

"Kind of . . . um . . . how long will this take? I have another
class this afternoon and then . . ." he decided to leave out his
plans on getting together with Amy.

"It shouldn't take long and if you want you could just meet us
there. That way you can leave if need be."

Mark thought about this for a few seconds and then agreed.
"Do you have the address?"

"Yeah, one second." In the background he heard someone
telling her the location, which she repeated to him. "You know
where that is?"

"I think so. Do you want to meet in the parking lot or something so that we all go in together?" He crossed his fingers with
this one, the idea of having to walk into a police station on his
own somewhat frightening.

"Yeah, that works."

"Okay, I'll leave right now."

"Excellent. See you soon."

"Yep."

Call ended, Mark started heading toward the building exit,
but then realized he had left the computer logged on Facebook to
take the call and quickly returned to it to sign out. Once that was
taken care of, he headed to his car, his mind going over everything that had occurred with Nikki so he could give valuable

information to the authorities.

11

NIU_Nikki was halfway out the door, a desire to get some food having gotten the better of her, when the connection clicked into place and knocked all thoughts of getting some lunch from her mind. Two minutes later, once she had gotten everything pulled up again, the connection was verified. The pictures that Kimberly had used on her blog to lure in men had been taken in the writer's apartment.

But why?

And what does it mean?

Several possibilities arrived, the most logical of which dealt with the fact that Kimberly was a whore and therefore would have been unable to resist starting up a sexual relationship with a guy living above her. What didn't seem logical was why he would have helped her with the pictures? Didn't he know it was so she could lure in other men to fuck her? Would he be okay with that?

Maybe he had no choice?

She could easily see Kimberly being the type of girl who would pretty much tell a guy that he was just a fuck toy and that if he wanted a one on one relationship he had better look elsewhere. Guys that just wanted sex would probably be fine with this, though they might still have a hint of jealousy present about the other men. Guys that weren't . . . well, she wasn't really sure how they would react. Some might still go for it in hopes that she would fall in love with them and end her whorish ways (unlikely, yet something she could see some men deceiving themselves with), and others might just look elsewhere.

Not Professor Moore.

Had he even hesitated in his answer?

She contemplated this for a while, but then realized it didn't even matter because he had obviously made the decision to push her away while pursuing Nikki.

An anger laced sadness followed.

Did he ever even really love me like he said he did or was it all a ploy to get under my skirt?

No answer arrived, nor would one.

And it's your fault.

If she hadn't freaked out and tried to fix things the entire series of events that had unfolded may have taken a different route. Instead, she had tried to pit Nikki up against his wife, her hope being the two would cause so much drama that he would just say 'fuck you' to both of them and come back to her.

Well, not come back to her because he had never left her, but shown more interest in her like he had in the beginning before Nikki had tried to lure him away.

12

The lecture Kimberly had been expecting from whatever police officer they were assigned never took place. Instead, the younger looking officer listened intently to everything that was told to him while taking notes, his eyes occasionally looking at the photographs Kimberly had brought in.

"Okay, so, the theory is that your interaction with Mr. Moore online caused his wife to snap and murder him. You then feel that since the mother had a few screws loose the daughter probably does as well and now is trying to seek revenge against the girl who she feels is responsible, which she believes to be you." He pointed to Kimberly. "And to achieve some of this she hijacked this Nikki persona you created – " he pointed at Bill " – so that she could lure men like you – " he shifted the finger toward Mark " – to the house to torment you." The finger returned to Kimberly.

"Yes," Kimberly said.

"Hmm." The officer put the finger to his lips. "I have to admit, it all does come together nicely."

But . . . Kimberly waited.

"What makes you think future harm is intended?"

Kimberly looked at Bill, who looked back and her. He then turned to the officer and asked, "You don't think she is going to try and hurt her?"

The officer shook his head. "I didn't say that. I'm just looking for something solid to combat that argument. Has a direct threat been made?"

Kimberly shook her head.

"There has been property damage, though," Bill said. "She cut the motion sensor lights."

"Yes, though as I'm sure you are aware one could easily argue that wasn't her." He held up a finger and quickly added, "I'm not saying that myself, but it can be argued."

"Yeah," Bill muttered.

"Is there anything you can do?" Kimberly asked.

"Oh yes. First things first we will contact the sites where this profile is being used and find out what we can about the user. We will then go speak with the party involved in the deception and make it known that this all has to stop."

"Is that it?"

"It depends. Several legal advances have been made in recent years to help with situations like this. There's no question you are being harassed and that an unauthorized surveillance of your life is taking place, which can help push this into the stalker category. The difficult part is proving the intent to cause harm. If we can do that then the legal consequences for this individual's actions become harsher."

An odd mix of disappointment and optimism filled Kimberly. Her hope had been that coming here to the police would have put a stop to things. Doubt that such an instant outcome would occur had been present, but somewhat ignorable. Now she had to accept that it would take time.

"In the meantime do your best not to provoke things, and keep a record of everything that occurs. Also, make sure you call us whenever anything happens, even if the incident seems unworthy of any attention. Okay?"

Kimberly nodded.

"Anything else you can think to add?" the officer asked.

Kimberly and Bill exchanged glances. She then looked at Mark who shook his head. "Guess not."

"Very well then." The officer stood up and withdrew three cards from a holder on the desk. "If you need anything or have any questions please don't hesitate to call me. I will also do my best to keep you updated on what we learn."

Kimberly gave him a weak smile.

"I know from where you are this all probably looks a little hopeless, but believe me; the information the three of you have given will go a long way in helping put an end to this. It just will take a little bit of time."

Kimberly nodded. "Thanks."

He turned to Mark. "Make sure to let your girlfriend know to contact us as well if she keeps getting messages. In fact, give her a card as well and have her call me as soon as possible just so she can fill me in on what has happened up until this point. In a case like this every little bit is important."

Mark took the card. "I will."

Two minutes later the three were standing in the parking lot, an uncomfortable silence hovering.

"So," Mark finally said while looking at Bill. "I was talking to you all that time."

Bill didn't seem to know how to reply to this and simply shrugged.

Mark shook his head. "I don't even know what to say. Do you have any idea how much heartache you caused me?"

Again, Bill didn't say anything.

"I sat in a motel room for six hours waiting for Nikki, my mind unable to do anything but contemplate the growing fear that I was being stood up again."

"I really don't know what to tell you," Bill said.

"I see." He turned to Kimberly. "I really hope everything works out okay with all this. Keep me posted."

"I will."

"And again, I apologize in advance for the boxes you will be getting. I completely freaked out when she threatened to tell Amy that I had been cheating on her."

"It's okay. I'm just glad I'll know who they all came from. Sorry you had to spend money like that though."

"Hey, not your fault." He shifted a glance at Bill. "Anyway, I gotta run. If I hurry I might be able to eat a quick snack before my next class starts."

With that, he got into his car and drove off.

Kimberly turned and glared at Bill.

"What?" he asked after a second. "I didn't force him to keep talking with Nikki online."

"Still – " she started, but then decided she didn't want to get into anything. "Never mind. What do we do now?"

"You still want to go check out the father's place and see if we can find out where the girl lives?" Bill asked.

"Do you really think that's a good idea?"

He shrugged. "It's an idea, that's all. There's no telling how long the police are going to be trying to locate her and in the meantime we might be able to confront her."

Kimberly was torn. On the one hand, it seemed like a good idea to simply let the police take over on this, but on the other, she liked the idea of coming face to face with the girl and telling her to stop.

"Or at the very least we can gather some information that might help them."

"Okay," Kimberly said. "Let's see what we can find out."

"Great." He pulled out a sheet of paper. "Here are the directions."

"I don't want to rush into confronting the daughter though, if we do find out where she lives." Kimberly waited a second for a reply and when none came asked, "Okay?"

"No problem. We'd want to think on that a bit anyway." He got into the passenger side of the car.

Kimberly followed suit and got behind the wheel. "By the way, when will your car be fixed?"

"Tomorrow morning. Would have been sooner but I guess some line beneath the engine tore." He tossed his arms up in an 'I don't know' gesture. "Then again, they could just be saying that so they can milk more money out of the insurance company."

"Hmm, maybe," Kimberly said, though she doubted things

like that really happened.

"Do you have class tomorrow?"

"Yeah, but I can swing you by the place on the way if you need me too."

"That would be great. Thanks."

"No problem." She pulled the car to the parking lot exit. "Okay, which way."

Bill looked down at the directions and said, "Take a right and then another right at the light."

13

Mark took a seat in the middle of the classroom auditorium several minutes before his class started and spent the waiting moments thinking about the writer guy. It all made perfect sense now. The website and profile that had seemed like it had been designed to drive traffic to the Adult Friend Finder site had been there to do just that, only it hadn't been created by the site itself.

He shook his head.

Never in the million years would he have figured individuals could make money by driving traffic to the site. Sure, he knew that places could make money from putting up ads, but actually taking in a percentage of the sign up fee, that was new to him.

It was clever too and helped explain why there were always so many ads for porn sites on other porn sites. In the past he had just assumed upfront payments were being made, but now it seemed that they were all probably getting a cut of the profits, which meant everyone was working hard to promote each other's sites.

Hell, you could probably set something like that up yourself and bring in a little extra cash. You could –

He cut himself off, his mind not liking the idea that he would do to someone else what had just happened to him, or the fact that he had actually given it some consideration.

Nope. He would never go that far.

Still, the possibility of making money from just directing people to porn sites was there. He could simply make a page that did nothing but review those sites. People would come to his site to see what sites were the best and then would follow the links to those sites.

His phone buzzed.

Amy?

Nope.

His mother wanted to know when he would be back.

GOING TO BE HANGING OUT HERE WITH SOME FRIENDS TONIGHT. NOT SURE WHEN I WILL BE BACK.

The MESSAGE SENT note appeared just as his class started, the female professor walking in and introducing herself.

Mark tucked the phone away and settled in to listen, his attempts at focusing on what was being said constantly usurped by the thoughts of Amy and what they would be doing later.

14

NIU_Nikki drove by the house twice in an attempt to see if anyone was home, but couldn't determine an answer. Adding to her uncertainty was the knowledge that the writer's car would not be there either way, thus its current absence couldn't really lend any weight toward coming to a conclusion.

A small bit of fear was present as well. In recent visits to the house and Steak and Shake, bad things had happened. Nothing but luck had kept her from being exposed during those horrible moments -- luck and some quick thinking.

She drove by a third time and then decided to pull around the block, park and investigate things on foot.

But why?

No answer followed, mostly because she didn't really have one; her current reason for surveillance nothing more than an attempt at trying to figure out a plan of action.

Memories surfaced.

The last time she had gone this route had been last spring when she had grown convinced that Professor Moore was involved with someone else. The theory, and the growing panic it instilled, had come about due to the lack of replies to the texts she sent him following her sudden awareness of how infrequently they were seeing each other. In the beginning, she had stayed with him every couple of nights, his arms wrapped around her as they slept together in the nice comfortable bed. When not together, he had always responded to the messages she sent, ones that often told him how much she loved him, which would then receive replies from him stating his own love for her. For several weeks she had enjoyed the relationship, her mind never feeling more at ease with the world. And then it started to crumble, first with a cutback in visits and then in the replies to her texts. Nothing was ever said to her, though. Adding to the confusion was that she still did get to see him occasionally and he did still reply from time to time. Had both of those things simply ended, she would have known something was wrong. Instead, she had to guess, which wasn't good because her mind never failed to dwell upon the worst possible scenario.

And then she had made the mistake of asking him, which had led to their first real argument, all because she mentioned that it seemed like he was losing interest in her. Actually, mentioning that had just been the fuel, his reply that he was busy with schoolwork, teaching, and his possible divorce the spark that ignited things. Oddly enough, they had then spent a wonderful night together once things had calmed down, and during that time he had told her not to worry so much. She agreed. By that time the next day, however, the worry was back, a lack of a reply to her text about what they had talked about starting it up. Several more messages were sent that day, but no replies ever came. On and on this went until her mind could focus on nothing else, her fear of what she was sure was happening overwhelming her to the point where she couldn't eat, sleep or go to class – the last of which never sparked any messages of concern from him.

And then she went to his house.

It was a moment she would never forget, both because it brought to life the fears she had been contemplating, and led to a decision she would always regret.

Thinking about it now brought tears to her eyes.

Letting herself into his place was easy, her ear having picked up upon the whereabouts of a hide-a-key one day as she approached his office at the school and overheard him talking to his daughter on the phone. *"Just please don't tell your mother where it is,"* he had urged. *"You know how crazy she can get at times."*

Crazy was right.

NIU_Nikki had once been at the house when the wife came by and stood outside the front door demanding that he remove her friends from his own Facebook friends list. *"I don't want you talking to them and spreading rumors about me!"* she had shouted over and over again, fists punctuating each word with a hard *THUNK!* upon the wood. *"You hear me! I'll call the police if you don't stop talking to them and making them un-friend me!"*

"I haven't messaged anyone but you on Facebook for a year," he whispered to her as they stood within the hallway. *"Her friends un-friend her because she is crazy and always causes drama."*

NIU_Nikki hadn't really known what to say to that and simply said, *"Maybe you should call the police?"*

"I would, but then you would have to get involved as well and that wouldn't look good."

At the time she hadn't understood what he had fully meant by it not looking good, and simply assumed he thought the police would side with the wife if they found out he had a young lady there. Later, once he started to become distant from her, a new theory appeared. He didn't want anyone to know about her because he never wanted a real relationship with her, just a sexual one that could be discarded quickly.

No, he wouldn't do that, an optimistic part of her brain insisted. *He just is keeping you secret until his divorce is final.*

The other part of her brain, the part that always seemed to understand situations better, didn't issue a rebuttal, mostly because one wasn't needed. The more she thought about things, the more she would realize the truth of the situation.

It was that constant thought that led her to the home office of Professor Moore, one where the two of them had frequently engaged in his role-play fantasies of what an innocent little schoolgirl like her would do to get a passing grade in his class.

I wish I could go back to that moment, she had thought to herself while logging into his computer. *I wish I could be kneeling beneath the desk once again with his cock in my mouth. I wish . . .* on and on the wishes had gone until she opened up his instant messenger and found what she had feared. Nothing before or since had ever caused her so much heartache. It was as if a black hole had opened inside of her and sucked every ounce of happiness from within. Nothing but hurt registered as she read the statements that had been made between him and Nikki, statements that talked about all the fun times that lay ahead and how, given her pictures and stories he could tell she would be the best partner he ever had.

A police car drove past as she sat there thinking about that moment, the officer giving her a good look before pulling his car to a stop in front of hers.

Panic set in.

She wiped the tears from her eyes and rolled the window down as he approached.

"Everything okay, ma'am?" he asked.

"Yeah," she said and wiped her eyes again, voice somehow calm despite the panic she felt.

"You sure?"

"Uh-huh." She nodded. "My boyfriend just broke up with me, that's all." Tears burst free as she said this, the memories of Mr. Moore betrayal helping bring them about.

"I'm sorry to hear that," the officer said. Then, unexpectedly, "May I please see your driver's license and registration."

"Oh, um . . ." she fumbled around inside her purse, which was on the seat next to her, and pulled her license free ". . . here is this." It took another minute to find the registration.

"I'll be right back."

She waited, concern growing.

If they knew anything about what you've done they would have come for you already, she said to herself. Sadly, it did little to distill the panic. Nothing short of getting her license and registration back and being told to have a good day would.

Several minutes passed before the officer returned.

"Here you are Ms. Baker. Hope the rest of your day goes a little better."

"Thank you," she said and returned the items to her purse, a thought about how good it was that she hadn't been lurking around Kimberly's place entering her head.

But is that why the officer was patrolling the area?

Have the police gotten involved?

Had the situation been reversed she knew she would have called the police fairly quickly. At the same time, she understood that many people often hesitated to bring the police in, an odd fear of law enforcement usually having been instilled since birth. It was something Professor Moore had actually taught the class during one of his lectures, his theory being that a parent's frequent concern and anxiety whenever they saw a radar patrol car while driving would help breed an all-encompassing fear of police in the children who were present.

Whether or not the theory was true was something she didn't know, but it made sense.

15

"Are you sure this is the place?" Kimberly asked.

"According to the address on Facebook it is," Bill said, his mind harboring the same doubt that he heard in Kimberly's voice.

"Then someone must be taking care of things, because there is no way this has sat empty since May."

Bill nodded, his eyes having noted the wheel impressions from a recently used lawnmower upon pulling up. All the bushes had been trimmed as well, and the landscaping around the front kept clean.

"You don't think someone moved in, do you?"

"I didn't even really consider that," Bill admitted and then wondered what the process for selling a house after a murder was. "But it sure looks like – "

"Like what?"

Shit, could it really have been that easy? he asked himself. *Could she have been living here all along?*

He thought about all the time he had spent on the computer that morning attempting to figure out a way of locating the daughter. Most of this search had occurred after he had located the father's address, yet never once had he even thought about the probability that the house had been handed down to the next of kin.

"Wait here a second," Bill said and started to open the door.

"Woah, hold up!" Kimberly pleaded. "What're you doing?"

"Gonna go check the mail and see who lives here, and if it is who I think it is, I'm going to see what they look like."

"Wait, what – "

He closed the door before she could finish and headed toward the front porch.

Kimberly followed.

"What're you doing?" she whispered as he reached into the mailbox.

"I told you, I want to see who lives here," he whispered back.

No mail was within; however, which meant it had probably been taken inside, and if that were the case then that meant someone was probably –

Movement in the window by the door caught his eye.

A moment later, the door opened enough for a face to peer out at them, the words, "Can I help you?" filtering through.

"Um, yes, I believe so," Bill said. "We're looking for Emily Moore. Do you know where she might be?"

"Why are you looking for her?"

The question pretty much confirmed to Bill that this young lady was Emily Moore. Chances were Kimberly had made the same connection. Now he just needed to get a better look at her so he could see if she was the girl from the other night. The space between the door edge and frame did not reveal enough.

"Ms. Moore, we have been receiving threats from someone who has also been in the habit of leaving information about your late father at our place for some unknown reason and we would really like to know if you have any idea who this person could be."

No reply.

"Do you know anyone who would do such a thing?" Bill added. "They seem to feel that she was somehow responsible for the murder."

Once again, there was no response and for several seconds he expected to hear a THUD! as the door slammed shut. No THUD! echoed.

"Why do they think this?" Emily asked.

"We don't really know," Bill lied. "Whoever it is just keeps leaving notes and pictures for her to find. She also destroyed my windshield and has been seen lurking outside our place many times."

Nothing.

Bill wanted to say more, but didn't know what to add. He also didn't want to overdo it.

"Is she one of them?" Emily eventually asked.

Bill looked at Kimberly and then back at the face in the door-way and asked, "One of them, who?"

"One of the students that was fucking my father?"

"No!" Kimberly cried before Bill could reply. "I never even heard of your father until these messages started to arrive."

Emily seemed to consider this for several seconds. She then opened the door wide enough to reveal herself. It was not the girl from the car. "I'm sorry; I really don't know what to say. Have you gone to the police?"

"Yeah," Bill said. "And to be honest they will probably come to talk to you, because until now everything seemed to point to you as the one who was behind all this."

"What?" Emily asked, her voice changing to one that con-tained worry. "Why?"

"Given the messages and the pictures and the accusations it seemed like someone was blaming her for your father's death and the only person we could really think of that would have a reason to be upset about this was you."

"But it isn't me."

"I know," Bill said. "I've actually come face to face with the girl that is doing it, and you don't look anything like her." He sighed. "Unfortunately, that leaves us with nothing once again." He looked at Kimberly for a second and then back at Emily. "You really don't have any idea who this could be?"

She shook her head. "Sorry. I pretty much stayed out of everything. My parents were . . . well . . . their marriage had been bad for many years, and once I was able to get away from it I rarely looked back because each one always wanted me to tell the other one they were wrong."

"You said your father had relations with several of his female students," Bill said. "Was that the cause of the marriage problems?"

"No," she said with a laugh. "That came after they had separated for the final time and was another reason I didn't visit him very much. Got a little awkward sometimes if you know what I mean."

Bill saw sadness in her eyes, but also saw that she had control over it. "I can understand that."

"Do you know who any of those students were?" Kimberly asked.

Emily shook her head. "Sorry."

An awkward silence settled.

Then, "If you don't have any more questions I – "

"Just one more," Bill said.

"Okay," she replied, voice heavy.

"How did your mother find out about the meeting between your father and Nikki at the hotel on Route 64?"

Emily stared at him for a long time, and, after a while, he started to think she wasn't going to answer, but then, "Someone sent her an email about it."

"Really?"

Emily nodded.

"But you don't know who?"

She shook her head. "And now, if you don't mind, I just got back home from work like ten minutes before you two showed up so I would kind of like to relax."

"Okay," Bill said.

"And I hope everything works out," she said.

"Same here," Bill said.

"Yeah, me too," Kimberly muttered.

"And if you do learn anything," Bill added, "do you think you could let us know?"

"Yeah, but chances are I won't learn anything."

Bill shrugged. "You never know." He pulled out his phone. "Do you have your phone? I'll give you my number."

"Hold on," Emily said and disappeared for a moment, door closing.

Nearly a minute passed before she returned.

"Okay, go ahead."

Bill did, then Kimberly.

"Are you two together?" Emily asked.

"Um . . . we live in the same apartment house," Bill said.

Kimberly added a nod to this.

"Okay, well, good luck." With that, Emily closed the door.

Bill and Kimberly exchanged glances and then, without a word, started toward the car. Once inside Kimberly said, "That wasn't what I expected."

"Same here."

"So, now what?" she asked.

"I really don't know."

He had been so convinced that Emily Moore was the one responsible for everything that he had never even considered another possibility. Of course, he hadn't been expecting to find her living here either, his thinking being that this little visit would have been the first step toward uncovering a trail that would lead them to her.

Kimberly started the car, but didn't pull out right away.

Bill looked at her.

"When did you come face to face with the girl?"

"What?" Bill asked.

"You told her that you came face to face with the girl, but the other night when you tackled her I never really saw you get a good look at her."

"Oh, it was last night. I saw her watching the house when I went for a walk and confronted her."

"And you didn't tell me?"

"I never got a chance. It was late and then you went to school this morning – "

"You could have still told me."

"Yeah, well, it was a disaster."

You should have called the police, he told himself again. *One simple call and this might have been over.*

"What happened?" Kimberly asked.

"She bit me."

"What?"

"I tried pulling her out of the car and she bit me." He lifted his arm so she could see the bandage. "I was kind of surprised you never asked about it, actually."

"Well, I figured you would have told me if it had anything to do with the situation."

He shrugged. "Next time I will."

"And why the fuck didn't you just call the police?"

"I don't know," he said. "At the time . . . well . . . I wish I had."

Kimberly shook her head and pulled away from the curb. Five miles came and went in silence. "By the way, I might go to my parents' place until this all comes to an end."

"Really?"

"I figure it might be the safest thing I can do if this girl decides to turn violent because there is no way she could figure out where I live."

"She could just follow you home, or look on Facebook like I did."

"My privacy settings are . . ." she didn't finish and instead simply said, "Fuck."

"What?"

"My Mom has everything visible and is on my friends list."

"You think she has looked at that by now?"

"Probably. It seems she has learned everything else there is to know about me, except the fact that I couldn't possibly be the girl from the website."

Bill didn't know how to reply to this.

"Dammit!" she suddenly snapped. "I was so convinced it was the daughter. Now, well, it could be anyone."

"Or it could still be the daughter," Bill said.

"What do you mean?"

"It didn't occur to me until now, but what if she hired someone to do this?" It seemed very plausible, especially if she was crazy like her mother, but also had enough sense to try to get away with everything.

"Like a hit person?"

"Yeah."

"Wouldn't they have just killed me and been done with it?"

"It all depends on what she paid them to do. If she wanted them to torment you first and make you suffer, I can't think of a better way than to get people sent to the house to try to have sex with you. It also would add to the suspect list once all is said and done."

"But we know it isn't one of those men because you've seen her."

"Yeah, but that was purely by chance."

Kimberly didn't reply.

"We just got lucky," Bill added.

16

Where in the world am I? Mark silently asked himself as the dark, unfamiliar room unfolded before him. A moment later his memories provided him with an answer, one that brought a smile to his face as he recalled all the different things he and Amy had done together.

A few days ago you were despairing over the possibility of never having sex and now . . . his mind didn't continue the statement.

BEEP!

Mark shifted himself toward the familiar sound, which belonged to his cell phone, and silently groaned. The beep was telling him he had a voicemail, and would continue to tell him this every five minutes until he opened the phone. He had to get up.

Unlike the other day, Amy and he were not entangled with each other, so slipping free from the bed was quite easy. The same could not be said of moving around the apartment, which was dark. Fortunately, he did manage to make it to his phone without crashing into anything.

The voicemail was from his mother, which didn't surprise him. He also had a text from Nikki letting him know that she knew he was with Amy.

I'M ENJOYING WATCHING YOU TWO BECOME INSEPA-RABLE.

God, will it ever end? he asked.

Thoughts of the police station and talking to the officer earlier came to mind, followed by thoughts of the writer guy being the real Nikki. Anger came next, but didn't stay very long. How could it when he had just spent the entire evening having sex with a beautiful young woman who seemed to like him very much?

Tell her to go fuck herself, his mind said.

Or better yet, tell her that you now know the truth behind the real Nikki and see what she says.

Does she know the truth?

From what it sounded like based on what Bill and Kimberly had said at the police station the answer seemed to be a solid NO. It also seemed that the new Nikki was pretty convinced that Kimberly was the same girl who had caused all the drama in her father's life, if their theory on who Nikki actually was turned out to be correct.

So, enlighten her.

She probably won't believe me.

Plus, given how crazy this girl had to be to do all this, telling her the truth could prove disastrous. Instead, it was probably better to leave things alone and just let the police deal with it. Once they had her in custody, they could explain the situation to her. Until then . . .

Fuck it!

He decided to tell her to leave him alone and that her messages no longer had any effect on him. Nothing good would come of it, and truth be told, not saying anything would probably be more of statement about the effect of the messages, but he didn't care. He also decided to tell her that Kimberly knew the items coming in the mail were from him, and that Amy knew that anything Nikki said to her would be a lie.

Message ready he hit SEND . . .

. . . and heard a faint BUZZ sound from somewhere near the front of the apartment.

Startled, Mark stared at his phone, his eyes trying to visualize the name AMY where the name NIKKI was displayed. It didn't work. He hadn't accidentally sent that message to Amy, which meant . . .

He didn't dare complete the thought.

Send another one.

Hope that it was all just a coincidence, yet fearing it was not, filled his mind as he typed the word TEST and hit SEND.

The BUZZ echoed again.

With it came an understanding of why Nikki had been able to know so much about Amy. The two were one and the same.

Or maybe not?

Maybe there really is an explanation?

Maybe . . .

The thought drifted away without completion.

Check it, a voice instructed.

Though he knew what he was going to find, the actual confirmation of the situation hit him hard. Making it worse, there was nothing his mind could do to argue against it. Looking at the phone there was no question that it was the one Nikki had used to message him, the SENT MESSAGE folder having all the texts within it. There also was no question of who the phone belonged too, its location inside Amy's purse pretty much solidifying things.

Now what?

He stared at the shadowy figure sleeping in the bed and wondered if everything had been real. Had she had sex with him because she really did like him, or because she wanted to continue messing with him?

The fact that he cared about this startled him because in the past if presented with such a situation he probably would have simply shrugged and said, *"At least I had sex."* Well, this is what he would have pictured himself doing. Now, given the interaction and statements Amy had made, and how good just being alongside her had made him feel, he wanted it all to be real. It went beyond the sex at this point.

Amy rolled over and said something in her sleep.

He then watched her lift her head and look over at where he had been, her hand quickly reaching around for him, and then, after she twisted back around, over to the lamp cord.

Light flooded this area of the apartment.

Confusion distorted her face as she caught sight of him sitting in the corner chair staring at her.

"What is it?" she asked.

Mark tried to think of something to say, but couldn't, and simply held up the phone.

Amy looked at it for a moment, her face puzzled, but then understanding dawned.

Seeing this helped Mark find his voice. "You're Nikki," he said. It was not a question.

Amy didn't reply.

Mark waited.

The two stared at each other for nearly a minute.

Mark then dropped the phone back in her purse and stood up. "I think I'll be going."

"No, wait," Amy said.

Mark reached for his pants.

"Mark, please!"

"Tell me why," he said once his pants were in place.

Nothing.

"Do you really like me like you said, or was it all just a ploy?"

"No, I really do like you, which is why I contacted you with my real profile. I wanted to get to know you and see if you really were as sweet as you sounded whenever you talked with me." Tears appeared in her eyes. "I'm sorry."

Confusion hit and once again, he didn't know what to say.

Amy's tears continued to fall. "Please don't go." She wiped away at some mucus. "Not after everything we've done."

Her emotions startled him. Confused him too. He didn't know what to do.

"Please," Amy repeated. "I love you."

"Then why did you keep sending me messages from the Nikki side of things?"

Amy rubbed at her eyes.

"And you made me spend a ton of money on those things for Kimberly," he added.

Nothing.

Mark waited.

"Because . . ." she started, but didn't finish.

Mark crossed his arms.

She sighed. "Let me just show you."

"Um . . . okay?" Mark said.

Amy stood up and headed into the kitchen area.

Mark followed.

"Open the fridge," she said.

"What?" he asked.

"Open the fridge and look inside the egg carton. It will help you understand."

Unsure what to think, Mark simply did as she suggested, his eyes squinting against the sudden brightness from within as he searched for the egg carton. Once found, he opened it. No eggs were present, just two . . .

Are those knotted condoms? he silently asked himself.

He turned toward Amy to ask her why in the world she had two used condoms in her egg carton, but the question never got a chance to leave his mouth as the large knife was plunged into his chest.

Shocked, and unable to comprehend what had just happened, Mark stood where he was for ten seconds, eyes focused on Amy who was still crying.

"I'm so sorry," she said. "You left me no choice."

He shifted his gaze from her to the knife handle and then, without warning, watched as the floor rose up to smash into him.

No pain arrived with the fall, just an odd type of numbness that had spread throughout his body.

"I love you," Amy said again. She then leaned down and pulled the knife free.

Blood spurted, followed by a hissing sound.

He tried to say something but couldn't get enough air to form the words. In fact, he couldn't really get much air at all.

Panic set in.

It felt like he was underwater.

"You really were a great guy," Amy said, the words somehow comforting him. "And I'm sorry it had to be this way."

That, mixed with the sound of the air hissing out of his punctured lung, was the last thing he ever heard.

17

Overwhelmed by the sudden turn of events, Amy was unable to do anything but sit on the kitchen floor, crying. Mark's hand was in her lap during this. She had taken hold of it shortly after pulling the knife free, but wasn't sure if he had even realized it. *What would go through one's head during a moment like that? Did the brain even allow for thought, or did it simply go into a reaction mode as it tried to comprehend the trauma and then fix it?*

No answer arrived.

This didn't stop similar questions from filling her head, their presence probably the result of her own brain entering into a type of survival mode, one that wanted a temporary distraction from the horror of what had just occurred. Not the horror of the violence. She could handle that without a problem. But the horror of having to kill a man she had fallen in love with, one who she had actually started to see herself with long into the future.

It would never have worked.

Even if she had decided to abort the part of the plan that called for his semen, chances were something would have happened down the road that would have made him leave her. That was what always happened it seemed. In the beginning, the two couldn't get enough of each other, but then, as time passed, the man would start to lose interest. It was part of the human condition according to her mother. Men were programmed to try to have sex with as many women as possible in order to populate the planet, while women were programmed to covet the men in their lives so that they would have a strong protective figure to help in the raising of their child.

Looking back this had been one of the last things her mother had ever shared with her. The conversation had taken place right after the divorce during a time when it had looked like she was going to live with her mother. Eventually she had decided her father would be better though, at which point her mother had refused to speak with her ever again, the word 'traitor' being used several times during her angry rant.

Better now than later, Amy said to herself as she shifted her thinking back to the situation at hand. Mark would have left her life at some point, of that there was no question, so at least this way she didn't have to experience the horror of a slow breakdown of their relationship. Plus his death would serve a purpose, which was an honor few ever got to have attached to their name.

But in the process you will tarnish his name.

That put a damper on the positivity she was trying to muster up.

It had to happen, she finally told herself. It was a bummer she had fallen for him the way she had, but that was life. Nothing could change it. Plus she could feel good about the fact that he had gotten to enjoy himself in the days leading up to this moment.

And that neither one of you has any bad memories from the time together. Everything was pretty positive and enjoyable.

With that thought, she carefully set his hand on the floor and stood up.

A yawn struck.

She endured it and then began devising a course of action for the body. Killing him in her kitchen had never been in her prior thoughts. Actually, killing him in her apartment had never been considered, her plan having been to take him out into a cornfield, or some other rural area of DeKalb.

Now, however, she had to figure out a way of removing him from her place. Simply bagging him up and taking him downstairs and out to her car was not possible. Even if she could carry him like that, the fact that she would have to travel through public parts of the house made it too risky. *Dismemberment.* It was her only option. No one would question her carrying down bags of trash. It was a sight everyone had seen countless times. Only her trash would not go into the dumpster outside, but into her trunk. After that . . .

Think about that later, she told herself. *Right now you have work to do.*

Heeding the suggestion, she reached down and grabbed Mark by the legs, her fingers marveling over the odd feeling his skin had already acquired, and began dragging him toward the bathroom. Once there she struggled to get him into the bathtub, her hands attempting to balance his upper half on the tub edge so she could lift the other side. In her mind, she figured he would just flop into the tub, but instead he kept sliding back toward her. Frustrated, she finally lifted his torso onto the edge and twisted him so that his head and shoulders would fall into the bottom of the tub. Once like that she lifted his legs and pushed the rest of him in, the body taking on a crazy handstand like appearance before crumbling down into the tub, the right ankle knocking down several of her bathing products in the process, and then slamming into the faucet.

Exhausted, she took a seat on the toilet, her body savoring the moment of relaxation.

I could fall asleep just like this, she realized.

Allowing that to happen would be a mistake. She needed to get this situation taken care of, for the longer it took the greater the risk became.

You also will need some rest if tomorrow night is going to be the night.

Though she had not originally had a specific date in mind for the death of Kimberly, and now the writer too, she had always known it would have to occur shortly after killing whoever the man was whose semen she planned to use for the DNA evidence. Ideally, she had hoped this would take place on a night when she, as Amy, contacted Mark while he was at home and begged him to come out to her because Nikki was harassing her. The reason for this was simple. She wanted his car being tagged going through the I-Pass on I-90 in the middle of the night so it would look like he had finally flipped out and driven out to Kimberly's place. Whether or not the bodies of Kimberly and the writer were found the next day wouldn't matter. All she wanted was for there to be evidence that Mark had raced out to the area. That, coupled with his DNA inside of Kimberly, would pretty much focus police attention on him.

Not having that one little bit of evidence wasn't a big deal, however, since she was sure the DNA she had acquired would be enough to focus that attention already.

Especially with the packages that should be arriving soon.

Those would be traced back to him.

There also would be evidence of his having traveled back and forth on I-90 quite a bit during the time of Kimberly's harassment thanks to his prior passes through the I-Pass. Amy wasn't sure if all those trips would match up nicely with the actual moments that she had done things at Kimberly's place, but she was sure they would be enough to add to the suspicion that he was to blame.

It's all going to work out nicely, she told herself. *And now get to work.*

A trip to the kitchen provided her with the tools she needed – or thought she needed. Cutting up the body was a lot more difficult that she had contemplated, and at no point prior to starting did she suspect that it would be an easy task.

I really need a saw.

She realized this while working on the legs. Given their length, she figured cutting them in half, or even thirds would be her best bet, but once the skin and muscle was cut away she realized the serrated edge she was using would not slice through the bone. Between bones on other parts of the body it had worked, its edge severing the connecting ligaments and tissues nicely.

Cutting through actual bone was another matter. It couldn't be done.

Maybe just separating them at the knee will be enough.

She gave this a go, her knife and hands having a tough time toward the end due to the kneecap. Being forced to reach down into the tub to do all this was awkward as well, especially given the limited amount of space between the tub, sink and toilet her tiny bathroom provided her. Adding to the mess was how slippery things were getting. Turning on the shower and rinsing everything off would take care of some of that, but she didn't want to go that route given how loud the water in the pipes was. The last thing she wanted was for all her neighbors to wonder what she was doing turning the shower on and off throughout the night.

As it turned out, separating the leg at the knee wasn't the most difficult task when dealing with the legs. That honor fell upon removing them from the hips. It also marked the first moment when she had to stop and get some fresh air thanks to the exposure of fecal matter that occurred when she cut the upper half of his pants free. Before this, she had occasionally noticed the smell, but for some reason hadn't allowed it to register. Once exposed there was no ignoring it. She also couldn't refuse to turn on the shower any longer, the need to wash all that shit down the drain overpowering the fear of waking her neighbors and having them wonder what she was doing up here.

Tuesday, August 23, 2011

Ugh, why? Bill demanded as he lay in bed with his eyes wide open at five thirty that morning. Having stayed up to almost three surfing the web he had figured he would sleep to at least ten today, but instead his body had decided upon five. And fighting it was out of the question, though he had tried. For the last half hour he had stayed curled around a pillow, eyes closed, body relaxed, yet sleep would not return. It was crazy. Several years ago when forced to get up so he could be on shift at six in the morning getting out of bed had been nearly impossible. In fact, he had been required to set his alarm to go off three or four times between four and five just in case he went back to sleep. He had also put the alarm clock out of reach so that he couldn't hit the snooze without having to walk over to it, which, of course, he never did because once he was on his feet he would be awake enough to realize he needed to stay up. Now, he had no reason to be awake, and actually wanted to sleep all morning, yet his body said NO.

He sat up.

Toby, who was curled at the foot of the bed, lifted his head and looked at him with eyes that were barely open.

Bill reached down and petted him for a few seconds and then shifted himself out from beneath the covers and went in search of a pair of pants. While doing this Toby put his head back on the bed and covered his eyes with his paws.

Dressed, Bill headed over to his computer and hit the power

button, and then headed into the kitchen to make some coffee. While that was brewing, he returned to the computer, typed in his password, and waited for the Windows screen to load up. Had this been a typical morning he would have then switched on the radio to listen to the Eric and Kathy show until the coffee was ready. Today, he simply signed onto the Internet, a statement of 'next week' echoing in his head on when he would once again get his writing back under control.

Or sooner if the Nikki situation is resolved.

And if it isn't?

It was this thought that had kept him up into the early morning hours, a sense of having suffered a setback plaguing him to the point where sleep was impossible.

How could it not be her?

Who else could it be?

The daughter, Emily, had voiced a thought that maybe it was one of her father's lovers, which, after thinking about it for a while, seemed plausible. The trouble was how would they figure out the identity of the girl. At least with Emily they had had a bit of a hook. Now, they really didn't have anything.

Even worse, Nicole's roommate's boyfriend hadn't been able to learn anything from the email address Bill had sent to him, a short apology having arrived last night in his own email inbox. *It is doubtful this is any type of government inspector or investigator,* had followed the statement of apology. Though nice to know, Bill had been fairly certain of this already.

If only you hadn't replied with the house address, he said to himself. *You had no choice.*

As true as the rebuttal was, it did little to help clear away the guilt he felt – not about the website itself, though, just the reply to the email. People (Kimberly and Mark) could bitch and moan about his creation of the site all they wanted, but the fact was that it had been necessary. Without it . . . well, he didn't want to think about that and quickly signed onto Facebook to distract himself a bit. Not long after that, the coffee pot beeped.

Moving slowly due to his exhaustion, Bill went from his desk to the kitchen and then, two minutes later, came back with a mug of coffee in hand. He then began browsing the web, his fingers first taking him to his normal everyday locations that he often visited when at the library. Once the information from those was gathered, he went onto some random sites to kill time, his mind lacking the motivation to do anything else. Actually, that wasn't true. If he could have, he would have been seeking out information on the NIU_Nikki girl, but since he had no idea where to begin with that, he didn't even bother to try. As the officer had said the first night, this was a *wait and see* situation.

Wait for what?

The possible answers that filled his head were chilling. Thankfully, the worst of them were so elaborate that he doubted such events would unfold. Plus, the police could be there quickly if needed.

But she probably knows that and will plan for it.

This thought troubled him.

Sadly, there was nothing he could do about it.

Wait and see.

He sighed.

Sitting back and letting things play out was not his style. He liked to be proactive. He liked to shape things around him rather than having them shape him.

But now he had no choice.

At least he didn't think he did.

If there was a path he could take that would help put an end to this situation he would follow it, but from where he sat it didn't look like that was the case.

Exhausted, frustrated, and bored, Bill soon found himself switching the Internet cord from his main computer to his porn computer. No sexual desire was really present when he did this, but that didn't matter. One would develop as he downloaded video after video and before he knew it, the day would probably be half over.

That was how things like this had always worked in the past, only then he hadn't wanted to kill time. Instead, he had been distracted by his addiction and eventually dismayed by the wasted hours. Now, it was just something to do. Had his writing been going well he probably wouldn't have even considered signing on to look at the porn until he was finished with his ten pages.

2

HEY MARK, JUST WANT TO LET YOU KNOW THAT IT ISN'T THE DAUGHTER LIKE WE THOUGHT IT WAS, Kimberly texted, a realization that she should do a better job of keeping him informed guiding her hand.

Five minutes later, her phone beeped.

She was eating a bowl of Life cereal at this point. Necessity rather than hunger had instigated the meal. A three-hour class followed by a six-hour Steak and Shake shift loomed before her. On the surface, it didn't seem like much, but for someone who had been dealing with the stress that she had endured these last few days, just the idea of leaving the house was almost too much to bear.

Cereal finished, she opened her phone. Sure enough, the message was from Mark. It read WOW! THANKS FOR LETTING ME KNOW. ANY IDEA WHO IT COULD BE?

NOT REALLY, she typed. SOUNDS LIKE THE GUY WAS SLEEPING WITH A LOT OF HIS FEMALE STUDENTS THOUGH SO IT COULD BE ONE OF THEM.

Kimberly waited for a reply, but none came so she cleaned out the cereal bowl and then headed up to knock on Bill's door to find out when he wanted to go to the car dealership.

"Anytime," he said.

Kimberly nodded and then asked, "You okay?"

"Yeah," he mumbled. "Didn't get much sleep last night."

"Hmm," was all she could think to say.

"We could go now if you want to get it out of the way," Bill said. "I'm sure they're open."

"Okay. Meet you down by the car?"

He nodded.

Kimberly returned to her apartment and went in search of her purse, which she eventually found next to the box she was using as a coffee table. *Gotta find a real one soon,* she noted to herself and then headed outside.

Bill was waiting in the garage.

"Anything left during the night?" she asked.

"Nope," he said. "Looks like she took the evening off."

Relief and disappointment arrived, the latter being due to the knowledge that something more needed to happen for the police to put a stop to this – unless they were able to uncover who she was through the dating site profiles. If that were the case then she would gladly welcome the lack of harassment from this point onward.

BEEP!

Kimberly paused in backing the car down the driveway to see who the text was from. "Oh, it's Mark again," she said.

"What's he want?" Bill asked.

"Your number actually."

"Really? Why?"

"Probably so we can all stay in touch and let each other know what is going on. Here." She handed him the phone. "Type in your number for him."

"Huh," Bill said.

"What?"

"Oh, nothing. I'm not used to people calling me William if they know me as Bill." With that, he typed in his number and then handed her the phone.

"Maybe he's just being polite?" Kimberly suggested.

"Could be."

Nothing else was said as Kimberly maneuvered them out of the neighborhood. Then, "Okay, tell me where I'm going."

Bill did.

Soon they were pulling into the parking lot of the car dealership.

"Want me to wait here just in case something is still wrong?" Kimberly asked.

"Good idea, thanks."

His phone buzzed.

He pulled it from his pocket and looked at the message. "HEY WILLIAM, IT'S MARK," he read aloud. "JUST WANTED TO TEST OUT THE NUMBER AND MAKE SURE YOU HAD MINE."

"William again," Kimberly said.

"Yeah," Bill said.

"Maybe that's his way of making sure you know he won't be friends with you given what you did to him with the Nikki profile."

"Could be," he said with a shrug, one that told her he was unfazed by this. "Okay, be right back."

"Yep."

Kimberly waited.

BEEP!

She opened her phone, eyes expecting to see that it was Bill telling her the car was good. It was Mark.

ANY IDEA WHO THE OTHER GIRLS WERE THAT WERE SLEEPING WITH PROFESSOR MOORE?

NO, Kimberly replied.

I WONDER IF KISH WOULD HAVE A LIST OF GIRLS THAT ATTENDED HIS CLASSES? came a minute later.

KISH? Kimberly asked.

No reply.

IS THAT WHERE HE WORKED? she asked.

Finally, after nearly five minutes, YEAH, DIDN'T YOU KNOW THAT?

NO, Kimberly replied. WHERE'D YOU LEARN IT?

FACEBOOK.

Shit, everyone is learning stuff there, she said to herself. She then wondered if Bill knew this too.

The answer came shortly after that once he returned to the car to tell her everything was good. "With the exception of my outrageous deductible," he added.

"That sucks," Kimberly said. "Hey, do you have any idea where Professor Moore taught?"

"I'm guessing NIU," he said.

"Huh."

"Why?"

"Oh, Mark says he worked over at Kish. Said he learned it on Facebook."

"Could be." He shrugged. "I didn't really look at employment, just his address."

Kimberly considered this.

"Anyhow, I'll see you back at the house," Bill said.

"Okay." Kimberly maneuvered herself around so that she could leave the parking lot. Not long after that, she was sitting at her desk looking at Professor Moore's Facebook profile. Sure enough, he was listed as being employed at the Kishwaukee Community College.

So, that's that, she said to herself.

Deep down inside, however, something didn't feel right. She couldn't pinpoint it, though, and didn't really have time to dwell on it, not if she actually wanted to participate in the classes she had forked over thousands of dollars to attend.

Outside Bill pulled up.

Kimberly quickly went out to meet him, a thought having occurred to her.

"You could probably recognize his girl if you saw her, right?" Kimberly asked.

"I think so."

"Well, why don't you take a look at Professor Moore's friends list and see if anyone jumps out at you."

"Not a bad idea," Bill admitted. "But do you think he'd really be so bold as to friend students on Facebook?"

"It's college, not high school. He could post a status that he was fuck buddies with some of his students and technically no one could say a thing." Truth be told, the school probably would take issue with it, but still, it got the point across.

"Okay, I'll take a look."

"Great."

"So, when do you go to class?"

"I'm going to leave in an hour."

"And then you work tonight as well?"

"Yep."

"Wow, long day."

"Yeah," Kimberly agreed. But at least it would keep her mind busy. Sitting around the apartment waiting for something to happen would be torture.

"Want me to come watch your car tonight and see if she does anything?"

Kimberly shrugged. "Up to you. Think she will?"

"Don't know, maybe?"

"If you do, and if she shows up, don't do anything yourself, okay? Just call the police."

Bill nodded.

"I'm serious," she said.

"Me too," Bill said. He held up his arm to show her the bandage where she had bit him, and then pointed to his windshield. "I've learned my lesson with this bitch."

3

Amy's day was not off to good start, if the word start could even really be used since she never officially went to bed. The trouble had arrived around two in the morning, once she had finally finished dismembering Mark. Thinking things nearly complete she had had gone into the kitchen to grab some garbage bags only to discover the box beneath the sink was empty. Even worse, a search of the apartment revealed she had nothing whatsoever to hold the pieces in until she could get a bag. She also knew she couldn't go shopping in her present condition, not when Mark's body had done a nice job staining her with blood.

Not wanting to climb into the shower with the pieces, she attempted to clean herself off at the sink, but then found another item that needed to be added to her shopping list: paper towels. Five sheets was all she had left and while they were of a good quality that could withstand quite a bit of abuse, they weren't enough to complete the entire job.

She had no choice. She had to shower with Mark's body.

First things first, she piled all the pieces toward the front of the tub so that she had room to stand. What she didn't realize, and never would have until this situation, was that the shower head wouldn't twist up far enough for the spray to reach the backside of the tub. Leaning forward, she tried to clean herself off, but it was no use, so she eventually decided to move the pieces to the back of the tub so she could point the shower head down upon herself while standing in the front. At first, this worked, but then, once the water soaked everything behind her, the pieces started to slide down toward the drain. Attempting to re-stack them proved disastrous, especially when the head rolled into her ankles, Mark's eyes looking up at her as the shower spray pummeled the lifeless pupils.

Seeing this, Amy couldn't help herself and vomited all over the body. It was the first time in nearly four years that she threw up, and it left her feeling hollow and useless.

Not long after that the hot water ran out and she was forced to finish cleaning off the blood in the cold spray. By the time she was finished she felt as if she had been standing in a freezer for hours, and barely spent anytime drying herself off before climbing beneath the bed sheets to warm up.

No sleep followed, though she was exhausted enough.

And then came the texts from Kimberly and the eventual information that Professor Moore had been sleeping with several of his students, not just her and, if things had worked out the way he wanted, Nikki.

Heartbroken all over again, Amy could do nothing but lay in her bed crying. It was all too much. Everything that had happened -- Professor Moore cheating on her, his death, Mark, her plans to kill Nikki, her dwindling finances -- she just couldn't hold back the growing despair that this mixture brought upon her.

I don't care if I die tonight.

Just as long as I make Kimberly pay.

Of course, she would still do her best to make sure everything went according to plan, but if things didn't, it wouldn't be much of a loss.

Just make sure you don't survive.

Spending the rest of her life in jail was not something she could handle, not when the thoughts about Professor Moore and Mark would be a constant companion. No. If things did end up taking a bad turn she would make sure the police ended things for her.

Mark's phone buzzed.

She picked it up and looked at it, her mind wishing he was still in bed with her so he could laugh about how annoying his mother was being.

If only you hadn't texted him from Nikki's phone last night, she told herself.

But you were going to kill him eventually anyway.

She wondered if this was true. Would she have done it? It was a question she had asked herself several times as their sudden relationship had blossomed; one that she had never really answered completely.

If only someone else had taken the bait, someone who you could have lured in, fucked and killed without any real thought.

If only . . .

She had been using this statement a lot in the last several months, her thoughts always directed backward in hopes of being able to change something.

Would it get better?

Once all was said and done and she moved on would she meet someone else and fall in love and this time have them all to herself so that the two could live happily ever after?

You probably could have with Mark.

The thought, like always, brought the sadness back up to the surface, which was something she didn't want.

If only I could shut down my mind and not think about anything! Or better yet, erase things that I never want to think about again.

Would such a thing ever be possible?

It isn't now, so don't dwell on it.

Taking this advice she sent a reply to Mark's mom telling her he was fine, and then decided to get up and go to the store so she could finish what she had started. After that, she would begin the final stages of her plan, one that might go more smoothly than previously thought thanks to the phone numbers she now had.

4

I FOUND HER.

Kimberly stared at the text while sitting in her class, the phone carefully tucked up under the desk so as not to be noticed by anyone else.

REALLY? she typed.

Why would he send this if he hadn't? she asked a second later.

YEAH, he replied. Then, CAN YOU TALK?

NOT YET, she typed.

Nothing followed.

She sat there for five minutes looking at the professor, ears hearing but failing to give meaning to his words, before she decided to leave class and talk to Bill.

Another five minutes came and went before she worked up the courage to stand and walk out, the attention she knew it would bring her something she didn't want to face. Naturally, she got her purse caught on the desk as well while trying to leave, which just added to the focus on her. Even the professor stopped talking.

"Sorry," she muttered, voice so low only those around could probably hear it. "Emergency."

Shortly after that, she was in the hallway heading to the nearest door so she could call Bill, mind trying its best to shake the embarrassment she had just endured.

"Hello," Bill said after a single ring.

"Hi," she replied. "I left class to talk."

"Oh, okay."

"So, you found her."

"Yeah, and believe it or not, it didn't take long at all. I don't know why, but she actually sent me a friend request the other day and I accepted it. So while looking at Mr. Moore's profile I saw we had a mutual friend."

"You didn't realize it was her when she friended you?" Kimberly asked. If he hadn't recognized her then, what made him so sure now?

"I didn't really look at the picture. I get quite a few friend requests from people who read my stuff, and since I don't go online that often they stack up."

"Oh."

"But this time I checked out the profile, because it seemed quite odd that we would share a friend and sure enough, it's her."

"You're positive?"

"Yep. Sadly, there is no address info."

"Still, if we know her name we can tell the police and I'm sure they can contact Facebook and find out everything they need to know." Excitement was coursing through her bloodstream. After everything that had occurred it finally felt like they had made a serious step toward putting a stop to things. Then again, she had felt this way a few times throughout this ordeal and nothing good had ever panned out. For some reason this time around felt more genuine than the previous moments. "Oh, by the way, what is her name?"

"Amy," he said. "Amy Baker."

"Amy?" Kimberly questioned, an 'uh oh' echoing within her head.

"Yeah."

"Wasn't that the same name as Mark's girlfriend?" Even as she asked this she knew it was, his words at the police station yesterday replaying themselves in her head. The words of the officer followed, the ones where he reminded him to have his girlfriend

Amy get in touch with them so she could report upon the harassment she had received as well.

"Um, was it?" Bill asked.

"Yes, it was."

But if NIU_Nikki was harassing her as well –

The thought ended as she realized that Amy could easily claim harassment. In fact, doing so would help keep suspicion off herself.

But why get involved with Mark?

Was it just another way of keeping tabs on her?

She remembered Mark informing her that he was going to claim the two of them got together -- as if she really were Nikki -- in hopes of somehow throwing NIU_Nikki off track and / or learning more about her. Maybe by doing this Amy had realized she should be close to Mark so she could stay up to date on what was unfolding from their end.

"Wow, I don't really know what to say," Bill said.

"Same here," Kimberly admitted.

"I suppose we should tell him, but – "

Kimberly waited and then, when he never finished, asked, "But what?"

"I don't think he'll want to hear this from me, so why don't you let him know."

Oh god. She didn't want to be the one to do this, not after being able to see how happy he was yesterday when talking about her. Mark and she didn't really know each other all that much, but from the beginning she had been able to tell he was a really sweet guy, one who had been jerked around quite a bit by Nikki (and Bill), so knowing he had found someone he enjoyed being with had been nice.

"You know, by telling him yourself maybe you will be able to patch things up with him a bit," Kimberly suggested.

"I don't care about patching things up with him," Bill said.

This startled her.

Anger appeared.

"You know, you're kind of a jerk," she said. Surprise at how easily the statement rolled from her tongue arrived. Normally she wasn't this direct with people, Kyle having been one of the few exceptions.

Bill didn't reply.

"I mean, it's one thing to do what you did. I don't agree with it, but I understand the money angle. But to be unapologetic about it after seeing the hurt you caused someone; and after learning you were somewhat responsible for a man's death -- " she shook her head even though he couldn't see " -- I don't even know what to say about all that."

"It is what it is," Bill said. "Look, if it would make you feel better I will let him know about Amy. I just want it to be clear that I'm not doing it to patch things up with him or so he will forgive me, because I really don't think I did anything wrong."

She sighed. "Whatever. Let me know what happens and if you learn anything else."

"Fine."

"Bye." She ended the call.

Dismay at how someone could be so unmoved by their own actions filled her, but then she wondered if he really was unmoved or just was acting unmoved. Maybe deep down inside he really did feel some guilt at what he had done, but just didn't want anyone to know. Maybe deep down inside he was conflicted by it given how it had helped him along, yet also had caused so many horrible things to occur.

Thinking about this she almost felt bad for the negative thoughts she had projected his way, and shared. Even so, she could not forgive him for what had happened in recent weeks, even if he wasn't the one behind the harassment. If not for him, none of this would have happened and therefore she couldn't help but hold him responsible. She also couldn't help but think he had to understand this himself; had to think about it while sitting up there all alone.

What if it plagues him?

All his statements about how he has no remorse could just be a shield. Inside his mind could be racked with guilt.

But will he ever admit it?

The question stuck with her for a while, but then faded as thoughts on what she should do next arrived. Going back to class was out of the question; she wasn't about to call attention to herself again. Going back to her place didn't seem appealing either, however, not when Bill would be right above.

An idea hit, one that she couldn't believe she hadn't thought about right away. A second later, after orienting herself and visualizing where she needed to go, she started walking toward the library. Once there she quickly found the nearest computer, which happened to be on the third floor, and logged into Facebook.

5

As was typical, Amy didn't stop browsing the aisles after she had grabbed a box of heavy-duty garbage bags and a new bundle of paper towels, and soon had a shopping cart nearly filled to the brim with items she didn't necessarily need, but would use in the coming days.

Unless I'm dead or in jail.

The thought soiled her journey through the candy aisle, yet also made her less worried about adding a few sweet treats to the cart. After all, why worry about the cost or the fat if this was one of her last days being alive or free?

No, just alive, because you won't allow yourself to be taken.

Thinking this, she wondered if there actually was a risk of being killed by either William or Kimberly. Would the two really be capable of putting up a struggle that could result in her death?

Not if you do things right.

The question was what was the right way? She had been thinking about this quite a bit, yet didn't really have much of a plan. Instead, she just saw herself subduing William at some point this afternoon and then waiting for Kimberly to come home from work. But how would she subdue him? This was the tricky part. However, once he was subdued she had a feeling everything else would be easy.

And fun.

Just thinking about the things she would do to Kimberly -- and the things she would have William do to her if he was still alive -- put a huge smile on her face.

And maybe, just maybe, it will all be enough to rid your mind of the horrible memories once and for all.

Maybe you will finally be able to get on with your life!

She crossed her fingers and hoped this would be the case.

If not . . .

Well, she just decided to wait and see what would happen. Honestly, there was nothing else she could do.

Wait and see.

Mark's phone beeped.

She was pushing the cart toward the Target checkout lane, her eyes looking for an open aisle amongst the dozen closed ones, when this occurred, and quickly pulled to the side to see who it was.

WILLIAM CELL.

Hmm. She had been expecting his mother again, who had already called twice this morning, the voicemails growing more and more worried with each unanswered call.

A lady pushing a cart that had even more items than her own passed her. Seeing this and also noting that only one checkout aisle was open -- why did they even bother having so many? -- Amy quickly started pushing the cart toward the register. Once there and her spot was secure she checked the message.

MARK. I HATE TO TELL YOU THIS, BUT YOUR GIRL-FRIEND AMY IS NIKKI.

Amy almost dropped the phone.

How?

It didn't make any sense.

"Miss?" a voice called. "Um, Miss?"

Amy looked up and saw that another register had opened.

Behind her a guy who was balancing several items in his hands hurried around to the register and dropped everything upon the conveyor belt. Amy slowly followed and began unloading the cart, her mind unable to comprehend how William could possibly know that she was Nikki?

Ask him.

But do it in a way that would sound like Mark.

What way is that?

The question bounced around for nearly a minute, a time during which the guy paid and the young cashier began scanning her items.

Amy watched all this, her hand unconsciously pulling her credit card free so she could swipe it, her other hand still holding onto the phone.

The cashier totaled everything.

Amy silently winced and then scanned her card.

Everything went through.

Two minutes later, she was pushing the cart toward the exit, a realization that she was going to need both hands spurring her into action with a message back to William.

BULLSHIT.

It was all she could think to say when trying to think up an appropriate response from Mark. However, what she really wanted to ask was HOW THE FUCK DID YOU LEARN THIS?

BEEP!

She pushed the cart up alongside the passenger side of her car and pulled out the phone.

BELIEVE WHAT YOU WANT, BUT IT'S TRUE. AMY IS NIKKI.

Now you can ask how he knows this, Amy said to herself.

Question sent she began loading the groceries into the car. The phone beeped while she did this, the reply being a single word: FACEBOOK.

Heart racing, Amy asked WHAT DO YOU MEAN FACEBOOK? and then went to put the cart in a cart return slot.

BEEP.

SHE FRIENDED ME AND I RECOGNIZED HER PICTURE.

Amy stared at this reply, anger toward herself growing.

You shouldn't have done that.

But I wanted to know more about him.

His profile was completely public.

She shook her head.

At the time, it had seemed like such a good idea, but now . . . well, now she couldn't believe she had been so stupid.

But at least he didn't send this to Mark the other day. That could have been a disaster.

This isn't?

Could she use this to her advantage somehow?

She thought long and hard about this while driving back home, the anger and frustration with herself slowly dissipating.

Maybe I can lure him away and then get inside his place?

Getting into the garage even though it was locked had been a piece of cake. Unfortunately, she doubted that getting into his apartment would be the same simply because most tenants wouldn't tolerate such a thing. She also doubted he would have a key hidden somewhere up there, especially after everything that had happened at the house.

Too bad you can't somehow get a hold of his key and have a copy made.

The idea was so implausible that she quickly pushed it from her mind so she could focus on other, more realistic possibilities.

6

Having accomplished everything he had set out to do in regards to the Nikki situation, Bill decided to call it quits with the computer for a while and pushed away from his desk.

Hunger guided him into the kitchen.

Nothing within was appealing though so he decided to put his car to good use and headed out, his mind unsure what he had a taste for until he drove by a Qdoba. Not long after that, he was sitting at one of the corner tables, waiting for the burrito insides to cool down, his eyes looking at the latest message on his phone. It was from Mark.

I THINK YOU MAY BE RIGHT. WHAT SHOULD I DO?

Bill thought about this for a while and typed, DON'T TELL HER YOU KNOW. JUST CALL THE OFFICER WE TALKED TO AND GIVE THEM HER ADDRESS. Once that was sent he typed up another message that said, OR GIVE ME THE ADDRESS AND I WILL TELL THEM.

DO YOU THINK THAT WILL WORK? Mark asked.

WHAT DO YOU MEAN?

WITHOUT ANY EVIDENCE WILL THE POLICE SIMPLY GO AND CONFRONT HER?

Bill thought about this for a while. THEY PROBABLY WILL GO AND TALK TO HER SINCE IT IS REALLY MY WORD AGAINST HERS. WITH A LITTLE DIGGING THEY SHOULD BE ABLE TO CONNECT ALL THE DOTS. MIGHT TAKE A WHILE.

Mark didn't reply to this.

Bill took a bite of his burrito, and, while chewing, had a new thought, one that might help cement things a bit.

WHAT KIND OF CAR DOES AMY DRIVE? he asked.

A SILVER HONDA, arrived a few minutes later.

Crap! Then, NOT A DARK BLUE CAR? He wanted to add the

make and model, but didn't really know what it was. All he could do was picture the car from the repeated confrontations, and recognize it if he saw it.

NO, Mark replied.

Bill didn't know how to reply.

A new message arrived. DOES THIS MEAN IT ISN'T HER?

I DON'T KNOW, Bill typed. COULD SHE HAVE A SECOND CAR?

NOT A CHANCE.

WOW, OKAY.

He took another bite of the burrito, his mouth savoring the flavor combinations while his mind played with this recent bit of news.

A new message arrived.

MAYBE WE SHOULD ALL MEET, Mark suggested.

WHAT DO YOU MEAN? Bill asked.

YOU ME AND AMY. MAYBE IN PERSON YOU WILL REALIZE IT ISN'T HER. PICTURES CAN SOMETIMES BE MISLEADING.

TRUE. YOU THOUGHT KIMBERLY WAS NIKKI WHEN REALLY THE PICTURES I USED WERE OF MY FRIEND NICOLE. AND IT WAS DARK WHEN I SAW HER.

Still, seeing the picture on Facebook and the fact that she was also friends with Professor Moore had been like a signal flare going off. It all fit together.

And didn't he just say he thinks I'm right?

HEY, he typed. WHAT MADE YOU THINK AMY WAS NIKKI A LITTLE WHILE AGO?

Mark didn't reply right away, so Bill set the phone down and focused on the burrito, his mouth methodically taking bites and chewing while his mind played over the idea of meeting Amy.

You'll need to clean your apartment.

And you should --

His phone beeped.

JUST MY INSECURITY, Mark's message said. I FIGURE WHY WOULD A GIRL REALLY BE INTERESTED IN ME. IF IT WAS BECAUSE SHE WAS MESSING WITH ME IT WOULD MAKE SENSE. BUT MAYBE SHE REALLY DID LIKE ME.

Once again, Bill didn't know what to say.

Another message arrived.

WHY DON'T I BRING HER BY YOUR PLACE TODAY? I
WON'T TELL HER WHERE WE ARE GOING AND WILL SEE
WHAT SHE SAYS ONCE SHE REALIZES WHERE WE ARE. IF
SHE REALLY IS NIKKI SHE WILL PANIC.

Bill considered this while wrapping up the last bites of his burrito, his stomach having protested the final bites. It was an interesting idea Mark had, one that might help them know for sure
what Amy's roll in all this was.

Could be dangerous for him though, he noted.

If it was Amy, she might snap and do something in the car.

*But either way we will then know for sure one way or the other if she is
Nikki.*

OKAY, THAT SOUNDS LIKE A GOOD IDEA, he typed.
BRING HER BY.

A minute later a reply came that simply said, OKAY.

JUST LET ME KNOW WHEN SO I KNOW TO BE HOME.

OKAY.

With that, Bill put his phone away and headed out to his car, his
leftover burrito in hand. Once home he would let Kimberly know
about the new developments and see what she thought.

7

TRUE. YOU THOUGHT KIMBERLY WAS NIKKI WHEN
REALLY THE PICTURES I USED WERE OF MY FRIEND
NICOLE. AND IT WAS DARK WHEN I SAW HER.

Amy couldn't help but stare at the message William had sent in
the middle of their text conversation, confusion at what exactly it
meant building with each second.

YOU THOUGHT KIMBERLY WAS NIKKI.

PICTURES I USED.

She didn't like the direction this was pointing.

If the pictures aren't of Kimberly . . .

Her mind let the thought fade as she pulled up the folder with
all the pictures she had downloaded from the blog. Also within
were the pictures she had taken a various points. While doing this
she had never really made any comparisons between the two, but
now she studied them and, after a few minutes, came to the star-

tling realization that the two were not the same girl.

But . . . what does it mean?

She pondered this for several minutes, a growing sense of un-ease filling her. And then she recalled something Mark had said about Kimberly not being the girl from the site, and how he felt really bad for her due to all the torment being inflicted upon her.

It might not be her in the pictures, but that doesn't mean she wasn't involved. In fact, she could have requested a really pretty girl be used so that she could lure in even more men.

And this would help explain the address situation.

After all, why would they use her address for the over eighteen age information if it wasn't the correct address? When going this route to uncover her address Dominick had showed her informa-tion on how much trouble webmasters could get in for not having the information on hand, thus she knew they could also get in seri-ous trouble for providing incorrect information on where it was all kept.

She shifted her thoughts to the agreement on meeting later in the day. With this came a smile. Figuring out a way of getting inside the writer's place had been daunting, but now, if things worked out the way she envisioned them, it would be simple. Of course, he would probably recognize her right away, but still, just the idea that she would show up at the door without issue might make him doubt his own thoughts on the matter. It was perfect. Everything was coming together.

Couldn't have planned it any better.

Actually, if she had tried to plan it all out she probably would never have gotten this far. Instead, she had mapped out a few simple steps, the most important of which was luring in Mark (when thinking about it she had just envisioned a guy desperate for sex) so she could get a hold of his semen. Little did she know his phone would be one of the most important tools, especially after he had already made contact with William and Kimberly.

It is almost like fate is helping guide things.

But to what end?

She pushed the thought from her mind and looked at the clock on her computer. According to the guy at Steak and Shake, Kim-berly worked a three to eight shift today, so sometime within that period would be perfect for meeting up with the writer.

HEY, HOW DOES FOUR SOUND FOR SWINGING BY WITH AMY? she sent to William's phone.

UM, KIM WORKS TONIGHT UNTIL EIGHT. WOULD IT BE BETTER TO WAIT FOR HER?

THAT IS TOO LATE FOR ME. THIS WILL JUST BE A QUICK POP IN SO YOU CAN SEE THAT I'M NOT NIKKI.

Time passed, during which Amy realized she had made a mistake in her message.

Will he catch it?

If so, what will you say?

As it turned out she didn't have to worry. His next reply was a simple OKAY, SEE YOU THEN.

Amy sighed, and then scolded herself for not re-reading everything before she sent it. One little slip could ruin everything.

It still could.

If he just decides to re-read his messages for some reason he could notice your slip-up and start to question things.

BEEP!

Great, he has noticed it, she said to herself while checking the message. It was from Mark's mom.

Another sigh escaped her lips.

She couldn't wait until tomorrow when all this would be over.

Speaking of which, you really need to dump Mark's body.

The thought was like an alarm clock going off in her head, one that told her she was running late. She had gotten so preoccupied with communicating with the writer and figuring out a way of getting into his apartment that she had totally forgotten about the need to bag up Mark.

No time like the present.

With that thought, she grabbed the box of garbage bags she had bought and headed into the bathroom, her mind and body not looking forward to the grim task that lay ahead.

8

WELL NOW IT MIGHT NOT BE HER ACCORDING TO MARK.

Kimberly looked at the message and asked, WHY NOT?

WRONG CAR.

BUT MAYBE SHE HAS TWO? Kimberly suggested after some

thought.

MARK SAYS IT ISN'T POSSIBLE.

Kimberly didn't know what to say.

Another message arrived.

HE IS BRINGING HER OVER LATER TODAY THOUGH SO I CAN MEET HER FACE TO FACE.

REALLY? AND SHE AGREED TO THIS? It seemed unlikely that Amy would agree to such a thing if she was the one responsible, especially knowing she had been seen.

HE ISN'T GOING TO TELL HER.

WHY?

SEE HOW SHE REACTS ONCE SHE SEES WHERE HE IS TAKING HER.

So, there is still some suspicion on Mark's part, Kimberly realized. A thought occurred. WHAT TIME?

AROUND FOUR. I TOLD THEM YOU WERE WORKING BUT IT WAS THE ONLY TIME POSSIBLE.

OKAY. Truth was she felt a bit better about not being there for this meeting.

And if anything is left upon your car during your shift it will be another sign that this Amy girl isn't the one responsible.

Naturally, this led her to ask who was responsible, a question that brought about quite a bit of despair since she once again couldn't point the finger at anyone. Making this worse was the confidence she had felt earlier at Bill's discovery. This girl Amy had seemed perfect. *Connections to the professor, connections to Mark, recognition by Bill -- how could it not be her?*

Frustration seeped into her system, along with a familiar sense of self-pity. *Why did things like this happen to her? Hadn't she been through enough?*

She shook her head.

Attempting to earn a college degree was difficult enough without all the shit life had thrown at her.

If only you hadn't gone to that party.

All those years ago, on a night where she had simply planned to study, her friend had convinced her to come along with her so that she wouldn't be all alone in an unfamiliar fraternity crowd. Being alone didn't seem to matter once she hooked up with a guy, however, especially if the 'alone' label was attached to Kimberly.

You should have left then and there.
You should have –
STOP!
Should have! Should have! Should have!

No matter how many times she told herself she *should have* done something different, she couldn't change what had actually occurred. It just wasn't possible. She also had no idea if things were actually better off this way. What would have happened if she hadn't gone to that party? Sure, the horrible event that had occurred that night wouldn't have happened, but maybe something even worse would have down the road, something that never got a chance to happen with her since she had flunked out after the miscarriage.

After you killed –

Again, she told herself to STOP!

Of course, this did little to prevent the sadness that overwhelmed her. Worse, the sadness was visible to anyone who looked at her, and given that she was still at the school and in a semi-crowded area, people did start to notice. No one said anything, but that didn't matter to her. Just knowing she was putting on a display was horrific. Thankfully, her car was not too far away. People still noticed her inside, but it wasn't as bad, and once the worst of the emotions passed she was able to head home.

If I could just stay home.

Unfortunately, going to work wasn't really optional, not if she wanted to keep the job. On the upside, she did have some time to relax before she had to get ready.

9

Body parts bagged, Amy went to her computer to see if anything needed her attention, but found that nothing new had really unfolded since her last check a few hours earlier. The only exception to this was on one of the dating sites where she had posted a profile, one that was dedicated to people who enjoyed rough sex and rape play. To her surprise, the email wasn't a solicitation for sex but a warning from a member of the site that she was being too risky. *You need to establish trust with the people you communicate with before handing out your address and telling them to try and follow you inside. Once that trust is established you will have scenes that are re-warding and very memorable rather than get yourself raped for real and forever live in fear and disgust of what occurred.*

Amy shook her head and then checked to see if this was some-one she had messaged in the past. It was. Then, even though it wouldn't really matter after tonight, she typed up a quick reply that read *I want it to be real.*

After that, she browsed Facebook for a while to kill some time, her focus being on William's friend list to see if she could find Nicole at all.

Do you want to kill her too?

The idea had appeal, yet also didn't feel all that necessary; not if her only role in this had been allowing her image to be used.

But what if she does it again for someone else?

What if through a twist of fate you once again find someone you love only to watch as they too start to neglect you thanks to another person using Nicole's image?

The thought was unsettling.

Thankfully, she also realized it was pretty far fetched.

Still might not be a bad idea to eliminate her at some point in the fu-ture.

Wait and see how tonight goes.

And make sure to ask him what her full name is.

Having scrolled through a third of his friends list, she realized the need for a full name. With people like Mark this wouldn't have been all that necessary, but when someone had over two thousand friends it was.

How many girls named Nicole are there?

She typed NICOLE up in the search box. Fifteen results ap-peared.

Out of curiosity, she looked at each picture, but again no one really jumped out at her. Even following some of the likely candi-dates to their own profile and checking out the rest of their pictures didn't produce a solid connection, though she did find one that carried a strong resemblance to the one in the pictures from the blog. She couldn't be certain, however, the trouble being the dif-ference in content between the two sets of pictures. In the ones from the blog she was trying to be sexy and provocative, and often had her hair pulled up and out of the way. In the pictures from

Facebook this wasn't the case. In fact, most were candid shots.

And this is why you simply thought Kimberly was the girl.

Seeing someone in a posed sexual situation was a lot different from everyday real life.

A thought on what she would have done if she had realized Kimberly wasn't the girl from the pictures entered her mind.

You would have gone about things the same way because she was involved.

The address proved this.

The two of them, Kimberly and William, had worked together. Nicole might have had a role that went beyond the pictures as well, though this she wouldn't know for sure until tonight.

Once William was secured, she would get some answers.

Secured . . .

A question on how to go about securing him entered her mind. It was something she hadn't really thought about until now, her focus always being on tormenting Kimberly and the eventual cutting of her throat.

Using a knife to subdue someone seemed a bit more complicated, almost improbable. Even with a gun it could prove difficult given that she would need to hold the weapon in one hand while using the other to tie the ropes.

And what if he decides to fight back despite the risk of injury or death to himself?

The outcome of such a decision on his part could ruin everything she hoped to achieve that evening. Both of them would still die, that outcome was not in question, but the look of the scene just wouldn't be right.

If only I had a taser.

Obtaining such an item between now and four o'clock was out of the question. Even if such an item were available in the local stores, she wouldn't want to go get one now because its use would leave a trace and the police might check to see who bought one in recent days. Nope. She needed to think up something practical; something she could do with the items on hand.

She wondered if the items she had instructed Mark to purchase had arrived. If so, she could use the handcuffs, which would make subduing William easier since she could instructed him to enclose his own wrists in the links behind his back while keeping a distance with the knife.

Relying on that possibility wouldn't be good, though; especially given the chance that Kimberly had taken those items inside -- if they even arrived. Even with the higher priced shipping she had instructed him to use, the arrival time could still be in question. One only knew for sure that it had been worth the cost when it actually arrived.

Think!

The demand forced her from the desk, but did little to solve the problem since nothing within her apartment jumped out at her.

She also doubted that Google would provide much help.

Maybe you should just kill him and then wait for her?

She did have Mark's semen, which would help set the scene. Still, if she could make it look like William and Kimberly had been sexual as well, and that Mark had gotten jealous, killed them and disappeared, it would be better, especially once the media condemned Kimberly for her sexual ways.

A glance at the clock told her she had an hour to think things over. Unsure what to do she got back on the computer and considered a search term for Google that might help her come up with something useful.

10

Bill heard Kimberly leaving for work while he was finishing with the dishes. Once that was done he did a quick check of the apartment to make sure it looked decent and then lit a scented Christmas candle that he found in his linen closet to mask the possible litter box odor. As a rule of thumb, he kept the box pretty clean, but one never really knew what the smell was like when living near it, so the scented candle seemed wise.

Four o'clock.

Anytime now.

Though he wasn't sure why, he was antsy about this visit. A part of it probably was due to the overall situation, another was due to him not having had anyone scheduled to come over in quite some time. This wasn't to say people hadn't been over, Kimberly being a perfect example; just that he hadn't had any advanced plans of guest in recent months. Not since Nicole, actually.

Memories of those days began to unfold.

He remembered always being excited for her visits (what guy wouldn't be?), but also constantly being overwhelmed by anxiety because of his financial situation, one that cast a shadow over everything and, eventually, killed the fun that he and Nicole had been having together.

Things would be different now.

If the two ever decided to get together again, or if he ever started working on a project like the blog with another girl, things wouldn't have such a serious 'we have to make this look good so it sells' feel to it.

Forget about building another site, just having a girl in your life who likes you would be different.

A sense of loss arrived.

Nicole had liked him.

Sure, they had started out just as business partners, but there had been a growing connection there as well, which was something that he hadn't really felt with anyone for a long time. Nor did he want to feel it then, which is why things had fallen apart with the two of them. Now he regretted that, though he wasn't sure why. Something within him had changed, something that now made him realize how alone he truly was.

Kimberly.

It didn't take a rocket scientist to know what it was that had stirred up these feelings, nor the reason why the feelings had appeared. If she had just moved in and been a neighbor, he might have continued being satisfied with his life, but instead she needed his help, his protection.

It seems so cliché, he said to himself, but then realized that maybe there was a good reason for that. *It happens!*

A sense of dismay followed, mostly because he didn't like the idea that he could fall into a situation that so many other people found themselves stumbling into. It made him too normal, too like everyone else, which was something he didn't really care for; not when he had always felt as if his abilities to rationalize and think things through had been a step above everyone else's.

He shook his head and started toward his computer to kill some time, but then stopped when he heard footsteps on the stairs outside.

They're here.

He went to the door and opened it.

The girl he now knew as Amy was standing there by herself, a shy smile upon her face.

It's her, he said to himself. *No question about it.*

"Hi," she said. "Um . . . William?"

"Yep, well, Bill actually," he said and held out a hand. *Be cool and don't give in that you know it's her.* "Amy?"

She nodded.

"So, where's Mark?"

"Oh, parking the car." She smiled. "Nothing was open in front of the house."

"Oops, I should have told him he could park in the driveway," Bill said. "Oh well, come on in."

He held the door for her as she stepped inside, his mind going over some options on what to say once Mark got there. As far as he was concerned, this girl was the one from the other night, the one who had bit him and the one who he had chased through the yards. Now he just needed to prove it.

Trip her up somehow.

Get her to spill something that kills any doubt.

"Um, can I get you something to drink?" he asked. "I have soda, juice, water. No Snapple though."

"Soda is good," she said. The word Snapple didn't earn a reaction at all.

Going to have to be a bit more clever it seems.

He grabbed two Cokes and handed one to her, and then motioned toward the couch in the other room.

She hesitated a moment, almost as if she wanted him to go first. He wasn't going to turn his back on her, however, and simply said, "I'll wait here for Mark, make yourself comfortable."

"Okay," she said and headed into the other room.

Bill waited, Coke unopened, but Mark never showed up.

11

He's going to know something is up soon when Mark doesn't show, Amy said to herself while sitting on the couch, panic rising. *You need to act soon.*

In her purse she had a kitchen knife, duct tape, a can of bug spray, and a sock with a potato in it, the last of which was a homemade knockout item she had read about online, one that was reportedly able to thump a person senseless without risking skull fracture. If that didn't work, she would spray him in the face with the bug stuff.

Gotta get close though, and if he is going to wait over there for Mark . .
.

The thought ended as a possible solution literally landed in her lap, one that she would never have thought of while sitting at home.

12

Something's wrong, Bill realized as the time without Mark's arrival stretched to five minutes. Never in the two years he had lived here had there ever been a total absence of parking spots on the roads around the house, the only exception being during the Memorial Day parade since the route was one road over. *He's not coming, which means –*

"Nice kitty."

The two words that the soft, almost sweet sounding voice carried pushed every thought from his mind and sent a chill slipping through his bowels.

He turned and looked through the doorway cutout toward the couch by the window where Amy was sitting. Toby was in her lap, his smiley face collar gripped in her left hand, while a large kitchen knife was in her right. No words were needed to share her intentions should he not comply with whatever demands she made.

"You might as well lock the door," Amy said. "Mark isn't coming."

Bill locked the door without a word and then turned back to her, his mind attempting to work around the growing panic to find a possible solution. Nothing came to him.

"Now, do you still have the handcuffs I saw in that one set of kinky blog pictures, or did those belong to Nicole?"

Bill considered lying, but feared the potential outcome, and said, "I have them."

"Where are they?"

"The dresser."

"Go get them and put them on behind your back and leave the key on the dresser."

Bill did as instructed, the only alteration being that he grabbed the second key himself and tucked it between his fingers before closing the links around his own wrists. Relief at the potential for escape arrived, though it wasn't enough to calm the panic. Nothing short of her releasing Toby would do that, and even then, he would still be on edge.

"Sit down on the floor," Amy said.

Bill did.

Toby was still in her lap, his stupidly friendly nature probably making him unaware that anything was even wrong. She wasn't even holding his collar anymore, yet he stayed right where he was.

13

Amy was caught off guard at how easy subduing the writer had been, her mind having expected something a bit more chaotic and, quite possibly, violent.

Now what?

The question went unanswered as she stroked the underside of the cat's chin, a steady stream of purrs reaching her ears.

"Is it a boy or a girl?" Amy asked.

"A boy," he said.

"And what's his name?"

"Toby."

She wondered if there would be anyone to take care of Toby once she finished with things here, or if taking him home with her would be her best option.

No, you can't do that, her mind snapped. *No connections between you and them.*

She would have to leave him behind.

"So, Kimberly gets off work at eight," Amy said.

"I believe so."

"That gives us three hours to get to know each other."

He didn't reply.

"Tell me about you and her."

"Why?"

"Because, you two ruined the greatest thing that ever happened to me, and I would like to know why."

"You're talking about your affair with Professor Moore?"

"It wasn't an affair," she said.

"Really?" he asked, body shifting a bit. "But wasn't he married?"

"Yes, but only because she kept refusing to sign the divorce papers." Anger developed, both at him and at the crazy bitch Professor Moore had been married to.

"You know, in this state that doesn't really matter, if only one really wants a divorce there are ways to go about it, especially if the two have been living apart from each other." He paused. "How long were they separated?"

"Why?"

"Because six months is all it takes to get a divorce based on abandonment." He shifted again. "Was it longer than six months?"

Amy didn't reply.

"Of course, I don't doubt that you loved him. I think your actions these past few days have proved that. The question is did he really love you?"

"Stop," she snapped.

"Stop what?" he asked.

"Stop trying to do what you're doing."

"What am I doing?"

"Making it so I'm really tempted to cut his throat," she said and moved the knife blade closer to Toby. "Or maybe I will just poke out an eye."

Bill didn't reply, though the panic she saw in his face was enough of a response.

"That's better." She set the knife down on the couch. "Tell me about Nicole."

"What do you want to know?"

"Was she just used for the pictures or did she play a bigger role in all this?"

"Just the pictures."

"And Kimberly?"

"She had nothing to do with anything. It was all me."

Amy considered this for several seconds and then shook her head. "Nope. I don't believe that for a second."

"Well, it's easy to prove. Just go take a look at her lease. It's sitting right on her desk downstairs. She just moved in earlier this month, yet, as you know, Nikki was talking to Professor Moore since Christmas of last year."

"What about the address?" Amy asked.

"What about it?"

"If she had nothing to do with this why did the age statement stuff say it could be found at her address and not yours."

"Because, many places don't recognize my address so I always just use the one downstairs."

"What?"

"Go look at the Netflix case on my desk if you don't believe me."

She looked at the red envelope sitting next to his laptop. *Would he lie about something that was so easily verified, especially in a situation like this?* An answer of NO arrived, which then made her wonder about Kimberly's lease. If she truly had moved in earlier this month then everything she had done had been a mistake. Even worse, it was a mistake she would have to see through to the end if she wanted to stay out of jail.

Or will I?

Could I just kill him and be done with it?

Amy stood up while thinking about this, and walked over to the dresser to grab the handcuff key, her mind noting at the last second that his desire to get her downstairs might simply be so he could go grab the key, which she had almost forgotten about.

"The lease is on her desk?" Amy asked.

"Yes."

"If you're lying I'm going to come up here and cut Toby," she warned.

"It's there," he said.

Knife in hand, she started toward the stairs, but then stopped and grabbed him by the hair and pulled his head back at a wicked angle and pressed the blade close to his throat.

"And when I get back you're going to answer every question I ask, or else I'll start cutting you."

He didn't reply, but once again, the expression on his face was enough.

She let go of his hair, and took a step toward the stairway door.

Bill twisted, his hands grabbing her legs before she even realized he had gotten free. The next thing she knew she was falling toward the floor, body bracing itself for impact.

14

For a moment, Bill feared his bluff had been called, his mind having forgotten until the last second that a mirror was behind him, and, if positioned properly, would have allowed Amy to see him working to free himself from the handcuffs. Thankfully, this wasn't the case, and once she released his hair and withdrew the blade he was able to act.

And down she went, a high-pitched squeal echoing from her lips, followed by a low grunt as she crashed into the floor.

Knife! his mind shouted. *Get the –*

Amy twisted from the floor and slashed at him with the blade, his eyes actually catching his own reflection seconds before the tip caught his retreating shoulder.

Pain!

First it was cold, almost as if a piece of ice had been forced into his pores, then it was hot as the blood opened up the two folds of skin.

"*Fucker!*" Amy cried and lunged at him from the floor, all while he scrambled backward like a crab.

The blade missed.

He hit the couch at an angle.

She grinned and thrust the blade at him.

He shifted as best he could, but wasn't quick enough and felt the point cut into the flesh of his stomach before continuing deep into the couch cushion.

The sound he made was unlike any sound that ever left his lips before, though it was more due to terror and surprise than actual pain.

Heart racing, he grabbed her wrist as she tried to pull the blade free and yanked it away from the couch.

The knife went flying.

He then slammed her hand down on the edge of the coffee table, which earned him a wonderful cry. Had his angle been better it would have been even more satisfying, because chances were he would have broken some bones. Instead, he just managed to bloody her knuckles a bit against the splintered edge.

Fingers came at his eyes.

He dodged them and then grabbed a boob with his free hand and squeezed, fingers really digging in while twisting.

She screamed.

He then threw all his body weight at her, forcing her back to the floor, one hand holding her wrist, the other one still squeezing the boob.

Another scream echoed, only this time it was followed up with a knee to his groin.

All thoughts and reasoning disappeared.

A hollow sensation followed, along with a horrible nauseous sensation.

During this, he was vaguely aware of her free hand fumbling around at something -- *her purse?* -- and then –

Recognition hit and he twisted his face away from the nozzle and closed his eyes just as a burst of mosquito spray came at him.

Unfortunately, he couldn't help but breathe in the spray, his lungs heaving from the exertion.

Get the handcuffs and end this, his mind cried as he scrambled away from her, arm wiping at his face to clear away the spray before he opened his eyes, all while his nose tried to flush out the irritant.

Another panicked burst shot his way, but the distance was too much for it to have any effect.

He opened his eyes and looked for the handcuffs, his thinking being he would grab them and then tackle her.

Rather than them, his eyes came upon the knife.

Get it!

Moving quickly, he went for it, his body slamming into the wall as he attempted to reach down and halt himself at the same time.

Pain from the two knife wounds echoed, but wasn't enough to sidetrack him from getting a grip on the handle.

Weapon in hand, he twisted back toward the living room, his eyes taking in everything just in time to catch sight of the object coming in from his left side.

A loud *thunk!* erupted within his head.

Several yellow explosions against a black backdrop came next.

A second *thunk!* and then nothing.

15

It worked! Amy's mind cried. *I can't believe –*

The writer groaned and started to move around a bit, which meant the blow hadn't completely knocked him unconscious.

Knowing she needed to act quickly, she hurried over to her purse for the duct tape -- wasn't going to risk the handcuffs again -- and quickly went to work taping his wrists together behind his back. She then taped his ankles and knees.

During this he struggled a bit, but no real strength was behind it, so it did little to hamper her progress.

Once finished, she took the knife over to the coffee table, along with her potato sock -- she still couldn't believe it had worked so well -- and began gathering up everything that had been thrown about in the struggle.

Blood stained the carpet by the couch.

You stabbed him, she reminded herself and quickly went to his body to check the damage. It was nothing, the blade having just caught the edge of his right side as he moved. The same was true of the shoulder wound. Had the two been worse than they were she would have put some tape over them to keep the blood flow to a minimum, but given that each looked as if it were already starting to clot, and knowing she didn't want to add anything to the body that could raise questions later on, she decided against it.

With that, she returned to the couch, her body completely exhausted from the fight, and finally opened the Coke he had offered her earlier.

Still cold, her mind noted as she guzzled down half of it, her taste buds enjoying the overly sweet liquid.

The little battle, which had seemed like quite the ordeal, had only last a few minutes. She realized this while checking the time on her phone, and then confirming it with the clock on his DVD player.

Everything was almost ruined during it, she warned herself. *Be more careful from this point on.*

A groan filled the room.

Toby then made an appearance, his small body having apparently fled under the bed during the fight.

"Here, kitty, kitty," she called as he walked over to sniff at the writer.

Toby cocked his head toward her, and then, with a happy sounding meow, hurried over and jumped up into her lap.

"Gah," she winced as he rubbed his check against her battered boob.

Twice, she silently said. *He grabbed the same one twice.*

She wasn't sure why this seemed so remarkable to her, yet it did. It also made her want to go over and hit him in the balls again. Once was probably enough though, especially given that she would want him to be able to perform later.

Gotta make it look like a lot of sexual depravity has been happening.

While thinking about this she reached into her purse with her free hand and pulled out the small Tupperware container that was holding Mark's semen filled condoms, and set it on the table.

"See that, Toby," she said while petting the sweet cat. "I've got some for Kimberly and some for William. Going to make it look like the three were all playing with each other before Mark snapped and went a little knife crazy."

Toby didn't reply, unless she counted his eyes rolling back and his jaw opening as she scratched him beneath the chin as one.

He's so adorable.

She really wished she could take him with her later.

Keep an eye on the animal shelter.

If he ended up there and she rescued him no one would think twice about the fact that she had his cat. It would be perfect.

"Poor guy would probably be really scared during all that," she said to the purring creature. "But don't worry. Momma would come and save you."

Toby stretched while she said this and then looked up at her with weary eyes before resting his head back on her knee.

"So cute," she whispered and then reached over for her Coke.

Finger prints, her mind reminded her.

Rather than taking a sip she reached into her purse and pulled out the small bag of gloves she had grabbed from the box she had purchased at Target. Wearing a pair while entering the apartment had been too risky given that William might have noticed, but now, with him secure, she could slip them on.

Gotta wipe this place down too.

First, she was going to relax a bit and calm down from the little scuffle that had taken place. After that, once she was rested, she would take care of things.

And look at the lease.

If it really is down there.

Chances were William had just wanted her to walk by him given that he had freed himself and wanted to grab her. The lease and the Netflix package had both been used as bait, nothing more.

And you fell for it big time.

Lesson learned.

It wouldn't happen again.

Gloves in place she took another sip of Coke and then went back to petting Toby. He didn't seem to mind the gloves, though he did take a moment to sniff them once he became aware of them a few minutes later.

It was cute.

16

Work was dreadfully slow that night. Making it worse was her exhaustion. Had all her tables been full and orders being placed left and right she wouldn't have had time to be tired, her mind and body simply working on some sort of autopilot until everything was taken care off. Without that situation, however, she was able to recognize her weariness, which wasn't good, because it added even more weight to the minute hand as it struggled to complete its circuits around the clock.

And then of course she fucked up.

One table and she mixed up the two flavored milk shake combinations on not just one of the shake orders, but three. The fourth was a simple chocolate shake, so that one was almost impossible to screw up. All the others had to be corrected, which upset the customers and her boss. It also tied up the shake machine, which earned some angry honks from the drive up window.

By the time the mess was all straightened out Kimberly wanted nothing more than to just go home, take a shower, and crash on the couch in front of the TV until her eyes rolled back.

Sadly, she still had a little over an hour and half to go.

17

At first, he was confused, and then he was scared. Having freed himself once, he doubted Amy would let her guard down a second time. Even if she did, he doubted he would be able to free himself from the duct tape, not without an edge of some kind that he could use to rip away at the thread-like adhesive.

But at least it isn't the handcuffs.

The first time around he had had an advantage given that she didn't know about the key. Without one, however, he would have been unable to get free. Of that, there was no question. With the tape he at least had a chance.

But she won't let you exploit that chance.

Or maybe she will?

Amy wasn't a professional at this. She was just a girl who was pissed off because she found out the 'love' of her life was just a man that had urges he wanted to indulge, she herself having been one of them.

Tell her this, he suggested to himself.

No, the better part of his judgment replied.

Life lessons like this were generally learned from having been through the experience itself. When it wasn't learned from it then that meant either something wasn't quite right with the person experiencing it, or they were going to need another couple of lessons before it sank in. Bill had the feeling Amy fell into the first category. Nothing he could say would make her realize how silly her fixation on the professor was, nor would she understand that her anger was misplaced. Professor Moore had obviously been a prick that used his position to seduce girls like her. It also seemed like he had been making up for lost time given the crazy bitch he had been married to for so long. Had he not created the Nikki blog and started talking to the professor, someone else would have come along. No matter what Amy would have been heartbroken at some point. The outcome was inevitable.

18

Eventually Toby tired of her pets and jumped down from her lap so he could go clean himself in the middle of the floor. Once that occurred Amy decided it was time to check on the lease William had told her about. She also wanted to talk to him, mostly because the silence was too much for her. Awkward even, which was somewhat funny given the situation.

Are you expecting him to just start telling you about his day and his writing and his life experiences?

No.

Then what do you expect?

She expected nothing, unless she asked him questions, yet even so, she still found the silence awkward. This was common though. Silent moments between her and another person had always been a source for discomfort. It worsened if the person was someone she was in a relationship with. Silent moments between her and Professor Moore had been torture, and almost always led to her making a fool of herself because she couldn't help but say something. At first, he had probably thought this was cute, but then, after a while, it had undoubtedly started to bug him.

"I'm going to go look at that lease you told me about," Amy said while standing. "If you try anything while I'm down there you'll be sorry." She lifted the kitchen knife to emphasize her warning, and relished the fear she saw in his eyes.

"You might need a pin," Bill said.

"What?"

"To open her stairway door." He shifted himself a bit so that he was now on his side and curled into somewhat of a fetal position. "Sometimes she locks it."

"Oh," she said.

"It's easy though, all you do is stick the pin in the small hole on the knob and push. Lock will pop right out."

Sounds like he has done this before, Amy noted. *He really is a creep.*

William shifted again and then asked, "You don't mind if I sit against the wall, do you? The carpet smells. I didn't get a chance to vacuum it before you showed up."

Amy considered this, her mind going over all the possible reasons he might want to be sitting rather than lying down, but couldn't really pinpoint any danger in it, and said, "Go ahead."

"Thanks." With that he shifted himself around until he was up against the wall next to the bathroom door and then struggled himself up into a sitting position.

Sweat dripped from his forehead.

"Do you have a pin?" Amy asked.

"Actually, a toothpick works just as well," William said. "I have some in the kitchen. Second cupboard next to the window."

Amy nodded and went to the cupboard. Sure enough, there was a box of toothpicks. She grabbed one and then went to what she assumed was the stairway door. It wasn't locked.

"Remember what I said," she warned.

He nodded.

The stairs squealed as she descended, each one seeming to protest the weight she put upon it, and then she was at Kimberly's door.

I wonder how many times she has come up here to suck his dick, she asked herself. *Hearing a person coming up the steps is probably enough to give him an erection these days.*

She smiled at the thought and then wondered if he would be able to get it up later once she instructed Kimberly to fuck him. It was something she hadn't really thought about earlier, but now the concern was there. If not –

A new sound echoed from up above.

She twisted and watched as the door to the writer's apartment closed.

What the --

Oh, shit!

She started back up, her hurried steps masking the sound of the lock clicking into place.

The knob would not turn.

She hurried down and tried the door at the bottom, but it too was locked.

Toothpick!

She stuck it in the small hole on the door, but despite what he had told her, the lock did not pop open.

Shit!

She went back up to the top and stuck the toothpick in that one, her mind knowing what the results would be, yet not admitting it until she failed to open it as well.

NO! NO! NO!

She slammed herself against the door.

The entire frame shook.

She did it again, her hope being that enough blows would eventually break something within it, the old wood unable to withstand the repeated impacts.

If it doesn't . . .

She didn't allow her mind to continue with the thought, though this didn't stop her from knowing what the outcome of being trapped in this stairway would be.

She slammed herself into the door again, her body wincing with the pain it caused; and then again, her ear listening but failing to hear the sound of wood splintering.

Frustrated, she stabbed the knife into the door, an angry cry escaping her lips.

The blade sunk about half an inch into the wood.

She wrenched it free and watched as a chunk came out with it.

She stabbed again and made another nice gouge.

You'll never cut a hole big enough to reach through.

But maybe . . .

Yes!

There was a gap. It wasn't as big as the one outside on the garage door had been, but with a couple cuts, she could probably fix that.

Knowing it would work, but also knowing she had to do it before he freed himself and got to a phone -- *does he have a house phone?* -- she began cutting away at the edge of the door where the inner door latch connected with the frame.

19

It worked! I can't believe it worked!

Using his shoulder after quietly getting to his feet, Bill had managed to close the stairway door, his eyes having first watched to make sure Amy was all the way at the bottom before attempting to spring the trap. He had then simply flicked the lock switch, his right thumb and index finger managing to maneuver around it and twist it seconds before she reached the top.

Had he failed, which had been a huge possibility given how hobbled he was by the duct tape, she would have killed him. Of this, he was certain.

And she still will if you don't get free.

Though it was a pretty solid door, Bill knew there was a good possibility that she would be able to get through it at some point, so waiting around for Kimberly to come home was out of the question. He had to free himself and then find a phone to call the police, who, hopefully, would arrive while she was still trapped. If not . . .

The entire second floor shook as Amy threw herself against the door, an odd, unintelligible statement reaching his ears. The words 'fuck' and 'kill' were there, of that he was certain, but everything else was jumbled.

A second blow landed, this one less forceful that the first and only shaking the frame.

Bill was halfway to the kitchen when this one occurred, his bound feet forcing him to shuffle his way across the carpet inch by inch all while his mind was screaming at him to *MOVE*.

No more body slams against the door echoed, which meant one of two things. Either she had given up, or she was attempting something new. He figured the second option was the more likely of the two. The question was what was she doing now and how effective would it be?

What if Kimberly's door isn't even locked?

What if –

He pushed the thoughts from his mind while pulling a small, yet sharp knife from the drawer near the window, his fingers trying to maneuver it into a position that would make it possible to cut away at the tape around his wrists.

Nothing seemed to work.

A rattle at the inner stairway door echoed, alleviating his fears that Kimberly's door was unlocked, yet doing nothing to calm the fear the she was making progress in getting back into his apartment.

Gotta get free.

The knife slipped from his fingers and bounced across the floor. "Fuck!"

He reached into the drawer to grab another, this one being a thinner, more flexible blade, but it to was impossible to maneuver around in such a way for him to cut at the tape and eventually joined the other knife on the floor.

What he needed was a fixed edge, one that he could hook and tear at the tape with.

The stairway door rattled again, and this time it sounded different, almost as if it had more room within its frame to move.

He looked around, eyes desperate to find something that would help him. Something close so that he wouldn't have to shuffle all the way --

YES! his mind cried.

The cabinet beneath the sink had a handle with a point-like tip; one that he was sure would puncture the tape if he applied enough pressure. All he had to do was get down on his knees and hook his wrists over it.

The door rattled again, followed by a frustrated scream.

Using the corner between the wall and the fridge, Bill lowered himself to his knees and then shuffled his way to the cabinet. Once in position he twisted his head around so that he could see what he was doing and carefully lowered his wrists so that the tape between them came to a rest on top of the point.

He pushed down.

At first, the tape resisted, the fabric-like weave stretching a bit, but not tearing, and then all at once the point popped through. Unfortunately, it was just a hole, not a tear, and given the strength of the tape, he couldn't pull at the handle to rip through the space between the hole and the edge, because it simply started to pull the handle off the cabinet.

Lifting his wrists free, he positioned the point between the hole and the edge and pushed down again.

Like before, the tape stretched before a hole opened up, only this time the hole turned into a tear as the strands between the edge and the first hole could no longer withstand the pressure.

With that he began twisting his wrists back and forth, each one pulling in a different direction than the other one was in hopes of tearing the tape.

It worked.

His hands were free!

He grabbed one of the knives and went to cut at his ankles.

In the other room, he heard the latch on the door pop, followed by a crash as the door was thrown open.

SHIT!

Legs free, he started cutting at the tape around his knees.

Amy dashed by the kitchen doorway cutout, body heading toward the apartment door.

She then reappeared, eyes probably having caught a glimpse of him but not fully registering the sight in time to stop herself in the actual doorway.

Bill pulled his knees apart and then quickly got to his feet, knife in hand. The blade was just over two inches long. The one she held was about twelve inches.

20

Just kill him and be done with it, Amy said to herself, her mind and body fed up and exhausted from everything that had already happened. *It isn't worth all this trouble.*

Yes it is, another part of her mind said. *At least, it will be.*

The second inner statement was correct, and no matter how much the other side protested she knew she had to do everything she could to keep him alive.

But if he forces the issues . . .

In the end, if she was forced to kill him, she could still salvage things. She could still –

Without warning, he came at her.

21

Switching the knife to his left hand, Bill charged toward Amy, his right hand grabbing and swinging a skillet that he had set on the stove to dry.

22

Having first focused on the knife, Amy didn't have time to react to the skillet he had grabbed and screamed as the solid metal surface connected with her right hand, the pain unlike anything she had ever felt before.

23

Knocking the knife from her hand, Bill brought the skillet back around and hit her in side of the face. It wasn't a solid blow like the first had been, but it was enough to scramble her senses and drop her to the kitchen floor.

Get the knife.

It was sitting in the sink, the skillet having sent it skipping across the counter and into the first of the two basins.

He reached for it . . .

. . . and then screamed with a mix of surprise and pain as Amy stabbed him in the lower back.

24

Work picked up a bit during the last hour of her shift, which was good because it forced her to focus on things to the point where she simply couldn't think about anything but the customers. Tips were good too for a change, which helped block out some of the dismal moments that had taken place earlier. It didn't erase them completely, though. Nothing ever did. Add in the probability they would call and complain, which was like lighting a fuse with an unknown length that would blow up near her during an unexpected moment, and chances were she would have a meeting with her supervisor in the near future. Right now, however, things were good, and that was all that mattered.

Eight o'clock arrived.

Outside, Kimberly looked around to see if Bill was keeping watch, but didn't see him, and headed to her car, which, thankfully, didn't have anything waiting for her.

A tiny debate began, one that concerned her dinner choices. Having gotten a decent amount of tips, she considered grabbing something rather than making something, but then realized there wasn't really anything appealing in the local drive through market. She also didn't relish the idea of going in anywhere to sit down and eat, not when she just wanted to go home, change out of her uniform, and relax.

Could always try that Ren's place Bill pointed out the other day.

The only problem was that she didn't have a menu or their

number.

Bill probably does.

Thinking this she opened her phone and called him, her hope being maybe he might be hungry and could place an order for the two of them.

He might even offer to pay.

The phone on his end rang a few times and then went to voice-mail.

Maybe he will call back.

She waited a few minutes, but no return call was made, so she said screw it and started heading home. It wasn't until she was turning from Barber Green onto Peace Road that she remembered she could have gotten one of the five-dollar ready pizzas from the Little Caesars that was within walking distance of the Steak and Shake.

Then again, she had a couple five dollar frozen pizzas in her freezer, and, chances were, they tasted a lot better.

Plus the Chinese food was still an option, and if she asked nicely, maybe Bill would go pick it up for them – unless they delivered which would be even better.

Not long after that, Kimberly was maneuvering the car into the driveway, her foot momentarily pushing the brake pedal as her eyes caught sight of a box waiting on the front steps.

Just the stuff Mark was forced to send.

Realizing this, she sighed and continued into the garage, parked, and headed toward the side door.

Inside she headed into her bedroom to change, her right hand flipping on lights as she made a path from the kitchen to the master bedroom. From there she headed around through the family room toward the front door, but rather than grabbing the boxes from out front, she turned toward the inner stairway door and opened it so she could go up and see if Bill had the Ren's menu and wanted anything.

Bill's door was open.

Puzzled, she took a few steps up the stairs, but then stopped and called out.

No response.

She took another step and asked, "Bill, you okay?"

Nothing.

Something wasn't right.

Unless he is on one of his walks.

That would explain why the car was still there.

But why was the door open?

Was that something that happened from time to time in this old house?

Or maybe something was wrong with the internet connection and he wanted to –

Movement!

First a shadow on the wall, and then Toby appeared, a meow leaving his tiny lips once he saw her.

"Hey, Toby," she said. "Is everything okay up – "

Blood.

It was all over Toby's face.

No!

Memories of waking up on the bathroom floor after the miscarriage and seeing Misty licking up the blood that had oozed out of her onto the white tiles arrived.

As usual, her attempts to hold back the unwanted thoughts failed, especially the ones where she kicked Misty.

Overwhelmed, she sank down onto the steps.

Toby came down and joined her, his bloodied cheek rubbing against her knee in one of his odd little greetings.

Seeing and feeling this brought everything back into focus. Something was wrong. The blood on Toby's face was proof of this. She needed too –

Up above the floor squeaked.

A large shadow then appeared on the wall.

Kimberly grabbed Toby and started to stand just as the girl appeared in the doorway. Like Toby, blood covered part of her face. Rather than focus on this, however, Kimberly's eyes were drawn down to her hand, which held a large carving knife.

"We've been waiting for you," the girl said. "Why don't you come up and join us."

Rather than reply, Kimberly took a step backward, and then another, her feet carefully planting themselves, so that her footing would be good if she had to suddenly haul ass.

"No?" the girl (Amy?) asked. "It'll be easier if you just come up."

"I don't think so," Kimberly said, voice a bit shaky.

"Oh, but Bill would really like your company," she said and took a step onto the stairs. "He isn't doing so well, by the way, and could use a friend right now."

Empathy toward Bill arrived, but it wasn't enough for her to simply give in. Not when she knew this girl was crazy. Nope.

The girl took another step toward her.

Kimberly turned and jumped down the rest of the steps, and then went to throw the door closed.

Toby panicked, his back claws digging into her flesh.

Kimberly opened her arms so Toby could flee, all while throwing her back into the door to close it, a hand going to the knob to twist the lock.

Something slammed the door, preventing it from closing all the way, and then, through the opening between it and the frame, the knife appeared and blindly slashed at her.

Kimberly tried moving out of the way, but failed, the blade catching the meat of her upper arm.

Teeth clenched, she tried grabbing at the wrist, but only managed to earn another cut as the blade twisted and got two of her fingers.

Pain and rage echoed from her lips.

25

Things were not going according to plan, mostly due to the writer, but also because of her quick, thoughtless moment of action in the kitchen after being knocked in the head by the frying pan.

But you really didn't have a choice.

She had told herself this several times while waiting for Kimberly to return home, her hope that the writer would still be alive and still be able to perform fading with each passing second.

You were also very lucky.

Though painful, the blow to the head she had suffered hadn't been as bad as it could have been. In fact, had he put enough force behind it he probably could have killed her. Instead, she had simply lost her footing for a moment as the world twisted around, and fell to the floor.

And there it was, a knife, sitting within reach.

Without really thinking about it, she grabbed it and drove the tiny blade into his lower back. Not just once, but three times, her anger toward him getting the better of her.

Later, she regretted this momentary loss of control. Other options had been present. Quickly standing and putting the knife to his throat would have done the trick. Or, if her legs had failed, stabbing him in the back of the leg, or the butt, or some other area that wouldn't have punctured an organ -- given the smell oozing from his wound she figured she had hit something.

But would it have really worked?

Twice she had had him subdued, and twice he had gotten the better of her. In the end, stabbing him might have been the only option. It was a debate that took up much of her time while sitting in the upstairs apartment, drinking soda and nursing her head.

He had also broken at least one of her fingers, maybe two. This realization had hit home when she had started patching up his wounds, her hope being that the tape would slow his decline down to the point where she could still force Kimberly to have sex with him.

Her pain was no match for his, however. She could see it in his eyes. The lack of protest as she bound him up nice and tight with the tape – before securing his wounds – was evidence of this as well. Earlier he had done everything he could to try to get away; now he barely moved.

And now things still weren't going according to plan.

Having finally subdued the writer, Amy had decided it would probably be a good idea to get into her apartment. In order to do this she would have to cut away at the door frame like she had done with William's door so that the blade could reach in and by-pass the lock by slipping the latch.

Doing this would take time and energy, one of which she was lacking. Sitting on the couch drinking the soda and resting her head for a few minutes would solve that. What she hadn't counted on was zoning out to the point where she wasn't even aware of her consciousness until Kimberly called out from the stairway. It was an unforgivable lapse, one that now seemed as if it would add another level of ruin to her plan.

26

Knowing she couldn't stay at the stairway door, not unless she wanted to suffer more agonizing knife cuts, Kimberly hurried toward the kitchen, her hope being to grab something that could be used as a weapon.

Once in there, however, she remembered that the largest knife she had, one that would probably match the dimensions of Amy's, was in the family room by the couch. Also on that side of the house, was her phone, though that was in her bedroom, which she didn't dare enter, not when she could become trapped.

Going for the knife was different. The layout of the first floor was like a donut, thus, it was impossible for Amy to corner her in one of the main rooms. The question was did she go for the knife or just flee the house screaming?

She chose the latter and went out the kitchen door.

27

NO! NO! NO! Amy's mind cried as she entered the kitchen in time to watch the door slam shut. A scream of "HELP ME!" followed.

She then saw that Kimberly was running toward the front of the house, probably so she could head down the street, which meant Amy had a chance to cut her off by going out the front.

Cut her off, stab her, and drag her back inside.

Once there she would smear Mark's semen on some object as if it were lube and then fuck her with it. Who knew, killing her first before fucking her might work to her advantage because it would make Mark look even sicker and thus really capture everyone's attention.

All these thoughts went through her head as she raced out the front door and actually brought a smile to her face. It didn't last. One moment she was going out the door, the next she was falling, her feet having tangled with something, a panicked cry escaping her lips.

28

Kimberly saw the front door fly open as she came around the

house and realized that the two were on a collision course with each other. And there was nothing she could do to stop it, not with the speed she was running at. All she could do was hope her body could somehow twist around out of the way once Amy was in position, twist around and keep running, lungs screaming until some form of help arrived.

Amy lunged at her from the top of the stairs.

At least this is what her mind concluded. Amy lunged, and since her timing was off, Kimberly was able to pass the point on the sidewalk that she thought Amy would intercept her at, and kept running.

29

Amy felt something pop in her chest seconds before she hit the sidewalk, followed by a sudden need to catch her breath, only she couldn't inhale.

Panic set in.

She tried for a second breath of air, but again her chest would not expand, almost as if some sort of restraint had been secured around her.

Get up.

Get Nikki.

BREATHE!

A small, quick gasp allowed some air to get through, but it wasn't enough. It was all she could manage, however.

Need to get up.

Need to –

An odd, ice like feeling began to expand within her chest, almost as if someone had speared her with an icicle.

And then she was drowning.

And choking.

Each small gasp for breath was bringing a horrible metallic taste to her mouth.

Blood!

It was rising up, kind of like vomit, only without the purge feeling.

She tried to get up, but her right arm wasn't functioning properly, almost as if she had slept on it.

Footsteps.

They grew closer and closer.

She tried looking up, but the tearing pain this caused in her upper back was unbearable, as was the pain in her chest that accompanied her gasp.

A pair of shoes appeared in her vision.

It was Nikki.

Kill her.

The desire was quickly replaced by her need for air, the tiny gasps no longer doing the trick.

And then a fuzzy border appeared around the edges of her vision and began to grow inward.

She tried blinking it away, but it would not clear. In fact, it was growing worse with each passing second. With it came a desire to sleep, one that she indulged in.

It didn't last.

People were lifting her, twisting her and then setting her down, this time on something soft and oddly shaped. Flashing lights were present, the red and blue dancing across every surface. No sounds though, not until something was forced down her throat.

"We got a critical one upstairs too."

It was all she heard before someone pinched her arm and she slipped away.

30

Kimberly had never seen anything like it, nor did she ever want to again.

Risking a look back while fleeing, she realized Amy was not giving chase and instead was lying on the sidewalk outside of the house.

It's a trick, her mind warned.

The thought faded.

Something had happened.

And if she is hurt, you might be able to subdue her for the police and then it will be over.

Subduing her was not necessary, not when Amy had impaled herself with her own knife.

Friday, August 26, 2011

1

"What box?" Bill asked. His voice was dry, but, thankfully, not weak, which meant he was recovering nicely from the two surgeries he had endured.

"The one with all the stuff she made Mark send to me," Kimberly said. "It was sitting in the middle of the front steps when I got home and I never got a chance to bring it in."

"Oh." Bill nodded. He then reached for the cup of ice and tipped some of the small pieces into his mouth, teeth crunching them until nothing was left.

"It was unbelievable," Kimberly said. "I've never seen anything like it. The knife tip was actually sticking out of her back."

Bill didn't reply.

"It was just awful," she added, voice solemn. "She kept gasping for air, but her right lung was punctured, so not much was getting in. She also couldn't take a deep breath because of the knife, not without a tremendous amount of pain."

"She was conscious?" Bill asked.

"Yeah. You didn't know that?"

He shook his head. "No one has told me anything, except that she was dead and that they found Mark." He closed his eyes for a second. "And they wanted to know why I had condoms full of semen on my coffee table."

"They asked me about that too, but . . ." she shrugged.

Silence settled.

Out in the hallway a cart was being pushed, one that brought with it the smell of food.

"Great," Bill said with a grimace. "Lunch time."

"Food sucks?" Kimberly asked.

"I don't know. They still won't let me eat. They want to make sure my small intestine gets a few days to heal." He sighed. "Thankfully I will be able to start drinking fluids later today, which reminds me. If you're still here then, can you bring me a Coke?"

"Will they allow that?" she asked.

"Once I can have fluids, yeah, though they will probably discourage it. It'll be up to me, though, and I want one."

Kimberly smiled. "Okay. If I'm still here, and if not, I'll bring you one when I come back."

"Thanks. How's Toby?"

"He's good. Misses you and I think he's confused as to why he can't go upstairs, but other than that he seems to be having a blast running in circles around my place."

"How bad is it up there?"

"Not as bad as it could have been, and don't worry about cleaning it up. I talked to the landlord and he's having someone come in to do it."

"Really?"

"Yeah." Kimberly had been surprised when the police had released the scene without having cleaned anything up, but then learned that this was standard. They weren't responsible for the aftercare required. Once finished with the crime scene they simply wiped their hands of it. Thankfully, when asked, they had provided a list of cleaning services that specialized in this sort of thing. "I think he wants to make sure it's done right, so that in the future people won't be asking about stains and then learning about what happened."

Bill didn't reply to this.

At first, Kimberly figured he didn't really have anything to say, but then she realized he had drifted off to sleep. Given the heavy dose of painkillers and antibiotics he was on, the nurse she had spoken too earlier said this would be common.

Unsure what to do, Kimberly eventually wrote a note telling him to call if he needed anything and then headed home.

2

For me, stalking is like foreplay. The more frightened I become, the wetter my pussy will be. And if you actually have the balls to come up behind me as I enter my apartment after a late night of working at Steak and Shake and push me inside, I'll forever be in your debt for the sexual ecstasy you will provide me. It has to feel real though, which means I don't want to talk about and discuss things; I don't want to meet with you beforehand and go over the scenario. That will kill the mood and any suggestions to do that will be met with rejection.

Her address followed the email, which had arrived a week earlier while he had been on vacation with his family. It was in reply to a message he had sent asking if she was for real and if so, to send him her address so he could provide her with the 'rape fantasy' she was looking for.

Many girls come to this site claiming they want to be raped, he had written to her in his introduction email. *But few really mean it. You, however, sound like you could be genuine based on your profile description. I hope this is true. If so, send me your address and I will do the rest.*

Opening a new tab he went to Google Maps and typed in the address she had sent.

She probably thinks I flaked out, he said to himself while printing out the directions to her place. *Little does she know it is just getting started.*

ABOUT THE AUTHOR

William Malmborg has been publishing short stories in horror magazines and dark fiction anthologies since 2002. In addition to TEXT MESSAGE, two of his novels, NIKKI'S SECRET and JIMMY, are both available, as is a short story collection titled SCRAPING THE BONE that features five previously published and five original tales of horror. When not writing William caters to the whims of Toby and Truman, two cats who reside with him in DeKalb, IL.

To learn more about William Malmborg check out his webpage at:

http://www.williammalmborg.com/

You can also friend him on Facebook at:

http://www.facebook.com/wlmalmborg

33534218R00204

Printed in Great Britain
by Amazon